DELTA 7

By
John Cathcart

10/21/08

HANK,

HOPE YOU ENJOY D7... ESPEC,
THE 'VARIL PART.

ALLY

ONCE I GET RICH AND
FAMOUS, YOU CAN SELL THIS
'UNIQUE" COPY FOR HUNDREDS!

JOHN CATHCART   ☺

Delta 7
All Rights Reserved.
Copyright © 2008 John Cathcart
V2.0

ISBN: 1438243901 EAN-13: 9781438243900

PRINTED IN THE UNITED STATES OF AMERICA

Forward

Why I wrote this book and a few caveats

I started thinking about writing this book while serving as a United States Air Force Attaché. For several months in 1994, I was temporarily assigned to the Defense Attaché Office (DAO) in Bogotá, Colombia. A year later, my family and I moved to Caracas, Venezuela where I also served as an Air Attaché. In conjunction with my attaché duties, the US government issued me a diplomatic passport, which facilitated access to places that might otherwise have been difficult to visit. As an attaché and a pilot, I flew a government-owned C-12 (Beech *Super King Air 200*) twin-engine turboprop. In this aircraft, my fellow attachés and I traveled to many locations in the vast and diverse area encompassing the countries of Colombia, Venezuela, and half-dozen islands in the Caribbean—where we were diplomatically accredited. During those months in Latin America, I learned about their cultures, geography, history, and military capabilities.

In the course of my two tours of attaché duty, I was also introduced to the sordid world of drug trafficking. Unfortunately, I was able to appreciate, first-hand, how the narcotics trade was slowly ravaging—even compromising the sovereignty of—these countries and their people. *Delta 7*, my first novel, is a fictional account of what can happen to individuals who get caught up in the world of drug trafficking and the mind-boggling quantities of illicit money it generates.

Finally, none of these characters is real—any similarity between any of the characters in this book and any living person (and especially any member of the US military with whom I served) is purely coincidental.

Military Jargon/Glossary

Although this book is entirely a work of fiction, it is based on 20 years of experiences as an officer in the United States Air Force. In an attempt to make this book accurate in its depiction of military life, I have tried to faithfully reproduce the same lexicon, jargon, acronyms and at times foul language one hears in the military. Although this use of jargon may add to realism, it will undoubtedly make it difficult to follow some of the dialog. To help explain what's being said, I have included a glossary at the end of the book with definitions for many of the words, acronyms and other expressions used in the novel.

The Situation in Colombia

From the time I lived in Colombia until I started writing this story (about 10 years later), it continued to be a tragically violent country. I think it's fair to say that in the past several years, Colombia has seen an appreciable reduction in the intensity of the fighting. Although the situation has improved, Colombia remains locked in battle with an armed insurgency, determined to impose its radical ideology on a largely unsupportive population. My hope is that one day this beautiful country will be as peaceful as my own and that its democracy will continue to adapt, survive and flourish.

The Past

The first thing you know our 'Varks are over there,
The Libyans said, "Let's shoot 'em from the air!"
But Ron says, "Gulf of Sidra is the place we wanna be."
So we took off from the 'Heath and we flew to Tripoli.

A slightly edited version of the second verse of a song entitled, "The Tripoli Hillbillies," which appeared in the extremely unofficial, unauthorized, uncouth and largely unprintable 494th Tactical Fighter Squadron "Black Panther Songbook." Several Panthers compiled and printed this songbook shortly after the raid on Libya—code-named "Operation El Dorado Canyon—in April of 1986.

The Past

15 April 1986
Over the Atlantic Ocean, off the West Coast of Spain

"We're not going to make it," US Air Force Captain Roger "Knife" North said matter-of-factly over the jet's intercom to his pilot, Captain John Carter.

North got his nickname shortly after joining the 494th Tactical Fighter Squadron at RAF Lakenheath, in the southeast of the UK. It was a fitting moniker, since the tall, muscular 32-year old always carried at least three of them. North was the squadron's top Weapon Systems Officer or *Wizzo*—completely at home staring into the infrared and radar screens arrayed in front of him in the cockpit of their F-111 Aardvark or *Vark*.

Unlike most tandem-seat fighters, the F-111's pilot and Wizzo sit side-by-side, allowing each crewmember to watch what the other was doing during flight. Although the Wizzo had his own control stick and throttles, he normally spent most of his time with his head in the *feedbag*—the hooded enclosure containing two screens presenting radar and infrared views of the surrounding terrain. Working with these systems—while flying along in a maneuvering jet—was very demanding. It was a challenge for the Wizzo to stay oriented and keep aiming at his target while the pilot yanked and banked the aircraft on its trajectory towards the target area. Many a Wizzo had *lost his cookies* during the often-violent maneuvering during low-altitude flying.

Captain John Carter was grateful that his Wizzo for that evening's mission seemed impervious to any of these problems. In fact, North was famous for chiding pilots into more aggressive maneuvering, and he was wont to say things like, "Come on you weak dick, put some Gs on this ole sonnova bitch! We're gonna get our asses shot down if you don't stop pullin' like a damned pussy!"

The F-111 was not a particularly sexy airplane—built for speed, not agility—but those who flew the *Vark* learned to love the smooth ride. She rode like a Cadillac with under-inflated tires at 540 knots and only 200 feet above the ground.

"What'ya mean, we're not gonna make it? We've got plenty of gas—or do you have to piss again?" replied Carter, glancing sideways at his Wizzo, a smile hidden behind his oxygen mask.

"Not gas, asshole, *time!*" replied North. "We're almost three minutes late right now, and by the time we get to X-Ray, we'll be even later. The HARM shooters will be finished before we even get there!"

Of the hundred-plus aircraft participating in tonight's mission—code-named *El Dorado Canyon*—Knife was referring to the Navy's F-18 and A-7 fighters. They would soon be launching off the catapults of the US carriers *America* and *Coral Sea*, flying to targets in Benghazi and Tripoli, on Libya's north coast. These initial attack aircraft would be carrying High-speed Anti-Radiation

2

Missiles—HARMs. Their job was to knock out any Libyan radar facility that might track the attacking jets.

"Damn! Knife, why didn't you say something sooner?" asked Carter.

"It's this friggin' comm silence crap. Everybody knows we're late, but nobody wants to say anything! What's the point of maintaining comm-friggin'-silence if the Libyans are gonna know we're comin' before we get there?"

Knife wasn't particularly articulate, but his point was valid. If they didn't alter course or speed up, the attacking F-111s would arrive several minutes after the HARM missiles had been launched—denying them the crucial element of surprise.

"Puffy Lead, Three," Carter transmitted to his flight lead—breaking radio silence and making the first radio transmission of the night.

"Yeah, I know," answered "Kaz," his flight lead. "Break... Debol 45, Puffy Lead, I show us three late. We need to speed up and cut some corners," he instructed the lead KC-135 tanker tersely.

Lieutenant Colonel Phil "Kaz" Kazakman was the only combat veteran in the formation. During the Vietnam War, Kaz had flown the F-111 during nighttime attacks on Hanoi. He was a fighter pilot's fighter pilot, and he flew the pants off the airplane, winning nearly all the squadron's top gun competitions, despite being twenty years older than the youngest lieutenants in the squadron. Tonight, as in Vietnam, he would be on time and on target.

In the cockpit of the lead KC-135, the subjects of timing, boom airspeed limitations, and upper-atmosphere winds had been the main topic of conversation for the last hour. The *weather guessers* had gotten it all wrong. Not only were the winds significantly stronger than predicted, they were in the opposite direction—giving the attacking formation a 75-knot headwind instead of a light tailwind. The lead tanker navigator had immediately noticed the difference in wind and had recommended a faster speed. They were leading the entire formation of KC-10s, KC-135s, F-111Fs and EF-111s. The tanker's aircraft commander, however, had initially resisted flying faster than the limiting speed of the tanker's air refueling boom.

The unpredicted winds were causing additional problems for the F-111s. Half of them had a weapons load of four 2000-pound laser guided bombs, while the others carried twelve 500-pound Mk-82 Airs each. All these weapons—hanging on the wings of the fighters—were causing a lot of air resistance or drag. That drag, combined with the increased airspeed to compensate for the winds, was causing the thirsty fighters to burn fuel at a much higher rate than they had planned.

"Booms, Pilot," said Major Tommy Wilson over the tanker's intercom, calling the plane's boom operator in the tail of the lead KC-135. "I'm gonna push this sucker up as fast as she'll go. Let me know if you're havin' trouble controlling the boom. For now, screw the boom limit, this is *combat*!" Everyone onboard the aircraft smiled at hearing those words. It was nice to be able to escape the rules of *Mother SAC*—the storied Strategic Air Command. They were determined to get their chicks to their targets on time; even if they had to break a few of *Mother's* rules in the process.

In Carter's F-111, the effect was immediate. The tanker, from which they were still receiving fuel, began to pull ahead of them and slowly banked to the left. Carter added power and matched the tanker's turn to stay in position. While Carter concentrated on staying in the refueling formation with the tanker, Knife made some quick calculations.

"Shit Hot!" exclaimed Knife, over the *Vark's* intercom. "They're cutting the corner on Spanish airspace too! I now show us 20 seconds late at *X-Ray*."

The governments of Spain and France had not allowed the Americans to overfly their countries to reach Libya that night. That had added a whole level of complication to the mission, and had almost doubled their flight time.

Of all the attacking F-111s, Carter's squadron had to fly the furthest to reach their target—the military airfield on the east side of Tripoli's international airport. After completing the final pre-attack air refueling off the north coast of Libya, they would continue east, past the city and outside of radar coverage. From that point, they would begin their descent to treetop level and head back through the desert toward Tripoli.

A particularly novel aspect of F-111 flying was the so-called TFR letdown. This maneuver could be especially unnerving for those new to the F-111—especially when accomplished at night. Immediately upon connecting the TFR, the aircraft would rapidly pitch over to a nearly 10 degrees nose-low attitude. It would maintain this gentle descent until about 5000 feet above the ground, when it would pitch over further and begin screaming towards the black void below. For the uninitiated, this maneuver appeared near suicidal—especially when descending into mountainous terrain. During this maneuver, a pilot caught occasional glimpses of potentially deadly hills gliding past the cockpit canopy, while wisps of clouds or lines of trees on these summits would compete for his attention. A seasoned F-111 pilot was well trained, and learned to concentrate on the information presented on the many dials, gauges and screens in the cockpit—rather than the potentially deadly terrain racing by outside his jet.

Carter had successfully completed his own TFR letdown only minutes before coasting-in over Libya's northern shoreline. As they streaked ever closer to their target, Carter pulled down his oxygen mask and took a sip of water from the small flask he was carrying in his anti-G suit. Ever since they had crossed over the Libyan coastline, he had begun to prepare himself mentally for what lay ahead. His stomach had been doing summersaults for the past several minutes, and the cool water helped calm him.

Carter and his squadron would be striking the east side of the airport, where the Libyan Air Force had its largest base. Satellite photography from the night before had shown that several Libyan military transport aircraft were parked on the tarmac. *Would they still be there? How much anti-aircraft artillery ("Triple A") would the Libyans fire at them? How many missiles would they launch? Would the missiles be guided? Will I make it through the target area alive?* As Carter continued to go over the mission in his mind, he kept repeating the most important mantra of every fighter pilot: *Don't let me screw up!*

As his F-111 continued along toward the target area—flying only 200 feet above the desert sands—Carter thought about his squadron mates flying along behind him. There was only one minute separating each jet in the formation, and all were heading to different targets around the International Airport. He wondered if their stomachs were churning as much as his was.

He glanced over at Knife—head buried in the *feedbag.*

"How's it going?" Carter asked.

"System looks pretty tight. Pave Tack's painting a great picture. I just saw a caravan of camels off to the right." Knife seemed to be enjoying the view outside the aircraft provided by the Pave Tack infrared and laser-targeting pod. True to form, Knife seemed immune to any concern for his safety. His voice was steady and calm—as if he were flying a regular training mission. There was little indication in their voices that these two airmen were minutes away from bombing military targets on the east side of Tripoli's International airport.

Carter tapped Knife's arm to get him to remove his head from the shroud around his radar and infrared screens. He silently pointed ahead to the lights on the horizon—the city of Tripoli.

"Guess it's too late to turn around now," joked Carter over the intercom.

"We didn't come all this way to screw it up or turn around," replied Knife.

Suddenly, off in the distance, they could see violent flashes augmenting the nighttime lights of the city. The intermittent bursts of light were the work of the HARM shooters—softening up the Libyan air defense network.

Carter knew that at this very moment the pilots from the Wing's other squadrons were on the final run to their targets in downtown Tripoli. The F-111's radio suddenly came to life. After hours of silence, there was now a cacophony of radio calls: "Jewell 61, Feet Wet, Tranquil Tiger." "Zulu Tango Four, up three looks good." "Karma 51, Feet Wet, Frosty Freezer."

As Carter listened to the frantic radio chatter, he tallied up the results. Jewell 61 and Karma 51 were calling "Feet Wet." That meant that they were returning north away from Libya. "Tranquil Tiger" indicated a successful strike.

"Frosty Freezer," on the other hand, indicated an unsuccessful target run. The other gibberish about "Zulu Tango" meant nothing to Carter. *Must be some Navy lingo*, he thought.

"Left turn, heading 342, push it up," barked Knife.

"Roger. Master Arm on," replied Carter, pushing up jet's throttles to increase the F-111's speed to 600 knots for the final run towards the target area. Now was not the time to think about the other aircrews in his Wing; he had enough to do in his own cockpit—his own target to hit.

"One minute," Carter said, calling out the readout from his heads-up display indicating the time remaining to weapons release.

In one minute, they would be over the airport tarmac releasing their twelve 500-pound, parachute-retarded bombs.

Carter watched the unbelievable light show unfolding ahead. It was almost beautiful, definitely surreal—but potentially lethal. Every single Libyan with a gun seemed to be firing wildly into the sky. Tracer rounds were scratching arcs of light all over. Eerily, he could see the bright illumination of the international terminal in the distance off to his left and could make out the individual civilian aircraft parked at the terminal. It would appear that no one on that side of airport was aware that an attack was underway and had not turned off any of the airport lighting. The attacking jets were fortunate; as it appeared that the Libyan gunners were shooting blindly. Carter realized that there was still an awful lot of lead in the sky ahead and he found himself fighting the urge to flinch.

Despite all the lethal mayhem around him, Carter's training kicked in. He took a deep breath and scanned his instruments. Airspeed: five knots slow; speed up... Steering bars: very slight deflection to the left, ease the stick over in that direction to center it up... Altitude: steady at 200 feet... Threat scope: clear... TFR Radar: normal.

In the distance, a continuing series of explosions were lighting up the night sky over downtown Tripoli. Carter's jet continued ever closer to the target; they were now within the airfield boundary. He could make out the blurred shadows of runways and taxiways whizzing by his speeding F-111.

"20 seconds," Carter called out.

Chaff, chaff, Carter thought to himself as he clicked the chaff dispenser lever with the tips of the fingers of his left hand—releasing bundles of aluminum strips to confuse the Libyan radar operators. He continued to dispense chaff, knowing that from this point on, he must fly straight ahead without defensive maneuvering in order to get to the exact weapons release point.

Meanwhile, Knife was trying to decipher the unexpected picture he was seeing in his infrared scope. Seconds earlier, he had done his last-minute radar work—refining his position based on the placement of his cursors on the radar reflection of the control tower on the other side of the field. Although the tower was not their objective, he used its radar reflection to fix the position of the aircraft close enough to be able to find their intended target on his infrared scope. His pre-flight target study had told him that their target—the tarmac where the Libyans normally parked their transport aircraft—might not be visible on the aircraft's radar. Seconds earlier, Knife had found the control tower on radar, and quickly updated the aircraft's position.

With only twenty seconds remaining until weapons release, Knife was confused. He was *not* looking at the wide expanse of concrete he expected to see. Instead, he was looking at a narrow strip of concrete with stripes in the middle. In a flash, Knife realized they were flying right down the airport's main runway, rather than the adjacent parking apron, which was his target.

With practiced skill, Knife's fingers swiftly pushed a series of buttons to expand the field of view on his infrared screen. Near the right edge of the screen, Knife could make out the beginning of the military aircraft parking area. He quickly moved the jet's infrared camera further to the right and could now see the wide expanse of the concrete apron. Knife knew that Carter would not see this change until he fired the F-111's laser—updating the aircraft's steering towards the target.

When the aircraft's navigation system registered this last-minute change, Carter's steering bars careened wildly to the right.

"What the—" was all Carter could get out before being interrupted by Knife's reply.

"Break right! Go for it! Go for it!" screamed Knife, nearly blowing the oxygen mask off his face.

Carter slammed the stick to the right—reorienting the jet's trajectory with the newly updated steering information. Just before the steering cue moved back toward the required position, Carter yanked the aircraft back to the left, rolling out on the perfect heading—while his right thumb pressed the pickle button, releasing their bombs.

"Oh Baby!" exclaimed Knife as the indistinguishable blobs on his scope transformed themselves into seven Soviet-built, IL-76 cargo aircraft neatly lined up on the ramp.

"Damn!" he blurted out, when his infrared screen erupted in a violent white flash of heat—the string of weapons exploding amongst the parked aircraft. Scores of weaponeers and intelligence experts would later evaluate his videotape to determine the extent of the damage. Although the battle damage assessment would happen later, Knife knew that most of those cargo aircraft would never fly again. Their flimsy aluminum outer skin no match for the explosive power of the string of Mk-82s he had just unleashed into their midst.

Suddenly, a violent explosion slammed the jet, tossing them brutally against their cockpit restraints. For the first time since their target run had started, Knife looked outside the jet's canopy—half-expecting to see a wing tearing away from the fuselage. The video game he had been watching on his scope had suddenly turned all too real. They had definitely pissed off the locals who were now earnestly trying to shoot them out of the sky.

"Let's get the hell out of here!" he yelled, his voice betraying fear for the first time.

Carter was totally focused on doing just that. From the moment the last bomb had left the jet's wings, he had been constantly jinking the aircraft and dropping metallic strips of chaff in an attempt to complicate the job of the Libyan anti-aircraft artillery gunners. Up to this point, Knife had been too intently focused on his Wizzo duties to appreciate—or even notice—the violent maneuvering that Carter was now commanding of their F-111.

As the jet screamed away from the target area, Knife switched off the Pave Tack system, causing the entire targeting pod to rotate back into its streamlined position in the jet's belly. They both scanned the sky for further Triple-A fire or missile launches.

Later that night, after returning home to their base in England, they would learn that the explosion they felt over the target area was caused by one of their own Mk-82s going slick. Because its parachute had failed to deploy, the bomb had glided along just below and behind them, exploding dangerously close behind the tail of the jet. Carter's textbook post-delivery hard turn had saved them from fragging themselves—from being blown up by their own bomb.

As the jet hurtled over the beach west of Tripoli, Carter could make out the twinkling of reflected starlight in the gentle waves of the Mediterranean. It was time for his delousing radio call.

"Puffy 61, Feet Wet, Tranquil Tiger," Carter transmitted over the jet's radio.

Once out of range of the Libyan defenses, Carter began a slow climb and scanned the instruments of his F-111 confirming his fuel status and making sure that the jet was still in good shape. The Libyan coast receding behind him and his heart rate slowly returning to normal, Carter took a deep breath and considered what had just happened.

Thank God! I'm alive... my jet is still flying. It looks like I did OK... I didn't screw up.

Captain John Carter was a now combat veteran.

8

15 April 1986
Guainía Department of Eastern Colombia

"¡Muévanse hijos de puta!"

"Keep moving you sons of whores!" screamed *Comandante Echo*, leader of this small group of the 38th *Cuadrilla*, of the 16th Front of the *Fuerzas Armadas Revolucionarias de Colombia* or FARC.

Carlos Hernández was about to participate in his first ambush. Under *Echo's* command, the 25 men in his guerilla unit had been moving through the thick vegetation since before dawn. It had rained earlier, which had made the going even more difficult and uncomfortable. The humidity was higher than normal, sapping his energy... or perhaps he was just sweating more in anticipation of his first actual combat.

Carlos thought back to how he had been pressed into service with the FARC only five weeks earlier—the day before his 16th birthday. He had been playing soccer with several boys from his village. Halfway through their game, a pickup truck had approached the field. Several armed men had gotten out of the truck and rounded up Carlos and three others.

Carlos and his friends had been beaten up and thrown into the back of the pickup. After several hours on the road, they had stopped at a remote gas station. One of his friends, Eduardo, had jumped from the small truck and run into the nearby woods. Two of the *guerrilleros* had run after him and had returned to the van a short time later. Once they were again on the road, Carlos watched as one of the two wiped fresh blood off his large hunting knife. Petrified, Carlos had remained silent and immobile for the remainder of the journey.

Over the next several days, Carlos' initial training with the FARC had been very rudimentary. He learned—with absolute certainty—that any attempt to escape would fail and that he would be killed for even trying to abandon his unit. They gave him an ancient, battered AK-47 that was covered with clumps of mud and dried blood. After he cleaned it, they showed him how to load and shoot his weapon.

In those early days, he also learned the truth about his country's history, the oppression of its people, and his duties in support of the FARC and the Revolution. As the days turned into weeks, the other members of his unit had become his family... his new brothers and sisters. The horrible aching in his heart began to subside and he thought less often about his own family back home.

The sudden snap of a branch slapping into his face interrupted Carlos' reverie.

"*¡Cuidado, bobo!*"

"Watch out, dummy!" he hissed to the comrade in front of him as the group continued their slow advance toward the ambush location.

The sun continued to climb into the morning sky, markedly improving the visibility. They no longer needed flashlights to guide them through the dense vegetation and the colors of the jungle were becoming visible. Through a clearing ahead, Carlos began to make out the outline of the road the Army used to transport troops for their regular patrols. Their informants in the *Muiscas* Counter-Guerilla Battalion of the Colombian Army had told them that one of their patrols would pass along this road around 9:00am.

"*¡Mantengan su formación!*"

"Stay in formation!" yelled *Comandante Echo.*

Everyone in the unit understood that they must follow *Echo's* orders without hesitation. He handled small infractions of the rules with a bellowed string of cuss words, threats, and other forms of abuse. During these tirades, he would often question the new recruits' parentage and at times their species. More often than not, verbal assaults were punctuated with a slap in the face. Sometimes he struck them with the butt of his AK-47. That was the easy part. Those who questioned his orders, failed to carry out an order unhesitatingly, or whom Echo considered untrainable, untrustworthy or unworthy were simply shot.

In the five weeks that Carlos Hernández had been with this group, he had seen two recruits dispatched in this way. The first time was when *Monito,* an elfish 13-year old, had complained that his feet hurt after a day's march through the jungle.

"*¿Podemos parar un ratito? Me duelen los pies.*"

"Can we stop for just a second? My feet hurt," *Monito* had asked no one in particular.

Echo calmly stopped the formation and walked up to the young boy.

"*¿Te duelen los pies, pobrecito Monito?*"

"Do your feet hurt, poor Little Monkey?" asked Echo, placing his hands on his hips.

Monito did not answer, and continued gazing down towards his feet.

"*¿Y la cabeza? ¿No tienes dolor de cabeza?*"

"How about your head? Have a headache?" he had asked calmly. *Monito* had stared silently at the ground, tears streaming down his cheeks.

"*¡A ver si ésto te sirve!*"

"Let's see if this fixes it!" sneered Echo, removing his pistol from his belt and calmly aiming it at the youngster's forehead. Without warning and with no further words, he fired.

Carlos had jumped at the loud crack of the pistol. He watched the spray of blood and brain tissue expand behind *Monito's* head, the sound of the gunshot quickly muffled by the dense jungle vegetation. The impact of the bullet had snapped *Monito's* head back and it seemed that his eyes were staring straight at Carlos—as if pleading for help. However, as the lifeless body began to collapse upon itself, Carlos realized that those eyes could no longer see. *Monito* was dead.

Carlos stared at the inert body lying in front of him. There was a gaping hole in *Monito's* forehead and a slowly expanding pool of blood mixing with the dirt and decayed vegetation on the jungle floor. He noticed the unnatural position of *Monito's* arms and legs—haphazardly folded at strange angles as his body had fallen. The tips of *Monito's* shoes were pointing at each other.

Carlos mind filled with a swirl of emotions and questions. *Those shoes killed him! Why did Echo have to hear his complaint? Why did Echo have to shoot him? Why had God let this happen?*

Carlos felt the jungle close in on him, and the air thickened, making it harder to breathe. He thought of crying; but feared that tears might seal his fate too. Showing any weakness might risk pushing *Echo* into another rage, and that might result in his lifeless body lying next to poor *Monito*. No. Carlos Hernández would not cry.

Carlos was jolted by the slap of *Echo's* hand on his shoulder.

"Bury him! We don't want those Army bastards to think *they* killed him and include him in some government body count. We must be strong to win! *Monito* was not strong, so he had to die. You are now students of the Revolutionary University. You will learn… or you will die. Guided by the Bolivarian Vision, we will win if we are strong!"

Comandante Echo was shouting, but his words barely broke into Carlos' consciousness. Carlos was only able to concentrate on *Monito's* unseeing eyes. Slowly, surreally, he picked up *Monito* by his wrists and started to drag the lifeless body away.

Carlos tried not to look at *Monito* and instead tried to search for a place to start digging; but was unable to look away. He gazed at the hole in *Monito's* forehead and the matted, still-dripping mass of hair/blood/brains/skull that was the exit wound. He saw the blank eyes—forever staring into nothingness. The offending shoes left twin furrows in the dirt as he dragged the lifeless body along the jungle floor.

Carlos surveyed the result of Echo's brutality and thought of his conversation with *Monito* the night before. Softly and tearfully, *Monito* had whispered his feelings and his fears. He missed his parents and wanted to go home. *Monito* had also complained that his shoes did not fit properly and were hurting his feet. He had explained how he had found them in the camp the day before; and had quickly grabbed them to replace the rotting, hole-filled sneakers that he had been wearing. The new shoes were too small, but at least were relatively free of holes and did a better job protecting his feet from the sharp rocks, twigs and branches that littered the jungle floor. In the darkness, *Monito* had removed the shoes, revealing several bloody, puss-filled blisters. Carlos had removed his own socks and given them to *Monito* to help cushion his feet and alleviate his suffering.

After lugging *Monito* unaided for a few meters, several members of the group joined him and helped drag the body towards an area of thick undergrowth. Together they cleared away the vegetation and carved out a shallow grave. Some used the butts of their machine guns—others used their hands to clear away the dirt.

Once the shallow grave was dug, one of the boys picked up *Monito's* body and starting moving him towards his grave. As he struggled with the corpse, *Monito's* head flopped backwards grotesquely—causing the massive exit wound to rub onto the guerilla's arm, smearing it with blood, bits of skull and brain matter.

"*¡Puta Madre!*" he screamed, throwing down the corpse in disgust, wiping the still-warm mixture off his arm.

"*¡Me duelen los pies!*" he said, mockingly imitating *Monito's* childish voice. As he said the words, he jostled *Monito's* lifeless body up and down—turning him into a gruesome marionette. Everyone laughed. It was perhaps the only acceptable way for them to react to the terror of what they had witnessed and what they were now being forced to do.

After a few seconds of this grisly theater, they had tossed their puppet into his grave and starting to cover the body with dirt. Carlos expected *Monito* to flinch when some of the handfuls of earth hit his still-open eyes; but he didn't move at all.

Monito was gone. It was better to make fun of his lifeless body, to laugh at his predicament, and to pretend that they were too macho, than suffer a similar fate themselves. They were members of the 38th *Cuadrilla* of the 16th Front of the FARC. They were warriors fighting against the oppression of a corrupt government. *Guided by the Bolivarian Vision—they would win if they were strong!*

"Listen up, you sons of whores!" it was *Echo*, giving instructions and forcing Carlos back to the present.

They had arrived at the ambush site and *Echo* began barking orders, sending each man into position. He was an experienced tactician, carefully noting everyone's field of fire. He set up each firing position with the correct weapon, and at the proper distance from the target. After guiding everyone into position, *Echo* placed two small bundles of branches about 40 meters apart along the sides of the road. He explained that the bundles would delineate the kill zone for the ambush.

Each member received his orders: Pedro and *Jonjo* had the RPGs (rocket-propelled grenades). They were deployed at the two ends of the ambush area, and were to disable the first and last vehicles of the convoy, trapping the enemy within the kill zone. All the others were deployed in a manner that ensured complete coverage of the ambush area. No one would escape. They would be victorious. *Guided by the Bolivarian Vision—they would win if they were strong!*

Carlos settled into his place near the center of the ambush position. He was to first single out the officers and then, once they were all gone, shoot at any soldier left alive. He would fire until he had only one clip of ammunition remaining, and then run back to the camp where they had stayed last night. Once there, everyone would re-assemble and re-group for their next attack.

As Carlos waited, he contemplated his role in the Revolution. The government was corrupt. The Army was a tool of the corrupt government. They must both be destroyed. He was an instrument of the Revolution. He would be strong. The Revolution would succeed and his country would be forever changed.

In the distance, Carlos heard the sound of approaching military vehicles. His heart started pounding and his hands shook enough to make him wonder if he'd be able to aim his weapon accurately. He checked the chamber of his AK-47—the first round was in position and the safety was off. He was ready.

The first vehicle, a Jeep Cherokee with four soldiers inside, came into view. A few meters behind the Cherokee was an Army truck with about 20 soldiers in the back.

Suddenly he heard a huge explosion. The Jeep Cherokee disappeared in a massive blast of sound, fire and smoke, just as it reached the second pile of branches. Pedro's aim had been perfect.

Carlos began firing his AK-47 in full automatic mode into the middle of the truck with the soldiers. After the first few rounds, he closed his eyes—stunned by the noise of his weapon, and the cacophony of fire seemingly coming from all directions. In the confusion, he completely forgot to seek out the officers as he had been ordered to do. There was so much happening. Smoke, screams, firing of weapons, flying shards of vegetation, confusion, noise, blood, and death—too much for his mind to process.

As he fired, several of the hot spent cartridges spitting out of his weapon bounced off a tree near his firing position and ricocheted onto his back. One of them hit his neck and rolled down into his shirt. He squirmed around trying to keep the hot shell casing from burning his chest. This movement caused his AK-47 to spray its bullets wildly high—way over the top of the truck and into the tops of the trees on the other side of the road. Then, without warning, his weapon went silent—out of ammunition.

Carlos quickly changed magazines, slammed the first round into the chamber and continued firing into the truck. He hoped he was doing what *Comandante Echo* expected of him—that he would perform with the bravery and skill required by the Revolution.

After firing for what seemed to be only an instant, his weapon again went silent. The second clip was empty. He had one clip remaining and it was time to go. As the firing continued behind him, Carlos jumped to his feet, turned and ran as fast as he could. As he sprinted away from the ambush area, the shooting continued behind him. The noise gradually subsided, as the ambush area grew more distant.

Reaching a clump of trees near the bottom of a small depression in the forest, Carlos turned around and stopped long enough to be sure no one was following him. He held his breath and listened for footsteps. He heard nothing but the pounding of his heart. In the distance, the firing had almost stopped and Carlos could just make out muffled shouting. He must get moving towards the rendezvous area. He felt sure that he had been strong and had done his duty.

Carlos Hernández was now a combat veteran.

1996
Hernández Family Farm—Near the Magdalena River, Santander Department of Colombia

Overwhelmed with emotion, María Luisa Hernández closed her eyes and lifted her face towards heaven—all the while, clutching the precious letter to her bosom. She said a silent prayer of thanksgiving to the Virgin Mary for keeping her son alive.

She had re-read her youngest son, Manuelito's letter dozens of times since it had arrived at their home two weeks earlier. That first day, the entire family—those who, because of God's mercy, were still alive and had remained at home—had sat together in their modest, two-room home, excitedly devouring every one of his carefully scribed words. Little Mani's letter recounted how pleased and proud he was to be completing his initial training with the Colombian Navy. He had made many new friends and was slowly adjusting to his new life. Upon graduation, he had told them, the Colombian Navy would send him for duty aboard a large ship, named *Antioquia.*

María Luisa would have loved to have her son close by, but recognized that it was more important that he be safe. Her little Mani's recent entry into the

Colombian Navy appeared to carry the promise of a relatively safe, although distant, environment.

Like so many mothers, her heart ached from the seemingly endless suffering Colombia's violence had caused her family. Ten years earlier, the *guerrilleros* had kidnapped her eldest son, Carlos. They had not heard from Carlos since that day. Occasionally, they heard rumors that he was still alive and fighting with the FARC.

José, her second son, was now 25. He had married and moved into a small house nearby. He was the only son who had remained in the area to help them on the family farm.

Her third son, Juan David, had been killed three years ago at the age of 18—caught in the crossfire during a paramilitary attack on a group of suspected *guerrilleros*.

Her daughter, Lida, left home years ago to find work as a house cleaner in Medellín. Lida returned every now and then to ask for money. Sadly, it was obvious that she only cared to be part of the family when her money ran out.

Nearly every day, Colombia's families were devastated by the armed struggle. Family members died in clashes with Colombian Army, were assassinated by death squads, murdered by the FARC, or they simply vanished, their killers or abductors unknown.

Holding Mani's letter tightly in her hands, María recalled that terrible night—shortly before Carlos had been taken from her—when she and her husband, Julio, had been drawn into the morass of Colombia's violence. Two armed men had come to the house and asked Julio to go outside with them. Too horrified to move, she had waited in the kitchen for the sound of the gunshot. She imagined herself running outside and seeing her beloved Julio lying in a pool of blood.

After twenty minutes of desperate waiting, Julio had returned. He was ashen-faced and his eyes wide open with fright, confusion and disbelief. For the next several minutes, they had discussed what had happened.

"Yes, María, the two men had rifles, but they never pointed them at me," said Julio, his voice unsteady, the bottom of his eyes coated with tears he fought desperately to restrain.

"The little black one was called *Nando* and he did all the talking," Julio said as he sat down on the stool in the corner of their kitchen. "The other one just stood there watching and listening."

"He kept his rifle on his shoulder and opened up a briefcase with two folders. The first folder had pictures of all our kids—even *Manuelito*. He lined up the pictures of our children on the table in the backyard. Then, the one called *Nando* told me how handsome they were and how they would one day grow up to be parents of their own families. He said that I must be very proud of them. The bastard knew everything about us, María. He knew how we owe money to the landlord, and about how we missed payments this year because of the dry season. He even knew about your trip to the clinic in *Barranca* last month for your surgery. He knew that we couldn't pay. He knew everything."

"Then he opened the other envelope. It had more money than I have ever seen. Maybe five million pesos—I was too afraid to count it. I'm still afraid," he said as he took the envelope from his jacket pocket and gave it to her.

"They gave you money, Julio?" she had asked him incredulously, looking at the envelope in her hand.

"They gave me the envelope with all the money inside, and then the one called Nando told me, 'It's very simple, my friend. You can take this envelope and make sure that your kids grow up to be healthy. Or you can refuse.' Then, the other one, who has still not said a word, takes his machine gun and points it at the pictures of our children."

At that part of the retelling, when they realized that the lives of their children had been threatened, they had both lost the ability to hold back their tears. They had urgently held each other—gently rocking back and forth while sharing their common dread for what tomorrow might bring. They finally left the kitchen for their bedroom, where they spent the rest of the sleepless night trying to figure out what to do.

After that horrible night, nothing had happened. No one made any further contact with any member of the family, nor did anyone ask them to do anything. Their life continued as before and they began to pray that it had all been a mistake.

About a month later, they were awakened in the middle of the night by the sound of trucks passing along the dirt road in front of their house. For the next several days, they also heard sounds of construction. The men doing the construction never told them what they were doing. After several days of this nocturnal activity, Julio became increasingly curious.

"What in the world is going on? What am I supposed to do?" he repeatedly asked his wife.

"You should do nothing and stay right here," she had insisted. "If they want you to do something, they will tell you. I don't want to risk losing you."

"I must find out what they're doing on our land, María," he told her.

Early the next morning after the sounds of construction had stopped; he had snuck through the woods behind his home to investigate. An hour later, he had returned, covered with sweat and mud-stained from sneaking about on his hands and knees. Mercifully, he was unhurt.

"Buildings," he told her simply and cryptically.

16

"What kind of buildings?" she asked.

"Surely they are building a factory for making *basuco,*" he said.

Basuco—Spanish for *trash*—is the less purified form of cocaine resulting from mixing chemicals together with coca leaves, which for the most part, are flown in from Bolivia and Peru. The coca leaf was a commodity that Julio and María's ancestors had used every day. For centuries, it had helped them endure the hard work and high altitudes in which they lived. Tragically, in modern times the simple coca leaf was being processed into a much more pure and dangerous derivative: cocaine.

That was why they had received the envelope. Their farm was to be used to manufacture cocaine. All they had to do was ignore the men with guns, the barrels of toxic chemicals and the trucks coming and going each night.

Julio could continue farming on the tract of land that had been farmed by his family for generations. However, the woods at the far end of their property were now under the control of the *Frente Armado Revolucionario de Colombia*—the FARC.

Julio César and María Luisa Hernández, like countless others before them, were the latest victims of the never-ending cycle of violence in their home country of Colombia.

The Present

Monday

Spies cannot be usefully employed without a certain intuitive sagacity; They cannot be properly managed without benevolence and straight forwardness; Without subtle ingenuity of mind, one cannot make certain of the truth of their reports; Be subtle! Be subtle! And use your spies for every kind of warfare; If a secret piece of news is divulged by a spy before the time is ripe, he must be put to death together with the man to whom the secret was told.

- Sun Tzu

5:33 PM AST
On board National Airlines Flight 986

National Airlines flight 986 had left Miami's International Airport almost three hours earlier, heading for Saint George International Airport on the Caribbean island of Grenada. The plane, along with its passengers and crew, droned along six miles above the calm Caribbean waters, towards their destination and the promise of palm trees, white sand beaches, rum punches, and bikinis.

Securely tucked inside the narrow aluminum tube of the Boeing 737, the two pilots of National Airlines flight 986 no longer needed their sunglasses, and had already removed their cockpit sunshades. The brilliant daytime colors were already beginning to fade and within an hour or so, the sun would once again lose its daily battle with the night sky.

John Carter was sitting in the left seat of the 737, having recently upgraded to captain after eight years with National Airlines. It seemed a lifetime ago that he had retired and left behind the more exciting and demanding world of flying in the US Air Force. In the mid-1980s—when he had been a Captain flying the venerable F-111 fighter-bomber—there had been over 100,000 Air Force personnel stationed in Europe. These dedicated men and women flew, maintained, and guarded more than 200 fighter jets in twelve fighter wings spread throughout Europe. A few short years later, the Berlin Wall had fallen, hastening the demise of the Soviet Union and bringing about the end of the Cold War. After a series of massive budget cuts, the Air Force in Europe had barely enough airplanes to form a single fighter wing. Suddenly, there was tremendous competition for the reduced number of fighter jock jobs throughout the USAF.

Unable to land a job in a fighter cockpit and unwilling to leave the military he so loved, Carter had begun to consider a job as a military attaché. One of his duties as an attaché would be to fly a twin-engine prop C-12, the military version of the Beech King Air 200. As it was the only way to keep flying, Carter had accepted an assignment as Assistant Air Attaché in Bogotá, Colombia.

"San Juan Center, Air Transat 2522, Position *FROST*, at 0211, flight level 350, *BALU* 0249, *ROMAN*." The crack of the radio brought him back from his reverie. It was another aircraft checking in with the San Juan Air Traffic Control Center.

"Roger, Air Transat 2522, report position *BALU*," replied the San Juan air traffic controller in a lazy, mid-western US accent.

Carter watched as his co-pilot adjusted the cabin temperature for the folks in the back of the airplane. At this hour—with the sun no longer shining through the windows—most of the passengers would nod off for the remaining hour of the flight. A few extra degrees would help them in their slumber and keep the flight attendants from calling up and asking to "put a few more logs on the fire."

From the time they had leveled off at their cruising altitude, Carter and his copilot had engaged in a wide-ranging discussion. First, they had confirmed that since Grenada did not use Daylight Savings Time, it was on Atlantic Standard Time (AST). That meant that they didn't have to reset their watches from Miami time. Once they had resolved that timing issue and passed it along to their passengers, they had then moved on to the airline's ongoing—and so far fruitless—contract negotiations. Then, since they were both former military pilots, they had swapped flying stories from their time in the service. A few minutes earlier, they had carried on an animated discussion of the relative merits of the A-6 versus the F-111 in the surface attack role. Now, they sat in silence as the plane droned on its southeasterly trajectory towards Grenada.

The just-completed discussion had Carter thinking about his days in the military. He remembered that there had been a big difference between the Air Force fighter community and that strange new world of the military attaché. The difference became quite clear during his first day of training when he showed up in civilian coat and tie, rather than his infinitely more comfortable flight suit. He had been ushered into a small room and asked to sit in a chair next to a machine with a tangled maze of wires and gauges.

It was Carter's initial polygraph test—a prerequisite for entrance into the highly classified world of the military attaché. The Defense Intelligence Agency (DIA) had administered the *poly* in the bowels of a non-descript building in Clarendon, Virginia.

"Major Carter, I'm going to ask you a series of questions. I'd like you to relax and answer them honestly," the technician had told him as he hooked Carter up to the machine. Then, the technician had badgered him with question after question about his past:

"What's your name?"

"When were you born?"

"Where were you born?"

"Where were your parents born?"

After a series of mundane questions concerning his background, the questions began to change—taking on a much more serious tone. It was clear that this was no "getting-to-know-you" chat. They were probing to find any evidence of unsuitability for the job. They needed to determine whether Carter would be a security risk... or worse.

After it was over, feeling emotionally drained after what seemed like hours of "interrogation," Carter began putting personal items (which had been removed for the polygraph) back into his pockets. Placing his watch back on his wrist,

Carter glanced at the time and shocked to discover that the *poly* had lasted barely thirty-five minutes.

The attaché training program had been longer and more arduous than Carter had anticipated. First, he had to complete four months of training with the DIA at Bolling Air Force Base in Washington, DC. Then, there were weeks of weapons and other specialized training at several different locations along the eastern seaboard, including the FBI's sprawling facilities in Quantico, Virginia.

"National 986, Descend and maintain flight level 190, contact Salines Approach on 119.4." The terse instructions from the *Piarco* controller snapped Carter back to the present. It was time to get ready for their descent and landing in Grenada.

5:02 PM EST
Carrera Siete—Bogotá, Colombia

Casa Medina's red brick façade made it appear more like a colonial home than a hotel. Originally built in 1945 as a private residence, it was now situated in the thriving international business section in the northern part of Bogotá. The rooms were decidedly five-star in size and amenities.

Sliding into the back seat of the limo waiting at the hotel's front entrance, Carlos Hernández sometimes had to remind himself that he hated the perks that came with his current position. It seemed a lifetime ago that he had toiled and sweated his way through the jungles of the Colombian countryside. *The battleground has changed, but the Revolution continues,* he thought to himself as the limo driver expertly merged the Mercedes S500 into the heavy rush-hour traffic. They were headed north on *Carrera Siete,* or Seventh Street, the main north-south thoroughfare in Colombia's capital city.

As a young boy, Carlos had done well enough in school. Like most boys his age, however, he lacked motivation. His only good grades were in mathematics. He had always felt at home with the order and exactitude of numbers and equations.

Then, Carlos had become a member of the FARC, and everything had changed. In jungle classrooms spread throughout Colombia, he had studied the Revolution. Over time, Carlos had come to understand the greatness of *el Libertador,* Simón Bolívar—the Liberator and hero of South America. As a fledgling member of the *Bolivarian Movement for a New Colombia,* Carlos had learned how the corrupt ruling class of Colombia would be replaced and the country steered towards a return to Bolivarian ideals. Through the FARC's armed struggle, Colombia would be great once again—its proud farmers and *campesinos* freed from the yoke of Imperialist/Capitalist dominance and control.

During his early years with the FARC, Carlos' cell leaders had been impressed with how quickly Carlos mastered each successive lesson. As his knowledge of the Revolution grew, he became increasingly involved in the administrative duties of his unit. In fact, if it weren't for the mandatory weekly training in guerrilla tactics and small arms marksmanship, he might have forgotten how to use his AK-47.

The further Carlos' duties had taken him from the actual armed struggle, the faster had been his movement up through the FARC's chain of command. While working at a remote base camp in the eastern province of *Arauca*, near the border with Venezuela, one of his superiors asked him to help unravel a new financial program on a laptop computer. Like any complex organization, the FARC needed to track its finances and the movement of money, drugs, weapons, and other supplies. His cell leader, Milton Reyes (known as *Tirofijo* or Sure-Shot) was responsible for the finances of the 10th and 16th Fronts of the FARC. Reyes had to submit detailed monthly reports to his superiors. However, as his nickname implied, *Tirofijo* was not happy pouring over financial documents on the damn, unreliable, antiquated, piece-of-shit laptop computer the FARC had given him. He was much happier with an AK-47 in his hands, going out on patrol, blowing up oil pipelines or setting up ambushes.

Since only the most trusted members were involved with this vital aspect of the Revolution, *Tirofijo* had initially been reluctant to share any information with Carlos. Over the months, however, he gained confidence in Carlos' commitment to the cause. More importantly, he had been impressed with his young assistant's ability to make sense out of the different sources of—and hiding places for—the organization's money. Over time, *Tirofijo* learned that he could safely delegate his financial management responsibilities to Carlos, who felt completely in his element when immersed in numbers, inventories, reports and any kind of paperwork.

In this way, Carlos Hernández became a moneymaker for the Revolution—mastering the intricacies of the corrupt capitalist financial system. Soon, he was creating new and innovative ways of exploiting that system for the Bolivarian cause. Carlos began to appreciate how the Revolution could accomplish two goals at once. It was the perfect solution: use the shameful degradation of the American population—reflected in their insatiable appetite for drugs—to raise money for the Revolution.

Carlos watched silently and contemptuously as a series of shopping malls and overpriced stores streaked by outside the limo window. They turned off *Carrera Siete* and continued north into *los Rosales*. This area, nestled at the foot of the towering mountains on the north side of the city, was Bogotá's most exclusive neighborhood. *Los Rosales* was filled with capitalist usurpers who were sucking the lifeblood from Colombia's exploited poor.

Carlos was heading to a meeting with one of the most important of these usurpers with whom he was forced to do business—an American named Marty Newmann. Newmann had been living in Colombia for years and had amassed a great fortune from the drug trade.

As the limo continued deeper into *los Rosales,* the scenery became increasingly residential. Carlos thoughts turned to the American's wife. What a beautiful creature she was. Born into the corrupt upper class of Colombia, her parents had obviously spoiled her and sent her to the most expensive schools and universities. In Carlos' opinion, they had wasted their money, as the woman appeared to have been educated beyond her intelligence. The American appeared to agree with this assessment, as he often belittled her in front of Carlos, his bodyguards and even the household help. The American also left his wife alone for long stretches of time while he traveled. Carlos did not understand why Newmann treated his woman the way he did or why he kept her. Perhaps her beauty had something to do with it.

He recalled the first time he had laid eyes on her. Even now, he was unable to stop thinking about that day and was incapable of excising the vivid image from his mind. Carlos and the American had been going over the initial stages of an annual financial planning document they were drafting for the FARC. At one point, the American had excused himself and walked into his private office to get some banking details stored in his computer. Seconds later, he had exploded out of the office, stormed straight past Carlos and violently torn open the sliding glass doors leading onto the back patio.

"Have you been using the computer in my office again?" he screamed at his wife, who had been sunning herself on a lounge chair by the pool. Carlos had shifted his position on the sofa to catch a better glimpse of the commotion. The American didn't seem to care if anyone heard his outburst, as he was yelling at the top of his lungs and had left the door to the patio wide open.

The American's wife had been wearing the skimpiest of bikinis. The bottom of the suit was comprised of an impossibly small patch of blue, metallic-looking fabric—that managed to cover only a small fraction of her bottom. Carlos remembered that delicious, olive-colored expanse of perfect skin, and the way it that glistened in the sunlight from the tanning lotion she had applied. As she turned and lifted her torso to look at her husband, the top to her bikini—which had been untied to allow for the tanning of her superbly-contoured back—had fallen off. The American's wife—that beautiful Colombian creature—had hastily stood to answer her husband.

Her gaze had been divided between her approaching husband; her arms, which were only partially successful in covering those wonderful breasts; and the ground. Carlos had watched, completely transfixed.

"I'm sorry, *mi vida*," she pleaded, an imploring, submissive expression on her face "I only wanted to check for some sale prices at the *Unicentro* Mall. I know you—"

"I bought you your *own* freakin' computer," he interrupted. "I've asked you a thousand times not to use mine. Why can't you do that one simple thing I've asked, you useless bitch?"

"I'm sorry," she said, sun-sparkled tears beginning to stream down her cheeks. "I can never get mine to connect to the Internet," she continued as Newmann turned and headed back into the house.

"Useless, dumb, Colombian bitch—I should beat the shit out of her until she pays attention to what I tell her," the American had grumbled as he stormed back into the room. The American was oblivious to the sight of his wife crossing the patio to reenter the house via the kitchen door. Carlos tried not to stare at the woman as she passed by the glass doors in front of him. After that violent outburst, Marty Newmann had gotten right back to business—as if nothing had happened.

Each time Carlos met with Newmann at his home, he remembered that beautiful body, but he knew better than to covet this woman. She was the enemy: rich, stupid, useless, and soft—living proof of the corruption and uselessness of the upper classes that still ruled his country. The demands of the Bolivarian Future left Carlos Hernández no time to crave any woman. The Revolution was his only mistress.

Over the past several months, he and Marty Newmann had been adding flesh and bone to what was initially only a general outline of an audacious plan of action. If successful, they would significantly increase the flow of arms and money into the national structure of the FARC. They had both agreed that if the Americans could spend billions of dollars in their imperialist "Plan Colombia," the Revolution would have to raise enough money to implement its own "Plan America."

5:13 PM EST
Panamax Office Supply Company—Panama City, Panama

The Panamax Office Supply Company was located in a complex of buildings in the *Bella Vista* section of Panama's capital city. This bustling community, lying just west of the scenic *Avenida Balboa*, used to be a staid residential area, composed primarily of colonial era homes. Today, it is peppered with a wide variety of businesses: jewelry stores, boutiques, small manufacturing operations, and office complexes mixed together with modern apartment buildings catering to Panama's growing number of middle class workers. Although only a mile from the luxurious high-rise apartment buildings, hotels, and expensive restaurants lining Balboa Avenue in the coastal area of

Paitilla, this neighborhood had a decidedly different, almost bohemian flavor.

Back in the 1990s, as the Americans pulled up stakes and left Panama, many Panamanians lost jobs they had held for decades working for the American military. Rafael Frontiza had been one of those who lost his job. He had been a logistics supply technician at Fort Amador until it was closed in 1997. Rather than despair over the loss of his once-secure employment, Frontiza had considered how he might benefit from the massive quantities of equipment left behind by the Americans. He knew where the equipment was stored, was aware of its condition, and was very familiar with both the American and Panamanian business communities. Frontiza began to think that he might be able to turn a reasonable profit by refurbishing and reselling what the Americans had left behind.

During his last days at Fort Amador, Frontiza had drawn up a business plan and approached a local banker for a start-up loan. The banker had been impressed with his idea, and had agreed to provide the requested financing. With this loan money in hand; Frontiza had been able to start the Panamax Office Supply Company. Frontiza's company had been profitable from the beginning, and it had expanded rapidly. As the company continued to grow, so did his client base, which now included businesses throughout Latin America—in particular, from neighboring Colombia.

Inside the main office building, Rafael Frontiza was escorting his long-time friend and fellow businessman, Jorge Dárdano, towards the reception area near front entrance. They had been talking business while sipping coffee in Frontiza's modest office.

"I'm sure this is going to work out well for us. Business has never been better," Frontiza confided to his old friend. "You should have invested more before the Americans left. I don't agree that all is lost without the bases."

"You may be right Raf, but I'm still afraid that these grandiose plans are designed only to line the pockets of government officials," replied Dárdano, draining the last drops of coffee from his cup and placing it on the receptionist's desk.

"Ah, you worry too much. There's enough money to go around!" Frontiza said with a laugh. "I don't seem to be doing too badly, do I?" he asked, pointing to the elegant office furniture and paintings on the wall of the entranceway. "Not only that, I've found the most beautiful and productive workers in the entire city," he said lustily, rubbing his receptionist's shoulder.

As the two friends reached the building's front door, they embraced each other in typical Latin, *abrazo*-style—the energetic slapping of each other's backs echoing through the large entranceway.

"Say hello to Margarita, and kisses to all the kids," he shouted as Dárdano walked away onto the sidewalk in front of the building.

"Until the next time, my friend," called Dárdano over his shoulder as he stepped into his waiting limousine.

Frontiza hurried back into the building and walked straight back towards his office—this time ignoring his receptionist. He had a large stack of paperwork waiting on his desk, a sure sign that it would be another late evening. Leaning back in his office chair, Frontiza stared at the offending stack of letters, bills, accounts receivable and shipping reports piled up on his desk. The paperwork represented a mixed blessing—more business and more work. It also represented a far more ominous portent of the future… a reminder of how drastically things had changed in so short a time.

A few months earlier, when the volume of business and the corresponding pile of paperwork on Frontiza's desk was significantly smaller, a well-mannered American had phoned Frontiza, and expressed a desire to set up a business meeting over dinner. He had assured Frontiza that the meeting would be well worth his time. They had dined at one of the most exclusive restaurants—located in the *Casco Viejo* section of colonial Panama City. The food and wine had been the best available—all on the American's tab. During the dinner, the American had explained how impressed he was with Frontiza's company. Frontiza had been proud to hear his business accomplishments praised so highly.

Once they had finished their sumptuous dinner, and the cognac had been poured, the American had gotten to the point. He was interested in purchasing Panamax. He proposed a very generous buyout and suggested that Frontiza should stay in charge of the day-to-day operations of the company. Frontiza could scarcely fathom the amount of money the American was offering—one hundred times his original business loan. The American had presented a contract for his signature, complete with the required permissions from Panamanian authorities.

That evening, as he drove home from the meeting with the American, Frontiza could scarcely believe his good fortune. It was almost too good to be true. He worried that the purchase might never come to fruition, or that the money might never actually materialize. However, the next morning when he called his bank, he learned—to his great pleasure—that the agreed amount had already been wired into his account. A total stranger had appeared, and in less than one day, his life had dramatically changed.

The American's plan over the past months had been simple and elegant. A subsidiary company based in Mobile, Alabama would ship old, discarded computers from the United States. Frontiza's operation in Panama would refurbish the computers (just as he had been doing for the last several years) and recycle them back to the States. Even the environmentalists would love the idea. The American had assured him that within a few months they would expand their operations to the UK, Holland, Germany, and perhaps even Russia. It was all a bit overwhelming.

Frontiza stared at the bill of lading in his hand and shook his head. He was still awed by the size of it—larger than any previous order. In two days, they'd be shipping the first huge batch of equipment from Panama City to Colón—on the Atlantic side of the Canal. From there, it would be loaded onto a waiting container ship. Frontiza, like most Panamanians, was accustomed to referring to the northern end of the canal as the *Atlantic* side of the Canal, even though technically that part of the canal flowed into the Caribbean.

Like all educated Panamanians, Frontiza knew there had always been some confusion as to the actual geographic layout of Panama and its Canal. Most people think of the Panama Canal as running east and west—linking the waters of the Pacific and the Caribbean. In fact, it is oriented in a north-south direction. Because that section of Panamanian isthmus runs in an east-west orientation, Panamanians are fond of explaining this geographic quirk as follows: a person can watch the sunrise in the east over the Pacific; while his brother, in Colón, can look to the west that evening and watch the sun set over the Caribbean. Normally, a quick glance at a map suffices to clarify the geography.

Once the shipment was loaded on the container ship, it would depart Colón and begin its nearly 1500-mile voyage to Mobile, Alabama. In a matter of days, the inaugural shipment would arrive in America. If everything went as planned, the local press would be there to record the occasion—providing free advertising.

Up until a week ago, things had gone exactly as planned. Just as the American had promised, extra cash had been pouring into the company's coffers. Orders were increasing and the company's profit margins and cash flow were improving exponentially. Frontiza's future was looking very bright indeed... until a week ago.

Out of the blue, the American had called him. This time, there was no dinner... no optimistic discussion of the future. The American was changing their arrangement. Frontiza was no longer in charge of the company.

The day after the phone call, a new group of "employees" had arrived. Speaking with Colombian accents, they had blocked all access to the warehouse and supervised the unannounced arrival of several truckloads of cargo.

As he glanced again over the paperwork for tomorrow's shipment, Frontiza hoped that no one would have reason to question it. He was sure that something illegal... something terrible was going on. The American had made it clear; from now on, none of this would be his concern. The secretive goings-on in his warehouse, and the new contents of tomorrow's shipment were making him extremely nervous. Rafael Frontiza was not only worried about his future of his company—he was worried about his future on the planet.

6:23 PM AST
Point Salines International Airport—Grenada

Shortly after the ground crew opened the main door of the 737, the passengers began the tediously slow process of gathering their belongings and bumping their way out of the airplane. Carter felt the moist, hot and heavy Grenadian air hit him through the open main cabin door—like a blast from an unseen furnace.

"The humidity must be higher than normal," remarked his copilot, wiping the sweat from his brow.

"Yeah, let's hurry up and get the hell out of here," Carter replied—his voice soft enough to be unheard by the passengers. "There are a couple of cold ones with our names on them waiting for us at the hotel bar!"

The bus ride from the airport to the hotel was a short one. As the crew left the small terminal in the left-hand drive Isuzu passenger van, Carter thought of the morning of October 25, 1983, when many young Americans saw the same scenery that he now watched outside the van's windows. Those brave, young soldiers had jumped out of C-130s lumbering along at only 150 knots, while facing the heavy barrage of anti-aircraft fire put up by Cubans operating Soviet-made S-70 machine guns. Nineteen of those Americans had breathed their last breath on this little speck in the Caribbean.

How calm and peaceful this corner of the world now seemed. The Grenadians—most of them anyway—still celebrate the anniversary of the US invasion, which saved the island from the last in a succession of Marxist leaders. In an earlier visit to the island, Carter had walked up the hill leading to Fort George, which had served as a prison and had been the location of the former Prime Minister's execution. One could still see the bullet holes and the eerie and fading graffiti from the gory days of the Grenadian Revolution: "No Pain No Gain, Brother."

Once the van reached the circular driveway of the Rex Grenadian Hotel, the crew waited while the driver carefully unloaded their bags and placed them in an orderly line beside the van. After collecting their belongings and tipping the driver, they headed towards the reception desk, where hotel employees greeted them with a complementary glass of rum punch.

"Anyone headed to the bar?" asked Carter.

"Nah," said the copilot as he filled out his check-in paperwork. "Now that I've polished off this rum concoction, I think I'm just gonna try to catch up on my beauty sleep. I'll probably head down for dinner in a couple of hours. But if not, I'll see you bright and early in the morning."

"Anyone else interested?" Carter asked the group of flight attendants busily chatting as they completed the hotel's paperwork.

"No thanks," said the most senior. "We're all dead tired. This was our fourth leg of flying today. I think we're all gonna *slam click*."

Slam-Click is both a noun and a verb in the airline world. The expression describes the noise made when shutting one's hotel door and locking the deadbolt. This meant that during the layover, one would enjoy a book, watch TV, or simply get a good night's sleep—rather than spend time socializing with the rest of the crew.

"OK, see everyone bright and early tomorrow," said Carter as he headed up to his room. "I think I'll just have one beer before I call it a night. I've been thinking about having a *Carib* all day!" Carter was determined to have at least a few sips of that tasty Grenadian beer—even if he'd have to enjoy it by himself.

5:24 PM EST
Onboard *Juguete del Calamar*—North of Cartagena, Colombia

It had been a perfect day for sailing. In the waters of the Caribbean Sea, 940 miles west of Grenada, the bright disk of the afternoon sun peeked through the scattered clouds, providing the perfect illumination for the great splashes of water that roared up on each side of the prow of the beautiful 50-foot Beneteau sailing yacht as it sliced surgically through the water. From the business end of this yacht, she was sleek and speedy—a beautiful compromise between speed and comfort. She was adequately equipped for open-ocean sailing and she was roomy and comfortable below decks.

Jack Zaworski loved the sea—as did the attractive, female shipmate by his side. Zaworski—known almost universally as "Z"—had served in the United States Navy for 15 years. For most of that time, he found it difficult to stomach the smug, incompetent, self-centered, careerist bastards who were calling the shots.

He started thinking seriously about leaving the Navy after his second assignment flying the F-14 *Tomcat* onboard the USS *Coral Sea*. Zaworski's first combat mission had been on an April morning back in 1986—flying combat air patrol over the Gulf of Sidra, north of Tripoli, Libya during operation *El Dorado Canyon*. His job had been to protect the fleet from any attempt at reprisal by the Libyans. He had been itching—almost praying—that the Libyan Air Force would be foolish enough to launch fighters against the American fleet. Instead, they had kept their airplanes parked on the ground. He had bored holes in the sky that night while the A-6 air-to-mud guys had gotten all the glory. He had to admit that the Air Force *prima donnas* had also done pretty well for themselves that night—finally quieting down that Libyan nutcase, Muammar Qadhafi.

After completing his tour on the *Coral Sea*, Z had gotten increasingly fed up with life in the Navy. The only exception to that boredom (outside of his

Tomcat cockpit) was the two years he spent at the Defense Attaché Office (DAO) in Bogotá, Colombia. His best friend during that tour of duty was the Assistant Air Attaché, John Carter—the only Air Force pilot he considered worth a damn.

After Bogotá, Zaworski had considered staying on active duty long enough to allow a full retirement. In the end, he had decided that it just wasn't worth it. After resigning his Navy commission, he had struggled through a couple of post-military jobs; but each one had proven to be a dead end. After spending so much time at sea with the Navy, Z realized that to be happy, he would have to maintain his maritime connection. For this reason, he decided he *must* have a sailboat large enough to double as his home. A few months after resigning his Navy commission, Z had sold his house, his car and most of his possessions, and used the proceeds to buy a used sailboat. He named it *Juguete del Calamar*—Spanish for "Squid's Toy."

Not long into his new, post-military life, the sad reality of his financial situation became impossible to ignore. He was quickly running through the money from the sale of his property and he could no longer afford to stay at his San Diego marina. After several weeks of soul-searching and investigating different options, he decided to leave the United States and make Cartagena, Colombia his home. The women were plentiful, the casinos liked foreign gamblers, the booze was cheap, and the low cost of living might preserve his rapidly dwindling supply of cash.

Shortly after sailing down in the *Juguete,* he had found an inexpensive berth and settled into one of his favorite watering holes in Cartagena from his attaché days: O'Reilly's Marina. He was quite happy, and it appeared that if he were careful, his money might last long enough to enjoy a lifetime of sailing, gambling and womanizing.

A few months into his new life in Cartagena, Z had been holding his own at a casino blackjack table when he had recognized Marty Newmann sitting at another table. He had gone over to Newmann, introduced himself and the two of them had talked about their time together at the DAO in Bogotá. At some point in the conversation, Newmann had off-handedly commented that he might be able to help Z with his somewhat meager financial situation, if he were interested in doing business together. Z had told him that the extra cash would certainly be helpful, and might even facilitate longer and less financially stressful stays at the casino.

About a month after their chance encounter, Newmann had once again appeared in Cartagena. This time, Newmann came to the marina and made a startling business proposition. He had purchased O'Reilly's Marina and Bar and asked Z to run the marina for a very handsome salary. Z couldn't believe his luck. Newmann's offer would provide him with exactly the life he wanted: sea, sun, sailing, and women. There also didn't appear to be too much work involved in running the marina, as it had been around long enough to almost run itself.

In very short order, the reality of Newmann's plans for the marina became clear. Zaworski's role was limited to keeping the marina's books open to Newmann's accountants and ignoring certain comings and goings. Boats began to show up late at night and leave within a few hours.

At the outset, Zaworski had tried to ignore what was happening. Childishly, he thought Newmann's offer might have been an act of kindness by a former comrade in arms. Deep in his heart, however, Z knew the truth. The marina purchase had been a business deal for Newmann—a way to secure Zaworski's cooperation in laundering money and to facilitate smuggling operations.

Over time, Z had learned to live with his decision to cooperate with Newmann. After all, he was not personally involved with any of the shady dealings going on at the marina. He never attempted to discover more about what was unfolding around him, and with the help of a little selective amnesia on his part, life was still good.

Once a quarter, one of Newmann's accountants would go over the marina's books and report on cash flow. The figures that emerged never seemed justified by the number of boats moored at the marina. Nor did the bar and restaurant patrons appear to be spending as much money as the books indicated. Newmann never asked anything else of Zaworski. Z simply showed up occasionally at the marina's office and pretended to be busy for a couple of hours each week.

During one of Newmann's subsequent visits to the marina, he had brought along his wife, Aliria. She was almost frighteningly beautiful, and even at that first meeting her piercing hazel eyes stared so deeply and hypnotically into Z's that they seemed capable of exploring his soul. Her long, jet-black hair framed a face worthy of any fashion magazine cover, and even the sparse amount of make-up she used seemed an unnecessary addition to near perfection.

She was several years younger than Marty, and more than a decade younger than Z. Her body was both voluptuous and athletic—all thanks to genes and regular exercise, not the result of some plastic surgeon's expertise with a scalpel.

As they sat drinking at O'Reilly's on that day he had first met her, Aliria had briefly mentioned that she had always dreamt of learning how to sail. In the ensuing conversation, Newmann had casually suggested that Z should teach her. At the time, it seemed like a random thought on Newmann's part, and Zaworski never expected to see Aliria again.

To his surprise, however, about a month later, she showed up at the marina, ready for her first sailing lesson. As they initially headed out in the *Juguete*, she had been silent and aloof—responding to Z's instructions with a simple nod of the head. After a few hours on the open ocean, however, she had slowly warmed to Zaworski's casual affability. Within a few hours, she began to open up and share some of the details of her life.

Z learned that Aliria was the only child of Ramón Escobedo Valeria—the head of one of Colombia's oldest and most successful banks. Her father had married his second cousin, Victoria Valeria Mejía—thereby combining parts of two banking empires. Despite the circumstances of their strategic partnership, her parents had surprisingly fallen deeply in love. Tragically, her mother had died shortly after Aliria's birth in a freak automobile accident. Her father never remarried, and Aliria had remained an only child. Aliria had had a pleasant enough life with her father; but because he was always at work, she spent more time with her governess. She and her father had remained somewhat distant through the years, even after she had grown up and started out on her own.

It was during her last year of college, that she had first met Marty Newmann at a party hosted by one of Bogotá's leading business families. She had been studying English and Business Administration—destined to work in her father's bank after graduation. That evening she had been nearly swept off her feet by the brash American businessman who was beginning to amass his fortune. She appreciated his outgoing, confident personality, and was impressed with his growing business empire. She also had to admit that she found his rapid-fire, totally-mangled Spanish quite endearing.

Once she had finished her university studies, she had gone to work at the bank. At first, she thought that her new job would give her a chance to see her father more often. However, seeing him more often at the bank did not alter their rather cold, emotionless relationship. It was during those first years at the bank that Marty had begun to court her more seriously. She had eventually succumbed and they were married.

After six months of bi-weekly sailing lessons, Aliria had told Z why she had initially become interested in sailing. During the last stages of their courtship, while discussing their plans for marriage, Marty had suggested they spend their honeymoon on a yacht or sailboat. With this fleeting outline of their post-nuptials, Aliria began to dream how she and Marty would sail around the Caribbean—her mind adding substance to the dry description her fiancé had provided.

During the first few months after the wedding, however, Marty had been in the middle of several important business transactions and the honeymoon was repeatedly postponed. Despite many promises over the years, it became clear that the honeymoon would never materialize. Slowly, Aliria's dream began to change, and Marty Newmann was no longer with her on that sailboat. Now, rather than an idyllic and romantic honeymoon together on the ocean, she sailed alone. The newly modified dream gave her an exhilarating feeling of escape and independence. In the blissful fantasy world she had contrived for herself, not only was she in control of a powerful sailing vessel, she was in control of her life.

Today, as the *Juguete* bounded along playfully in the waves, Aliria struggled to come to grips with a long-dormant emotion. She could no longer deny it. Unexpectedly—almost inexplicably—it was there in her heart: a warm, glowing ember of happiness. Unfortunately, it was a feeling she felt compelled to keep locked away inside. She was still married to another man—a cold, calculating man, for whom she no longer felt any love.

"Look at your jib. See how it's fluttering?" asked Z, interrupting Aliria's thoughts and forcing her to concentrate on her sailing lesson. "You're losing air on that sail. Bring in that line some. There. That's it!"

"Jack, I think we better start heading back," her face no longer graced by the faint smile it held only moments earlier. "Marty's supposed to be back in Bogotá tonight. Plus, I've got a couple of errands I need to take care of."

"OK. Let's see if you've got this tacking thing down," said Z as Aliria deftly steered the craft back towards the north coast and Cartagena.

They sat close together in silence at the helm. Z marveled at how much at ease they were with each other, despite the fact that she was his boss's wife. It was also a bit out of the ordinary that he had been alone with this woman for long stretches of time without ever having gotten her into bed. For Zaworski, a relationship with a woman that did not include sex was a perplexing novelty.

"Penny for your thoughts," Z said, noticing that Aliria seemed pre-occupied—her mind was definitely *not* into the sailing.

"I was thinking about my father. I can't believe it's been less than two weeks since he died. I wish we had been able to spend more time together. He was always busy... too busy to be involved in my life. Oh, I was always well cared for. He sent me to the best schools, bought me the latest fashions from Paris, you name it. But I would have traded it all for a real family."

"I wish I could help," Z sympathized.

"You *do* help, Z. That's why I come up to Cartagena to sail with you on the *Juguete*. It's an escape for me. These days, I feel like... it's like a memory I have, from a long time ago. It was Christmas morning, when I was about nine years old. I was sitting there amongst mountains of presents. I had gotten everything I asked for, and more. After I had opened all the gifts, Papa told me he had to leave for some terribly important meeting at the bank. So he left me alone in that huge, empty house with the servants. I should have been happy, but all I could do was cry. That's how I feel right now. I have all the *things* I want; but not the *life* I want. Do you understand?"

"Of course I do."

"Last week, when I was at the lawyer's office for the reading of Papa's will,

I learned many things... many, many things. Papa was a very good banker. Although it'll probably take me weeks to figure out all the trust funds and financial instruments that he's set up for me, I know I'll always have more than enough money. Oh, it's not as big as the fortune Marty has amassed, but it would be more than enough for my purposes. It seems silly to say, but I'm only now realizing that money isn't everything. And it's true that it can't buy happiness. I wish I could use that money to turn back the clock... to change some of the decisions I've made."

"What will you do, buy a time machine?" Z asked whimsically, trying to lift her out of her dark mood.

"No. But I will finally *do* something to change my life," she said, ignoring Z's attempt at cheering her up.

"Aliria, it's not your fault. Your father probably did the best he could. I'm sure he did what he thought was right for you."

"Yes, that's probably true. I loved my father, and I know he loved me. I thought I knew everything about him—even though most of our time together was spent in *his* world. It was a cold place of leveraged takeovers, bank ledgers, money, and investments. But now that he's gone, I've been able to unravel unexpected aspects of his finances. As I've gone deeper into his world, I've found out I didn't know him at all. He led a secret life that was off limits to me."

"Aliria, he's gone now, and you can't go back to re-live... or change your past. You have to find a way to live for today, and to try to plan for a better tomorrow."

"I know," she said simply. "For today, I need to get *Juguete* and me back to the marina so I can get back to Bogotá."

"With these winds," said Z, glancing at his watch. "It'll take us a little over an hour."

"That'll be just fine."

6:52 PM AST
Rex Grenadian Hotel—St. Georges, Grenada

Carter made his way up to his hotel room. He then accomplished his layover unpacking ritual—tie off, shirt unbuttoned, pants off, roll-on travel bag hefted up onto left side of bed, unzip bag, remove toilet kit, carry to bathroom. It was always the same. After years of practice, Carter had gotten the process of moving in and out of hotel rooms down to a science.

In five minutes, he had taken a quick shower and changed into a short-sleeved shirt and khaki pants. Before leaving the room, he glanced at the bed where he had placed his suitcase along with tomorrow's clothes and smiled wistfully. As usual, he had lined up everything on *her* side of the bed. No matter where he was—at home or away on a trip—he could only sleep comfortably on *his* side of the bed. Although she had been gone for years now, it still seemed somehow inappropriate to encroach on her territory, even in slumber. Just like the territorial partition of sleeping space, Carter preserved an indelible and inviolate part of his heart for her.

Realizing that he was a hopeless creature of habit, Carter amusedly shook his head, turned around and walked out of the room, heading for the hotel bar. He hurried down the stairs—skipping the elevator. At least taking the stairs would provide a *little* exercise to offset the upcoming beer consumption, Carter rationalized.

The Rex Grenadian was *Caribbean Standard*. The bar area, which connected with the lobby on one end and the pool area on the other, was filed with white wicker tables and chairs. Scattered amongst the tables were evenly spaced, long-leafed plants, gently swaying in the gentle but persistent onshore breeze. Ceiling fans, suspended by lengthy tubes, rotated slowly enough to give the illusion of adding to the flow of air. Barely audible over the Reggae music piped from the hotel sound system, he could make out the intermittent sound of the surf, pounding away at the beach right behind the hotel.

Grenada had always been one of Carter's favorite layover locations. Grenadians were unfailingly friendly and appeared genuinely appreciative of their American visitors. Grenada's powdery white-sand beaches were paired with crystal-clear, blue-green ocean water. Together, they represented one of Grenada's most treasured assets, and made it one the Caribbean's most beautiful tourist destinations.

Uncharacteristically, the hotel's first floor and lobby area were sparsely populated. There were two couples sitting at one table near the bar. The volume of their discussion and the quantity of empty beer bottles at the table, gave testimony to the seriousness of these vacationers. From the accents and the fragments of conversation that he overheard, Carter guessed that they were Canadians, escaping the dreary cold and snow of their native land. Near the back of the room, a family of four was playing cards.

Out by the pool bar were the usual local suspects, laughing as they stood with bottles of beer and cigarettes playing *Swing Ring*. The object of the game—which was frequently punctuated with much shouting and laughing— was to carefully release a ring suspended by fishing line attached to the top of a wooden column and try and have it catch on a hook placed about chest-height on the column. Each of the men playing the game seemed vaguely familiar to Carter. They were regulars, spending an evening together over a few beers at the hotel's pool bar. On closer scrutiny, Carter recognized one of the men as the driver who had driven his crew to the hotel that evening.

At the bar, a bartender—wearing the obligatory, garishly colorful, tropical shirt—was wiping the deserted counter clean. Carter walked over and asked for a beer.

"What kind of beer would you like, Mon?" he asked.

"Make it a *Carib*, please, Reginald" replied Carter, noticing the name on his nametag. "Is the beer nice and cold tonight?"

"Always cold, sir! As long as de ice don't run out."

Reginald reached into the icebox under the bar and removed a bottle of beer. He wiped off the ice clinging to the outside of the bottle, and poured half of it into one of the small glasses that had been stacked neatly on the corner of the bar. After wrapping a paper napkin around the glass, he placed it front of Carter.

"You come here before... wid da crew from National, right?" Reginald asked with a smile.

"Yes, I have. And yes I did," replied Carter, reaching out to shake Reginald's hand. "The name's John Carter. Nice to see you again, Reginald."

Carter continued chatting casually with Reginald while he savored the ice-cold glass of beer. They discussed the weather, which as usual, was pronounced quite hot and providing plenty of rain. Their conversation also covered the upcoming elections, the recent fire at the prison, and the new Pina Cola road, which had recently been finished up in Saint Andrews. Clearly, nothing earth-shattering had happened since his last layover.

In an effort to continue the now-lagging conversation, Carter tried to remember some of the Grenadian politicians and military leaders he had met during his visits as an attaché. Perhaps this bartender would have heard of some of the people Carter had met at the time.

"Is Fitzroy George still the head of the Coast Guard?" Carter asked, finally remembering the affable head of the Royal Grenadian Coast Guard and wondering if he might still be in the position.

"Yes, Mon, he's still at it."

"I'd like to get back in touch with him some day. I met with him several times... but that was years ago; he probably doesn't even remember me," Carter explained.

"Well, I don't know," continued the bartender. "I tink he's gone off to sea for a while. You can call the Coast Guard tomorrow."

"Maybe on another trip... when I've got more time," replied Carter, polishing off the last of his *Carib*.

Carter glanced at his watch, quickly calculating how much time was remaining before his alarm clock would go off the next morning. His flight back to Miami would leave at 8:55 a.m. He'd have to be at the airport an hour before that, and allowing for the five-minute drive to the airport, he'd have to set the alarm very early indeed, if he planned on having a quick jog along the beach before they left.

"Another?"

"No thanks, Reginald. I gotta get up early tomorrow... just the check please."

Carter paid for the beer, leaving a tip equal to the cost of the beer. He then shook the bartender's hand and walked away from the bar.

"See you later," said Carter, over his shoulder as he started back to his room.

"Good evening, Mon, an I hope you sleep well," wafted the reply.

As Carter rounded the corner and headed up the stairs to his room, Reginald put away the empty glass and wiped off the countertop. Then, glancing around the room, he picked up a telephone and dialed a local number.

"Hello sir, it's Reginald over at da Rex. Thought you'd like to know that an American was just here askin' 'bout Superintendent George." Reginald said in a near-whisper, cupping his hand over the phone.

"No sir, he said sometin 'bout meeting him before, and wantin' ta get in touch."

"His name? John Carter. I'll check wid reception, if you want, but I'm sure he's leavin' tomorrow."

Reginald then hung up the phone and got back to polishing his already spotless bar.

7:15 PM EDT
National Security Agency—Fort Meade, Maryland

"I don't know what he's doin' down there, *Mon*, but I don't like it." A voice with a pronounced Caribbean island patois complained. "I remember he and that *Z-Mon* character used to come down here all the time checking out the RGPF and the SSU. Now, when he's supposed to be out of the military, the man comes back here asking for me—personally! I don't like it a bit... and it's making me very nervous."

"Calm down, I'll look into it," replied the steady voice.

"I'd appreciate that. Now is definitely *not* a good time for anyone to be snoopin' around askin' 'bout me."

"OK, hang tight, and I'll get back to you," responded *Mr. N*, ending the phone call.

Bill Hargrove and Steve Young continued their note taking while listening to the static at the end of the satellite phone conversation they had just intercepted. The two were sitting at their computer consoles in the South

American Communications Assessment Division of the National Security Agency. NSA's headquarters was located in a large complex of buildings between Washington and Baltimore. Their office was crammed full of computers, sound equipment, and lined with scores of file cabinets. They proudly considered it *organized* chaos.

For the last three decades, their unit had been primarily concerned with counter drug operations, handling communication intercepts from the tip of *Tierra del Fuego* to the southern border of the United States. Over the years, their job had become more difficult due to the increasingly sophisticated encryption technology used by drug smugglers.

Bill Hargrove and Steve Young had been at the Agency in the "good old days"—the 80s and early 90s—when it was a piece of cake to intercept conversations lifted from commercial satellite communication systems like *Inmarsat.* In those days, the bad guys thought they enjoyed total privacy with these new toys—but they were wrong. The NSA (or anyone else with enough money and a nearby Radio Shack) could easily intercept these conversations. Later on, as demand increased for global communications, the industry brought new systems on line, like the *Iridium* network of satellites, first launched in 1997.

Over the years, to meet its need to collect these snippets of conversations, the NSA had launched its own constellation of spy satellites. NSA analysts and technicians had access to mountains of information gleaned from a whole spectrum of intercept systems with exotic code names like *White Cloud, Aquacade,* and *Trumpet.* Each system had very specific capabilities designed to match the various requirements of America's premier electronic spying agency.

The electronic cat and mouse game continued apace as vast drug smuggling profits allowed the bad guys to engage in an encryption hardware and software arms race. Often, they used complex technology to defeat NSA's considerable computing power. Drug dealers—and terrorists, for that matter—also used simple codes in open e-mail messages sent from the Internet's vast network of private and public computers. At times, they used the simplest systems to avoid detection by NSA's snoopers. Runners or messengers on foot were particularly effective and almost impossible to detect or intercept.

This was not the first time that Hargrove and Young had intercepted one of *Mr. N's* calls. In fact, over the past few months, they had been following him quite actively, and his dossier had grown to fill several drawers of the file cabinets in their large office complex. *Mr. N* had several aliases: *Nacho, November,* and occasionally, simply *N.* Nearly all of intercepted cell phone calls they had collected, originated from Colombia, and were made to points all over the globe. Recently, his preferred calling destinations were New York, Switzerland, Panama, and Washington, DC.

Through coordination with their counterparts at the FBI, the two had learned that the satellite phone number that *Mr. N* had been calling in New York was the same number that the FBI had been following in one of their ongoing investigations. Pending legal authorization to share the content of their intercepts, their contact at the Bureau had simply told them that their Organized Crime Section had a roving wiretap authorized by a District Court Judge in New York. That tidbit of information gave them ample reason to suspect that *Mr. N* was in contact with organized crime elements.

Apparently, *Mr. N* had plenty of money to spend on encrypting his communications and was changing encryption packages every couple of weeks. This was problematic for Young and Hargrove, who had to use more and more time on one of the big supercomputers in the basement of this top-secret facility. At the NSA, computer time was an even more precious commodity than money. Hargrove and Young were convinced that *Mr. N* was the key to a large drug smuggling and money laundering organization operating out of Colombia.

"So, did we get any new code words this time?" asked Young, beginning the post-intercept analysis and cataloging process.

"Nope. *Z-Man* we've heard before—still no positive ID on that one. But on the caller, we have a 98% positive rating on voiceprint ID. It's definitely George again. I can't believe that dummy makes it so easy for us—talking about the Royal Grenadian Police Force and the Special Services Unit. I mean, what else are the RGPF and the SSU supposed to be? He might as well take out an ad in the *Washington Post!*"

"You'd think he'd never heard about the NSA's rather awesome computing ability," Young said with a smile.

"Yeah... and the awesome super analysts who never tire of chasing the bad guys," replied Hargrove, continuing the sophomoric superhero-crime-fighter shtick that had peppered their office conversation for years. It helped them cope with the tedium of their job, involving long hours poring over snippets of phone conversations, purloined e-mails, and other electronic transmissions.

"I still get a bad feeling about that guy," said Young. "I don't care if the Pentagon's Counter Drug Division vouches for Superintendant George, or that he's helped them out in a couple of counter-drug ops. I can't shake the feeling that he's a bad apple. Oh well, I guess it's all above our pay grade, we'll just have to let someone else keep track of which guys are wearing the black hats."

Suddenly, an alarm bell sounded and a red light flashed at the main intercept console. *Mr. N* was at it again. NSA's extensive voice recognition programs had matched his voice imprint, and its vast computing power was allowing them near real-time access to another electronic conversation. The voices coming out of their main monitoring station had a strange, electronically muffled tinge to them, as the computer worked to restore the voice signal from the sophisticated encryption algorithm that was attempting to keep this phone conversation private.

"*Delta One*, we've got a problem," said *Mr. N*, without preamble.

"Oh really?" came the reply, the voice carrying an unmistakable touch of sarcasm.

"Yes, really. *Delta Seven* has come up on radar, asking questions about our guy in Goldmine. I need him checked out, and if necessary…" the voice trailed off mid-sentence, as if enough had been said.

"How'd we find that out?"

"He was actually *in* Goldmine when he asked about our man."

"No shit!"

"Yes, shit. Get *Delta Two* involved on this. I'll get back to you tonight, when I've got more details."

"OK, don't worry; I'll handle it up here."

With those words, the line went dead. Young and Hargrove continued their frantic note taking as the computer dutifully waited to translate any further transmissions. Finally, a computer-generated voice announced, "Connection terminated, transcription complete. Ready for auto-save and cross-reference keywords."

Young moved over to a console keyboard and began to enter various code words and cross-reference keywords that would help them file and keep track of this conversation. The computer would automatically file a transcript of the dialogue in the same file location along with the other intercept transcriptions for *Mr. N*. Young would add keywords and notes to help identify this conversation. Eventually, they hoped to piece together all the intercepts and tidbits of information in such a way that would allow them to discern the big picture.

"Get anything?" Hargrove called over his shoulder toward the far side of the office.

"Yep. Got a partial," replied the intercept and tracking specialist from his desk, across the office from Hargrove.

The preliminary trace had narrowed the number down to a location in northern Virginia, maybe DC. The specialist continued to frantically type at one of the many keyboards at his station.

"Son of a bitch!" he cried, turning around in his chair to face Hargrove and Young. "It's the goddamn Pentagon. I'll have a name for you shortly. I've got to crosscheck with the Pentagon phone directory."

Despite the assurances from DOD, Young and Hargrove had long ago surmised that the connection for many of the drug transshipments through Grenada was Coast Guard Superintendent Fitzroy George. Once they had made that connection, it had been relatively easy for them to figure out that "Goldmine" was their code word for Grenada. Based on the input from military sources, the Interagency Task Force following this group of traffickers was not yet convinced that there was enough evidence to go after George. Experience taught them that time was on their side—George or one of the others would eventually make a mistake, and they'd all go down.

For weeks, there had been growing indications that they were up to something *big*. Furthermore, this latest intercept suggested that the traffickers were being assisted by someone inside the Pentagon. Clearly, the time was rapidly approaching when they'd have to talk to a judge and get permission for a domestic phone tap. The NSA was constrained by law from spying on US citizens. Someone working in the Pentagon, on the other hand, would be "easy pickings" once they got the required approval from Departments of Justice and Defense.

"OK, here it is guys… the call was made to a Colonel James K. Elmore, US Army. He's currently assigned to the Counter Drug Division of the Joint Staff at the Pentagon. The number checks out as current."

"Well I'll be damned," said Young. "First, let's get the paperwork started to have Legal approve a full spectrum of surveillance on Elmore—work, home… the works. Second, let's pull Elmore's service records, finance history, tax returns—everything we can get—and run it all against what we have so far. Maybe the computer will come up with something."

"Agreed… let's get a move on," added Hargrove. "It's gonna take some time to get approval from DOD to let us get at that Pentagon phone line."

As he picked up his phone to call the DOD liaison office, Young looked at his watch and then at Hargrove, "Looks like this already long day is about to get longer."

"You got *that* right," agreed Hargrove, shaking his head.

6:17 PM EST
Onboard *Juguete del Calamar*—North of Cartagena, Colombia

Jack and Aliria had continued sailing southward uttering hardly a word for the last 45 minutes. As the Colombian shoreline came back into view, Aliria began to prepare emotionally for leaving the *Juguete* and Z. Every time she left Cartagena, she felt like a part of her was being torn away. She dreaded going back to being Mrs. Marty Newmann. Finally, she broke the silence and raised the topic haunting her present: her husband.

"You know, I have never liked all this cloak and dagger stuff that Marty's into," she confided. "I know he's heavily involved with the drug and money laundering business. At first, I thought he must be a genius—everything he touched seemed to turn into gold. He had succeeded in the Colombian financial system, even as an outsider. In the beginning, I found that exciting and appealing. Now, life seems so different from my dreams. He insists on keeping bimbos all over the world—you know, a woman in every port. Well, I just can't accept the machismo, Z. Oh, sometimes he's almost civil with me; and he certainly gives me all the money I need. Still, I'm just his trophy wife—selected for *what* I was, rather than *who* I was. He saw me as a means of securing his access into Colombian society."

"All I know, honey, is that if you were married to *me*, I sure wouldn't need any other women in any damn ports of call!" Z leaned over and kissed Aliria on her forehead. For an instant, their eyes met. Just as quickly, Z averted his eyes and shifted his gaze up at the sails.

"My father never liked nor trusted him; but I didn't feel like I needed to listen to my father's opinions," continued Aliria. "Now I've come to realize that my father was right. I don't think Marty ever loved me. I was merely a means to an end. I know I'm well provided for. I have everything I ever wanted... and more. But..." she trailed off.

"I know, I know," said Z.

They were both beholden to Marty Newmann, and trapped in a relationship with someone for whom they felt both loathing and fear.

7:35 PM EDT
Director of Counter Drug Operations—Joint Staff, the Pentagon, Washington, DC

"Asshole!" Colonel Elmore bellowed to his empty office, slamming down the phone in disgust. *First, it's the damn Congressional visit, and now this!*

The many photos, plaques, and awards hanging on Elmore's office walls bore witness to a career served largely overseas. Nearly all those postings were in Latin America: Bolivia, Peru, Guatemala and two tours of duty in Colombia.

The wooden nametag on his desk read as follows:

COLONEL JAMES K. ELMORE, USA
ASSISTANT DIRECTOR, COUNTER DRUG PLANS AND OPERATIONS
JOINT STAFF, J 36
PENTAGON, WASHINGTON, DC 20301

Elmore had risen rapidly enough during the first two decades of his career. "Rapidly enough for a FAO," Elmore would have added. FAO, (pronounced "fay-oh") was yet another of an unending supply of military acronyms. This one stood for Foreign Area Officer. Unfortunately—for those assigned to Spanish-speaking countries—FAO is pronounced the same as *feo*, which meant *ugly* in Spanish.

The Army selected and trained officers for duty as FAOs due in large part to their language and cross-cultural skills. A FAO could expect to spend his career serving in overseas, non-combat posts. The Army assigned these officers to US Military Groups, to liaise with foreign military organizations; in Defense Attaché Offices, where they provided military intelligence and advice to ambassadors; and other politico-military organizations throughout the world where their specific knowledge of language and culture came in handy.

Despite their repeated protestations to the contrary, the Army did not hold the contributions of FAOs in as high esteem as they did their warfighters. Every Army officer knew that he must have "muddy boots" to continue moving up in rank. An officer muddied his boots by serving in combat and combat-support companies, battalions, and divisions. Although it might sound exotic to serve in overseas locations, the FAO career track was certainly *not* a preferred (or expeditious) route to the top.

Those who did become FAOs, however, knew that if they didn't screw up too badly, they could rise to the rank of full Colonel. Another potential benefit, given the frequency of their contact with defense contractors, was that their career field often paved the way for a lucrative job in that sector of the industry at the conclusion of their stint in the military.

Elmore couldn't stand the thought of working for a defense contractor. Even more unsavory to him would be working for one of the many think tanks that recruited retiring military officers. Most of these think tanks were located around the beltway surrounding metropolitan Washington, DC; and were commonly known as *Beltway Bandits*.

Elmore knew that based on the phone call he had just received; he had to get in touch with Colonel Michael Kennedy down at the US Southern Command in Miami. Kennedy had served with Elmore at the Embassy in Bogotá Colombia ten years earlier. Back then, Kennedy had been a hard-charging Captain—one of two Assistant Army Attachés. He too had gone on to serve several tours in various Latin American countries in his career.

Many years ago, Kennedy and Elmore had decided—at different times and for different motives—that the military compensation system was not sufficient for their needs. For this reason, they both had moonlighted for someone other than Uncle Sam: a successful but secretive American businessman operating out of Colombia.

Elmore walked over to his office safe, reached into the top drawer and removed the black plastic key containing the cipher that allowed the STU-3 classified telephone on his desk to operate in an encrypted mode. He then walked back to his desk, opened his palm pilot to the directory page and found the number for the SOUTHCOM Deputy J2, (the Southern Command's Deputy Director of Intelligence). Elmore knew that Kennedy would be sitting at his desk, in the Joint Operations Intelligence Center (JOIC), which maintained a 24-hour watch over all intelligence operations for SOUTHCOM. He dialed the number.

"SOUTHCOM JOIC, Staff Sergeant Parker speaking. May I help you Ma'am or Sir?" came the crisp military phone greeting. Elmore still winced each time he heard that *Ma'am/Sir* crap, as it represented yet another unnecessary concession to political correctness. It was one of many irritants endured by the old-school Elmore, who infinitely preferred just plain *Sir*.

"Colonel Kennedy please, this is Colonel Elmore calling, from the Joint Staff."

"Yes sir, Standby one. I'll transfer you."

There was a short pause as the Sergeant transferred the call to the desk of the Senior Watch Officer for the JOIC—a position that rotated amongst the senior officers of the directorate. Each officer served a 12-hour shift, and had to remain in this office—away from his or her normal workspace—for the duration of his shift.

The Senior Watch Officer was separated from the large cavernous room of the JOIC by a glass wall. The office door was fitted with large panels of glass, affording the occupant an unrestricted view of the "big board"—with its maps and situation displays. The members of the JOIC staff could see the watch officer, but could not hear any conversation through the double-paned glass.

"Colonel Kennedy," he answered simply, while glancing at the clock on the wall.

"Can you talk?" said Elmore, knowing that Kennedy would recognize his voice.

"Sure. What's up?" replied Kennedy.

"Let's go classified," replied Elmore, indicating that he was ready to transform their current un-encrypted conversation into a more private one.

"Roger, going classified," said Kennedy, turning the key in his STU 3 to the classified position.

Simultaneously, in the Pentagon, Elmore turned the key in his phone. As usual, the line appeared to go dead as the two mini-computers in each phone checked their authorizations and compared the cipher codes in each of the plastic keys inserted into each phone. Seconds later, the message, "TOP SECRET: JT STAFF J36 PNT, WASH DC" appeared in a small LED screen on the top of Kennedy's phone. A similar indication was displayed on Elmore's phone in the Pentagon: "TOP SECRET: JOIC SNR WO USSOUTHCOM," and they each heard the familiar electronic crackling noise as the encrypted connection was completed.

"I'm showing TS," said Kennedy's slightly distorted and electronically altered voice.

"Hey Mike, we need to talk," said Elmore, skipping the required confirmation of his phone's transfer into the classified mode. Over the years, Kennedy and Elmore had become quite accustomed to this form of communication. When they first began using the STU 3s, they had still used codes and code names to discuss "business." Over time, however, they had grown complacent. They thought that since everyone was so interested in chasing terrorists these days, no one would want to intercept their conversations. If they had known about recent goings-on at the NSA—a few miles to the north of the Pentagon—they would not have felt so secure.

"I just got a call from *Asshole*," said Elmore, using the nickname they often used for Newmann. "He wants us to check up on a retired military type. Remember John Carter, the Assistant Air Attaché who worked at the DAO in Bogotá?"

"Sure I remember him. I thought he retired a while ago and was flying with an airline."

"Yep, that's the one... and yes, he did. He's apparently living down in Miami Beach. Butthead says he's been in contact with Zaworski recently. Also, seems as though he's been asking about Fitzroy George down in Grenada."

"Holy Shit! That's not good! Do you think he's back working for DIA, or maybe DEA?"

"Nope, I've already asked around and nobody knows him."

"You don't think Z has told him anything, do you?"

"No, my guess is he's just fishing; but we need to find out for sure. Can you arrange for one of your DEA contacts to watch him? Something like... there is suspicion that he's using his airline job as a cover for smuggling. You'll think of something."

"Yeah, sure. Surveillance and phone tap?"

"Yes. Can you handle it?"

"No problem. I'll get with the Dade County cops for the tap—no use raising any suspicions with the FBI. They'll be able to get a warrant and place the bug within a couple of days... hopefully before Saturday. Is that fast enough, or should I try and get some outside help?"

"No, a couple of days will be fine. This is probably much ado about nothing. Give me a call if you find anything interesting."

6:38 PM EST
O'Reilly's Marina—Cartagena, Colombia

The sun was nearing the horizon and had transformed the distant clouds, rendering them a beautiful, nearly blood-red hue. Overhead, the clouds were turning gray—losing the playful white color they had displayed earlier. Along with the diminishing evening light, the winds had died down to the point where the sailing was less exhilarating; but still strong enough to carry them at a comfortable clip towards Cartagena and the marina.

After furling the sails, Z guided the sailboat into its berth using its inboard diesel motor. Once they had securely tied down the *Juguete*, Z checked his cell phone. There was a message waiting from Marty.

"He wants to know if I've been in touch with John Carter and if I have any idea why John would be nosing around Grenada asking questions about the Coast Guard Superintendent," Z explained, after listening to the message and putting the cell phone back into his pocket.

"Why would Marty be interested in John?"

"I don't have the foggiest notion. But there was something in his voice. He sounded more pissed than usual," replied Z, beginning to feel a sense of foreboding for his friend.

"I don't recall him ever mentioning John before—not once," she volunteered, noticing Z's concern. Over the months of their sailing together, Z had mentioned John Carter and the times the two of them shared during their attaché days. Given Marty's reputation for violence, Aliria shared Z's concern for his friend's safety.

"Well, I can't believe he's asking now. About a month ago, I was going over the old times with Ben O'Reilly. I told him about John being my closest friend. Hell, he's almost like family… even though we don't stay in touch that often or anything like that. We e-mail each other every now and then, and he sends me an occasional letter. Still, I owe him."

"You've talked about him before, Z, but I didn't realize you two were *that* close."

"Shit, I guess *I* didn't even know it. Not really. I mean I just don't have a lot of people who are… you know, close. But it's strange. After that talk with Ben, well, I've been thinking a lot recently about what would happen if I were to kick the bucket or something. I mean he'd be the closest thing to family for me. So, he'd probably get the *Juguete* and all my stuff if I croaked. No kidding, I've even started writing a damn will. Me, thinking about a will… can you believe it?"

"Yes, I can," she said, reaching out to touch his arm. "And that's always a good idea."

"This is so weird," Z continued. "For the past couple of weeks, I've had a feeling that I needed to get my shit together—to get my life a little more organized... you know what I mean? I've thought about a couple of my old Navy buddies; but mostly I've thought about touching base with John. And now this... I... Damn!" exclaimed Z, as he paced back and forth in the *Juguete's* cockpit area. "It can't be a good thing that Marty is asking about him. People that Marty starts worrying about sometimes end up disappearing. I don't think I can stand by and let that happen to John. I've got to figure out why he's got Marty interested in him, and the best way to figure *that* out is by going to Miami to ask him face-to-face."

Z's mind raced—considering the list of things that needed to happen in the next few hours. First, he'd have to call Carter in Miami and set up a time for them to get together. Next, he'd need to make reservations for the flight and make hotel reservations. No matter what, he had to warn his friend.

Zaworski hurriedly escorted Aliria out of the marina and past the bar to the parking lot, where her limousine was waiting. He told Aliria he would call her in Bogotá as soon as he had met with Carter in Miami. As Aliria got ready to get into the limo, they both felt a bit awkward. He felt close enough to her for a goodbye kiss, but neither of them dared show affection for the other in public. Instead, Zaworski simply opened the door for Aliria, helped her into the limo, and waved goodbye as the car pulled off into the night. He then headed back inside the marina to call John Carter.

6:52 PM EST
Onboard *Juguete del Calamar*—O'Reilly's Marina—Cartagena, Colombia

While Aliria and Z had been saying goodbye in the parking lot, there was activity elsewhere in the marina.

Back at the *Juguete*, a shadowy figure had approached the empty boat, quickly scanned the immediate vicinity, and confirmed that no one had seen him. The man then walked down the gangplank connecting the boat to the pier and continued toward the *Juguete's* stern. After glancing around one more time, he reached over and removed a cushion covering the seat near the helm. Next, he opened the hatch under the seat. There, just out of view, velcroed to one of the supporting beams under the seat, he removed a small electronic device. He checked the tiny LED on the bottom. The steady green light ensured him that the device was functioning. He reached into his pocket and pulled out an exact replica of the one he had just removed and placed the new one under the seat.

He slowly closed the hatch, replaced the seat cover, and calmly walked down the plank onto the dock. He continued at a relaxed pace along the row of berthed boats towards the entrance of the marina.

His job had become ridiculously easy. To complete this evening's work, all he had to do was go across the street from his house and use the key they had given him to open the mailbox for apartment five. He would place the device—a combination receiver and recorder—in the mailbox, trading it for another one already inside the box. Alongside the new one would be an envelope containing the payment for the past week: 180,000 pesos. Someone was actually paying him about one hundred dollars US for an hour of work each week.

If that someone wanted to listen to what that *bellísima criatura* and the gringo were saying on that yacht—it was none of his business, and he would not ask questions. He could only wonder why someone would pay him so much for so little effort. In the end, it didn't matter. For as long as the peso-filled envelope appeared in that mailbox he would continue to do exactly what he had been doing for the past two years.

Tuesday

"It's a commodities business… you're not moving pork, not moving cows, not moving petroleum—you're moving coke or pot."

From PBS interview with drug dealer

11:40 AM EDT
Joint Staff Briefing Room—Pentagon, Washington DC

"Ladies and gentlemen, welcome to the *Puzzle Palace*!" Elmore always got a laugh by starting his briefings off using his favorite nickname for the Pentagon. "My name is Colonel James Elmore and I'll be talking to you briefly about the Joint Staff's Counter Drug program."

Colonel James "Kelly" Elmore was briefing the new members of the Congressional Caucus on International Narcotics Control. Although Elmore preferred *Kelly* to *James*, the former was reserved for family, close friends, and military workmates who had the rank to use a *Full Bull's* first name.

After years of briefing visitors from "the Hill," Elmore had learned that many of the newer Congressional committee members had no idea what they were getting into. They knew next-to-nothing about the drug trade. They came from many different backgrounds, and from all points along the political spectrum. In fact, most of them were more likely to be recreational drug users themselves, rather than being committed to the "war against drugs." Some of them, especially those from the "left coast," even supported the legalization of drugs.

What a bunch of idiots! Elmore thought, as he surveyed the smiling faces around the U-shaped table of the briefing room. The staff had placed pitchers of water and glasses meticulously around the table at precise intervals. Each member had a personalized place card, embossed with the Department of Defense shield. Behind each place card was a paper copy of the unclassified version of the slides he would use during his presentation.

Elmore had given this briefing many times, and by now could almost do it in his sleep. He updated its content and focus periodically so it conformed to the prevailing inclinations of each Presidential Administration; but the main story line remained the same over the years. He'd give an overview of the massive demand for drugs on the streets of America. He'd talk about the wild '80s, when the Medellín and Cali cartels were duking it out to see who would dominate the cocaine market. He would tell them about Pablo Escobar and his exploits. He would explain how the countries in the area—and their fragile democracies— were slowly drowning under the weight of all that drug-tainted cash. He would then switch to the fight against narcotics, outlining the roles of the various government agencies involved. By the end of his presentation, he'd leave no doubt in the minds of his audience that the Pentagon's drug warrior team was totally committed and professional.

In order to help his audience understand the wild excesses of the early 80s drug scene, Elmore would bring up Norman's Cay; the small Bahamian island located a little over 200 miles east of Florida. For at least four years, it was

Delta 7

under control of Carlos Lehder and the Medellín Cartel. At this point in the briefing, Elmore would put up a slide with a photo of Carlos Lehder, dressed in shorts and bare-chested, getting out of a small Cessna. In his hands was a large bail of cocaine. He had a wide smile; as if displaying a fish he had just caught. Under the photo was the following quote from Lehder:

NORMAN'S CAY WAS A PLAYGROUND. I HAVE A VIVID PICTURE OF BEING PICKED UP IN A LAND ROVER WITH THE TOP DOWN AND NAKED WOMEN DRIVING TO COME AND WELCOME ME FROM MY AIRPLANE... AND THERE WE PARTIED. AND IT WAS A SODOM AND GOMORRAH... DRUGS, SEX, NO POLICE... YOU MADE THE RULES... AND IT WAS FUN.

"Those were the days we all remember about drug trafficking—the 'Wild West' atmosphere," continued Elmore, after giving the group time to read the quote and develop their own mental picture. "We remember the names: Pablo Escobar, the Ochoa brothers, Carlos Lehder... But who do you remember now? What big drug kingpins come to mind today?" Elmore waited, looking at the puzzled expression on each Congressman's face. "You can't think of any names, can you?" he asked rhetorically. "Well that's because things are different now. You don't have flamboyant cowboys running the major cartels anymore. You don't have wild parties on the beach. The major drug lord of the past has been replaced by seemingly respectable businessmen and women. They still generate mountains of cash... still launder vast quantities of drug money... still pay off politicians, judges, the military, and everyone else. The difference is that now they're smarter, more efficient, less flamboyant, harder to identify and—"

"I was a teacher before I was elected this November," interrupted the new Congressman from Kentucky, "and don't have much of a background in this area. To tell you the truth, I'm a little unclear on how money laundering actually works. Could you please explain the process to those of us who aren't investment bankers?" The use of the expression "investment bankers" drew a smile or two from around the table.

"I'd be happy to," said Elmore. "Perhaps it would be easiest to give you an example. A drug dealer in... let's say New York, generates a lot of cash—a *lot* of cash. Remember, conservative estimates tell us that the United States has about 13 million folks who see no problem wandering down to their local pusher to purchase the occasional gram of coke or maybe a little weed or ecstasy with which to party. Add to those 13 million, the five to six million hard-core drug addicts in our country—spending as much as $500 a week to support their habit—and you're talking about $60 *billion* dollars a year... and they ain't payin' with their American Express card!" For the last bit, Elmore changed his accent to mimic his idea of a person of the street—bringing a few chuckles from the group.

"$60 billion makes a fairly large pile of cash... and it needs to go somewhere. So, let's return to our drug dealer in New York. He has several million in cash he needs to launder. First, he'll divide the original amount into separate lots of around $1 million cash. Next, he'll divvy up the lots amongst a group of his smugglers and money runners. Each of these folks is promised $5,000 to $10,000 to make the trip down south. Half a percent commission, that's not too steep! The runners will then head down towards the Mexican border in their cars. At a prearranged time—before they get to the border crossing point—they'll check their cell phones for text messages from spotters at the border. These spotters are looking for evidence that ICE or DEA agents are checking cars leaving the US. By the way, they never worry about being caught on the Mexican side, because they know that they can bribe their way out of trouble and recover most of the cash. If the runner gets a text message with all sixes—the sign of the devil—he'll wait. If, on the other hand, he gets 7777—Lucky Sevens—the coast is clear and he breezes through."

"Next the runner will go to a Mexican bank—where he's done business many times before. Some of these banks will even allow the runners to have codes for remote-controlled gates that allow access to special sections of the bank reserved for their use. Using these gates, they can drive in unobserved. The runner, the drug dealer, and the banker will have already arranged—a verbal contract, if you will—for the delivery of the cash. Sometimes the drivers will simply leave the keys to the car at the bank, and fly back to the States. They might also take a bus... or use another vehicle that was left during a prior visit. The banker does not pay them. Instead, the contract they have with the drug dealer says they'll be paid when they get back. As part of the prearranged deal, the banker has agreed to wire $800,000 into the account or accounts used by the drug trafficker. That 20% discount still allows for a great profit—and *voila*, the trafficker doesn't have to worry about dirty money any more."

"Speaking of dirty money, it's rather ironic; but that cash actually is *dirty!* Nearly all of it will be tainted with a residue of drugs. Much of it will have been stored underground for some time, so it's literally covered with dirt. In fact, it's so dirty that the cash won't even go through electronic counting machines without gumming up the works. To get around this problem, our Mexican banker will employ a small group of trustworthy, poorly paid and exceedingly well-monitored ladies to count the cash by hand. This tedious task can take several hours. Sometimes the runners will stay and monitor the counters during their work to avoid any 'losses.' They do that because everyone knows that these ladies are very adept at making a bit of cash 'disappear' during the counting. It's simply considered part of the cost of doing business."

"So, now our not-so-ethical Mexican banker has close to a million dollars cash in his account. In the preceding days, that same banker has gotten calls from a similarly—shall we say—'integrity-challenged' banker from Medellín, Colombia. Our Colombian banker has several clients who want to buy caseloads of American cigarettes or Johnny Walker Black Label scotch... or perhaps even a couple dozen US refrigerators—goods not easily obtainable in Colombia. These clients have learned that they don't have to pay the official exchange rate to convert their Colombian pesos into US dollars if they go to this particular banker. In fact, these lucky Colombians will pay about twenty percent less than the official exchange rate to get their dollars... *and*, they will be getting the American products without hassling with those nasty old import duties, taxes or customs forms. That's a good deal for them—and a *great* deal for the banker! It's a not such great deal for the country of Colombia—but those folks sure will enjoy sipping their Johnny Walker, or *Juanito Caminante* as they call it, while smoking their Marlboros!"

"These days, laundering drug money is a multi-billion dollar, world-wide business—and you'd be surprised how widespread it is. We find evidence all the time that international criminal organizations are finding constantly changing and ingenious ways to launder these mountains of cash. They invest in businesses, buy real estate, make legitimate investments, deal in stolen artwork, trade drugs directly for arms, etc. You name the commodity and someone has probably traded it for drugs or drug money!"

"Well, that's basically how it works, ladies and gentlemen. Each and every day, in every corner of the world—thanks to the planet's voracious appetite for illegal substances—the same dirty game is replayed again and again. Welcome to the exciting world of Counter-Drug. Thank you very much for listening and that concludes the formal part of my briefing. I'd now be happy to take any of your questions."

There were a few inane questions to be answered, but the group's schedule indicated that it was time to enjoy the unparalleled culinary pleasure of the Pentagon's main cafeteria. As Elmore watched the military escorts guide the group out of the briefing room and down the hallway to the cafeteria, he thought to himself...

If they only knew how truly simple and profitable it was.

1:50 PM EDT
Playa Mirador Condominiums—Miami Beach, Florida

Carter had just arrived at his condo in Miami Beach (just north of the more famous and exotic South Beach) after the 30-minute bus ride home from the airport. He quickly removed his uniform, changing into shorts and a tee shirt.

Tuesday

He had lived in the area long enough to adopt the *south-Florida-casual* style of dress, which was appropriate attire almost anywhere. Getting "dressed up" in south Florida meant wearing trousers and socks.

Carter thumbed through the pile of mail he had removed from his mailbox; quickly confirming that he had received nothing of import. Next, he walked over to his answering machine and noticed he had four messages.

In the first message, a breathlessly excited salesperson from Sun Estates was proud to let him know that he had been selected for a free cruise to the Bahamas. All he had to do was to spend a couple of days experiencing their gorgeous new condominiums in Tequesta Beach.

The second was from his friend Bill. A fellow pilot from National, he wanted to know if they could get together for some diving next weekend. According to his message, Bill had found a great spot about an hour south of Miami and had lined up two flight attendants who wanted to go boating with them.

His daughter, Rachel, was the third caller, making her weekly call. "Hi Dad! I guess you're away on a trip again. Sorry I missed you. Ummm... not much going on up here. Working my butt off as usual. Oh, Gloria and I got together last week. You'll be happy to know we had lots of fun barhopping in Georgetown. Anyway, I'm glad you gave her my number; she's so cute. I *really* like her, Dad. Don't worry, I didn't tell her all the family secrets! Well, I hope you're OK. Give me a call when you get back. Love you... bye!"

Almost immediately after finishing college, Rachel had landed a job with a company doing contract work for the Pentagon. She was now living in Arlington, just south of Washington, DC. Despite her always-hectic schedule, she never failed to call her father each week to keep up with what had been going on.

During several of their recent phone conversations, they had discussed the new woman in Carter's life—a flight attendant, named Gloria Saenz, who worked with the Colombian airline, *Avianca*. For the past six months, they had seen each other nearly every time Gloria had a layover in Miami.

Rachel had been surprisingly supportive of her father's tentative steps back into the dating scene since the death of her mother. She wanted to hear everything he had to say about Gloria and let him know that she would very much wanted to meet her.

Last week, when Carter had told Gloria about his daughter's desire that the two get together, Gloria had been very receptive. In fact, she had told him that since she had a long Washington layover coming up, she would try to see Rachel while there. His daughter's message confirmed that they had indeed gotten together and that they had obviously hit it off quite well.

Carter had *not* told his daughter that he had first met Gloria almost a decade earlier, during his assignment to Colombia. He had been on an unaccompanied tour, while his wife, Sally, had stayed at their home back in the States with Rachel. Although they were slowly getting used to seeing each other again after so many years apart, Carter still maintained an emotional distance. He was not yet ready for another serious relationship—even with a woman as fun and attractive as Gloria.

Carter stayed busy—flying and trying to forget. Someday, he'd get around to more serious dating... perhaps his heart would heal enough. Still, he wondered how long it would take the aching pain to subside. He and Sally had been married for just over twenty years. She'd been by his side during all the difficult times.

He and Sally were just getting used to this new phase of their lives as "empty nesters," when she started getting headaches. The headaches had gotten progressively worse until they'd finally done an MRI. The horrible verdict: she had an inoperable brain tumor. They had tried to be optimistic at first, hoping they would prove the doctors wrong. However, as predicted, the tumor failed to respond to treatment. The end had come quickly—in six weeks, she was gone.

Carter stared down through his tear-blurred vision at the answering machine. He wondered how long he'd been lost in thought, thinking about the wonderful times he had had with Sally, his soul mate. She was the only woman he had loved for nearly 25 years, and he just couldn't imagine finding another woman to take her place, much less getting back into the world of dating.

The blinking light and number came back into focus as he wiped the tears from his eyes. There was one message left.

"John? John Carter? This is Jack Zaworski calling. Wow, it seems like a thousand years! Anyway, I'll be in Miami tomorrow. I got your number from John White up in DC a couple of years ago—just never seemed to find the time to actually call you. So, you're an airline puke now. I remember White said you were in Miami flyin' the big metal, rather than our snappy little C-12. Anyway, I've had... well... I've got some stuff that I need to chat with you about. Ah, well, I hope we can get together. I'll be staying at the Blue Moon Hotel until Tuesday evening, so if you get in tonight, give me a call at the marina. If not, I'm leaving real early tomorrow, so I guess I'll talk to you when I get into Miami. I *really* need to talk to you, man. The number at the hotel is 305 459-2100. Here at the marina, it's 384-2673. You'll have to figure out the codes for Colombia and for Cartagena... damn if I know what they are. Give me call, man. This is important."

What a blast from the past. Carter hadn't seen "Z" in almost ten years—since Bogotá. Funny, he'd just been thinking about those days: trips to the Caribbean, to Cartagena, the bars, the playful banter with the local call girls, the bottles of scotch packed in his overnight bag. Why was Zaworski calling him now? What was the "stuff" that he had to talk about?

Carter dialed the hotel's number, and the operator put him through to Zaworski's room.

"Hello," the voice was familiar.

"Jack, is that you?"

"Oh yeah, John. I'm glad you're finally home. I was starting to think I was going to miss you. So can you make it for lunch?"

"Hell yes, Jack! I just got back from a trip. Where do you want to meet?"

"I'm staying at a place here in South Beach—on the main drag, called the Blue Moon. Have you heard of it?"

"Not really," answered John, his mind going through the many bars and restaurants on the strip by the beach, "I don't spend that much time down there in South Beach—it's a little too wild for my taste. Are you right on Collins Avenue?"

"I don't know man, it's smack in the middle of South Beach. I saw a place right down the street where we can eat. It's called the Sushi Rock or something," said Zaworski.

"Don't worry, I'll find it. Although I'm not sure I'm in the mood for Sushi!"

"That's fine. Forget about the Sushi; let's just have a few beers and eat at the hotel. I'm kinda pressed for time... and we've got a lot to talk about."

"OK, I gotta jump in the shower. I'll meet you in an hour."

"Good, I'll be at the bar downstairs by the swimming pool. Think you'll be able to recognize me after all these years?" asked Zaworski.

"Sure, you'll probably be the one with the 'Thomas Magnum' Hawaiian shirt, with two—no three gorgeous babes hangin' all over him, right?"

"Yeah sure, that'll be me. Hurry up and get here, I gotta talk to you about some pretty weird shit that's been happening lately. Things you really should know about." The concern in his voice was obvious and Carter noticed that some of the bravado he had displayed earlier in the conversation was gone.

"I'll see you in an hour. Don't drink all the booze in the bar before I get there!"

Carter hung up. *I wonder what in the hell is going on. That sure wasn't the Jack Zaworski that I remember*, he thought as he stepped into the shower.

2:25 PM EST
Los Rosales—**Bogotá, Colombia**

Marty Newmann was sitting outside in the shade on his back patio, enjoying a break from his work. He savored a Cuban *Cohiba* cigar and a glass of incredibly smooth, aged rum. The *Cohiba* brand name had been adopted by Che Guevara back in the 60s when he took over the recently nationalized Cuban cigar-manufacturing sector. If these cigars were good enough for Che, they were good enough for Marty Newmann.

Newmann had purchased his home in Bogotá several years ago. Although it was certainly a good investment, it also served as a place where he could keep his wife out of his hair. Aliria often stayed by herself in *Los Rosales*, while Newmann preferred to stay at his large ranch north of Cali.

He had several reasons for his short stay in Bogotá, but later this evening he'd be heading back to Cali. Yesterday, he had had the whole house to himself for the planning session with Carlos. Aliria's short trip up to Cartagena had guaranteed the privacy of that meeting. Last night, he'd spent the night at his girlfriend's apartment. Newmann had originally planned to head back to his home in *Los Rosales* after getting his rocks off. However, she had surprised him by inviting one of her friends to spend the night too. In the end, Newmann had been much too tired to return home and the three of them had stayed at his girlfriend's apartment.

As he surveyed the large heated pool and the immaculately manicured garden, Newmann was pleased. Long gone were the days of taking orders from incompetents in the US Army. Having left the Army as a Sergeant, he was now near the top of his own chain of command. Some of those who had once been his superiors were now taking orders from him.

Newmann had been able to create his financial empire in less than a decade after leaving the military. He set up so many successful and diverse businesses that it was a chore just to keep track of how many he currently owned or controlled. Marty Newmann's Midas touch was aided immeasurably by a single fact—he had become one of the most successful money launderers for Colombia's drug traffickers.

His life had gone through an amazing transformation in the past decade, when he was a Sergeant, serving as an administrative specialist at Bogotá's Defense Attaché Office. When he had first arrived in Colombia (and for the previous eight years of military service), Marty Newmann had been a dedicated and conscientious soldier. His performance had begun to deteriorate almost immediately after his arrival in Colombia. The problem was his new bride, Karen.

He had met her at a raucous two-week vacation at an all-inclusive resort in the Caribbean. Marty had finished training for his new job in Colombia just prior to leaving on that vacation. He was in the mood for celebration and so was Karen. She was a gorgeous, brash and energetic California blonde with a serious thirst for thrill seeking. The two weeks they spent on holiday had been a constant, wild party. The sex was unlike anything Marty had ever experienced: passionate, unbridled, and non-stop. As the end of the vacation drew closer, they both dreaded the thought of having to part company. On a whim—and aided by the amazing clarity of purpose that countless tropical rum drinks can bring—they had decided that they must immediate marry. They had found a small chapel outside the resort and paid the local priest to marry them.

After flying home, Marty assumed that once the vacation hangover was over, the non-stop merrymaking would subside and they would return to a somewhat more sedate lifestyle. It was soon obvious, however, that Karen's proclivity for partying was not the least bit changed by the end of the vacation, nor by the alteration of her marital status. She remained the same wanton party animal from the resort, even after the newlyweds had settled in amongst the more serious men and women of the US military.

Newmann began having serious misgivings about his new bride. Karen seemed incapable of controlling herself. She wanted it all: new clothes, parties, new shoes, more parties, dinner out on the town, and then another party or two. The fact that his income came nowhere close to covering their expenses was of no interest to her.

Newmann had hoped that the move to Bogotá might prove to be the catalyst leading to a moderation in Karen's comportment. Instead, things got worse. Many times, she brought home drunken strangers or presented Marty with outrageous bar bills—often after going missing for days at a time. He begged her to stay at home and to spend money a little less wantonly. However, she was her own woman, and completely dismissed his attempts at controlling her impulses.

Rather than accept that his marriage might have been a mistake, Newmann let Karen do whatever she wanted. This somehow seemed easier and less expensive than divorce. At the same time, he began actively and openly searching for alternative female companionship of his own. Their freewheeling relationship continued in this manner until one night, Newmann had picked up a local girl and taken her back to the apartment. Karen had unexpectedly returned home after an absence of nearly a week and found the two of them in bed. Rather than the expected fight, Newmann was surprised when, far from yelling at him, Karen had immediately thrown off her clothing and enthusiastically joined them in bed.

As his debts mounted, Newmann realized that he desperately needed more income to support his wife and their various extracurricular activities. Their out-of-control, train-wreck of a marriage continued in this fashion for months. Just when he thought his life couldn't get any more complicated, Karen brought home an astounding new houseguest.

This guest was monumentally different from any of the others. The difference did not stem from the fact that Karen had brought home a woman to serve as a sexual partner for both of them. Nor was it particularly shocking that she had subtly coaxed their guest into acting out a long-held, secret desire to spend time in bed with representatives of both sexes. What was novel and astonishing was that their new houseguest was Mrs. Joyce Elmore—the wife of Colonel Kelly Elmore, his boss.

Earlier that afternoon Joyce had paid her first visit to Newmann's apartment. Since Colonel Elmore had left on a weeklong conference at the Pentagon, Joyce and Karen had decided to spend an afternoon experiencing Bogotá's many tourist and shopping areas. In between the stores, museums and other attractions, they had taken several breaks to enjoy a glass of wine or two. Therefore, in addition to their many bags of purchases, they were also enjoying a pleasant buzz.

The day's shopping marathon complete, Joyce had driven back to Karen's apartment building to drop off her new friend. It hadn't taken much arm-twisting for Karen to talk Joyce into going upstairs for one last glass of wine to celebrate the afternoon. That *one glass* had turned into two more bottles, accompanied by much giggling and storytelling. At one point, Karen had related how much she enjoyed skinny-dipping in the apartment's small and always deserted swimming pool. Joyce had demurred, unwilling to risk being caught unclothed in a public place. Always persistent in these matters, Karen recognized that her guest's resolve was fading with each successive glass of wine.

Since skinny-dipping seemed out of the question, Karen had topped off their wine glasses and brought out a deck of cards for a game of poker. After losing the first hand, Karen had playfully removed her blouse and begged Joyce to join her in a game of strip poker. Although it made her heart pound wildly in her chest, Joyce had been almost surprised to hear herself agree to play.

Shortly after the game started, Newmann had returned home from the Embassy to find two giggling and partially clothed women in his living room. They had run up to him and embraced him, insisting that he join the game. As the women had had such a head start on Newmann in their consumption of wine, he had enjoyed winning nearly all of the succeeding hands. Due largely to his sobriety—aided by Karen's creative card dealing—he had been the last one to lose all his clothing.

To celebrate his final hand, Joyce had enthusiastically offered to help remove the last remaining item of his clothing—with her teeth. After assisting

59

with the removal of his underwear, she began using her mouth for an even more pleasant purpose. As Newmann put his hands on top of her head, bobbing up and down at his waist, he glanced at his wife. She was kneeling next to Joyce, alternatively kissing and fondling her more-than-ample breasts. When Karen noticed that Marty was looking at her, she smiled broadly. She then briefly looked down at Joyce's breasts and back at Marty winking, as if to say, "Aren't you pleased with the present I've brought home for us?"

Newmann had gone to work the next morning trying to figure out how he was going to survive this latest development. Once again, Karen had made his life more complicated. He was confident that he would find a way to play this to his benefit. Still, there was no escaping the fact that his current cash flow situation was untenable. Clearly, he was one bounced check away from total financial meltdown.

While half-heartedly transcribing one of the office's classified reports into the required electronic message format, he struggled to come up with a way out of his precarious financial and marital situation. As he scanned the report on his computer screen one last time before sending it to DIA headquarters, the solution to his problems hit him right between the eyes.

Because of his job in the DAO, Newmann had access to every report written by the attachés, many of which dealt with drug smuggling activities. The reports provided detailed information on the players involved in the illicit trade: crooked port inspection officials, corrupt National Police and Colombian military officers, politicians on the take, and judges being bribed or threatened. The detailed reports described exactly how and by whom drugs were being smuggled out of the country. They also reported on the Colombian government's largely futile efforts at stopping this illegal trade.

The report he had been transcribing that morning detailed a new smuggling operation that the attachés and DEA agents had uncovered between Cartagena and the Caribbean island country of Grenada. The DEA's investigation had been very thorough and had reached the point where arrests were imminent. Newmann was sure that information would be extremely valuable to someone— he had only to find that *someone*.

Armed with the details of the report, Newmann had made cautious inquiries in both Colombia and Grenada. After a few phone calls, Newmann found several individuals quite willing to pay for a sneak preview. He was soon $10,000 richer for his efforts.

Newmann had used this seed cash to finance a little drug smuggling of his own. In his second operation, Newmann contacted a crooked National Police Officer he had read about in one of the reports. The two of them came up with a scheme using a boat from a small marina in Cartagena to smuggle several hundred kilos of cocaine to his new—and very appreciative—friends in Grenada.

From there, the cocaine traveled to Puerto Rico and on to the United States. Newmann also had access to nearly all the Embassy's reporting on friendly counter-drug operations, and this greatly increased the probability that his own smuggling activities would be successful.

The drug business and its related financing had been a natural progression for the young Sergeant—each successive deal had made him ever-larger sums of money. Over the following months, he took on riskier and more audacious drug deals. One day, his luck ran out.

After a series of planned drug busts were compromised, his boss, Colonel Kelly Elmore, began to suspect that the leaks might be coming from his office. He quietly began his own investigation and it didn't take long for Newmann to come under suspicion. His lifestyle certainly fit the typical profile of someone who might be tempted to stray from the straight and narrow. He was in serious debt, and often went missing from the office for unexplained reasons.

Before starting an official investigation, Elmore had decided to confront Newmann with what he had uncovered. He ordered Newmann into his office and outlined what his own probing had revealed. Newmann sat quietly, listening to the overwhelming evidence of his complicity in the failed drug busts. When Elmore had finished, Newmann calmly and brazenly ordered the Colonel to back off, insisting that a formal investigation would not be in anyone's best interest. In the ensuing confrontation, Colonel Elmore had been shocked to learn that not only had this cocky, enterprising young bastard been having an affair with Joyce; he had used her personal checking account for several of the drug transactions.

Newmann had proven to be a very worthy adversary for his military superior. Elmore was trapped and could do nothing about Newmann's activities without jeopardizing his *own* career. He was too close to retirement to risk everything to go after Newmann. There could be no formal investigation.

Initially, Elmore tried to ignore what Newmann was doing—to pretend that nothing had ever happened. That option quickly became untenable for him. He could not sit by and let one of his own enlisted men call the shots. After all, *he* was the superior officer and Newmann was only a sergeant, for God's sake.

As if that weren't enough, there was the matter of the continuing sexual relationship between Joyce and Newmann and his wife, Karen. Elmore could no longer listen to Joyce's invented excuses and pretexts to meet with the younger couple. He was well aware that his wife's visits had nothing to do with normal military or Embassy social responsibilities and activities.

Trapped by both Newmann's treachery and his wife's unfaithfulness, Elmore began to drink heavily. The only way he found to assuage his hurt feelings at having been cuckolded by this enlisted man was to join them in their sexual escapades. He saw it as a way to punish his cheating wife. Surely, once she was forced to watch him couple with Karen—who was much younger, more attractive and vivacious—Joyce would see the error of her ways and repent.

To Elmore's shock and despair, his wife considered none of their varied sexual encounters as punishment. Rather, she had become a willing and enthusiastic participant. Even worse, they all seemed feed on the group dynamics—each taking turns having sex in front of each other in various groupings and positions. Their weekly orgies, combined with the soothing escape provided by Colombia's cheap and powerful *Aguardiente* liquor, helped Elmore blind himself to the fact that he was no longer in charge of his life.

Thoroughly disgraced and outmaneuvered—both at home and at work—Elmore realized that he must do something to regain at least partial control of his fate. One day, after showing up at work with a horrible hangover, Elmore recognized that he was reaching the nadir of his life. That day, alone in his office, he had decided that he would no longer look the other way. Instead, he would profit from the situation that had been forced upon him. Until he could think of a better solution, he would work *with* Newmann, rather than against him.

With Elmore's help—or at least with his tacit ignorance—Newmann's finances had continued to grow exponentially. In less than a year, Newmann's various enterprises were successful enough that he no longer required even the pretence of his military job. He had resigned from the Army at the end of that first tour in Bogotá.

Once he had un-tethered himself from both DAO and the military, Newmann began to see Karen as a liability. Her life seemed to revolve around sex and non-stop partying. Money was not a concern to her. *His* needs had changed, however, and like so many successful men in Latin America, Newmann wanted to have it all. Once Karen was out of his life, he would find a suitably respectable wife to increase his standing in Colombian society. It was conceivable that at some point in the future, he might even permit that wife bear him children. More importantly, with all the money flowing in from his rapidly growing drug-smuggling operations, he could afford to indulge himself with a nearly unlimited quantity and variety of sexual partners. Unlike a wife, these women could be used discretely and later discarded once the novelty wore off.

Six months after leaving the Army, he had unceremoniously dumped Karen at the Los Angeles International Airport. She was told that he would never see her again and she was forbidden to attempt any contact with him in the future. Once he had returned to Colombia, he had immediately set about looking for an updated version. He deserved a woman more befitting his newfound wealth and social position. After all, he was no longer a lowly Sergeant.

Before the ink had dried on his divorce decree, Newmann had zeroed in on the daughter of one of Colombia's most successful banking families. She was well connected and beautiful—perfect for his needs.

The smooth taste of the rum and a noise from within the house brought Newmann back from thoughts of his past. He heard the sound of his wife's voice greeting the bodyguards and household help—as she always did.

"Marty?" she called from the kitchen.

Newmann ignored her.

"Marty? *¿Dónde estás?*" Aliria called again, near the open door leading to the patio where he sat enjoying his cigar.

"I'm out in the back," he answered—at last.

"Where were you last night?" she asked, emerging through the door leading outside to the back yard patio. "I thought you were going to be here."

Aliria was dressed in a modest black dress, dark stockings, and *Ferragamo* pumps. As always, she was exquisitely attired—a true representative of Colombia's upper class.

"I had business last night," he said dismissively, his voice making it clear that she had no right to know where he was.

"Why did you leave Jack that message about John Carter and Grenada? Is something wrong?" she asked, walking over to the table where Newmann was sitting.

"No, nothing's wrong. I heard Carter was asking questions in Grenada. I just wanted to see if Z knew why he was all of a sudden interested in the island and some of its government officials. That's all. Don't worry about it."

"Will you be home for dinner tonight?" she asked, changing the subject in an attempt to hide any display of the concern she felt for Z's friend.

"No, I've got a meeting in a couple of hours, and then I'm off to Cali."

"Oh, but you just got here," she said placing her purse on the table and sitting in one of the deck chairs across from Newmann.

"Somebody's got to make money in this house, you know," he hissed. "I can't sit around and play 'Ken and Barbie' with you, Aliria, I've got businesses to run. There's a lot going on right now, so don't give me any shit."

"But I..." she attempted meekly, staring down at the ashtray on the table as she rotated it with her slender fingers.

Newmann jumped up, threw the cigar towards the ashtray on the table, and stormed back into the house. His cigar bounced off the table with a shower of ashes and fell into her lap.

"I'm sorry," she called to his back as he stormed off, while she frantically brushed the cigar and its ashes off her dress.

On his way into the house, the phone rang. *Another business call*, Aliria thought, fighting back tears. *I guess we're finished talking... yet another tender and romantic interlude with my husband has ended.*

As Marty continued his phone conversation, she wondered what he was planning to do about John Carter.

3:30 PM EDT
Blue Moon Hotel—South Beach, Florida

The Blue Moon Hotel and Restaurant on South Beach was famous for its hard-bodied clientele and soft-shelled crabs. The trendy restaurant was located on the famous stretch of Art Deco buildings in South Beach. Carter parked his weather-beaten, but trustworthy Saab in one of the lots located off the main thoroughfare: Collins Avenue.

Running parallel to the beach, this wide, palm tree-lined avenue was always bustling with a constant procession of vehicles and pedestrians. Couples engaged in animated discussions while dodging the obstacle course of packed tables jutting haphazardly onto the sidewalk. A steady stream of humanity ducked under the lower fronds of the potted palms as they made their way alongside the busy avenue. One could hear snippets of conversations in every conceivable language. An elderly couple stopped to admire the black, 1920s-vintage gangster car parked on the side of the street with a Bogart-looking mannequin at the wheel. Every few seconds, a magnificent male or female would glide by on roller blades, sweat glistening off his or her carefully sculpted body. The rollerbladers' attire consisted of very short cutoff jeans with no tops for the men and incredibly skimpy bikini tops for the women. They all had immaculately smooth and bronze skin, stretched tautly over well-muscled frames—as if they had no other concern in life but tanning and weightlifting.

As he walked up the stairs into the Blue Moon for his meeting with Zaworski, Carter wondered what had brought Jack to Miami. He was curious how the years had treated his friend. Zaworski had been a robust man with a large handle bar mustache—clearly unauthorized by the US Navy. He was outgoing, always smiling, and forever plotting his next "drinking adventure."

Carter fondly recalled their many trips to the northern Colombian seaport of Cartagena. Zaworski had been the Naval Attaché (or ALUSNA in DIA-speak) in Bogotá. In addition to keeping tabs on the Colombian Navy, the ALUSNA had other peripheral and decidedly more pleasant duties. One of these duties occurred when the US Navy conducted ship visits to Cartagena. At first, these visits were time-consuming and tedious—requiring constant coordination with port authority officials, the Colombian Coast Guard, and numerous companies and organizations providing fuel, food, and other services to the visiting warships. After the first few visits, however, the Navy had contracted with a local company to manage these details. Thus, during their last several trips to Cartagena, Jack's presence had been mostly ceremonial. Zaworski relished any opportunity to leave the stifling atmosphere at the Embassy, and escape to this sultry, tropical port and resort town.

Since the Embassy's C-12 aircraft required two pilots, he needed to take along one of the other attachés qualified to fly the plane. Carter was always delighted to accompany Zaworski on these sojourns. The visits to Cartagena settled into a familiar routine. They would arrive at the Cartagena International airport located on the northeast side of town and take a taxi directly to the Hilton. It goes without saying that the Hilton was chosen for its relative safety—certainly not for the spectacular view of the beach and the beautiful women that frequented its pool and bar. After cocktails, they'd head out for a busy night of gambling at one of the many casinos nearby. Then, happily exhausted and having contributed to the casinos' profit margins, they'd head back to the hotel.

The following morning, they'd drag themselves out of bed and head to the Colombian Naval Base, which was located on the outskirts of the town, near the ruins of the 16th Century fort of *San Felipe de Barajas*. At the base, they'd meet with various Colombian Naval officers to ensure that all the arrangements for the arrival of the US Navy ships the next day were complete. Zaworski developed close relationships with many of these officers. Due to his unaffected, affable style—undoubtedly helped by bottles of Johnny Walker Black Label Scotch, which he handed out as gifts—Zaworski won the trust of his Colombian counterparts and became quite familiar with their activities and level of readiness. In other words, Commander Jack Zaworski did his attaché job very well, while also managing to make the process quite pleasant and enjoyable for everyone.

Off to the left side of the Blue Moon Hotel's lobby, Carter saw the entrance to its restaurant. He scanned the bar area for his friend, and finally spotted Zaworski sitting alone at a small table near the back of the room. Carter had the odd feeling that Z didn't want to be seen from the street.

He had recognized Zaworski immediately. Except for evidence of an extra pound or two around his waist and the swath of gray hair around his temples, he appeared to have aged little over the years. A large smile came over Z's face as he recognized Carter approaching, and pushed back his chair to greet his friend. After embracing in a big bear hug, they stood back—each giving the other a quick "once over."

"What's that hanging over your belt, young man?" Carter asked, playfully slapping Z's gut.

"It's a sign of the quality of beer I've been drinking, asshole! Maybe you still have those Colombian amoebas in your gut keeping you slim and trim."

"Well, at least neither of us has to be embarrassed by running with those young Marine Guard studs like we used to."

"Yep, I sure don't miss that military torture routine," agreed Zaworski.

"Come on, sit down. Let's have a drink!" he said, pointing out the chair across the table from his own.

As they took their seats at the table, a young Latin waiter sauntered over to their table. "My name is Tito. I'll be your waiter. Can I bring you something to drink before you order?"

"Two beers!" replied Zaworski, not bothering to ask what Carter wanted.

While the waiter fetched their drinks, Carter looked at his old friend. Despite his jovial outward appearance, Carter sensed an underlying anxiety. Zaworski's eyes continuously darted about the room, as if looking for someone tailing him. In accordance with their training, he had picked a defensible position: facing the bar's entrance, his back to the wall. *Why was he being so cautious? Was he in danger?*

"So... what the hell have you been doing since our heroic days together fighting the forces of evil in Colombia?" asked Zaworski.

"Well, since I retired, I've been flying for National. To tell you the truth, I haven't missed the military at all. I really am glad I retired when I did," answered Carter.

"Do you ever fly to Bogotá or Cartagena?"

"Nah. We don't fly to Colombia any more. We used to have a couple of flights a day to *Barranquilla;* but they stopped those about a year ago. I haven't been back since you and I were there. Mostly, I fly to the Caribbean islands and Central America."

"How about that cute little flight attendant you mentioned in that e-mail a couple of months ago... the one who flew with Avianca? Do you still see her?"

"Gloria? She's been up here to Miami a couple of times on layovers. We've gone out to dinner every now and then... nothing spectacular. I have to admit it's always nice to see her, but I guess I just can't get used to the dating scene. After all those years with Sally... well, I'm just not sure how it works any more. How about you?" asked Carter, remembering Zaworski's cryptic phone message. "What's all this mysterious crap about you *having* to speak with me about something? Did you find a hoard of Spanish gold or something?"

"No. It's nothing like that. I... I just had to fill you in on some recent goings on. My life... well, things have been getting kinda strange down in Cartagena," Zaworski struggled to put his thoughts into words. "I think we should get together... down at the marina," he finally managed to say.

"Damn, Z, what's all the intrigue? Frankly, you're not making a visit seem very appealing. Although, I guess it would be nice to get the hell out of Miami and see how much things have changed down there. I do have some vacation time saved up. Maybe I could head down there for a couple of days. Is what's his name, the Aussie, is he still there?"

"Ben O'Reilly? Sure, they'll have to carry that Irish-Aussie bastard out of that place feet first."

"No surprise there! The two of you certainly did love that place. So, I guess that's what you've been doing in your post-Squid life—staying close to O'Reilly's... the perfect place to shiver your timbers and wet your whistle at the same time, huh?"

"Yeah, but it's been a real bitch there recently. Lots of strange stuff's been going on." Z continued to scan the room, as if he half-expected someone to come charging in off the street after them. He quickly changed the subject. "So have you kept in touch with the old gang from the Embassy?"

"Are you kidding? I couldn't even get *you* to return my letters. To tell you the truth, I haven't heard from anyone since I left. What's it been... ten years ago now? How about Meyer? Do you know what he's been up to?"

"Dunno," said Z, suddenly more interested in the cocktail napkin that he had been busily folding and unfolding—like a confused origami artist. Carter noticed that Z's eyes seemed to glaze over as he glanced around the room—avoiding looking directly at Carter.

"What about Elmore?" Carter asked.

"I don't know, I assume he's retired by now," Z answered.

"Oh well, I guess it really doesn't matter. Hell, you and that *Coastie*, the guy who sounded like a California surfer dude, were the only ones I gave a shit about anyway. Never did like the rest of those characters. Especially what's-his-name—that slimy admin type that was always hanging around with Elmore. What was his name? Sergeant Newburg or something?"

"Yeah, Sergeant Marty Newmann," replied Z, still avoiding eye contact. "What a nutcase—and he still *is* one!"

"I always thought it was strange how an Army enlisted guy spent so much time with his full Colonel boss. I felt like the two of them were wife swapping or something. How 'bout you... been in touch with anyone?"

"Nah, not me. Newmann's back in Colombia. He's a big shot business guy now. For me, it's the same old thing: sleeping late in the morning; sailing lessons during the day; drinking and screwing lessons at night. It's paradise—pure, unadulterated paradise," said Z, rubbing the stubble on his cheeks.

He was not convincing. Despite the description of his life in *paradise*, it was clear that something was bugging Z... something was wrong. He just wasn't the same happy-go-lucky guy from the Bogotá days.

"Speaking of Newmann," Z continued, after a nervous pause. "Well, we've sort of gone into business together. I'm actually in charge of the marina now."

"Are you kidding me? You've turned into a marina operator in Carta-friggin-gena? What about O'Reilly—wasn't he the owner?" asked Carter, surprised at Z's revelation.

"Well, Newmann bought him out. He's happy, has a pot full of money; and still gets to work in the bar. He just couldn't stand to leave the place. But, uh… back to Newmann. I heard that he was asking about you recently… something about you trying to find someone in Grenada."

"You're kidding! I was just there on a layover last night. I was thinking about getting in touch with Fitzroy George. You remember him?"

"I guess. It's just that Marty isn't an Admin Sergeant any more. He's a real big shot now, and he's involved in some serious shit. When Marty Newmann gets *interested* in someone, that 'someone' better be careful. Sometimes people go missing after Marty Newmann shows an interest in them. Do you understand what I'm saying?"

"You gotta be shitting me, Z!" Carter said, sensing that this meeting with Z was not a simple get-together with an old friend. "Why would Newmann be interested in me? What the hell are you guys doing down there?"

"Nothing! It's just that… well, I had to warn you. You need to be careful. Don't worry about me. And… well, I knew what I was getting into. Frankly, I've got to figure out how to make some serious changes in my life. I just can't let things continue the way they have been. I have been thinking a lot recently about you and our times together. You remember Leticia? You saved my life on that trip."

"Saved your life? Come on," Carter said with a chuckle. "It was a friggin' bar fight… hell, more like a *possible* bar fight. I just stood by you when things got a little testy, that's all."

"Well, you didn't run off. You stayed there and I'll never forget it. In fact, you know you're the closest thing I have to family. Everyone else is dead, or gone, or doesn't give a shit. I know we haven't stayed in touch that much, but to tell you the truth, I just started writing my will… and well, you get everything if I croak."

"Really?" Carter stammered, caught off guard by this news. He struggled to say something appropriate. "I don't know what to say. I'm honored. Surprised… but honored, that you'd think of—"

"Don't worry," Z interrupted. "It's not much. In fact, all I have is my boat, the *Juguete*—and all my crap crammed inside. It really doesn't add up to much. It's just that I feel like I need to have someone around me that I can trust. Someone who can… who may save my life again. And, well, even if you can't make to Cartagena, I had to let you know that your name is coming up down there… I had to tell you about it."

"Damn, Z! I don't know what I can do to help. I mean, I've been out of the attaché business for a long time now. What can *I* do to help you?"

"I don't know, John. I just don't know. I feel like maybe the two of us could figure something out if you came down to Cartagena. I'll understand if you can't make it. You've got quite a setup here in Miami."

Carter was about to say that he'd think about it, when Zaworski looked at his watch and suddenly stood up, reached into his pocket and tossed a fifty-dollar bill on the table.

"Hey, I really gotta go. My flight back leaves in a little over an hour. I've got too much crap to take care of back at the marina."

Carter was stunned, "What the... Where the hell are you going? We haven't even eaten yet. Why are you in such a hurry? Hell, we've only had a couple of minutes together. After all these years... five minutes and you're gone?" asked Carter, trying to decipher the strange look in Z's eyes.

"Promise me you'll try to come to Colombia. When you get there, I'll fill in some more details."

Carter stood up and grabbed Zaworski's outstretched hand. Carter tried to make eye contact with Z, but his friend's eyes remained focused on their hands. Then, as if driven by fear, Zaworski pulled his hand from Carter's, turned and hurried out of the restaurant. Carter stood next to the table, bewildered.

His conversation with Zaworski—their entire meeting—seemed disjointed and bizarre. One moment he was talking to the confident, humorous, irreverent *Z-Man* from the Bogotá days—and the next, to some paranoid stranger, checking the restaurant's exits like a marked man. Then, there was Newmann. That he might be interested in Carter was odd enough, but that he might *harm* him just didn't make any sense at all.

3:32 PM EST
Cristóbal Docks Customs Facility—near Colón, Panamá

Years of neglect and a miniscule maintenance budget had taken an obvious toll on the Cristóbal Dock facilities. Inside the Customs warehouse, electrical power was intermittent and even when it was available, the outlets often didn't work. As the installation of central air conditioning seemed about as likely as winning the *Lotería Nacional*, the facility's workers had pieced together a jumbled patchwork of extension cords for the intermittent functioning of two ancient and noisy fans. They had little impact on the stifling heat and humidity inside the warehouse, but did succeed in blowing ashes, trash and the occasional stack of paperwork around the area.

A dozen customs agents shared five filthy desks, each covered with overflowing ashtrays, used coffee cups, and piles of disorganized paperwork. Overhead—due to the large number of burned out ceiling lights—an eerie, half-illumination made it difficult to read any of the forms, manifests or other paperwork. Each desk had a telephone on it, but none of them worked with any regularity. Instead, the only reliable phone service was provided by the pay phone on a wall at the rear of the building. Not only was that phone more reliable; it also afforded agents additional privacy for "bargaining sessions." Anyone using the Cristóbal port facility needed to haggle and make payments to various outstretched palms to ensure that their shipments flowed with any alacrity. These "additional fees" allowed inspectors to live above the poverty-level existence their government salary alone would have guaranteed. That was the system. It had always worked this way—and always would. For as long as anyone could remember, the customs operation had been a steamy jungle of incompetence and petty corruption.

For fifteen years, Fernando García Luna had worked in this warehouse as a customs inspector for the government of Panama. Bleary-eyed, he sat idly chatting with his fellow inspectors. García had barely managed to keep up with the ongoing conversation, and had already thrown up twice this morning. He had not yet recovered from the celebration the night before.

Last night had been his first meeting with the Colombian, who had promised him an unbelievable sum of money. All Fernando García had to do, the Colombian had explained, was allow certain containers to pass through customs without "unnecessary inspection or delay." It was not the money, however, that was responsible for his heavy drinking and the very unpleasant hangover from which he was still suffering. It was the threat the Colombian had made that had turned García's world upside-down.

In the end, there had been no choice between the money and the threat. He must let the containers pass. Any alternative course of action on his part—the Colombian had made this exceedingly clear—would have led to long and painful deaths for him and his extended family.

Only an hour earlier, García had dutifully signed for and sealed each of the special containers with an official seal of the Panamanian Customs Authority. The containers were at this moment awaiting shipment to the Unites States in another section of the warehouse. They would remain there until the trucks came to load them onto a Danish ship, which was scheduled to depart sometime tomorrow evening. In four hours, he would once again meet with the Colombian. At that time, he was expected to confirm that the containers had passed through Customs without incident. According to their agreement, he would receive his final payment when the shipment reached its final destination.

García tried desperately to hide his anxiety from the other agents. He prayed that no one would conduct a snap inspection—or that the damn American DEA wouldn't come snooping around the warehouse. He prayed that he and his family would survive the next few days. All the while, he fought back the horrible, churning feeling in his stomach, which seemed determined to empty its contents violently onto the desk in front of him. Only a couple of days more and this would all be over. *Please God, let it end soon!*

5:02 PM EDT: Playa Mirador Condominiums—Miami Beach, Florida

Returning to his condo after his surreal meeting with Z, Carter put his keys on the table near the front entrance and walked into his small kitchen. He shook his head silently as he confronted the unorganized clutter inside. He was never very good at cooking—much less cleaning—and the mess in the kitchen bore witness to that fact.

As he set about cleaning the stacks of dirty dishes strewn about, Carter struggled to make some sense of his friend's recent behavior. He certainly hadn't acted like the carefree jokester from the Colombia days. He was preoccupied about something, even afraid. What did he expect Carter to do for him? Why would Z want him down in Cartagena?

After pondering these and other questions, Carter considered that he might learn more by getting in touch with the other members of the Defense Attaché Office in Bogotá. Even if they were unable to explain Z's behavior, perhaps one of his former workmates could shed some light on what might be going on in Colombia.

Carter walked over to the desk in his bedroom and opened his address book. As he tried to recall names from that long-ago time in his life, Carter realized that with the exception of Jack Zaworski, he had lost touch with almost everyone he'd known during his attaché service. Some would have stayed in the military, but most probably would have retired or moved on.

After a few seconds of flipping randomly through the pages, he found a promising entry for Lieutenant Colonel Bruce & MinJung Meyer. Meyer had been the Assistant Army Attaché in Bogotá. Prior to Colombia, he had served as a company commander with the Second Infantry Division, at Camp Casey—near Seoul, Korea. While there, Meyer had met and eventually married MinJung. Nearing the end of his tour in Korea, Meyer had been notified of his follow-on unaccompanied assignment to the attaché office in Colombia. Since an unaccompanied assignment meant the military did not encourage—nor pay for—married personnel to bring their spouses, Meyer had first tried to get the assignment changed or canceled. Despite his repeated pleas, the Army hadn't budged and Meyer had arranged to have MinJung come with him on his own dime. "I'll protect her myself," he had said at the time, "but I'll be damned if

I'm going to take her from her home in Korea and have her spend the first year of our marriage by herself in the States while I'm in Colombia."

The last time they had spoken, Meyer had retired from the Army at the rank of Lieutenant Colonel. At that time, he was working with a company setting up security for foreign corporations doing business in Colombia.

Carter dialed the number written in his address book.

"Hallo?" It was a female voice with an almost impenetrable Korean accent.

"*Kam sam me da*! MinJung?" Carter said, trying out the one Korean phrase he could remember—and fairly certain he had butchered the pronunciation.

"Yes, I am MinJung. What you want?"

"Hello, MinJung, this is John Carter. I worked with your husband, Bruce, while you were stationed in Bogotá."

"Oh, John very good. I so glad to hear from you. Very long time, I don't hear anything from you. Are you OK now, please?"

"I'm doing very well, MinJung. I was just thinking about my time in Bogotá, and thought I might have a chat with Bruce. Is he there?"

There was no response.

"MinJung?"

"Bruce, he dead now," said MinJung, almost whispering.

"Oh my God, MinJung, I'm so sorry!" said Carter, staggered by the news. "What happened to him?"

"He was driving his car and he die in crash. I don't know. I very scared for him. He always go to Corombia. I no like. Very… dangerous there. I tell him, stay home, we don't need money so bad to go to Corombia so much and get killed."

"Killed, MinJung?" said Carter, struggling to follow what MinJung was saying. "I thought you said he was killed in a car crash?"

"Car crash, yes. But he killed. I know."

"MinJung, I just can't believe it. Is there anything I can do to help you?"

"No. My mother come from Korea. She help with children. You no worry, John."

"MinJung, when did Bruce die?"

"He die three days ago. In Corombia. Oh, he gone all the time. Very secret tings he doing in Corombia. He never talk to me about. We always fight. He tell me not to worry, but I worry plenty. And now he dead."

"MinJung, I can't believe it. I'm very glad that your mother could be there to help you. I hope everything works out for you. Again, please let me know if I can do anything."

"You help youself, you no go to Corombia. Very bad place. Goodbye, John," she said, her voice trembling as she fought to maintain control of her voice.

"Goodbye, MinJung," said Carter, but the line was already dead.

Bruce Meyer killed three days ago! Did this have anything to do with Z's strange behavior? Carter thought back to the meeting with Z. When he had asked about Meyer, Z had stared forlornly at the floor. Carter now remembered having the feeling that he knew something had happened to Meyer, but their conversation had moved on before he had the chance to press Z for more information.

Hoping to find another person who might be helpful, Carter continued to thumb through the address book. The next name he found surprised him— Michael Kennedy. Carter had completely forgotten that he had bumped into Kennedy about a year ago on one of his flights from Washington to Miami. Although Kennedy had served as an Assistant Army Attaché with Carter in Bogotá, their tours had overlapped only a couple of months.

When they had met on the airplane, Kennedy—now a full colonel—had told Carter that he was returning from a meeting at the Pentagon and that he was working at the Southern Command headquarters in Miami. If he had not been re-assigned, Kennedy might still be there.

The listing had only Kennedy's name, with a question mark for his wife. Even if he had once known her name, Carter had never met her, as Kennedy's wife had not been with her husband during his assignment to Colombia.

Carter decided to *google* the US Southern Command's Miami headquarters to find the main phone number and then spoke with one of the Command's operators. After a quick search, the operator confirmed that there was indeed a listing for Colonel Michael Kennedy and put the call through to his office.

After exchanging pleasantries, they began to fill each other in on what they'd been doing since the Bogotá days. Kennedy gave a brief chronological overview of his Army career in the intervening years, ending with his current job, working counter-drug operations at SOUTHCOM.

"Gonna stay in for as long as you can?" Carter asked.

"I guess so. All I know how to do is dress up in my shiny uniform, salute smartly, and kill people. You know, like the saying goes: 'go out and visit the world, find interesting people from all over... and kill them!' Isn't that what our new 'Army of One' is all about?" chuckled Kennedy.

"Too bad you can't work my hours and suffer through layovers with all the nubile young flight attendants I'm forced to work with." Carter then described his current flying job with National, discussing routes, airplanes and describing how much more time off he now enjoyed compared to his military years.

"Yeah, tough life you're living there big boy. Are you sure you've left the military and the counter-drug thing for good? Don't miss the good old days?" asked Kennedy—subtly fishing for information.

"Nope, I've never even looked back since I retired," replied Carter, truthfully.

Finally, Carter brought up the bizarre meeting he had just had with Zaworski at the South Beach restaurant. He covered Z's weird behavior and the comments he'd made about recent goings-on in Colombia and the marina.

"Kinda strange, isn't it?" agreed Kennedy. "Sorry, but I don't know what to tell you, John. I don't know why he'd act that way. But then, I pretty much lost track of him after Bogotá. In fact, I don't think I've run into any of the old Bogotá crowd... just Kelly Elmore every now and then. He's up on the Joint Staff. He's retiring the end of this year, if I'm not mistaken."

"It gets even worse, Mike. I just spoke with Bruce Meyer's wife, MinJung. Remember her?" asked Carter.

"Korean girl, right?" replied Kennedy.

"That's her. Anyway, she told me Bruce was killed down in Colombia a couple of days ago. Have you heard about that?"

"I heard he died in a car crash or something, not that he was killed. What else did she say?" asked Kennedy.

"She *did* say that he had died in a crash, but she seemed sure that he was killed. She kept telling me how dangerous Colombia is these days."

"Well, she's right about Colombia being dangerous. I'm glad I don't have to live there anymore," replied Kennedy.

"So you don't know about anything unusual going on down in Colombia... anything that might explain Bruce's death... or Z's strange behavior?"

"No, I don't, John. I guess I don't have to tell you that it's always been a screwed up and dangerous place. I'd say Bruce's security company might have pissed off the wrong people... or maybe it *was* just an accident, and his wife just has it wrong. I don't know; I haven't heard anything. Nor do I know what might be Z's problem. Sorry, but as far as I'm concerned, it's just a screwed up country. That's all I can say," confided Kennedy, with a resigned sigh.

"Oh well, I figured I'd try to get in touch with the guys from the DAO and see if I could make any sense of this. Guess I'm just going to have to go to Colombia as Z suggested if I'm going to figure anything out. I've got the next few days off, and there are certainly worse places to spend a couple of days than Cartagena."

"Colombia's still a pretty dangerous place, John. Not the ideal vacation spot," cautioned Kennedy.

"I know, I just—"

"Hey you're a big boy now," interrupted Kennedy. "I'm sure you know how to stay out of trouble."

"Guess I do," replied Carter, recognizing that Kennedy did not appear to have any answers to his questions.

"Well, John, thanks for getting in touch… it was great to hear from you. I'll certainly give you a call if I hear anything that might help you. For the time being, I'd say you should just chalk it up to Colombian 'ops normal.' I gotta run though. I've got three minutes to get upstairs for another meeting. Keep in touch, OK?"

"Sure thing. See you later," replied Carter hanging up the phone.

Carter went over what he knew so far: something was bothering Zaworski in Colombia. Bruce Meyer was dead—under what his wife considered unusual circumstances. Carter had not learned anything from Kennedy, but at least *he* was still alive, and stationed nearby at the Miami headquarters of the US Southern Command.

Since Zaworski had promised to tell him more about what was going on if he went down to Cartagena, it was obvious that he'd have to go there if he was going to have any realistic expectation of solving this mystery. Glancing at the calendar on the wall in his kitchen, Carter confirmed that he had nothing planned for the next several days. Clearly, it was time for a short trip to Colombia.

5:58 PM EDT
US Southern Command—Miami, Florida

"You'll never guess who just called me," said Colonel Michael Kennedy, calling Kelly Elmore at the Pentagon on his office STU 3 telephone.

"Today's not a good day for guessing games, Mike. Just tell me what's up!" demanded Elmore—obviously not in the mood for humor.

"OK. John Carter just called asking about Zaworski. I spoke with him for about 10 minutes. He said that Zaworski came up to see him in Miami, and that Zaworski said that things were *weird* in Cartagena. Carter also mentioned that he had spoken with Bruce Meyers' wife—who told him she thought Bruce was killed. I don't think he knows anything about the plan or us. I think Carter was just fishing for information."

"What did you tell him?"

"I pretty much wrote it all off to the violence in Colombia," replied Kennedy.

"Anything else?"

"He said something about going to Cartagena. Said he'd look up Zaworski and try to figure out what was going on."

"Well, I guess we can't stop him from heading to Cartagena. He won't find anything there anyway. But I'll have to let Newmann know that he's going. You don't think he's working for the government again, do you?"

"No, he's still working for the airlines. Just to be sure, I made inquiries here in Miami—called my contacts in the other agencies. Unless it's under some pretty deep cover, he's not working for anyone else. He appears to be an airline pilot, just like he says."

"All right. Keep an eye on him and keep me posted. We can't afford any screw ups right now."

As Kennedy hung up the phone, he thought about John Carter. Even though their tours at the DAO in Bogotá had only overlapped for a couple of months, they had flown a trip or two together in the Embassy's C-12 airplane.

Not a bad guy for an Air Force Prima Donna. Poor bastard better be careful, though. He risks pissing off the wrong people and could end up getting his ass in a crack.

8:28 PM EST
Newmann's Hacienda—Cali, Colombia

The walls of the library were lined with floor-to-ceiling bookshelves filled with expensive, leather-bound books. Smoke from non-stop cigar smoking enveloped the room like a thick blanket, muffling the conversation going on inside.

Carlos Hernández and Marty Newmann had been updating and refining the plan. It was the most complex operation the two of them had ever conceived. There were literally hundreds of moving parts, and scores of people (in several different countries) with whom they needed to coordinate. Bills had to be paid, bribes offered, threats made—all synchronized to occur at the appropriate times.

Meticulous planning was required to pull off something on this scale. They had to consider security options and contingency plans. Although they had already started setting things into motion, they still had questions too. How were they going to be certain that the New York group was on board? Had they allowed the Panamanian welding crew enough time to construct the wall? How secure were the plans for the transfer of funds? Were all the bank accounts set up? Were their military contacts in position? Had any part of the plan been exposed?

In addition to mulling over these questions, Carlos had come up with a promising new addition—a way to kill two birds with one stone. Through

Carlos' stroke of genius, they would now be able to take care of a pain-in-the-ass cocaine dealer in Los Angeles, named Douglas Veith, who was refusing to pay for a shipment. Veith initially claimed that the cocaine was not as pure as promised. After almost a month of lame and ever-changing excuses, he had yet to pay the full amount due. Rather than send someone up to take care of the asshole, they would plant evidence implicating him in their upcoming operation. As a result, Veith would almost certainly be nabbed by American law enforcement authorities—diverting attention away from the real culprits and teaching the greedy bastard a lesson.

Based on the new information they'd gotten in Elmore's most recent phone call, Carlos and Newmann had to iron out a new wrinkle. In addition to working out the myriad details of the operation, they had to contend with Zaworski and his friend John Carter. They knew that Carter had shown up recently in Grenada—asking about Fitzroy George. Later, Elmore had called with the news that Zaworski had gone to Miami to see Carter and that Carter had known about Bruce Meyer's death. Did this mean that either Carter or Zaworski had somehow learned about their plan? Did either of them constitute a threat? Would killing one or both of them direct more attention to them or the operation? Newmann and Carlos had spent the last twenty minutes wrestling with those questions.

"What are we going to do about Zaworski?" asked Carlos.

"He's been talking to my wife about things he shouldn't," said Newmann, his head surrounded by smoke as he relit his *Cohiba*. "I know he's not screwing her, or he'd already be dead. I just can't afford to have him slip up and let something out that jeopardizes our plans."

"I agree completely, Marty. The FARC doesn't want to lose the opportunity that this deal represents for the Revolution. You must consider the security of our operation ahead of the life of a former military acquaintance," said Carlos. "And since we now know that he's met with Carter, I believe that our security is definitely at risk of compromise."

"I know," said Newmann, tapping a non-existent ash from his cigar as he considered his next move. "It's just that he's been useful to me running the marina. Up to now, I have not questioned his loyalty nor have I worried about his discretion as far as my ongoing operations."

Newmann twirled the cigar around the inside of the ashtray in silence for a few seconds as his mind settled on the obvious course of action to be taken. "I guess that's the way it's going to have to be. Too bad, I used to like the guy," he said finally.

"Yes. It's for the best," agreed Carlos.

Newmann made the phone call. The various alternatives had been weighed and Jack Zaworski was judged to be too much of a risk and therefore expendable. The first thing in the morning, a long-term business relationship would end—no gold watch, no fanfare and certainly without a retirement ceremony.

Wednesday

Hymn of the Colombian Navy

Viva Colombia, soy marinero;
por mi bandera, por mi heredad
vivo en las olas celoso y fiero,
soy caballero del ancho mar. (bis)

Bajo la gloria de un sol de fuego,
bebiendo brisa, gustando sal,
todo lo grande, todo lo bello
me va enseñando la inmensidad.

De oros brillantes, de azul de cielo
de ocasos rojos torna el singlar,
el gallardete de mi crucero
sus tres colores de libertad.

Besos fugases me dan los puertos;
locos vaivenes el vendaval,
más la que alumbra mi pensamiento
como una estrella rumbos me da.

Por eso canto cuando navego,
poco me importa la tempestad,
siempre me alumbran mis dos luceros,
el de mi patria y el de mi hogar.

Viva Colombia, soy marinero;
por mi bandera, por mi heredad
vivo en las olas celoso y fiero,
soy caballero del ancho mar. (bis)

Wednesday

9:23 AM EST
BarcoMundo—Cartagena, Colombia

Jack Zaworski emerged from the *BarcoMundo* boating supply store in downtown Cartagena. His bloodshot eyes were having trouble adjusting to the bright morning sun. Zaworski had arrived back in Cartagena very late the night before—barely catching the last connecting flight from Bogotá. He had spent the abbreviated time he had in the sack tossing and turning, while going over what he was going to do if and when Carter came to Colombia.

Unable to sleep, he had gotten up early and decided to purchase a few replacement parts for the air-conditioning system on his boat. The damn thing never seemed to keep up with the high humidity. He had to tinker with it constantly to make it work at all. Despite the lack of sleep, he had driven over to the store that morning, arriving shortly after it opened.

Zaworski was surprised to discover that the store had everything he needed for the *Juguete* in stock—an unusual occurrence in Cartagena. After paying for the parts, he loaded everything into a large cardboard box, which clanked and clattered as he made his way out of the store. Oblivious to the noisy traffic that streamed by him on this busy morning, Zaworski adjusted his grip on the heavy box and walked away from the store towards his car, just down the street.

Concentrating on maneuvering the unwieldy box into the back seat of his car, he did not pay any attention to the van that pulled up next to him. Suddenly, the doors of the van exploded open and three men pounced on him. Before his mind could register what was happening, the box was stripped from his hands and tossed on the ground. He was lifted off his feet and manhandled away from his car. He tried to free himself—struggling against the hands locked onto him like powerful vices. His abductors were too strong. Easily overpowering him, they continued carrying him towards the open van door.

They threw him violently onto the floor of the van, and two of the men sat on top of him—pinning his arms and legs, and forcing his face into the van's filthy carpet. They sped away from the parking lot and merged into the morning traffic. After several minutes of struggling to free himself, Zaworski recognized that escape was not an option. He stayed still, realizing that his fate was sealed. It would appear that Marty Newmann had decided that he was too dangerous.

Strangely calm and resolved to his fate, Zaworski wondered how they would do it. *Would it be a knife? A gunshot? Would it be painful?* He also thought of his friend. *Would he come to Cartagena? Would Newmann kill him too?*

As the van sped down the main road leading out of Cartagena, he thought of to John Carter. *I'm sorry, I was in way over my head. I tried to warn you. What else could I do?*

80

9:54 AM EST
Avianca Flight 2984 Bogotá to Cartagena

Contrary to the predictions of the flight attendant on the Miami-to-Bogotá leg of his journey, the 45-minute flight to Cartagena had been completely full. Fortunately, Carter had been able to sit in the jump seat—directly behind the two *Avianca* pilots in the cockpit of the McDonnell Douglas MD-83 aircraft. The flight crew had been very chatty during the short flight from Bogotá.

"What are you going to do in Cartagena?" asked the Captain, his face bearing a good-natured smile as the autopilot controlled the jet while they cruised, "You got a Colombian girlfriend there, maybe?" The captain and first officer broke out laughing. Like most Colombians, they were quite proud of the reputation their county's women had for beauty.

"I wish," said Carter bemused. "No, nothing that exciting or fun. I'll be visiting with a friend of mine who's living at a marina in Cartagena. Ever heard of O'Reilly's Bar?"

"No," said the captain, looking over at his first officer, who shook his head indicating that he too had not heard of it.

"We layover at the Hilton, and spend all our money at the casinos!" laughed the first officer.

"Yeah, I think I was personally responsible for a good part of the casinos' profits when I used to go there," joked Carter, receiving knowing nods and chuckles from the Colombian flight crew.

Shortly after this exchange, the cockpit became busy as the crew prepared for their arrival at the *Rafael Núñez* Airport in Cartagena. Carter sat quietly and watched the crew as they completed their pre-landing checks and slowly banked the aircraft out over the water to the north of the city. As the jet made its final descending turn back to the south for their landing on runway 19, Carter recognized the airport, along with the surrounding city and port in the distance. In the past, he had always been filled with a sense of eager anticipation when approaching this lively port city. Today, Cartagena seemed much less inviting, and as he heard the sound of the landing gear falling into position, Carter couldn't shake the feeling that this visit would not be as pleasant as the ones in his past.

11:05 AM EDT
Office of the Joint Staff, Director of Counter Drug Operations—
the Pentagon, Washington, DC

Colonel Kelly Elmore calmly walked over to the door of his office and looked out into the hallway. No one was in sight. As he closed and locked the door, he thought about his conversation with Kennedy the day before. He knew that John Carter's recent actions represented a possible threat to the operation, and that Newmann had to be told. He also understood that informing Newmann might very well lead to Carter's death. Although he liked Carter, in the end, he resigned himself to the fact that Carter's fate—like that of Bruce Meyer—was in Newmann's hands.

Sitting down at his desk, Elmore removed the high-tech satellite phone from his briefcase and dialed the number in Colombia.

"I just got off the phone with *Delta Two*. *Delta Seven* is on his way down there. Arriving today or tomorrow."

"Down where?" Newmann snapped angrily.

"Down to Cartagena, apparently to meet with *Six*," replied Elmore.

"You've got to be shitting me," screamed Newmann. "When did you find out about this?"

"Late last night. But I don't think we need to get all lathered up about it. The two of them were pretty tight when we were down there together. I think he's just visiting an old friend. I'll admit that the timing is troubling; but I don't see how he could know squat. Yes, he's been in contact with *Delta Six*; but if *Six* wasn't read in on the plan... then he couldn't have told *Seven* anything."

"I can't have a trail leading back to me. *Delta Six* is already out of the picture. I'm afraid that if *Delta Seven* was also taken out, somebody might connect the dots."

"You mean Jack's—" Elmore started to say, neglecting to use Zaworski's codename.

"Yes. It's already done," Newmann replied, before Elmore could finish the question.

"That's too bad. Are you sure you had to do that?" asked Elmore, unsettled, but not surprised at hearing the news that Newmann had murdered yet another former military officer.

"I run things down here, not you," snapped Newmann dismissively, before hanging up.

Delta 7

1:15 PM EST
Rafael Núñez Airport—Cartagena, Colombia

After thanking the cockpit crew, Carter quickly exited the terminal and hailed the first available cab. Nearly before he closed his door, the driver accelerated out of the airport area and turned onto the main road leading southwest along the coast towards the town center. Along the way, brightly colored busses chugged along, belching out thick, black clouds of exhaust. They were all impossibly full of passengers—with people of all ages hanging out of the open doors and windows. In their former lives, the busses had transported schoolchildren throughout the United States. Long past their useful service lives, they had been sold throughout Latin America and taken on new personalities in their adopted home. They were garishly repainted and given expressive names reflecting the personalities of their owners and drivers. The busses stopped at various locations along the coast road—pausing just long enough for passengers to jostle frenetically on and off the over-crowded antiques.

Carter's taxi was an ancient Toyota with moldy, dirty, worn-out seats. As Carter wiped the sweat from his brow, he scanned the taxi's instrument panel—guessing that the air conditioner had probably not worked for years. The driver seemed unfazed by the temperature as he bolted down the road, dodging in and out between the busses, cars and trucks.

Fortunately, the clouds rolling in with the ocean breeze were blocking out the blazing sun. This, combined with the air rushing in the taxi's open windows, kept the temperature just bearable. As they continued on the short trip from the airport, Carter smelled the pungent smell of salty sea air rolling off the ocean... Cartagena! As they passed each landmark, memories began to flood into his mind. He saw the old wall surrounding the city, the entrance to the Colombian Navy base, and finally the area of casinos and hotels around *El Laguito* and its peninsula in the southwestern tip of the city.

"Driver, have you ever heard of the O'Reilly's Marina and Bar?" he asked in Spanish.

"Sure, I can take you there," answered the driver, eager to augment his fare. Having waited nearly two hours at the airport for his first customer, he hoped that Carter was one of the Americans who tipped well. "You want to go there now?" he asked.

"No, please take me to the Hilton first. I need to change and make a few phone calls. Can you meet me at the hotel in an hour?"

"Sure. No problem, *Señor*. I will wait at the hotel for you. My name is Angel, and I can take you for a tour of the city too, if you like," he added,

83

handing Carter a sweaty and wrinkled business card yanked from his pants pocket.

"We'll see about that," Carter said noncommittally as they pulled up to the entrance of the Cartagena Hilton.

1:26 PM CDT
Onboard *Antioquia*—Gulf of Mexico, 200 miles west of Key West

It was a typically bright and sunny day in the Gulf of Mexico—smooth seas with a steady easterly breeze. Below decks, near the center of the Colombian Navy frigate, *Antioquia*, Royal Grenadian Coast Guard Superintendent Fitzroy George could scarcely discern he was at sea. From the relatively spacious cabin accommodations the Colombians had provided him, George was preparing to execute his first contribution to the mission. He would be nominally in charge of this impressive armada once they starting boarding the container ship. George and his Grenadian and Colombian shipmates considered themselves *nominally* in charge because as usual, the damn Americans were acting as if they were masters of the world's oceans.

During his many years working with the Americans, George had become familiar with their sense of superiority. Whenever the Americans contributed a ship or two to an exercise, they always ran the show. The readiness and training of their crews, the capabilities and condition of their ships, and the vast financial resources at their command were always manifestly superior to those of the other participating countries.

Despite a tendency for arrogance and condescension, George couldn't help liking the Americans based on his experiences working with them during a 30-plus year career. They were competent sailors and were firmly committed to the counter-drug effort. However, unlike the Americans, George recognized long ago that they were fighting a losing battle. He was convinced that Americans would be better off spending their money trying to control the massive *consumption* of illegal drugs, rather than their supply chain. Surely, the world's largest capitalist empire should have recognized by now that they couldn't overcome the forces of a free market. Despite the overwhelming evidence, George was sure that his American friends would never have such an epiphany and would blindly continue this unproductive and costly charade.

Superintendent Fitzroy George and his fellow Grenadian Coast Guard members had just begun the last week of their month-long participation in *UNITAS*—a series of exercises and practice operations throughout Latin America. For the last three weeks, the various members of their Task Force had learned about each country's respective rules of engagement and methodology for interdiction of maritime drug shipments. Although only an exercise, the Task

Force was also carrying out "real world" surveillance. In addition, if they were to encounter an *actual* drug smuggling operation, they would be called into service to interdict the traffickers.

The Task Force consisted of five vessels. Sadly, his own Grenadian flagship, the 106-foot patrol boat, *Tyrrel Bay* was not up to such a long journey. She was a grand old lady, lovingly maintained by the members of the Royal Grenadian Coast Guard. However, their current patrol area—in the north-central Caribbean—was too far away from her home port. Although Grenada did not contribute a vessel, Superintendent George had pulled strings to make sure that his men could still participate in this particular exercise. The Grenadian contingent had all embarked on the Colombian Navy frigate, *Antioquia*.

The Task Force was further augmented by the destroyer *Admirable* from the Dominican Republic. The Canadians contributed the frigate, HMCS *St. Johns*. The other two ships were both American: the guided missile frigate USS *Doyle*, and the destroyer USS *O'Bannon*.

Yesterday had been a high point in the exercise for George. The Canadians had sent down an oiler, the HMCS *Preserver*, which carried out an underway replenishment, or UNREP. It was an amazing thing to behold—each ship maintaining a distance of only 125-150 feet from each other. George had watched, transfixed, as they stretched the refueling hose between the ships and transferred nearly 20,000 gallons of fuel.

As if the impressive display of seamanship weren't enough, the Canadians had also provided the entire armada with a unique serenade. During the entire UNREP maneuver, the *Preserver* piped a series of traditional Canadian folk songs over its public address system—complete with bagpipes.

Since the Grenadian Coast Guard contingent was the largest, George would be in charge of any boarding operation. He would begin to exercise Tactical Control (or *TACON* as it was universally known) the moment any boarding procedure began and would do so from the control center aboard the *Antioquia*. Each country used its Coast Guard Detachment for this purpose because, unlike the Navy, the Coast Guard had civilian arrest and other law enforcement capabilities and authorizations.

Later this afternoon, George and his men would carry out their second practice maritime interdiction or ship boarding. Superintendent Fitzroy George was keenly interested in how well his men performed in this afternoon's exercise, and had meticulously overseen every detail of the boarding scenario. He was especially interested in today's practice boarding because he, along with a handful of co-conspirators onboard *Antioquia,* were the only members of the Task Force who knew that this would be their last trial run. Within the next few days, instead of *practicing* a ship boarding—they would be doing the real thing.

5:38 PM EST
O'Reilly's Bar—Cartagena, Colombia

Ben O'Reilly's face bore the marks of 62 years' exposure to sun, salty air, strong sea breezes and cheap rum. He strolled amongst the dozen or so customers of the *O'Reilly's Marina y Bar* with his normal gusto and good cheer, dispensing drinks, food, and sea stories with an ease practiced over the last two decades at this popular establishment.

O'Reilly's ancestors had been part of the mass exodus from Ireland's potato famine in 1849. Ben's great grandfather—a farmer from near *Lough Derg* north of Limerick—had been unhappy with the prospect of living "elbow-to-elbow" with all the displaced Irish now streaming towards America. After reading a newspaper article about the new colonies and farming opportunities in Australia, he had decided that Perth would be a better place to settle. Two generations of Ben's family had toiled on a sprawling, 1000-acre ranch 100 miles east of Perth. Ben had never gotten used to the life of a rancher or farmer, and had quickly tired of the land-locked life. Shortly after his sixteenth birthday, he had run away from home and headed to Sidney and the promise of adventure at sea. His travels had eventually taken him to the north coast of Colombia, and Cartagena. He had fallen in love with the port city, and had been living here for the last 40-plus years.

Carter walked up to the bar and introduced himself to O'Reilly, who at first did not remember him. Finally, after Carter recounted several visits to Cartagena with Zaworski, a smile of recognition came over O'Reilly's face.

"Now I remember you!" said O'Reilly. "You two blighters used to come up during the ship visits. *Now* I remember! Sure... back then, Z recommended the place to all the Yank sailors on shore leave. They used to show up by the busload. We had to hire three extra barmaids whenever the American Navy was in town," O'Reilly shook his head and chuckled—recalling the wild visits of the large contingent of sailors.

"Z mentioned that you might be stopping by when he left this morning," continued O'Reilly. "I didn't recognize the name when he brought it up— wasn't payin' too much attention to tell you the truth. Said he was off to buy some parts for the *Juguete* or something."

"So, where is the lug? Is he back? Taking a quick *siesta* on his boat?" asked Carter with a chuckle.

"No. In fact, I'm surprised he hasn't called yet. When he left this morning, he said he'd be right back. But it's been... what, eight hours now?" said O'Reilly, glancing at his wristwatch. He then turned towards the passageway behind the bar and shouted, "Hey Daniela, have you heard from Z?"

"No! Hasn't called since I've been here," Carter heard a muffled female voice from the marina's small office.

"Knowing Z, he probably found some girlie at the store. He's probably showing her the sights of the city or something. I wouldn't worry too much; nobody can keep track of the man anyway. He'll probably show up in a little while. Can I offer you a little something to wet your whistle while you wait?"

"Sure, I'll take an *Águila*, please," said Carter, referring to the brand of Colombian beer he remembered from his many attaché visits.

O'Reilly placed the ice-cold beer on the bar in front of Carter, who took a large swig and then continued their conversation. "So anyway, Jack came up to Miami yesterday and convinced me that I absolutely *had* to come down here to visit. Said he had some strange stuff he had to share with me. So… here I am. Have you noticed anything weird going on lately?"

"Weird? Here at the marina? You mean other than the normal weirdness?" he said, laughing energetically. "Nah. It's the same old thing. Hell, Z's always marched to a different drummer. He probably got nostalgic for the old days and wanted to see you. He had to go to Miami to look into buying a new compressor for our walk-in fridge. The bloody thing's been off and on for years now, and I know he was thinking of getting a new one. In fact, it's hard to keep any kind of air conditioner working around here. The AC on his sailboat is apparently also on the fritz."

As O'Reilly was finishing his sentence, another patron came in and sat at the bar. O'Reilly excused himself, and went over to attend the new customer. As they chatted, Carter looked around the bar and thought of the many hours he had spent here with Z. O'Reilly's Bar had not changed one iota. It was graced with the same, rickety barstools, encircled by about fifteen tables. Above his head, the rafters were filled with fishing nets, model sailboats, and other nautical paraphernalia. As he looked around, Carter took in the various fragrances—an exotic mixture of sea air, spilled beer, and the delicious aromas wafting from the kitchen.

Although O'Reilly's was open nearly 24 hours a day, the place didn't get lively until right before sunset. Many of the regular customers couldn't resist enjoying the sunset over a cocktail or two at the bar. Each night the place would fill with adventurers who loved to swap stories about their greatest passion—the sea. Most of the patrons were rich in experiences, but not in possessions or wealth. Nearly every spare penny went into their sailing and boating.

A few yards past the bar area, Carter scanned the marina. Although it had berths for about 50 boats of various sizes, today it appeared that only half of them were occupied. He wondered if "Rebecca the Loon," from the story he'd heard so long ago would still be there amongst the boats he saw lined up at the marina.

He remembered the story O'Reilly had told years ago. Rebecca, a middle-aged woman with many years of experience at sea, had been sailing solo, 480 miles north of Colombia and 130 miles off the coast of Nicaragua, headed for the Colombian island of *San Andrés*. Almost within sight of the island, a freak gust of wind from a storm had splintered her main mast. Unable to start her backup engine, she had radioed for help.

As luck would have it, Ben O'Reilly had been in the area—hired to captain a rich couple and their yacht from Puerto Lempira, Honduras down to Cartagena. When he first heard the distress call, O'Reilly had just passed southwest of San Andres. Since no one else appeared willing and/or able to answer her emergency call, he had come about and headed north to render assistance. Fortunately, due to the ample size and power of the yacht, they had been able to tow Rebecca and her crippled sailboat all the way to Cartagena. A plentiful supply of booze and non-stop storytelling helped fill the hours during their southward journey. Everyone had thoroughly enjoyed this unexpected rescue mission.

When O'Reilly had told this story, he cheerfully pointed out that Rebecca had promised to reimburse him fully for his expenses as soon as she was able. Carter remembered how O'Reilly had laughingly explained that she had yet to make good on that promise, and that he was still waiting for his money!

Most of the other guests berthed at the marina had much shorter stays than Rebecca's had been. Some stayed a few days and never returned. Others returned for a two or three week vacation at the same time each year. No matter how long their visit, nearly all were bewitched by the beauty of the Caribbean and appreciative of O'Reilly and his patrons' camaraderie. They were further enticed by the marina's very reasonable dockage fees and its even more reasonable prices for food and alcohol.

Carter's reminiscences were interrupted as he felt a pair of arms reach gently around him from behind. Two hands then covered his eyes.

"*¡Hola marinero! ¿Dónde has estado todo mi vida?*"

"Hello Sailor! Where have you been all my life," said the soft, now recognizable feminine voice of Gloria Saenz. Carter stood up and gathered her into his arms.

"Ah, it's so good to see you, Gloria! You're looking absolutely spectacular, as always!"

"Be careful, Gringo, flattery will get you anywhere!" she replied, kissing both Carter's cheeks, European style.

"How in the world did you find me here?" asked Carter, who although quite pleased with Gloria's surprise apparition, could not imagine how she could have found out about his last-minute trip to Cartagena.

"A little bird from DC told me, that's how I knew," she answered with a wink and a smile.

"Oh!" said Carter, remembering that before he left Miami, he had called his daughter, Rachel, to let her know he'd be leaving the country for a few days on an unplanned trip to Cartagena. Since his daughter and Gloria had apparently hit it off, it appeared that they had gotten in touch and that Gloria had found out about the journey.

"Where's that silly friend of yours? Was it Z-man?" asked Gloria, changing the subject.

"I don't know," said Carter, taking in the enticing smell of her perfume. "It would appear that he's waiting to make a grand entrance or something."

They moved away from the bar to sit at a table. Carter watched as she gracefully and confidently moved over to a table a few feet from the bar. She was very well put-together, raven-haired, and about five feet nine inches tall. The simple cotton dress she wore was understated—feminine, but not consciously sexy. Carter felt that many Latina women tended to reveal too much in an attempt to be feminine. Gloria, on the other hand, turned heads without even trying.

As if that weren't enough, perhaps most impressive were her eyes. They were a deep, mysterious brown—a perfect complement to her jet-black hair. And when Gloria smiled—something she did almost constantly—her eyes had a certain twinkle that conveyed a deep sense of confident and infectious happiness. She was always cheerful and full of life. Carter couldn't help feeling energized by her presence.

"So, tell me everything that's happened to you since I last saw you in Miami. Is your flying still good?" Gloria's accent was noticeable, but it never detracted from their conversation. She was obviously well educated and quite comfortable speaking in English.

"Oh, same old thing: Fly, layover, fly… keeps me out of trouble," replied Carter, taking another swig from his beer.

"I've been flying a lot lately too, and I've got a couple of layovers in Miami next month. I was hoping that maybe we might get together again." She stared intently—almost intensely—into Carter's eyes.

"I'd like that very much. Guess we'll have to coordinate our schedules to make that happen," Carter said, smiling as he thought about how much he'd enjoy seeing more of her.

Averting his eyes from her penetrating gaze, Carter thought of the first time they'd met. He was attending one of the many cocktail socials at the Ambassador's sprawling official residence. Since no Colombian military officers had been invited that evening, Carter had no official duties and had looked forward to socializing with the Embassy staff. After about an hour, one of the Embassy's secretaries had come over to the table and introduced Gloria to the group. As chance would have it, Gloria had taken the open seat next to him. While the others recounted inane rumors concerning who was *doing* whom at the Embassy, Carter and Gloria had begun to talk about current events in Colombia.

They had hit it off from the start. She had been impressed with Carter's understanding of the political situation in her country. He knew the important names and places, and was genuinely appreciative of her country's history. Carter had been impressed with Gloria's ever-present smile and quick wit, and he could not deny that her sultry good looks were also an asset. They became so engrossed in conversation that they seemed to be in their own private world— oblivious to the various conversations going on around them.

It was during that evening, that Gloria had given Carter a short synopsis of her life. She came from a middle class family and had always lived in Bogotá. Her father had died when she was an infant, and she was living with her mother in a two-bedroom apartment near the airport. Her mother had managed to save enough money to allow her to attend the National University of Colombia. Shortly after graduation, she had been hired by one of Colombia's largest and most prestigious banks, where she was still working.

At the end of the evening, as the crowd started to thin, Gloria had quietly passed Carter a napkin with her phone number. After standing in line together near the front door to thank and bid farewell to the Ambassador, they walked outside the residence, still engaged in conversation.

Carter had escorted her to a large, black—and obviously well armored— limousine, where a waiting driver opened the door to the rear seat. As he held open the door, the driver's jacket opened enough to reveal that he was armed. Seeing the puzzled look on Carter's face, Gloria had explained that the limo belonged to the bank's president, who was waiting in the back seat along with his daughter. At that point, Carter had leaned over enough to see an older gentleman and a very attractive woman sitting together inside. He smiled and waved at the two, but was more intent on watching Gloria slide gracefully into the limo. As she did so, he stood transfixed noticing the way her dress moved up her long slender legs as she settled into the large back seat. He waved goodbye through the limo's darkened windows as it pulled out of the driveway of the Ambassador's residence.

As Carter headed to his Embassy-provided armored car for the ride back to his apartment, he looked down at the napkin upon which Gloria had written her name and phone number. All the way home—and all through that night—Carter kept thinking of Gloria. He also thought of his wife and child back home in Virginia. Alone in bed that night, he considered what might happen if he were to get in touch with Gloria. He then imagined her naked body lying next to him in bed. As his mind conjured up all the delicious details, part of his body responded under the sheets. *It's only a dream*, he thought to himself as he finally drifted off to sleep.

The next morning when Carter had arrived at the attaché office in the Embassy, he saw Z sitting at his desk enjoying a cup of coffee—the first of countless cups of black coffee Z downed each day. Without preamble, Z began to give Carter a hard time.

"So, did you sneak off and get laid last night? Has the family man finally decided to play the field a bit... to partake of the local culture?"

"Screw you!" Carter said with a smile. "But I'll tell you what... she certainly made it difficult to stay faithful."

"Yeah, well you two sure seemed to be enjoying each other last night. Everybody's talking about it!"

"Damn," said Carter as he considered the ramifications, "That's all I need... the Embassy rumor mill running full speed. The word will surely get back through the wives' comm net and before you know it, I'll be judged guilty, convicted and sentenced—without actually doing the crime!"

"Ah, the world's just not fair, is it my man?" said Zaworski with a broad smile, taking great pleasure in Carter's discomfort.

"No shit! Meanwhile, you're certainly enjoying your bachelor status. Hell, you're getting more ass than the toilets seats in the airport bathroom!"

In the middle of this high-minded debate, their boss, Colonel Kelly Elmore had walked in. He had just returned from an Embassy staff meeting, where the head of the Econ section and the CIA station chief had been interested in learning more about one of Colombia's largest banks. The two departments of the Embassy had been conducting an investigation and following up leads that indicated the bank might be involved with money laundering. One of the Econ section's staff members had seen Carter and Gloria at the Ambassador's residence the night before. Recognizing that Gloria held a mid-level management position at the bank, he thought she might be in a position to accelerate their investigation. Therefore, they had decided that Carter should try to arrange further contact with Gloria to see what he could learn about the bank's operations.

Secretly, Carter had been happy for the assignment, as it gave him an excuse to see Gloria again. For the next several weeks, they saw each other nearly every day. They met after work and went out to dinner, or visited one of Bogotá's many attractions.

Most of the other men Gloria had known seemed to be acting out a courtship ritual designed to entice her to have sex with them as expeditiously as possible. In this respect, Carter seemed very different: intent on getting to know her, rather than simply getting her into bed. They talked about his family and his relationship with his daughter. For the first time, Gloria had openly talked about her childhood without a father.

Therefore, without really trying, he put Gloria at ease, and she found herself falling in love with a married man. When Carter steered the discussion toward Gloria's bank, she had described how she had received a surprisingly rapid series of promotions in her first few years. She also mentioned that the bank's president seemed overly interested in her section of the bank: the international division. Like any well-educated Colombian, Gloria was well aware of the impact drug trafficking was having on her country and its banking industry. She told Carter that she assumed that there might be some degree of money laundering going on, but that she saw little evidence of that kind of activity in her job. Despite his repeated probing for information, it became clear that she would provide no new evidence for the Embassy's investigation.

As the date for Carter's return to the US drew near, he had invited Gloria out for dinner at one of Bogotá's most exclusive restaurants. From the outset, they both recognized that their relationship would be short-lived—its end tied to Carter's fixed departure date. Up to that point, they had ignored that fact and concentrated solely on the present.

As far as the Embassy was concerned, he was breaking off their relationship because he had learned little about the bank's operations from her. That night at the restaurant, however, Gloria would hear a different, but more honest reason for them to stop seeing each other. He had told her that he was happily married and was finding it increasingly difficult to stay faithful to his wife back home. Within a week, he had returned home to the US.

This magnificent evening in Cartagena, as the sun continued its journey below the horizon, they were together once again—and for that, John Carter was very grateful indeed.

7:23 PM EST
Cristóbal Docks—near Colón, Panamá

Powerful floodlights were now providing illumination for the Cristóbal dock area—their harsh white light replacing the soft pink glow of the evening twilight. The port facility never slept—keeping pace with the hectic choreography of ships transiting the Panama Canal. Tonight, as usual, the docks were a beehive of frenetic activity. Four massive container ships were in the process of being loaded and unloaded.

In an open storage area just outside the glare of the busy dock area, a few hundred feet from the *Billesborg III*, Customs Agent Fernando García pretended to inspect a row of crates. García was not the least bit interested in the contents of the long-abandoned property at the edge of the customs yard. A few hours earlier, trucks had transported the Colombian's containers to the dock area. A pair of huge cranes was now lifting them off an orderly lineup of trucks and hoisting them up into position on the ship.

Checking his watch for the hundredth time that evening, Fernando García Luna desperately prayed that time would pass more quickly. Once that monstrous ship got underway, he might finally be able to sleep.

9:05 PM EST
O'Reilly's Marina—Cartagena, Colombia

Carter and Gloria spent the evening in rapt conversation, slowly building on their recently rekindled relationship. They sat alone at a table, far enough away from the other patrons to talk in private.

"You know, Gloria, I've wondered ever since we ran into each other in Miami, why you're working as a flight attendant. I would have thought that by now you'd be a bank vice president or something."

"Well, actually it's all your fault," she said with a smile. "Remember when we were seeing each other in Bogotá, you used to ask about money laundering and other bad things going on at the bank? I told you that there was nothing going on... that the bank was on firm financial and moral ground. Well, that was true... or at least I thought it was. After you left Colombia, I received several other promotions and after a couple of years, began working on projects where I had access to certain special account transactions. What I discovered was very disturbing. There *was* a lot of currency manipulation going on. I really didn't know... I mean while you were there," she said, reaching out to touch Carter's arm.

"Of course you didn't. I believed you then... just as I do now," Carter said, taking her hand into his own. "So what happened?"

"I eventually worked up the nerve to confront the bank president. He seemed genuinely surprised. Surprised with the details of the transactions, the extent to which the bank was involved, and surprised that I'd mention any of it to him. He refused to answer any of my questions. He never got angry, but appeared unable or unwilling to admit what was going on in his bank. Anyway, I felt sick knowing that a good part of the bank's profits was coming from financing drug deals and laundering money. For a while, I considered going to the police or the banking regulators; but I knew that would come to nothing. So I just quit. They tried to talk me out of it, but I just couldn't see myself being part of that system."

"After I left the bank, I got a couple of secretarial jobs in Bogotá. But every time, after a couple of months on the job, I'd get restless and moved on.

Eventually, I decided to get away from it all... at least for a while. I wanted to take a break... to go out and see the world. I figured that since I wasn't independently wealthy, the only way I could afford to travel was to work for an airline. At the time, I thought it would be a short-term thing. You know... that I'd give it a try for a couple of months. But I started to like my new life without a desk... and I still do. So, there you have it," she finished with a smile and that gleam in her eye that Carter found so irresistible.

"Wow, I had no idea," he managed to say. The more he learned about this woman, the more impressed he was. Noticing her empty glass, he added, "Would you like another drink?"

"No thank you, I've had more than enough. We should go see if there's any news from Z."

Carter had been so engrossed in his conversation with Gloria that he had forgotten all about his friend. They got up from the table and headed back to the bar, where O'Reilly was regaling a customer with another of his seemingly endless supply of stories. Seeing the two of them approach, O'Reilly walked over to where they were standing and leaned over towards them, both hands on the counter.

"So, mates, how may I be of service?" he asked cheerfully.

"I think we're both OK on the drink front, Ben. We were just wondering if you'd heard anything from Jack," Carter said.

"Not a thing. And although I certainly would have guessed he'd be back by now, it's like I said this afternoon—he's probably off with some girlie," opined O'Reilly, with a smile. "Come to think of it, since our friend has screwed up mightily and left you two here to fend for yourselves, I suggest that you ought to crash on his boat tonight to get even!"

"I don't know... maybe I should head back to my hotel," Carter protested without conviction.

"Nonsense!" insisted O'Reilly, who then reached under the bar and pulled out a spare set of keys to the *Juguete*. Tossing them across the bar to Carter, he added, "What the Hell... leave a big mess—it'd serve him right!"

"No way we're going to that fancy hotel, Mr. Carter," Gloria agreed playfully. She grabbed him by the arm and the two turned away from the bar and headed out towards the line of boats moored in the marina.

Reaching the *Juguete,* Carter first jumped the short distance from the dock and then turned around to hold Gloria's hand, helping her onto the deck. Using the key O'Reilly had given them; he opened the hatch leading down to the main cabin and walked downstairs. It was stifling hot—having been closed up during the heat of the day. The two of them quickly set about opening the various portholes and hatches to allow some of the fresh evening breeze to cool off the stuffy interior. From the other side of the small cabin, Carter admired Gloria's body as she kneeled on a padded bench, struggling with a hatch.

The humid cabin interior had caused both of them to start perspiring. Carter's gaze was drawn to the miniscule droplets of sweat coating Gloria's body. Admiring the view, he zeroed in on the delicate gold necklace and pendant, temporarily affixed to her right breast by the moisture.

"Here, let me help you," said Carter, walking over and kneeling in front of her on the same padded bench. As they pushed rhythmically upwards together, Carter's eyes moved away from the hatch and down towards her. As she struggled, her breasts swayed with her exertions—barely contained inside the cotton dress she was wearing. Carter tried to avert his gaze and concentrate on the job at hand, but was unable to keep his eyes off her. Then, foregoing any pretense of helping her, Carter openly devoted his entire attention to Gloria's ample cleavage.

"Are you going to stare at my boobs, or help me with this hatch, Mister?" she said playfully, finally able to divert Carter's glance away from her breasts.

"I'm sorry," he whispered, staring into her eyes.

"No need to be sorry," she murmured as they locked in a warm, sweat-moistened embrace, exploring each other's lips and mouths with a deep kiss. They pressed their bodies together ever more urgently as they slowly and clumsily negotiated their way, their bodies interlocked, into a horizontal position on the narrow bench. After several minutes of struggling to keep from falling off the narrow bench, they both seemed to reach a wordless consensus on two points—they needed more room and less clothing.

Carter stopped kissing Gloria long enough to grab her hand and guide her aft into the main stateroom, where he helped pull her dress over her head. Slightly dazed and with quickening breaths, he watched as she slowly removed her bra and slid off her panties. Carter stared at her voluptuous body—thinking of nothing but giving it as much pleasure as possible. He quickly ushered Gloria onto the spacious bunk, tore off his own clothes and joined her. He then slowly moved on top of her, again exploring her lips with his own, enjoying the sensation of her naked body against his own.

Gradually, he shifted his attention from her lips and moved down her body, alternatively tracing with his tongue and planting kisses along each side of her neck and shoulders. After slowly exploring her waist and stomach, breathing her in with every kiss, he returned to those wonderful breasts that had so captured his attention earlier. He gently kissed and caressed each one, his mouth savoring the salt-tinged taste of her. She began to moan her appreciation. Again, he moved slowly down her body toward the wonderful triangle of her pubic mound. Gloria wiggled her legs apart, allowing Carter unrestricted access to her. He playfully explored her sex; constantly varying the pressure and movement of his tongue in response to her moans.

Eyes closed in pleasure; Gloria rhythmically raised and lowered her pelvis off the cushion, giving herself up to Carter. Their sweat mixed with the moisture of her passion as her body began to shiver. Gloria frantically reached for Carter's manhood to guide it inside her.

She quickly discovered, however, that Carter was unable to consummate the passion of the evening. His mind had uncontrollably returned to his past—to another time and another woman.

"It's OK. Come here," she softly insisted, pulling him up into her arms, her body still trembling.

As they laid together wordlessly in each other's arms, listening to the sound of the other's breathing along with the gentle rhythmic lapping of waves against the hull, each of them pondered what tomorrow would bring.

Carter half-smiled in the darkness, frustrated at the realization that even death did not easily overcome so many years of faithfulness. Part of him wanted to run out of the *Juguete* in shame. The other enjoyed having this beautiful and caring woman in his arms. For the time being, it was impossible to deny that he was right where he wanted to be.

Lost in her own thoughts, Gloria understood that there was another woman on his mind. Confident and patient, she realized that she loved him enough to wait until he could make room for her in his heart.

10:44 PM EST
Newmann's Hacienda—Cali, Colombia

"*Señor*, you have a phone call from Cartagena," said one of the household security guards.

"I'll take it in my office," Newmann replied.

Newmann had just returned to his ranch after taking his private jet for the short flight from Bogotá to Cali. He needed to be here at his large estate in Cali, where he could more easily monitor the progress of the operation.

"Is it done?" asked Newmann without preamble—already aware of who was on the other end of the phone.

"*Sí, mi Jefe*, it is done. We will dispose of the body later tonight."

"Did you find out what he knows?"

"I'm sorry, *Jefe*, but he didn't talk too much before his heart stopped. He said he would never betray you... that he wanted only to be left alone. He denied talking to police anywhere. He did admit to going to Miami; but said that he only needed to buy a new compressor for the big refrigerator at the marina."

"Did you ask about Carter?"

"*Sí mi Jefe.* He insisted that he only visited Carter because he lived in Miami, and that's where he had to buy the compressor. He said they were friends from the American Embassy in Bogotá. He swore that he told Carter nothing about you or the Cartel. I'm pretty sure he was telling the truth, *Señor.*"

"And my wife?" Newmann asked, off-handedly.

"Same thing, *Jefe.* He insisted that they were only going out on sailing lessons. I believe this too, *Jefe*, and the surveillance and recordings we've been doing back him up."

"Good! Make sure there is no evidence."

"Of that you can be sure—the sharks will have only small pieces to eat. It will be finished tonight."

Newmann considered what he had just been told. He had known Zaworski for more than ten years. Until recently, he had done nothing to indicate that his interests went beyond a desire to live a comfortable retirement, close to the sea. Still, Newmann could not afford to take any chances. Taking risks got one jailed, or killed, in his line of business. He had been happy to buy Zaworski's cooperation and ensure his silence with respect to operations in Cartagena. Their arrangement had worked well over the years and he had been able to use the marina for many important shipments. Then, there was that unexpected trip to Miami... along with those lingering doubts about his wife's fidelity. There was no longer a reason for concern on either account.

The last item on the agenda was John Carter. His continued meddling and snooping around might represent a threat to the operation and to Newmann's organization.

"Has Carter arrived yet? Have you found out why he has come to Colombia?"

"He is here, *Jefe*... but we don't yet know why. He has been waiting for Zaworski at the marina and has met with a Colombian girl there... an *Avianca* flight attendant named Gloria Saenz. We're looking into her right now. I'll get back to you as soon as we've checked her out. So far, we've seen nothing that causes us concern."

"OK. Keep an eye on both of them and let me know if anything changes," he ordered.

Newmann continued pacing the room in silence—the phone connection still open—while he considered his next move. He needed Carter out of his hair. Ordinarily, arranging the death of an enemy was a simple matter; and he had plenty of underlings who could easily handle the task. Newmann remained convinced, however, that the death of yet another former member of the Defense

Attaché Office in Colombia would raise his profile. Carter's death might allow the Colombian national police (or even worse, an American law enforcement agency) to discover the connection amongst those killed. That connection would lead them to him—and he couldn't afford to take that risk. Therefore, rather than kill Carter, he must persuade him to leave Colombia.

"In fact," he continued, after getting his thoughts together, "have a couple of your men pay him a visit. Don't hurt him too much; just make it clear that he must leave Colombia immediately."

"*¡Entendido! ¿Alguna otra instrucción?*"

"No. Give me a call tomorrow, and let me know of your progress."

"Consider it done, *mi Jefe! Hasta luego.*"

Newmann hung up and stared at the wall of his office. He would not allow anything, or anyone, to stop him. Zaworski had become a liability and had to disappear. That was done—he was no longer a threat. Carter was now the only remaining dark cloud on the horizon. If he were lucky, Carter would give up after a good ass kicking. If that failed to convince him to stop snooping around and leave Colombia, then Carter—like his friend, Zaworski—would also have to disappear.

11:57 PM EST
Onboard *Billesborg III*—Cristóbal, Panamá

The giant ship slipped quietly away from the pier area and slowly—almost imperceptibly—started to pick up speed. She had just been released by the two tugs that had gently maneuvered her away from the dock. It was a few minutes before midnight, and the Master had just ordered his communications specialist to send the first report of the voyage. Since the home company in Denmark constantly monitored their position via satellite, the report was merely a formality.

Thankfully, they were right on schedule as the loading process in Cristóbal had been more efficient than normal. A merchant ship might sit at a dock facility for days on end if its paperwork was not in order. In Panama, the process of ensuring that the paperwork was "in order" was expensive and time-consuming. At each step of a shipping transaction, there were various officials waiting with outstretched palms: Panama Canal Authority and other government officials in Panama City, port agents, and customs officers assigned to the docks in Cristóbal—the list was seemingly endless.

Over the years, the Danish shipping conglomerate—*Dana-Dafra*, which owned the *Billesborg*—had accumulated enough experience to identify the officials with the necessary connections to ensure an expeditious transit through the Canal. These types of extra-official expenditures were made through a subsidiary with accounts at several banks operating in Panama. The shadowy cash transactions were just part of doing business. If you did things "by the book," your ship might lay idle and your profit margins would slowly evaporate while you waited. Your competitors, who would not hesitate to play by the rules of the game, would garner all the business. Things worked that way in Panama.

Thursday

"No plan survives first contact with the enemy."

Prussian Field Marshall Helmuth von Moltke

7:34 AM EST
Onboard *Juguete del Calamar*—O'Reilly's Marina; Cartagena, Colombia

Carter awoke to the smell of brewing coffee. He wanted to keep his eyes closed—shielding them from the brilliant early-morning sunlight shining through the portholes of the *Juguete*. Fighting to open his eyes and climb out of his slumber towards consciousness, Carter struggled to recall where he was. He tried to remember in which foreign country he was laying over, and when he'd have to get dressed to head downstairs to meet with the crew for their next flight.

I'm late! Suddenly, with his heart racing, Carter nearly bolted out of his bed. As the sights and sounds finally came into focus, Carter realized where he was... *Cartagena, the Juguete del Calamar... Gloria.*

As his pounding heart slowly returned to normal, he remembered his pitiful attempt at lovemaking last night. Things had certainly not gone well. His thoughts were interrupted by the sound of bare feet walking on the floor approaching the main stateroom.

"Good morning, sleepy head!" said Gloria, wearing nothing but a smile.

"Good morning," replied Carter stretching his arms and legs while slowly taking in each contour of her perfectly sculpted body.

"Care for a little *café con leche?*" she asked, gesturing back towards the *Juguete's* simple, almost-Spartan galley.

"Why thank you. I'd love some. Gloria?" he said as she turned to the galley.

"Yes?" she said, turning around to face him again.

"I'm sorry about last night," he said.

"Don't be sorry, silly. I certainly enjoyed myself. And besides, we have plenty of time to practice, no?" she replied with a wink and a mischievous smile. Once again, Carter saw that lively twinkle in her eyes.

"Have you heard anything about Jack?" he asked.

"Well, I don't think I'm in appropriate attire to be wandering about the marina asking questions," she replied, gesturing down towards her naked body.

"I guess not," said Carter smiling. "This look really works for you. You are a beautiful woman, Gloria. Looking at you like this... well, it's a pretty tremendous way to start the day," he admitted.

"I'm glad you like the show," she said bemusedly, playfully shaking her hips for his benefit, all the while staring straight into his eyes. After a few seconds, Gloria's impromptu dance ended and the smile left her face.

"What's the matter?" Carter asked.

"Do you have the slightest idea how much I care for you, John Carter?"

"I... I care for you very much too, Gloria," Carter stammered, trying to choreograph a tap dance of words to convey what he didn't even understand. "I've enjoyed every single moment we've had together. It's just—"

"I know," Gloria interrupted, walking over and putting her finger over his lips. Moving her hand slowly away from his mouth, she kissed him, pulled back and looked into his eyes. The long, silent stare communicated more than any words either of them might have been able to put together.

Gloria knew exactly how she felt, and desperately wished she could blurt out the words trapped in her heart: *I love you! I love you!* At that very moment, looking deep into his eyes, she was sure that he felt the same. He was not yet ready to admit it to her, or perhaps even to himself. Whatever his reasons, she would continue to give him the space he seemed to need and let him set the pace of their relationship.

"Well," Carter said with a sigh. "I guess we really should get dressed, have some of that coffee, and head to the restaurant. Maybe someone's finally heard from Jack."

"Whatever you say, sir," said Gloria with a playful salute before heading back to the galley for the coffee.

After sharing a cup of coffee, they got dressed and left the *Juguete*. On the way through the marina, they waved at a few early-risers enjoying the morning sun on the decks of their boats. Reaching the deserted bar area, they saw one of the local bus boys hosing down the area. There was no sign of Zaworski.

Continuing past the tables, they found the manager doing paperwork in the office behind the bar. Daniela—who had worked at the marina for the past 15 years—preferred to work in the quiet early-morning hours, before her small, un-air conditioned office became unbearably hot. Although he had heard her voice the night before, Carter had never actually *met* Daniela. However, that wasn't particularly surprising since he'd never been awake this early at the marina.

They spoke with Daniela for a few minutes, sharing a growing apprehension that something might have happened to Zaworski. Everyone knew that Jack would often head to Cartagena's casino district where he was wont to enjoy the company of any number of women with whom he might hook up while there. He always seemed able to attract good-looking women—visiting tourists or locals—willing to help him celebrate and spend his winnings from the blackjack table.

Carter imagined that Z was sleeping late after a raucous evening of gambling and sex. He tried to bolster that scenario in his mind—that his friend was safely recuperating after another long night—to keep the other, more troubling alternatives out of play. Daniela did not share his outward optimism, however, saying that it was unusual for Z to be gone this long without so much as a phone call. In the end, they all agreed that the best thing would be to head downtown to see if they could find him.

As they got ready to leave, Carter tried to clear his mind of a disturbing thought—a foreboding premonition—that it was already too late.

1:17 PM CDT
Onboard *Antioquia*—400 miles south of Mobile

Royal Grenadian Coast Guard Superintendent Fitzroy George was sitting at the head of the small table in his cabin. With him were three others—men who had spent the last several days preparing for the upcoming operation.

First, there was Manuel "Mani" Hernández—Carlos' younger brother. Although he was youthful and headstrong, George knew that Mani harbored no divided loyalty. Not only had Carlos assured him of his brother's commitment to the operation, George had seen Mani's utter devotion to and admiration for his beloved older brother. If it came time for Mani to choose between the Colombian Navy and his brother... there was no question where his allegiance lay. For the past several weeks, he had been eager to help in any way he could.

Early on, Carlos had decided that Mani would help with security and communications for the operation. He had also decided that the *Antioquia* would be the most appropriate ship in the Colombian Navy to carry out their part of the plan. Carlos had arranged with one of his contacts in the upper echelons of the Colombian Navy to have Mani assigned to the ship. He had further insisted that Mani attend night classes in Cartagena to improve his English language skills. Mani had taken his brother's admonitions to heart and had studied conscientiously. For the last three weeks at sea, he was having no trouble keeping up with the English conversations going on around him.

During a late night phone call just before the *Antioquia* had left port, Carlos had left word that he would meet his brother shortly after their arrival in Mobile. He had given Mani his cell phone number and the name of the local bar where they would meet. Mani could hardly wait until the boarding was over. After all these years apart, he would finally be able to see his brother again. His excitement was also intensified by the visit to the United States, as this was his first trip outside Colombia.

Also present in the cabin were two accomplices from the Grenadian Coast Guard: Assistant Inspector Samuel Toppin and Corporal Patrick Ogilvie. As the ranking enlisted member of the detachment, Inspector Toppin would be in charge of the boarding party—directing all boarding operations and leading the team at the container ship's bridge. Toppin would also ensure that the incriminating evidence was properly placed, and subsequently found, in the First

Mate's cabin. Corporal Ogilvie was to head the team searching for drugs below decks.

During this short meeting, they had ironed out the final details of the boarding—clearing up the division of labor between the groups and agreeing to various backup and contingency plans. They had all concurred that if anything happened that couldn't be handled onboard the container ship, they would transmit the code word "curious," indicating that they needed Superintendent George's direct participation.

"Nothing will go wrong. We control the two main boarding teams. Just don't get in too much of a hurry; it's got to look good... like you just stumbled on it. Got it?" George asked.

Heads nodded in agreement. Everyone knew his part in the mission. They would do their jobs and would soon be rich.

"Don't worry," George had assured them as he got up. "We've gone over every possible contingency. It should not be necessary; but if anything should happen, I'll get there as fast as I can. Just stay calm. Any questions?"

There had been no questions, and after the men had walked out of his room, George continued to pour over the details in his mind. He felt certain that his men would be able to keep ahead of the Americans, control the pace of the boarding and search of the vessel—that everything would go according to their carefully conceived plan. Now it was nearly time for the real thing.

The plan was simple enough, albeit expensive. The financial arrangements were up to Newmann and his Colombian connections. George imagined that if Newmann could afford to pay the agreed amount for his services, he must have been making a hell of a lot of money on this deal. They always did.

George's experience had taught him that the simplest plans had the best chance for success; and their plan was indeed simple. First, Carlos would make an anonymous phone call alerting the Americans to a large shipment of cocaine—ironically, the property of a competing cartel—hidden in a container ship steaming near the Task Force's location. George and his men would be tasked to board the *Billesborg*, where they would "find" the smuggled drug shipment. The entire Task Force would then escort the ship and its cargo of confiscated drugs to Mobile, Alabama.

Superintendant George would be directly responsible for one of the largest-ever seizures of cocaine. There was sure to be stories in the Grenadian press— where the news would likely turn him into a national hero.

During the boarding, Ogilvie's team had the easiest job: discovering the cocaine. It would be easy because they already had blueprints of the *Billesborg*, showing the exact location of the fake wall behind which it was hidden. Toppin's job was only slightly more complicated and therefore entailed more risk. Toppin would plant an envelope containing incriminating evidence in the First Mate's cabin. During each of their meetings, Toppin had practiced lifting the mattress in George's cabin as if searching for something. Making sure that his back was facing everyone else in the cabin, he lifted the mattress with one hand, while using the other to drop the envelope from his shirt pocket—making it appear to have fallen from underneath the mattress. No one would be watching Toppin closely enough to notice the deception.

The time for planning and rehearsing was nearly over. George and his men would soon turn themselves into "drug-fighting heroes."

7:22 PM EST
Cartagena, Colombia

Carter and Gloria spent the entire day searching Cartagena for Jack Zaworski. After breakfast, they had borrowed O'Reilly's small outboard motor boat and headed to Fort San Fernando, which protected the smaller of the two entrances to Cartagena's harbor, known as *Bocachica*.

After returning to the marina, they had taken a taxi and explored the downtown area—walking along the dark-sand beaches and visiting many of the city's attractions from the colonial period: the Church and Convent of Santo Domingo, the Plaza Bolivar, the Clock Tower, and finally the impressive Castle of San Felipe de Barajas.

They picked out a small sidewalk café near the beach for a leisurely lunch, where they reminisced about their time together back in the "Embassy days." Try as they might to keep the conversation light, however, they had frequently returned to recent troubling events, and were becoming increasingly concerned about Jack. Several times during the day, Gloria had called back to the marina. Each time, the answer had been the same—Jack had not returned, nor had he called to let anyone know his whereabouts.

Near sunset, they had returned to marina. Exhausted after spending most of the day on their feet, they headed straight for the bar, and once again asked O'Reilly if he had heard anything.

"Ah, you two are worrying too much about old Mr. Z. Like I said before, he's probably found something more interesting to keep him busy," said O'Reilly unconvincingly.

"Well, I sure hope you're right, Ben," Carter said. Then, turning to Gloria, he asked, "Would you like to have a drink?"

"Yes, I *am* quite thirsty after all that walking around today. We might as well have something while we're waiting. It would be a shame not to enjoy this magnificent sunset," she replied, gesturing towards the west.

Thursday

It was indeed an impressive display—in the foreground, the marina's boats sat gracefully in their slips, while the clouds in the distant horizon framed the shoreline on the opposite side of the bay.

As the sun began to disappear below the horizon, Carter drained his beer and told Gloria, "My dear, I feel positively *crusty* and must admit that I'm in great need of a shower!"

"Yes you are, Mister," said Gloria, playfully holding her nose.

"We better call a cab," said Carter, looking at his watch.

"I've got a better idea," said Gloria, her hand covering his. "I feel rejuvenated by that sunset. Or maybe it's the alcohol. Why don't we just walk back to your hotel? It should take us less than an hour to get there, it's a nice walk, *and,*" she said, smiling devilishly and grabbing Carter by his arm, "the night is still quite young!"

"All right, you've talked me into it!" Carter agreed with a chuckle.

He turned toward O'Reilly, and asked for the bill.

"Your money, is quite useless here, Mr. Carter!" replied O'Reilly with a wink and a grin.

"Thank you, my friend," Carter said, moving closer to shake the man's hand. "You have Gloria's cell phone number, and we'll be staying at the Hilton. Please call us the minute our unreliable friend decides to grace us with his presence."

"You can count on it. I hope you and the lovely lady have a very pleasant evening," said O'Reilly, vigorously pumping Carter's hand.

Carter turned and took Gloria by the hand as they walked out of the bar and onto the street leading back toward the Hilton. As they strolled hand-in-hand, conversation came easily. Engrossed with each other, they covered their past in Bogotá as well as the many sights they had shared earlier that day while searching for Z throughout the city.

Suddenly, Carter felt a sharp pain in the back of his neck. Simultaneously, a strong hand grabbed his arm and his legs were kicked out from under him. As he hit the sidewalk, unseen arms and legs had already immobilized him—painfully pressing in his face into the still-warm concrete. All the while, he was pelted with punches. Carter struggled with all his strength, but was unable to free himself or protect his head and body from the onslaught—he was helpless.

There were five of them, as best as he could tell. Two of the bastards kept kicking him in the stomach and head. He looked for Gloria. She was lying on the ground near him, one of the men was placing what looked like duct tape over her mouth, and had already secured her legs and arms. Other than the tape, she appeared uninjured. *She must be alive*, he thought to himself, *otherwise why would they be taping her mouth shut?*

"¡Déjela tranquila! ¡Toma mi dinero!"

"Leave her alone! Take my money!" Carter yelled in an attempt to get the attackers to leave Gloria and concentrate on him.

It was obvious, even through his increasingly dazed and groggy state, that he would not be able to do much. He would not be able to protect himself—much less Gloria.

The attackers' punishment stopped long enough for one of them to reach inside the rear pocket of Carter's pants to remove his wallet. He took out the cash, and then looked at his National Airlines ID.

"John Carter," he spat venomously while examining the ID. "Too bad you don't have an airplane to fly away from us. None of your flight attendants are here to help you, *hijo de puta!*" The last punctuated with a kick in his side.

"We don't want to see you here anymore. Do you understand!" said another voice.

He struggled to maintain consciousness. Unable to hold his arms over his face for protection, he felt a hard kick connect with his nose. He only dimly felt the pain, but could feel the warm blood flowing from his nose. Through the haze, Carter sensed that his attackers had stopped hitting him. He tried to concentrate. They were still there... and were talking to him; but he couldn't quite understand what they were saying.

"You fucked up. Go back home. Forget about Colombia. Forget or die, it's up to you."

Carter struggled to piece together what they were saying. It didn't make any sense. Why didn't they just take his money and leave? Why were they still talking to him?

Suddenly, one of the attackers grabbed him by the collar and starting yelling at him. He was close enough that Carter noticed the warmth of his breath and the strong odor of garlic. The attacker then moved even closer to Carter's face, saying nothing, only staring with emotionless eyes. With his face only inches away, he slowly and deliberately whispered chilling words—confirmation that this was not a simple mugging.

"Both of your friends are dead, asshole. You'll be dead too if you don't get your ass out of here!"

With his required message delivered, the assailant grabbed Carter by his hair and violently slammed his head into the pavement, causing Carter's world to go black.

Friday

Therefore do not be anxious about tomorrow,
for tomorrow will be anxious for itself.
Each day has enough trouble of its own.

Matthew 6:34

3:34 AM EST
Hilton Hotel—Cartagena, Colombia

Through a throbbing headache, Carter attempted to locate the rays of sun that should have been shining into the *Juguete*. But there was no light, and the cabin appeared larger than he remembered. He was in a large bed... there were large pieces of furniture around him... paintings on the wall. He was covered with sheets and surrounded by fluffy pillows.

"Where am I?" muttered Carter, his entire body aching.

Carter heard hushed footsteps. As his mind took in the welcome sight of Gloria walking towards him, he realized that he was not on the *Juguete*, but in his hotel room at the Cartagena Hilton.

"Gloria," he whispered, wincing with pain, but delighted to see her. "What happened? How did I get here?" Carter then reached up and felt the swelling that covered the left side of his face. It came back to him—the mugging. He had survived... *they* had survived.

Gloria leaned over the bed and gently kissed him, looking relieved.

"I'm so glad you're awake! I was beginning to wonder how long I should let you sleep, before taking you to a hospital."

After insisting that he was all right and that he would get by just fine without medical attention, Carter had asked Gloria fill in the blanks from their violent encounter. She began at the end of the attack.

Shortly after their attackers had left, Gloria had been able to remove the duct tape covering her arms, legs and mouth. She had rushed over to Carter and found him drifting in and out of consciousness—his face and head covered with blood. She had hurriedly checked his condition, confirming that he was able to move his arms and legs, and that his eyes followed her moving finger. After a hasty cleaning, she quickly determined that he had no life-threatening injuries.

She had elected not to call the authorities and to take care of Carter herself. After their not so random attack, there was no telling whom they could trust. Finding her purse near where she had been bound, Gloria had used her cell phone to call a taxi. As she had waited for the cab, she had sat next to Carter—pondering where to take him. She had ruled out heading back to the marina and the *Juguete*. Carter's hotel would be a much more public and therefore safer location for them to spend the night.

Once the cab had arrived, she had explained to the driver that Carter had had too much to drink, fallen down and cut open his head. Hotel security had reluctantly accepted the same tale after checking Gloria's identity card and confirming that she was indeed flight attendant for *Avianca*.

The hotel management reasoned that if Gloria's intent had been to rob Mr.

Carter, she would not have brought him back to the hotel in his current condition. They decided to let the two of them go up to Carter's room.

Listening intently as she recounted what had happened; Carter was impressed with her strength and quick thinking under pressure. He was seeing a new side of Gloria, and was quite awed and even humbled by this courageous, yet still caring and stunningly beautiful woman.

"Wow! I'm sure glad you were there last night," he said, holding out his arms, silently beckoning her into the bed. She slid under the covers and moved into his waiting arms. As they lay holding each other tightly, Gloria began to sob—letting go the built-up flood of emotions. Now that he was finally conscious again, she was tremendously relieved to see that the attack had not caused him serious injury.

"I'm so glad you're alive... and that I'm here with you," she said through the tears, burying her head into his shoulder.

"Thank you," he said simply, continuing to hold her tightly, almost urgently close to him. After several minutes in silence, he gently removed her head from his shoulder so he could look at her. He brushed away a strand of hair that had fallen over her eyes. Still lying next to each other, they stared into each other's eyes in silence for several more minutes, until Gloria finally asked, "Are you sure you're all right, John?"

"Well, I *have* felt better. To tell you the truth, I wish I could stay here in bed with you for the next week or so," he answered honesty. "But, I've got to find out what the hell's going on."

"I would like to know too. All I know is that we need help."

"Well, I don't know who's going to help us. I don't even have a gun. And after last night, I feel like I need a dozen armed men around for protection," admitted Carter. "But who *can* I trust? There seems to be some kind of connection between my attaché assignment and what's been going on. I need to find someone who can help me figure this out. That wasn't just a mugging last night, it was a warning. That guy said both my friends were dead. But why? Why did they kill Jack and Bruce? Who *were* those guys? I just can't believe that Jack was involved in the drug business—it's not like him. Hell, look at the simple life he was living. Would he live like that if he were dirty? What made him come to the States to warn me? What have I done to piss these people off? There's got to be something or someone linking all this together."

"None of it makes any sense to me either. But I *do* know something," Gloria said, her face determined and her eyes almost fiercely focused on Carter's. "You need protection from these animals—whoever they are. There are too many people in my country willing to kill for a few hundred dollars. I'm afraid Colombia is still a very dangerous place. And as you say, you don't even have a gun. We can't go to the police; most of them are not trustworthy. We could go stay with my mother in Bogotá...and I have some uncles there who could find—"

"I just can't do that," Carter interrupted. "Thank you Gloria, but I can't hide out with anyone here. I no longer have the Embassy support structure I once had. I must head back to the States."

"OK. I was... I just want to keep you safe. I don't want anything to happen to you. And yes, I agree that you probably need to leave Colombia, but I'm going with you."

"I'm sorry, Gloria, but I don't want to put you in danger too. I have to go alone," said Carter, getting out of bed and heading, a bit unsteadily, over to the low table where he had left his overnight bag. He began folding his clothes and putting them back into the bag. As he packed, he continued, "This whole thing seems to have something to do with the DAO in Bogotá. I still know some people at the DIA who might be able to help. That's where I may find some answers. I don't think they'll let you into the places I'm going. Hell, I'm not even sure they'll let *me* in. But it's time to call in some chips, and put some of the training they gave me to use."

"But John, I'm worried that—"

"I'm sorry Gloria, but I need to do this alone. I'll get in touch with you as soon as I start getting some answers... I promise," he said, leaning over to kiss her. "There's a flight leaving for Miami in a few hours. I can be in Washington by lunchtime, but I've gotta get going."

"I understand," said Gloria, tears welling up in her eyes.

Gloria rose from the bed, pulled Carter away from his packing and embraced him. For that moment, they both pretended they were in some other place and time. They stood together in each other's arms, so much said in the intense silence.

"I've got a lot to work to do if I'm gonna catch that flight, and a shower is pretty damn high on the list," said Carter as he tried to focus on the immediate tasks at hand. "Do you mind calling and checking on the flights to Washington?"

As she turned and walked towards the phone, Carter stopped and called after her, "Thank you, Gloria. I mean it. I can't thank you enough—for everything." He walked into the bathroom and turned on the shower's hot water.

Slowly, the steam began to fill the small bathroom. He added cold water to the mixture until the temperature was just tolerable. Carter then got into the shower and let the soothing hot water flow over his head and revive him. After finishing his shower, Carter turned off the water and pulled back the curtain. There at the door of the bathroom, Gloria was waiting for him.

They embraced as he stepped out of the shower—still dripping water. Their kiss was long, urgent, and passionate. Carter felt a familiar stirring in his loins—and so could Gloria. They both knew there was no time. If he was going to get to Washington, DC, and the Defense Intelligence Agency, he had to leave *now*.

12:47 PM EDT
Reagan National Airport—Washington, DC

Carter had a lot to accomplish in Washington, and no clear plan on how to do it. It had been years since he had been in the military circles of DC, and he knew it might be difficult to catch up with *anyone* he knew—much less find someone with information to help him figure out who was behind the deaths of two former members of the Defense Attaché Office.

On the flight from Miami, he recalled the abbreviated phone conversation he'd had with Mike Kennedy before he left for Cartagena. Kennedy had told him that Kelly Elmore was working on the Joint Staff in the Pentagon. Since Elmore had been Carter's boss and Defense Attaché in Bogotá, he would certainly be in a position to know about current events in Colombia. Carter decided that Elmore would be the first person he'd attempt to contact in Washington.

Next, he had thought of the folks at the Defense Intelligence Agency's satellite office in Arlington, just across the Potomac River and west of the city of Washington. Perhaps he'd get a lucky break, and someone there would remember him and be able to help.

After his flight arrived, Carter walked outside the terminal and continued up to the airport's elevated metro station. Three stops to the north, he arrived at Pentagon Station. He exited the metro and took the incredibly lengthy escalators to the building's huge main concourse. Carter's mind flooded with memories of his two tours of duty at the Pentagon.

Even though he had worked there for several years, the mammoth building still impressed him. Sitting on almost thirty acres of land, the Pentagon's circumference was just shy of a mile. Yet despite its massive size, you could reach any location in the building in about ten minutes. Always clogged with people, the main concourse was nearly a city unto itself. It had bookstores, restaurants, a post office, dry cleaning, florist, jewelry, film processing and many other stores and shops.

As Carter watched the be-medaled men and women stride confidently in their services' uniforms, he tried to spot a familiar face. They all looked so young... and unfamiliar. He made a beeline for a bank of payphones where he knew he'd be able to find a Pentagon phone book.

Reaching one of the payphones, he opened the phone book and found five entries for "Elmore." Luckily, only two of them worked on the Joint Staff and only one was a full colonel in the US Army. Carter dialed the number.

"J36, Petty Officer Jones speaking, may I help you Ma'am or Sir?"

"Hello, my name is John Carter. I'd like to speak with Colonel Elmore, please."

"One moment sir, I'll put you through."

"Colonel Elmore here. Is this the John Carter from DAO Bogotá?"

"Yes sir. How've you been?"

"Good; and you?"

"Well, to tell you the truth, sir, things have been a little confusing lately. I had a strange visit from Jack Zaworski, the other day. We met for lunch back on Tuesday down in Miami. He seemed very preoccupied and nervous; and tried to warn me about something. Well, before I could figure out what the heck he was talking about, he ups and almost runs out of the restaurant. Said he had to catch a plane back to Cartagena. He mentioned that things were *weird* in Colombia, and suggested that the two of us get together in Cartagena. I guess I was intrigued enough to take him up on his offer. Before I left for Colombia, I made a few phone calls to try and get in touch with some of the old crowd. First, I tried Bruce Meyer, and got through to his wife, MinJung. She told me he was dead and that she was sure there was foul play involved."

"Did she mention anything specific?" asked Elmore.

"Not really. She was convinced that Bruce had been killed, though. Anyway, I took a couple of days off and headed down to Cartagena to see Z— who was a no-show... most likely, because he had been killed too. Then, as if things weren't screwed up enough already, I get beat up and told to get my ass out of Colombia. The guys who attacked me were definitely pros. They had me off my feet and immobilized before I knew what hit me. Then they made sure I knew that Zaworski was dead. There's got to be—"

"Mugged?" Elmore asked, before Carter could finish his thought. "It always was a little wild down there in Cartagena, especially around that marina area. Are you OK?"

"They roughed me up pretty good, but I'm fine—just a couple of bruises, and the remnants of a pretty serious headache. Anyway, they seemed to be very intent on making sure that I got the message to leave Colombia. I got that message, loud and clear!"

"What a screwed up place. I'd say you're lucky to be alive!" said Elmore.

"You're right about Colombia. Although, despite my recent experience, it's certainly not as bad as when we were there," added Carter. "Speaking of our time in Bogotá, what about some of the other guys at the DAO? Are you still in touch with any of them?"

"No, John... sorry, but I haven't stayed in touch with that gang," Elmore lied.

"Oh well..." Carter sighed, disappointed at how little he had learned from Elmore. He began to think that he had been too optimistic about finding answers in DC.

"I'd say you've had an exciting couple of days. I'm sorry to hear about Zaworski and Meyer; but I can't think of anything that could help you figure out what's going on. Nothing's come up on my scope, anyway. Tell you what, I'll ask our Colombian desk officer, and see if he's heard anything that might be of use. However, if you're still retired from the military, and not working for any government agency, I won't be able to share anything classified... you know how it is."

"Sure Colonel Elmore, I just figured I'd ask. I have no idea which way to turn."

"Sorry I couldn't have been more helpful, but I've got to run. The J3's keeping me real busy these days. Maybe we could have lunch sometime," Elmore said without meaning it. "You got my number. If anything comes up, give me a call. Take care, John," the line went dead before Carter could respond.

Well, that wasn't very helpful, Carter thought as he paged through the phone book, hoping a name would jump out at him. It was—of course—a lost cause as the Pentagon had over 23,000 employees. Crestfallen and fatigued, Carter retraced his steps back down to the metro station and his next destination, the Clarendon Building.

1:32 PM EDT
National Security Agency—Fort Meade, Maryland

As usual, Hargrove and Young were having lunch at their desks. They had long ago tired of the bland fare at the agency's cafeteria, and for years, sandwiches from home were their preferred culinary option. The only drawback to their desk-bound lunch break was that they lost a good excuse to get away from the frenetic pace of their office. Even if they had been inclined towards a more social meal at the agency cafeteria, neither of them ever seemed to have the time. This was especially true over the past few days, as a certain American in Colombia had been occupying much of their time.

They felt sure that the increasing number of intercepted communications indicated that *Mr. N* was up to something big. It was a familiar pattern—as they'd often see an increase in communications a few days before major drug trafficking operations. This certainly was the case with the suddenly very talkative *Mr. N.*

A few hours earlier, they had come very close to nailing down *Mr. N's* identity. After NSA computers had been fed details of Elmore's service and personnel records, they spit out several possible candidates. The list included foreign nationals, active-duty and retired military officers, and finally… a former sergeant, named Marty Newmann, who had worked with Elmore in Colombia. Because of this lead, government operatives had been deployed to Colombia to try to gather more details on Newmann's business activities. As he was still an American citizen, they were awaiting legal authorization to tap his phone lines in Colombia. Pending the results of this investigation, Newmann appeared to be their prime suspect.

"So, *N's* guy, Elmore—AKA *Delta One*—is working in the Pentagon and wants his boss to know that *Delta Seven* is in DC," said Hargrove, pushing the hanging piece of sandwich meat back into his mouth.

"Yep, and that tidbit was definitely *not* good news for our man," agreed Young, sipping on the soup he had just heated up in the division's break room microwave.

"So, *Delta Seven* is a threat to them."

"Yes, but who is he… Colombian National Police?"

"Why would they call him a '*Delta* something' if he was a cop?" replied Hargrove with another question. "Why wouldn't they give him some other code name? I mean, they seem to have good *Deltas* and bad *Deltas*. And, I doubt he's Colombian National Police—that doesn't jibe with the *Delta* thing they've got going."

"You're right, and I think we're talking about Gringos. Except for the Grenadian, all the accents are American," said Young.

"OK, so maybe *Delta Seven* is DEA… does that make any sense?" Hargrove hypothesized.

"No, we've already run the transcripts by DEA and they came up empty. Although we certainly got their attention," said Young, his voice muffled by the plastic soup bowl covering his mouth as he finished off the remnants of his lunch.

"Gringos, drugs, Pentagon, Grenada—something's definitely about to go down," said Hargrove.

Friday

Carter rode the escalator from the main concourse down into the depths of the Pentagon Metro station. Reaching the bottom of the escalator, he walked over to a large map of the Metro route system to figure out how he would get to his next destination. The map indicated that he would take the Blue Line to the Rosslyn station and then transfer to the Orange Line. Two stops west would take him to the Clarendon stop—right across the street from the DIA's Clarendon Building in the city of Arlington.

Continuing downstairs, he arrived at the platform just as a train was pulling noisily into the station. As soon as the doors opened, he walked inside and found an empty seat. As the train accelerated, Carter reviewed a couple of details from the conversation he had just had with Elmore that were troubling him. First, he seemed unfazed by the news of Zaworski and Meyer's murders. It was if he already knew. The second nagging issue involved Elmore's response to Carter's description of the mugging in Cartagena. Elmore had volunteered that the area around the *marina* was dangerous. Although he couldn't remember precisely what he had told Elmore, Carter was pretty sure that he had never mentioned *where* the mugging had taken place. Perhaps Elmore had just assumed that Carter had been mugged at that location, since Zaworski was living at the marina.

Carter struggled to read a sign coming into view as the metro train slowed down approaching the next station. It read Clarendon—his stop.

Carter emerged from the metro station escalator in a pedestrian island between Clarendon and Wilson Boulevards. The 15-story building was right across the street to the south. After crossing the busy street, he entered the building and walked to the back of the lobby. As he approached the security screening area that served as the single entrance to those floors controlled by the DIA, Carter wondered if they'd let him inside. He hoped that John White—DIA's senior Latin American analyst—would still be there, remember who he was, and be able to help make sense of recent events.

Carter walked up to one of the armed guards and introduced himself, "Good afternoon, my name is John Carter. I'm a retired lieutenant colonel, and I used to work for the DIA several years ago. I'd like to speak with Mr. John White. If I'm lucky, he'll still be working in the Latin American Division. I'm sorry, but I don't have his office or phone number anymore."

"Just a moment, sir, I'll check our roster," said the guard heading over to the small desk to the side of the entranceway. He pulled one of several loose-leafed binders from the top of the desk, and started searching for White's name.

"I'm sorry, but I don't see his name. Is there anyone else you'd like to see?"

"Would it be possible for you to call someone in the Latin American Division, and let them know that a former colleague is downstairs, and would like to chat very briefly with someone?" Carter was beginning to feel this visit might also be unproductive. Things change and people move on. What were the chances that there'd still be someone there who remembered an attaché who served more than a decade ago?

"I'll give it a try, sir, but I don't think I'll be able to make more than one call for you. Those folks are pretty busy up there."

Carter was actually surprised at how helpful this guard had been so far. Most other government security guards probably wouldn't have been as accommodating. Carter listened as the guard spoke to one of the receptionists upstairs. After a brief conversation, the guard cupped the phone and told Carter that the person answering the call had been working with DIA only a few years, and was trying to find one of the "old heads" in the division. A few moments later, the guard put the phone back to his ear, listened for a few seconds and handed the phone to Carter.

"Hi, thanks very much for speaking with me," said Carter hopefully.

"I'm sorry, Colonel Carter, I've asked those within earshot of my desk here, and no one remembers you. However, there is one more possibility. I know someone down in the East European division, and I'm pretty sure he worked the Colombian desk right after John White died. Maybe he remembers you and can help."

"John White is dead?" asked Carter with a sinking feeling.

"Yes, about five years ago. The cancer finally got the best of him. Just a minute and I'll put you through to Mr. Fred Dunsmore. Good Luck, Colonel." The line went silent as she transferred the call.

Sadly, it was not much of a surprise to learn that John White had died. When Carter had worked with him, the topic of White's chemotherapy sessions came up frequently. White had been a fighter—fighting both the disease and the DIA bureaucracy. Now he was gone, and Carter had lost a potential ally. Still, there was this last hope... *Fred Dunsmore... Fred Dunsmore...* Carter repeated the name in his mind—hoping to shake loose a helpful memory. The name seemed familiar, but he couldn't place it.

The phone came to life in his hand.

"John Carter? Is that you? From the DIAC?" asked Dunsmore.

Carter struggled to remember the name and to connect it to a face.

"I'm sorry Mr. Dunsmore, but I don't remember you," Carter said, frustrated that he was unable to recognize the voice.

"Aw, come on, John, we used to have lunch together all the time at the DIAC. You were going through initial attaché training, and I gave you a couple of briefings on Colombia. I was still in the Air Force then—a Captain."

That last piece of information lit the proverbial floodlight of recognition in Carter's mind. "Yeah, Fred, now I remember! I'm sorry; my mind was drawing a total blank. Well, shoot! What are you doing now?"

"Heck, John, I'll tell you in a little bit. I'll be right down. You got time for lunch?"

"Sure, I'm starving. Lunch would be great."

After Dunsmore arrived in the lobby, he and Carter walked across Clarendon Boulevard to a Vietnamese restaurant. After they sat down and ordered, they quickly covered the basics of each other's lives for the past decade. After nine years of active duty, Dunsmore was passed over for promotion to major and decided to leave the Air Force. With the strong recommendations of all his former superiors at DIA; his knowledge of Latin America; and Top Secret, code-word security clearances, Dunsmore had been hired as a civilian intelligence specialist for the DIA.

"After the Colombia desk, I spent a while covering Guatemala and Honduras. Then, just when I was getting comfortable with the area, the DIA, in all its wisdom decided to transfer me to the FSU section," Dunsmore said. Seeing the quizzical look on Carter's face, he laughed and clarified, "That's Former Soviet Union—not Florida State University."

"You know how it goes: you get your Spanish up to speed, learn a little Portuguese, become an expert in several of the countries in the region, and they move you somewhere else. Same old shit," complained Dunsmore, with a smile.

"Thanks to old commies and new Mafia types, looks like Russia is headed for the same kind of nihilism as our buddies, the Colombians. Speaking of Colombians, seems like I can't get rid of them no matter what office I work for. We've been collaborating with the NSA on a possible connection between some mafia types up in Saint Petersburg, and the Cali Cartel. We're fairly certain they're working on a coke-for-arms deal. In the past month or two, there's been a spike in communications between the two groups."

"Enough about me, John," Dunsmore continued. "Tell me what brings you back to your old DIA *Alma Mater* here at Clarendon?"

"To tell you the truth, Fred, I just got the strangest visit from a guy I served with in Bogotá, named Jack Zaworski. He gave me a cryptic warning and acted so weird that I followed him to Colombia to figure out what was going on." Carter went on to describe the entire meeting with Zaworski in Miami and his trip to Cartagena—including the deaths of Zaworski and Meyers and his mugging.

"Wow, so you think they killed him... those guys in Cartagena?"

"Well, I can't be 100% certain they did it, but they sure wanted me to *think* they did. And they made it painfully clear that they didn't want me nosing around Colombia either."

"Damn!" exclaimed Dunsmore, shaking his head. "I remember Z; and you're right, the way you described him acting in Miami—that sure sounds a bit out of character. Have you gotten in touch with any of the other guys from the DAO? Have they been able to shed some light on what might be going on?"

"Frankly, Fred, I was going to ask John White the same thing. I didn't know until today that he had passed away."

"Yeah, too bad about that cancer... really tore him up. He was a good egg and we miss him around here. Well, let me see, the guy who was the DATT down there, Elmore, is still on active duty—and still a colonel. He *must* have more than 30 years by now. Last I heard, he was over at the Joint Staff, working counter drug."

"I spoke with him for a couple of minutes this morning at the Pentagon. Unfortunately, he couldn't shed any light on what's happened... or add anything to what I already knew. What about that enlisted guy, Newmann... do you know anything about him?"

"Well, normally I wouldn't have any contact with the enlisted folks at the different Defense Attaché Offices—but Newmann was different. Ends up he got out of the Army about the same time I left the Air Force. Within a few weeks, he was back in Bogotá—starting up an import-export business and raking in the cash. The DEA looked into Newmann's business—they felt he was a bit *too* good at making money, especially since he had no prior entrepreneurial experience. Anyway, they investigated him for a while, but the whole thing seemed to fizzle out. Apparently, they never could pin anything on him. Why do you ask?"

"Oh, it's just that I've always thought something strange was going on between Elmore and Newmann. Elmore was a nice enough guy, but it just seemed weird for an Army colonel to have such a close relationship with a sergeant. We all noticed how those two couples—Elmore and his wife and Newmann and his wife—spent way too much time together. There were all kinds of rumors going around at the time that the two of them were into swapping wives or something."

"Well, from what I remember of Elmore's wife, I think I might enjoy some swapping with her myself. She had some pretty *bodacious ta-tas* as I recall," admitted Dunsmore with an appropriately lecherous chuckle.

"You've got *that* right," laughed Carter, enjoying Dunsmore's earthy sense of humor.

"Anyway," continued Dunsmore, "as I recall, right before I moved off the Colombian desk, Newmann dumped wife number one, and got himself a newer model—a well-bred Colombian woman."

"So, based on what you're telling me, Newmann is probably dirty... involved in narcotics? Jack Zaworski mentioned that he had gone into some sort of business arrangement with Newmann in Cartagena. He didn't say what they were doing, but based on what you've said, it looks like maybe he was involved in something shady."

"Maybe Zaworski found out what kind of crap Newmann was up to, and that's what got him killed," said Dunsmore.

"Sergeant Newmann kill Jack Zaworski? It's almost too screwed up to—"

"You might want to consider it a distinct possibility, John," Dunsmore interrupted. "Newmann's a big player down there now. He's doing well enough to cover his tracks and to be dangerous to his adversaries. I'd watch out if I were you."

"Damn," said Dunsmore, looking at his watch. "I better get back to the office. I've been gone for over an hour and a half."

"We obviously had too many war stories to catch up on," agreed Carter. "Thanks very much for the intel—don't worry, I'll be careful. Hopefully, I'll be able to figure out what happened to *Z-Man* before too long."

They walked over to the counter to pay the bill. On the way out the restaurant door, they exchanged phone numbers and shook hands.

"Hey, John, you need to stay in touch. And if there's anything I can do to help—anything at all—please let me know. Day or night, just give me a shout!"

"I will," said Carter, as he turned and walked away.

Walking along the busy sidewalk, Carter racked his brain, trying to think of someone he could trust. Perhaps he could get in touch with his old boss, General Charles Wilcox. The retired Marine four-star was a man who Carter trusted completely. But how would he get in touch with him? Where was he now? Would he even be interested in helping Carter after all these years?

Less than a block from the restaurant, Carter noticed an unmarked van parked on the opposite side of the street. It had blacked-out windows and extra antennas on top. Inside the van, he imagined there might be men wearing headsets, looking at computer screens and coordinating with their compatriots conducting surveillance nearby. He wondered if they were government, or perhaps someone in Colombia might be interested in tracking his movements.

Carter recalled the way Zaworski had behaved in Miami. His head had been on a swivel, and he had repeatedly checked the exits, as if he were being followed. Carter considered the possibility that whomever Z thought was tailing him could now be on *his* tail. After the events of the past few days, anything seemed possible.

He considered walking over to the van, knocking on its windows, and simply asking those inside what they were doing. *What if the occupants were armed? What if no one answered his knocking? Geez, am I becoming paranoid?* Carter thought.

The events of the past few days were resurrecting thoughts of his past... of Colombia and his attaché training. Carter was starting to see danger lurking around every corner. In the end, he decided that maintaining some kind of balance between caution and paranoia might help him stay alive for a while longer.

2:43 PM EST
Newmann's Hacienda—Cali, Colombia

In the suburbs to the north of Cali, there are many large ranches, farms and haciendas—homes for the upper class families of Colombia's second largest city. One of the most impressive properties belonged to Marty Newmann. His large estate was not accessible from the main highway that ran north of the city. It could only be reached by a dirt road that exited from the main highway. There were no signs marking the road, and although it wasn't paved, the road was well maintained.

Exiting the main thoroughfare and continuing toward the hacienda, there were numerous non-distinct hovels thrown together with wood and discarded sheets of aluminum and tin. Wooden stakes protruding from the ground held rusty strands of barbed wire—better suited for delineating property lines than discouraging trespassers. A multitude of colors festooned the clotheslines outside these houses; and music blasted from several small radios. Even a careful observer would consider these small dwellings as typical of Colombia's lower class neighborhoods. However, upon closer examination, one would discover that the ostensive poor in this *barrio* had cell phones, radio equipment and automatic weapons. They were, in fact, Marty Newmann's first line of defense.

The second line of defense was the ten-foot high wall surrounding the entire estate. About a half mile down the dirt road from the highway, there was a substantial gate—which at first glance appeared deserted. Hidden behind the large steel gate, however, was a guard post, manned with well-armed guards. In addition to automatic weapons and RPGs, they had a dedicated phone line connected to the hacienda, two-way radios and backup cell phones.

Inside the hacienda, Marty Newmann was talking to Carlos Hernández.

"So you're sure Carter is back in the US?" asked Carlos.

"Yes. He arrived in Washington earlier today. In fact, he's been in touch with Elmore," replied Newmann confidently. "And, after speaking with Carter,

Elmore told me he was convinced that Carter has no idea what's going on down here. He doesn't know about the plan... it's that simple."

"Don't you think we should have killed him, instead of just beating him up, while he was in Cartagena?" asked Carlos, concerned about the potential security breach.

"As long as he stays in the US, we're fine," replied Newmann confidently. "I don't want to leave a trail of dead bodies. The stink would draw flies— Colombian police, DEA and the Agency. We don't need that right now. We have people in DC following him. They'll be able to keep an eye on him."

"I'll trust your instincts, Marty; however, I am still very concerned. Are you sure we can afford to let him continue nosing around?" Carlos asked, pacing back and forth in Newmann's living room.

"Like I said, we'll keep an eye on him until the deal goes down. After that, we'll see what he does and decide if he continues breathing. For the time being, I don't want him killed."

"As long as you're sure," replied Carlos, unconvinced.

"Enough about Carter!" Newmann snapped. "Get me New York on the Satphone," Newmann ordered one of the guards at the back of the room. "I want to make sure everything's ready on that end."

2:50 PM EST
El Dorado International Airport—Bogotá, Colombia

It had been almost ten hours since Carter had gotten into the cab outside the Cartagena Hilton and headed to the airport for his flight back to the US. Watching him leave had been one of the most difficult moments in Gloria's life—as if a part of her body was being ripped from her. She felt an almost irresistible urge to be by his side as he continued his fight against an unknown and dangerous enemy.

That morning she had almost begged to go with him. The thought of him being in danger—or even worse, losing him—was almost too much for her to bear. However, he had insisted on leaving by himself, and in the end, she had reluctantly respected his wishes.

After Carter's cab had disappeared out of the hotel parking lot, Gloria had gone back up to their hotel room. Exhausted, she had hoped to get a couple of hours sleep before taking her own flight back home to Bogotá.

Despite having been awake for the past 36 hours, she had been unable to sleep. She could not stop thinking of him. After an hour of tossing and turning in the bed, she had decided that there was no reason for her to stay in Cartagena any longer. She decided to catch the next flight home.

For every minute of the past ten hours, she had thought about him. Not only did she have an overwhelming urge to be with him and to try to help him, she also desperately wanted him to figure out a way to open up his heart to her. She understood that he had strong feelings for her—perhaps he even loved her—but she still wondered exactly what his feelings were. She didn't want to appear too needy; but she could no longer deny that she *did* need him.

On the short flight from Cartagena to Bogotá, it became clear that she had to share her feelings with someone else. She needed to bounce her many conflicting thoughts off someone she trusted completely. The choice was obvious, for when it came to advice, no one knew her better than her mother did. Her mother always seemed to have the big picture, and even when she didn't have answers, she always listened and helped Gloria navigate her way through life's occasional obstacle course.

Gloria missed the regular long talks she used to have with her mother. Growing up as an only child, the two had become very close. Since her mid-teens, they often seemed more like sisters than mother and daughter and were comfortable discussing even the most intimate details of their lives. For the last several years working with *Avianca*, Gloria was often away from Colombia on trips, and their conversations had become less frequent. They remained very close emotionally; they just had less time to share their lives.

At this moment, she felt an urgent need to hear her mother's voice. As soon as the plane touched down in Bogotá and began taxiing toward the gate, she turned on her cell phone and called her.

"*Hola Mamá*, it's Gloria," she said fighting back tears.

"Oh, Gloria, *mi vida, como estas*? Are you crying?" her mother asked, immediately noticing her daughter's emotional distress.

"There's a man, the American we talked about long ago. I love him very much. He's in danger, and I don't know what to do," the words tumbled urgently out of her mouth.

"I told you then, and I'll say it again: you must stay away from a married man. You deserve—"

"No *Mamá*, his wife died more than a year ago, he's not married now. We've been seeing each other again," she continued, oblivious to the curious stares of the eavesdropping passengers sitting around her in the taxiing plane.

As her mother listened silently, Gloria told her everything, her pent-up emotions pouring out like a dam overflowing. She explained again how she had fallen in love with him almost from that first night together at the American Ambassador's residence. She described the way he had treated her so kindly during those weeks while he was working at the US Embassy. After all that time together and all those romantic dinners, she knew she loved him enough that she might have accepted the relationship without preconditions... even if he stayed married to another woman. But that had not happened. He had left Colombia and returned to his family.

Things were different now. He was a widower and he was once again in her life. She told her mother that she felt sure that God himself had guided the two of them back together. In her soul, she knew they were destined to be together.

When she finished, there was no response.

"*Mamá,* are you there?" Gloria said into the silent cell phone.

Finally, her mother answered, almost whispering, "You must come here right this second. There are things that I must tell you right now... to your face, not on the phone."

"All right, *Mamá.* I will be there in about half an hour."

3:02 PM CDT
Onboard *Billesborg III*—Caribbean Sea, 90 miles east of Cozumel, Mexico

First Mate Philip Handfield surveyed the water ahead of the *Billesborg III,* as she steamed northbound towards the northwestern-most extent of the Caribbean. They were about to enter the Yucatan Channel, which separated Mexico's Yucatan Peninsula from the island of Cuba. The sea was thankfully gentle and the *Billesborg* was making good headway toward their destination of Mobile.

Handfield was thankful for the gentle seas because he had spent a good part of the last two days hugging his toilet and praying for a more expeditious recovery. Although the details of the evening remained rather cloudy, he certainly didn't recall drinking enough on Tuesday night and well into Wednesday morning to justify the seriousness of this hangover. Now that his survival seemed assured, he hoped that the rest of the crew would remain oblivious to his extended absence from the ship.

Handfield was supposed to have been on duty while the welding team repaired the bulkhead below decks starting on Tuesday afternoon. However, several hours after the work had started, he had been approached by the supervisor of the work group—a burly, mustachioed Panamanian, named Arturo. The two immediately began comparing sexual exploits. Arturo had regaled him with stories of wild nights he'd spent at a whorehouse near the old district of Colón. He bragged that the girls were the most beautiful in the country and promised that the owner—a distant cousin—would grant them huge discounts. He further offered to call a cab to pick them up at the port and take them there. Although suspecting that Arturo was exaggerating wildly, Handfield agreed to escape the ship for a couple of hours to have a few drinks and check the place out. Surprisingly, Arturo had understated the quality of the talent. The night had been unbelievable.

After slipping away from the *Billesborg* just before two in the morning, he and Arturo had gone to a cab waiting just outside the port facility. Inside, Handfield was amazed to discover three of the most beautiful women he had ever seen. They were not "local talent," but high-class European hookers.

After arriving at the establishment, Arturo had escorted Handfield and the three women into a small, private room. Once the first round of drinks had been served, he had left to see his cousin. The drinks had flowed freely the entire evening. And the women... my God, had they been talented. Not only had Handfield missed the remainder of his shift that night, he had almost missed the *Billesborg's* departure on Wednesday. They had dropped him off at the port, and he had just managed to stumble back into his cabin a few hours before the tugs started nudging the giant ship away from the pier.

Although it was not uncommon for the ship's officers to disappear during port visits, it was a bit irregular that a senior member of the crew would spend so long away from the ship without permission. Nevertheless, no one seemed to notice his absence, and Handfield was confident that his incredible night out on the town would not lead to any worrisome consequences.

Philip Handfield was completely unaware that his incredible night of debauchery had been bankrolled by a certain American businessman in Colombia. Marty Newmann considered the cost of the evening a small price to pay to get the job done. In a little over 30 hours, First Mate Philip Handfield would learn just how expensive that night would prove to be.

3:25 PM EST
Alma Saenz' apartment—*Barrio Modelia;* Bogotá, Colombia

Gloria paid the cab driver and walked into the familiar nine-story apartment building where her mother had lived for as long as she could remember. As soon as she walked into the apartment, her mother ran to her and the two embraced in silence, tears flowing freely down both sets of cheeks.

"Let me make us some coffee," said Alma Saenz, turning towards the kitchen. "We have a lot to talk about."

Gloria sat quietly at the small kitchen table while her mother scurried about the kitchen preparing the coffee.

"You know, until you called me this afternoon, I thought we might never have this conversation. Now, I see that we *must* have this conversation. You must know the truth... and I should have told you long ago."

"But *Mamá*, we have shared everything, ever since I was a little girl. We have had no secrets from each other. You are like a best friend to me, you could have told me anything and it wouldn't matter. I will always love you."

"I know, *mi vida*, and I will always love you too. I never told you the truth about your father because I was ashamed. I was ashamed of myself, not of him. I was ashamed, and still am, because your father was a married man. He was married to another woman... and he could not... no, *would* not leave her to marry me. All the years we were together, I let *him* set the rules. *He* was in charge—not me. I was afraid. I had no money. He gave me this," she said gesturing around the kitchen. "He paid for all this. He paid for your education, and he still pays."

"You mean Papa is not dead?" Gloria implored.

"He is no longer alive, but his money still comes each month. The money comes, but he has been out of our lives for a long, long time. He might have been a part of our lives if I had been more insistent. Perhaps if I had done more. I should never have fallen in love with him... a married man. But, God forgive me, if I had not fallen in love with him, you would not have come into this world. That, my love, is a part of my life I cannot wish to have changed. You must know that you are the center of my world," she turned away from Gloria, struggling mightily to hold back the tears.

Gloria got up from the table and walked up to her mother, embracing her.

"Why, *Mamá*... Why did he leave?" Gloria asked, wiping a tear from her mother's face.

"He had his reasons. We were from different worlds, and he could not leave his world to be a part of mine. Once I became pregnant with you, he seemed less willing to see me. Maybe we both decided that the money he kept sending was enough. He paid. He left. That's it."

"Did you love him, *Mamá*?"

"Of course I did."

"And did he love you?"

"In his way, I'm sure he did."

"Then why did he leave?"

"Maybe he was not able to love me enough. Maybe our love was cursed by God. Maybe he was too weak... or I was too weak. I don't know. I let him leave us and go back to his life. He gave me you... and that's enough for me," she said turning back to the boiling water in the coffee machine.

Gloria returned to the table and sat down. She watched as her mother unhurriedly poured the coffee into her cup.

"Tell me about my father, *Mamá*."

126

"We have many years in the future to talk about him, Gloria. That will come. Have you forgotten why you called me? As I recall, you have a man in your life now... a man that you love with all your heart. I think it's more important that we concentrate on that man, and save your father for later."

"If you truly love this man," she continued determinedly, her voice now steady and no longer wavering. "You must do whatever it takes to keep him. You must fight to be by his side. Never let him go. If you fail, and he leaves you, at least you will know you've done everything you can to be with him... to deserve his love. I failed to do this with your father, and both of us have paid the price. I loved you and raised you as best I could; but you never knew your father. I let him leave me, and I let *him* set the rules of our relationship. Don't make the same mistake I made, my love. Go and be with him!"

"I will. I will. Thank you, *Mamá*. I guess I already knew what I needed to do. I just needed to hear you say it. I love you very much."

"I love you too my darling," said her mother, kissing her forehead. "But you need to hurry up and finish your coffee; I believe you have another plane to catch."

9:30 PM EDT
Playa Mirador Condominiums—Miami Beach, Florida

Leaving the Miami International Airport, Carter had been able to bum a ride in the *Port Frontenac Hotel's* courtesy van filled with a Swiss airline crew headed towards the beach and a long layover. The van lumbered across the palm-lined MacArthur Causeway towards Miami Beach, while the street lamps streaked across its windows in a rhythmic pattern. Inside, the radio blasted out a lively Puerto Rican salsa. Carter ignored both the music and the animated conversation in the bus.

Carter's head throbbed and his eyes stung—his body suffering from both a lack of sleep and from the pummeling he had received in Cartagena. He had learned very little during his short visit to DC, and he still had more questions than answers. One thing was certain—he'd need to get a little sleep before he'd have any chance thinking clearly. As they arrived at the hotel, Carter tipped the van driver, said goodbye to the Swiss aircrew and walked off towards his condo.

He traversed the six blocks in less than ten minutes. After checking his mailbox, he proceeded to the elevator in the building's main lobby. Fortunately, the elevator arrived quickly and unoccupied. He was certainly not in the mood for chitchatting with another tenant... not tonight. He had too much on his mind.

When the elevator doors opened on his floor, he exited and turned the corner heading towards his condo at the end of the corridor. In the darkness, just outside his door, he saw her waiting for him. Gloria! Leaving his bag in the hallway, he raced to her, gathering her up into his arms.

"Let me get you inside. You poor thing! How long have you been waiting out in my hallway?" Carter asked, his eyes reflecting his obvious concern.

"Not long. I was going to meet you at the airport, but thought that you might prefer to meet me here."

"Well, I sure am glad to see you! Come in," he said as he carried her roll-on bag into the entrance hall of his condo. He pointed to the chairs in the kitchen, and guided her over to one of them. "Make yourself at home. Let me get my bag. I'll be right back."

As he walked out to get his luggage, Carter realized that he was no longer tired. The sight of her and their quick embrace in the hallway had made him forget how long he'd gone without sleep.

8:40 PM EST
Tocumen International Airport— Panamá

Despite the Tocumen International Airport terminal building's well-functioning air conditioning system, Fernando García Luna was sweating profusely as he stood in line waiting to board his flight. García fought back the waves of nausea that swept over him every few minutes. He was losing control and knew that he had to leave Panama. The day before, unable to take the stressful uncertainty, he had decided that the only way to ensure his family's survival was to escape. Australia seemed like the most distant location in which he might settle—far enough to be out of the Colombian's reach.

At least a thousand times over the past several days, García had tried to wake up from his nightmare. He was quite happy with his country, his job, and his family. He only wanted to be left alone. However, it was inescapable—the Colombian had taken away his comfortable life. He would never again be safe, and had to come up with a way to protect himself and his family.

As the long line inched forward along the jet bridge and the waiting airliner, he thought of his wife and children. He had told his wife what had happened and insisted that she and the children leave their home, family and friends. The children had been terrified, unable to fathom what was happening to them. His wife had reluctantly agreed to drive to her sister's house outside the city of Panama. She and the children would stay there until García could arrange a new home for them in Australia. He had given her $2000 from the stack of cash he had received from the Colombian.

"You must stay with your sister and not contact anyone!" he had told her before they had started the long trip from Colón to the Tocumen Airport on the opposite side of the isthmus.

"But Fernando, why must we leave Panama? Why must we go so far away, to a place where they do not even speak Spanish? At least let us go to a country in Latin America," she had pleaded with him tearfully.

"We must move far away from the Colombian. We cannot live where he will find us… where he will be able to kill us. I fear that I have ruined our lives. We will start a new life. We will be together, my wife, we will be all right." García had tried to be convincing, strong, and comforting. He was not successful, however, and had been unable to console her. She had cried during the entire trip to the airport.

After his family had left, he had proceeded through the airport check in, paid his departure tax, and gone through the outbound Customs line. Fortunately, none of the agents at the airport had known who he was, and had let him pass without inspecting his carry-on bag.

As García handed his boarding pass to the airline agent at the gate, he kept the bag clutched tightly to his chest. If his prayers were answered, the cash in that bag would allow him to start a new life in another country—far away from the Colombian.

9:45 PM EDT
Playa Mirador Condominiums—Miami Beach, Florida

"The more I find out, the worse things look," said Carter, pacing back and forth in his living room. "Someone has killed Z—the same people killed Bruce Meyer. Whoever did the killing was probably taking orders from a former sergeant in the Bogotá DAO, Marty Newmann. I found out that after he left the Army, Newmann turned into some kind of business tycoon in Colombia—almost certainly involved in drug trafficking. Until I heard his name mentioned while I was up in DC, I'd forgotten that Z talked about him when he came up to Miami. Z told me he was working with Newmann in Cartagena and that Newmann became interested in *me* after my visit to Grenada. But I was only there on a short layover. I didn't do anything, and didn't see anybody. I had a beer and went to bed early, that's it. I have no idea why my layover in Grenada would be of interest to anyone… not a clue. For some reason though, that's why Z came to Miami—to warn me."

"But why are they killing people like Z and Meyer? And why would they threaten us?" asked Gloria.

"I still can't figure that out, Gloria," confided Carter, shaking his head. "Maybe they did something to piss somebody off. Maybe Newmann thinks I was working with Z-Man and/or Meyer or something. I mean, except for our meeting here in Miami, I hadn't seen or talked to any of them since I left Bogotá. And Z and I have only e-mailed each other every now and then. I think we've spoken on the phone maybe twice since I left Colombia."

"Did you find out anything else in Washington?" implored Gloria. "It scares me that the guys who mugged us talked openly about killing Z. They didn't seem to care that we knew they killed him... as if they're not afraid of being caught."

"Yes, these are dangerous people who kill with impunity in Colombia—and maybe here too. And no, I didn't learn anything else up in DC... nothing more than I've already told you."

"Did Z mention *anyone* else, other than Newmann when he was in Miami?" she asked.

"Well, he didn't give me much else to go on... except... I remember Z said that everything started when I asked about Fitzroy George while I was in Grenada on my last trip. For some reason, that was somehow important—or perhaps even threatening—to Marty Newmann. But that doesn't make any sense either. Fitzroy George was the Commander of the Grenadian Coast Guard when I was an attaché, and I guess he still is today. Why in the world would my asking about George bother Newmann?" asked Carter, continuing his pacing as Gloria watched him silently from the couch.

"Damn! It seems like weeks ago that I was in Grenada. But it was only, what... three days ago?" Carter shook his head, mentally juggling all the details. "Maybe George is somehow involved with Newmann in Colombia. If that's true, it means we're talking about drugs. I still don't believe Z was involved in that kind of thing. Plus, if Z *were* involved, why would he come up to Miami to warn me? I think Bruce Meyer was even less likely to have gone dirty. He was a real straight shooter. I have to admit that Z always had his wild side, but not Meyer. They're both dead now... why? Why?" Carter said as he stopped pacing and sat down next to Gloria, rubbing his face with his hands.

"We've been talking about your co-workers from the attaché office, John," said Gloria, grabbing hold of Carter's arms and pulling them away from his face—forcing him to look into her eyes. "As much as you find it difficult to believe, it appears certain that some of them were, or maybe still are, involved with something illegal. And now, that means *you're* involved. These are dangerous people, John—you can't keep fighting this alone. We need help."

"Yes, of course... you're right," he said, pulling away from Gloria's grasp and standing up again—unable to concentrate with those beautiful eyes of hers staring into his own. "I can't accept where this is taking me."

"There must be *someone* you trust, John," said Gloria, looking up at him from the couch. "...someone—like you—who would not be tempted by drug money."

"Well, I've thought about General Wilcox. I think he's retired now. I'm certain that he's a good man. Even though I haven't seen him in years, I feel certain that I could trust him with my life. It's a feeling I've always had about him—that he was genuine and completely incorruptible. Maybe he could help. All I have to do is figure out how to get in touch with him."

"I'll bet Rachel would have that kind of information. After all, she's working in DC and is in touch with the military all the time."

"You're right. I'll bet if her company doesn't have it, she'll know someone who does. I owe her a call anyway," Carter said while picking up the phone to call his daughter.

"Hi Dad. What are you doing up so late, isn't it way past your bedtime?" she asked cheerfully, recognizing her father's caller ID.

"I'm here in Miami with Gloria," he said, ignoring his daughter's good-natured ribbing.

"Oh good... tell her I said 'Hi.' So, how was Cartagena?"

"Well, it wasn't exactly what either of us expected... but I'll tell you about that later. Listen, I'm a bit pressed for time, and I need to get in touch with an old boss from my days at SOUTHCOM. His name is General Charles Wilcox... almost certainly retired by now. Do you think you could find out how to get in contact with him?"

"I don't see why not. The company has a whole database of military personnel, and we're in touch with retired Generals all the time. Let me check it out, and I'll call you right back."

Less than five minutes later, she had called with the information. General Charles Wilcox had retired, and as luck would have it, was currently living right there in Florida. In fact, he was living in Coral Gables—a short drive from Carter's condo.

"It's almost 10 PM, Gloria. I think it's too late to call," said Carter, glancing at his wristwatch.

"No it's *not* too late, John. If he can help us—and if we're right about what's been going on—we need to call him right this second," she insisted.

"OK, I guess you're right. I'll call right now."

He picked up the phone and dialed General Wilcox's number. He desperately needed an ally... someone in whom he could place his complete trust. As a retired four-star General, Wilcox would almost certainly have a network of connections with the Pentagon and Washington political circles. As the phone started ringing, Carter prayed that the General would be at home and would be willing to help him make sense of the events of the past few days.

9:02 PM CDT
Onboard *Antioquia*—300 miles south of Mobile

The Operations Order (OPORD) had arrived from the Joint Interagency Task Force - South in Key West earlier that afternoon. The OPORD stated that the DEA had received a tip-off about a possible shipment of drugs on a container ship. The *Antioquia* and the Task Force were ordered to intercept and board the *Billesborg III*, a Panamanian-registered container ship that had departed from Cristóbal, Panama just before midnight on Wednesday. The Task Force was now steaming towards an intercept point, a little over 200 miles ahead, and would conduct the boarding at a point south of Mobile, Alabama.

Fitzroy George had just finished a meeting with the various sub-commanders of the Task Force. He had insisted that as they were in international waters, the Grenadians should continue to be in charge of the actual ship boarding. Just as they had done in their practice boardings, the American Coast Guard Law Enforcement Detachment (LEDET) would *monitor* the activity of the boarding party, but would not be in charge. In the end, even the Americans had agreed that it was appropriate for George's men to maintain operational control.

Moving on to the next topic, the American Navy commander had explained that while the Task Force continued steaming towards the intercept point, the US Coast Guard and Customs would fly non-stop aerial surveillance of the *Billesborg*. He had also pointed out that at this very moment, a specially designed US Customs Cessna Citation aircraft was shadowing the lumbering container ship—carefully monitoring its every move with its radar, infrared and low-light TV sensors.

At the conclusion of the meeting, George was confident. Nothing new or unexpected had come out of the briefing by the American commander. Everything was unfolding exactly as planned, and George and his men would be ready.

10:30 PM EDT
House of General Wilcox, USMC, Retired—Coral Gables, Florida.

General Charles Wilcox, USMC (retired) had been quite surprised to hear from his former executive officer—especially at such a late hour. The General had been persuaded by Carter's urgent outline of his situation. He had agreed to meet with Carter and Gloria as soon as they could get to his home in Coral Gables.

As Carter and Gloria walked up to front stoop and were about to reach for the doorbell, General Wilcox emerged to greet them enthusiastically. He was casually dressed in a yellow button-down shirt and brown Dockers pants. Wilcox was still in excellent physical condition—his six foot four inch frame was trim and well-muscled—exuding good health and vitality.

Wilcox—like all proud *Devil Dogs*—strongly believed that there was no such thing as a "former Marine." Amongst the men and women for whom *Semper Fi* is much more than a slogan, there were retired Marines, dead Marines, and even incarcerated Marines; they were, however, unwilling to accept that there might be any "former Marines." Wilcox accepted that part of his duty in retirement, was to remain connected with his country's military. Wilcox stayed actively involved with a network of fellow General Officers. They discussed the structure and readiness of the nation's military on golf courses, during phone calls and while attending cocktail parties. Many also maintained their contacts on Capitol Hill. Wilcox had never been fond of that last type of duty. Rather than concentrate on the battles taking place on *the Hill*, Wilcox involved himself with the battles his Marines were fighting today. Those battles were fought on real hills, beaches, and increasingly the inhospitable streets of faraway cities and towns.

If what Carter had just told him was true, there were rotten elements in *his* military that must be flushed out and taken down. Wilcox considered himself duty-bound to listen to what his former subordinate had to say. His wife had immediately understood and accepted the interruption of their movie watching— just as she had countless times in the past when her husband had been called away from her side. His mistress was the United States of America, and no one came before her.

After introductions and a quick synopsis of Carter's life since his retirement, they moved to the General's study. There, Carter outlined the unbelievable and confusing swirl of events of the last few days. After listening to his monologue, the General asked Carter and Gloria to leave his office and wait for a few minutes in the den with Mrs. Wilcox. General Wilcox then closed the door, sat at the desk, and got out a pen and paper. He had many phone calls to make in the next several minutes.

Nearly forty-five minutes later, the General emerged from the office and beckoned Carter and Gloria back in. Over the next couple of minutes, the two came to appreciate the extent to which General Charles Wilcox remained an active member of the General Officer network.

Wilcox had energized contacts in the National Security Council at the White House. He had also called the Vice Chairman of the Joint Chiefs of Staff (who was himself a former commander of the Southern Command), the current Commander of the Southern Command, and the Director of the National Security Agency. During those calls, he had pieced together a compelling—and extremely troubling—picture.

Evidence from various sources indicated that several former members of the US Defense Attaché Office in Bogotá were aiding and abetting organized criminal activity, and that two of them had been murdered. Wilcox learned that a series of NSA wiretaps suggested that there was a connection between those military members and an imminent drug-smuggling operation. This illegal enterprise was apparently being orchestrated by another former DAO member, Marty Newmann. Next, Wilcox's contacts had informed him of an ongoing FBI investigation that linked Newmann with organized crime syndicates in New York.

Wilcox's final phone call—with the current SOUTHCOM Commander, General Stuart—had proved most interesting. According to Stuart, US officials had recently been tipped off about a major drug-smuggling operation, which might be thwarted in a matter of hours. Stuart had briefly outlined the events leading up to tomorrow's planned boarding of the *Billesborg*. According to Stuart, a Customs P-3 aircraft had just started a surveillance orbit over the suspect Danish container ship and that the Task Force was at this moment steaming toward the intercept point.

Perhaps it was only a coincidence that all these disparate pieces of information were coming together only hours before tomorrow's ship boarding. However, the information Carter had shared with General Wilcox added a new layer of detail to what was already known in Washington.

Based on Carter's inputs—along with General Wilcox's vigorous vouching for him and Gloria—Stuart had invited the three of them to meet in his Southern Command office the following morning. The meeting was set for 0715—less than an hour before the *Billesborg* boarding was scheduled to begin.

"If you two will hand me some kind of photo ID, I'll fax them up to Washington. I've arranged to have the Pentagon secure temporary SECRET security clearances for both of you. That'll probably take some doing in Miss Saenz' case; but I'm sure my friends in the White House will have the necessary horsepower to expedite the process. I propose that the two of you bunk here with the Mrs. and me tonight. General Stuart's driver will be picking us up in less than seven hours," said Wilcox authoritatively.

Thoroughly impressed, Carter and Gloria watched Wilcox walk ramrod-straight out of the office towards his wife of nearly 40 years, who had been waiting patiently in the den. He informed her that they'd be having last-minute guests for the night and they needed two separate bedrooms. Although his words indicated that it had been a request, the invitation for Carter and Gloria to stay the night was clearly an order. There was no question where they'd be sleeping that night—and that they would be doing so in separate bedrooms.

General Charles Wilcox was in his element: collecting intelligence, making plans, giving orders, directing subordinates, preparing for battle. The steady resolve of this highly decorated, combat veteran came through loud and clear. For the first time in the past several days, Carter felt that he had finally found a highly skilled and powerful ally.

Saturday

Far better it is to dare mighty things, even though checkered by failure, than to take rank with those who neither enjoy much or suffer much, because they live in the gray twilight that knows not victory nor defeat.

--Theodore Roosevelt

6:44 AM EDT
House of General Wilcox, USMC, Retired—Coral Gables, Florida.

Even at this early hour, the sun—shining brightly in the nearly cloudless sky—was already warming up the hazy morning air. Throughout the neighborhood, a multitude of automatic lawn sprinklers hissed and sputtered to life, adding to the lushness of the vegetation around each carefully manicured lawn.

Having arrived several minutes earlier, a dark blue SOUTHCOM staff car sat idling quietly on the General's driveway. The driver stayed inside the air-conditioned interior, waiting to exit and ring the General's doorbell at precisely 0645, as he had been instructed.

Once he had done so, his passengers proceeded orderly out of the house. Reaching the driveway, the General ushered Gloria into the back seat of the staff car and indicated that Carter was to sit up front with the driver. Carter smiled to himself as he got into the front seat. *He's still the same gentleman I remember when I worked for him.*

They quickly left the General's house and sped off towards the Southern Command headquarters, located just west of the Miami International Airport. Despite the early hour, the traffic was already building to the normal crazy crescendo that occurred each morning on Miami's busy thoroughfares. At least it was a Saturday, and they would be spared from having to crawl along at the normally glacial pace associated with the weekday rush hour.

From the back seat, General Wilcox began to review what he expected to happen once they arrived at the Southern Command.

"John, based on the fact that we're not sure who's involved in this mess, I think we should keep your information from everyone except General Stuart," said Wilcox.

"Yes, sir," agreed Carter. "I was just thinking about the fact that Michael Kennedy is currently working at the headquarters, and that he too was assigned with me at the DAO. It's certainly possible that he's not on our side. Frankly, I just don't know who to trust."

"I think that's a healthy and appropriate feeling for you to have, John. I think it's prudent that we not share anything with Colonel Kennedy—or anyone else for that matter—until we're sure who's on our side," agreed General Wilcox with a calm, reassuring, yet commanding voice. "I'll probably be invited to see General Stuart first, since they'll want to give us Generals some time together."

"I feel like my stomach is turning summersaults," confided Carter. "I hope I haven't gotten you involved in a wild goose chase."

"Don't worry, John. I believe you've found some geese that need chasing."

Saturday

7:09 AM EDT
Southern Command Headquarters —Miami, Florida

Shortly after arriving at his office that morning, Colonel Michael Kennedy had been called up to the headquarters' command section. At the reception desk outside of the General's corner office, he had run into the Chief of Staff, Brigadier General John Peabody. Peabody told him that the former Commander of the Southern Command, General Charles Wilcox, was on his way for a visit that he had arranged late last night.

"That's a little strange, isn't it?" Kennedy asked the always-busy Chief of Staff.

"I guess," Peabody said brusquely, continuing to look down at his notebook. "We'd like you to go out and escort him to General Stuart's office. Our protocol officer has been held up in traffic, and everyone else is caught up in the ship-boarding... or couldn't make it on time. Here," continued Peabody, handing Kennedy a small radio, "take this with you, and give me a call once the staff car shows up at the gate. They should be arriving any minute now."

"Yes, sir," said Kennedy walking off briskly towards the exit. He headed downstairs and turned toward the building's front entrance. As Kennedy stepped outside, his eyes squinted against the blazing sun in the nearly cloudless sky. The hot, humid air made him start sweating almost instantly—ruining the sharp creases of his freshly pressed, short-sleeved military shirt.

I'm just a damned errand boy for these assholes—playing escort for some retired General who decides that he needs to come here today... just before the Billesborg is boarded. What incredibly screwed up timing!

Kennedy reached the front gate just as the staff car turned the corner heading to the guard shack at the main entrance. Kennedy made a quick transmission on his radio to alert Peabody that the General had arrived. He then quickly glanced down to check the "gig line" formed by lining up his shirt and his belt buckle with the flap that covered his pants' zipper. Although possessing a flawless gig line, the quick self-examination also revealed the growing circles of perspiration forming under his armpits.

Standing just behind the guard at the gate, Kennedy stood at attention and saluted the staff car as it glided to a stop in front of them. As the windows opened, Kennedy was stunned to see John Carter seated in the front passenger seat.

What the fuck is he going here? Kennedy attempted to comprehend what he was seeing—racking his mind to imagine a plausible reason why John Carter might be in *this* staff car, with *this* retired four-star General, on *this* morning!

"Good morning, General Wilcox. Welcome to SOUTHCOM," he said, laboring mightily to hide his astonishment.

"Good morning, Colonel," replied General Wilcox, returning Kennedy's salute.

Kennedy glanced at Carter in the front seat. "Hi, John. I must admit that I'm surprised to see *you* here this morning!" he said, desperately trying to convey a sense of calm and assurance that he did not feel.

"I'm kinda surprised myself, Colonel Kennedy. Suffice it to say that it's been a long couple of days for me," Carter said, offering little information to clear up Kennedy's confusion.

"Colonel, why don't you join us?" General Wilcox offered—gesturing toward the open place in the back seat, as Gloria moved over next to him. "There's no reason for you to have to *walk* all the way back in this heat. We've got plenty of room."

"Thank you, sir," Kennedy said as he got into the car, for the first time noticing the gorgeous woman in the back with Wilcox.

As the staff car covered the distance from the front gate to the entrance of the building, Kennedy's heart continued to pound in his chest. He kept repeating to himself, *Stay calm! Stay flexible. If they're being this nice to me, they don't know what's going on. As soon as I can, I must get a hold of Elmore.*

Just as they were getting out of the car, General Stuart walked out the building's front entrance. He rendered a salute to his retired fellow four-star General.

"Welcome back to your old stomping grounds, General Wilcox," said Stuart has he extended his hand towards General Wilcox.

"Well, I certainly appreciate your agreeing to see me on such short notice, Bill," Wilcox replied, after returning Stuart's salute and shaking his hand.

"Not a problem—*mi headquarters es su headquarters,*" joked Stuart in *Spanglish.*

As the group proceeded inside, and climbed the stairs leading to the Commanding General's office suite, Wilcox introduced Carter and Gloria to General Stuart. Kennedy bounded up the stairs and squeezed in next to Carter.

"So John, what in the world brings you here so early on a Saturday morning? Chasing bad guys?" Kennedy asked breathlessly.

"I'm just trying to figure out why someone would want me out of Colombia. I thought General Wilcox might be able to help me figure it out. Plus, I haven't been back to these hallowed halls since I retired," Carter continued with a smile. "I wanted to see what you guys have done to the place!" They both were laughing as they reached the top of the stairs, and headed across the hall to the Command Section's reception area.

As they moved through the hallway leading to the General's office, General Stuart stepped to one side, motioned for Carter, Gloria and Wilcox to enter, and then stepped in front of Colonel Kennedy—making it obvious that he was not to be included.

"Thanks for the help, Mike. I guess you better head back to the JOIC and see how things are going with the *Billesborg*. I should make it down there in a few minutes," said General Stuart as he turned into his office and closed the door.

Kennedy knew he must get in touch with Elmore immediately. He considered heading directly to his office; but decided that there would be too many people there monitoring the boarding of the *Billesborg*. Instead, he would go downstairs and use one of the pay phones just outside the command's small *Shoppette*. He could pass a quick message to Elmore using their code words. It wouldn't be necessary to risk suspicion by throwing everyone out of his office and using the classified STU 3 phone.

Still breathless from running down the stairs, Kennedy inserted the necessary coins and dialed Elmore's number at the Pentagon.

6:15 AM CDT
Onboard *Billesborg III*—Gulf of Mexico, 380 miles south of Mobile

The *Billesborg's* Master, *Torben Olsgaard*, was not pleased.

"What do you mean hold my position?" he had asked the shipping company's main office over the vessel's satellite communications system. "I've got a schedule to meet."

Minutes earlier, the *Dana-Dafra* headquarters had contacted the *Billesborg III* and told them to hold their position and await further instructions. Starting at their current 20-knot speed, it would take five miles for this 100,000-ton ship to come to a stop. Even worse, the delay would take *hours*. It was all so pointless.

However, the written orders that *Olsgaard* held in his hand were clear, unassailable, and beyond his power to change.

```
TO: BILLESBORG III
FROM:  DANA-DAFRA SHIPPING COMPANY, LLC
SUBJECT:  AUTHORIZATION FOR BOARDING AT SEA

    CORPORATE HEADQUARTERS HAS BEEN IN TOUCH WITH
THE FLAGGING COUNTRY, AND HAS RECEIVED
AUTHORIZATION FROM THE GOVERNMENT OF PANAMA TO
ALLOW THE BOARDING OF THE BILLESBORG III BY AN
INTERNATIONAL NAVAL TASK FORCE OPERATING NEAR YOUR
CURRENT POSITION.  THE GOVERNMENT OF PANAMA
```

CONSIDERS THIS BOARDING TO BE AUTHORIZED UNDER
THEIR EXISTING MARITIME COUNTER-DRUG AGREEMENT
WITH THE UNITED STATES OF AMERICA.

THE US GOVERNMENT HAS INFORMED US THAT THEY
HAVE RECEIVED CREDIBLE INFORMATION LEADING THEM TO
BELIEVE THAT THERE MAY BE A SIGNIFICANT QUANTITY
OF ILLEGAL NARCOTICS HIDDEN ONBOARD.

THE TASK FORCE VESSELS WILL REACH YOUR CURRENT
POSITION IN ABOUT ONE HOUR.

YOU ARE THEREFORE DIRECTED TO CUT YOUR ENGINES,
STAND TO, AND ALLOW YOURSELF TO BE BOARDED.

YOU AND YOUR CREW ARE FURTHER DIRECTED TO
COOPERATE FULLY WITH THE BOARDING PARTY. PLEASE
KEEP CORPORATE HEADQUARTERS APPRISED OF THE
PROGRESS OF THE BOARDING AND SEARCH, AND ADVISE
WHEN YOU ARE AGAIN UNDERWAY TO MOBILE.

DO NOT AGREE TO ANY POTENTIALLY DESTRUCTIVE
SEARCH (PDS) WITHOUT FURTHER AUTHORIZATION FROM
CORPORATE HEADQUARTERS IN COPENHAGEN.

WE ARE IN TOUCH WITH US AND PANAMANIAN
EMBASSIES HERE IN COPENHAGEN, AS WELL AS THE US
SOUTHERN COMMAND IN MIAMI AND THE JOINT INTER-
AGENCY TASK FORCE SOUTH IN KEY WEST.

"Damn," grumbled the Master through gritted teeth, throwing the crumpled message on the floor of the bridge. "I just can't believe this is happening. Helm, all engines full stop!"

"All this wasted time and money for a search that will find nothing. We will now watch the US Navy and the US Coast Guard flex their muscles and show us, yet again, that this is *their* blasted Gulf."

High above the *Billesborg*, the orbiting Citation jet noted the speed reduction and relayed this information to its headquarters. The jet had been on-station for several hours—trailing the ship in a constantly updated orbit. Keeping watch with sophisticated surveillance equipment, the crew was watching for any sign of trouble. They were especially vigilant for any attempt by the *Billesborg's* crew to dump anything overboard. So far, they had seen no suspicious activity. In less than an hour, the Task Force would catch up with this ship and put an end to their interminable orbiting.

Saturday

6:23 AM EST
Newmann's Hacienda—Cali, Colombia

Newmann rubbed his chin as he replaced the phone into its receptacle. Kelly Elmore had just informed him that John Carter was at this very moment in the Southern Command headquarters. This was certainly a very troubling development and Newmann's initial reaction was a feeling of doom. *Is the plan compromised? Should they continue? Maybe Carlos was right... I should have killed the son of a bitch while he was in Cartagena.*

As Newmann went over each detail in his mind, he considered how Carter could have discovered what they were doing. Zaworski knew nothing about the upcoming operation—so Carter could not have learned anything from him. If Carter *had* discovered anything about the operation, surely he would have told someone in the military or in law enforcement. If that were the case, Kennedy or Elmore would have heard by now and passed it along. That had not happened. Therefore, despite the very troubling appearance of John Carter at SOUTHCOM that morning, Newmann remained reasonably confident that the authorities in Colombia and the US didn't know enough to be a threat.

Just to be sure, Newmann decided to call his contacts in New York to see if their network of snitches or police informants had any inkling that the plan had been exposed. If a law enforcement agency had learned anything, his New York associates would probably be aware of it.

As Newmann picked up the phone to make the call, he steeled himself. He needed to sound more confident than he actually felt. As he waited for the call to go through, Newmann tried to force a nagging question out of his mind—had he underestimated John Carter?

7:26 AM EDT
JOIC, SOUTHCOM—Miami, Florida

Five minutes earlier, when Michael Kennedy had arrived at the row of pay phones on the headquarters' first floor, he had been relieved to discover that the area was unpopulated. There would be no one to overhear his call. During his abbreviated phone conversation, he had told Elmore about Carter's arrival at SOUTHCOM. He had also conveyed his belief that Carter was still unaware of their plan.

Although surprised that Kennedy had called on an open phone line, Elmore had replied simply, "Roger, I'll let *November* know. Out here."

Kennedy had then returned to his office, scanned the JOIC's status boards and determined that he had not missed anything—the boarding had not yet begun. Having successfully informed his superior, Kennedy strode confidently out of his office towards the main console of the sprawling JOIC complex. There, he would watch the next act of the play unfold.

"OK, Chief Brown, tell me where we are so far," Kennedy said to the senior enlisted watch officer.

"Well, sir, the DEA received an anonymous phone call this morning, indicating that within the last couple of days, a major shipment of cocaine was loaded in Colón and shipped to Mobile, Alabama. The Coast Guard confirmed that there were only two vessels making the trip between those ports during that timeframe. The first vessel, the *Seaborne Pride*, has not yet left Colón. Panamanian police and port authorities conducted a thorough search, which turned up nothing."

"The other ship was the *Billesborg III*—operated by the *Dana-Dafra* Shipping Company based in Copenhagen. As the ship is Panamanian-flagged, our Embassy got in contact with the government of Panama late last night, briefed them on the situation, and received permission for the intercept and boarding in accordance with our bilateral maritime counter-drug agreement."

"The Joint Interagency Task Force in Washington was briefed on the situation, and authorized the Grenadian Coast Guard to assume tactical control once the boarding process begins. The USS *O'Bannon's* onboard US Coast Guard Law Enforcement Detachment will accompany and monitor the Grenadian Coast Guard Detachment. The boarding team will be augmented by three Colombian Navy enlisted men. Once Tactical Control is transferred to the Grenadians, the US LEDET will be in an advisory role only. However, Superintendent George has agreed to transfer control back to our LEDET, if he considers it necessary."

"The ship's Master has cooperated fully so far, and the *Billesborg* is currently dead in the water at the indicated coordinates."

"All Task Force ships report full operational readiness; and the estimated time of boarding is now 1140 Zulu—0640 Mobile or Central Daylight Time."

"We just received a photo of the ship, sir, from Denmark," said Chief Petty Officer Brown, completing his situation briefing.

Projected on one of the large screens on the front wall of the operation center was a large digital photo of the *Billesborg III*. It was massive in size and would be carrying more than two thousand 40-foot cargo containers—each the size of an 18-wheeler's rig.

Considering what he'd heard, Kennedy guessed that the ship's Master would be pretty pissed right about now—not at all happy with the prospect of a bunch of well-armed military types running around his ship. These container ship Masters were used to getting their way and being in total control of their universe.

Furthermore, Kennedy appreciated why the *Dana-Dafra* Shipping Company would be extremely reluctant to let any of the boarding party run around poking holes or otherwise breaking their ship. The Potentially Destructive Search (PDS)—referred to in the Operation Order—was the procedure used for a more thorough search. This PDS could involve drilling holes or even using blowtorches to gain access to various compartments of the ship to facilitate the search for drugs. Although the boarding party will have been given access to the ship's detailed plans, one had to be 100 percent certain that they weren't drilling a hole into the wrong place... such as a bulkhead forming part of one of the ship's massive fuel tanks. For this reason, the boarding party would need the approval of the ship's Master and the home company before doing anything so potentially dangerous.

Before proceeding with any PDS, they would first accomplish a thorough "space accountability check." By comparing the ship's blueprints—which every cargo ship was required by international maritime law to have in their possession—with measurements taken during the search, they might be able to locate any suspicious alteration that might have been used to hide smuggled items.

The ship boarding would also include a careful inspection of the outside of each container. They would be checking for any evidence that the seals placed on them by Panamanian customs officials had been tampered with or altered. Kennedy knew that any inspection of the containers would be limited to their exteriors—because they were almost never opened while at sea. It was simply too dangerous to open them while the ship was away from port. Today's modern container ships held thousands of these 40-foot containers—each one carefully secured and stacked as tall as a 12-story building. Since there was almost no space between the individual containers, getting in a position to open them on a ship, would be extremely dangerous—especially while the ship was listing and tipping about in ocean swells. Furthermore, even if they *could* be opened, the containers' interiors were likely to have a hazardous, oxygen-deficient atmosphere. These conditions would be too dangerous for anyone carrying out the search.

Kennedy—along with the men and women in the JOIC and other teams sitting in similar operations centers in various locations throughout the US— were very familiar with all these facts. Kennedy, however, was privy to certain facts that were *not* well known.

He was a member of a select group of individuals who were counting on the fact that the *Billesborg's* containers would not be searched this morning. Paradoxically, they *were* counting on the boarding party finding a large shipment of cocaine in another part of the ship.

Delta 7

6:38 AM CDT
Onboard *Billesborg III*

In the dawn twilight, *Torben Olsgaard* watched the approaching Zodiacs through his binoculars. Each one appeared to have about eight men aboard. He could just make out the barrels of their M-16 rifles protruding over the sides of the speeding Rigid Inflatable Boats or "RIBs." He then scanned back to the military ships that had surrounded him. He knew that they would be at battle stations—weapons armed and ready to fire.

As the boarding party quickly traversed the distance to the *Billesborg*, he had made a broadcast throughout the ship, demanding that all crewmembers cooperate fully. He had also explained that the more they cooperated, the sooner they could get back underway. That was his only concern—getting back underway as expeditiously as possible.

He was quite familiar with what was about to happen. After arriving alongside his ship, the team leader would introduce himself and receive permission to come aboard. The boarding party would then split into separate groups to search different sections of the ship. Members of his crew would escort one of the groups to the bridge. Once there, he would show them the ship's cargo and crew manifests. They would muster the crew to crosscheck their identities with the ship's crew complement list. They would then review the ship's engineering drawings for their space accountability check.

Olsgaard was quite confident that they would find nothing. He ran a tight ship and was sure that no illegal cargo had been hidden onboard. Perhaps one of the crew had been stupid enough to sneak aboard his own personal stash of drugs. That would certainly not be unprecedented. A smile came across his face as he imagined that several of those personal stashes were at this very moment being hastily flushed down toilets throughout the ship in preparation for the search.

"Let me know when they're ready to board," he said over the intercom to the men standing by at the ship's retractable *Jacob's Ladder*. The crew had already lowered the rope ladder with wooden slats over the side of the ship to allow access by the boarding party.

Shortly after the Zodiacs disappeared under the port side of the ship, the intercom crackled to life, "The boarding party has requested permission to come aboard, sir."

"Permission granted. Please show them to the bridge."

Looking down near the access point of the ship, the Master noticed that a three-man team was already being escorted around the outside of the containers on the port side. Soon, he saw another team approaching the bridge. *Olsgaard* glanced at his watch. *Hopefully, this will be over in a couple of hours.*

145

Saturday

6:48 AM CDT
Operations Center, Onboard the *Antioquia*

Superintendant George listened as the boarding team submitted its first update—the terse report blaring out of several wall-mounted speakers in the *Antioquia's* Ops Center.

"The teams have been granted permission to board. We have been informed that the Master intends to cooperate fully. All secure so far. Topside crew commencing external inspection of containers. Our team is proceeding to the pilothouse. Will update on arrival, over."

"So far so good," said George to the assembly in the operations center. His voice tinged with a sense of urgency and excitement. This was, after all, a *real world* boarding of a ship at sea and as such, was considered very serious business.

"Captain, JIATF-East and SOUTHCOM report a copy on aerial and seaborne transmissions," said the watch officer of the deck—repeating what he had just heard from the ship's communications center. The two military headquarters had just acknowledged that they were receiving both the live video feed from a US Coast Guard C-130—which had just replaced the Customs Citation orbiting overhead—as well as repeater audio from the short-distance radios being used by the boarding party.

So far, so good. George repeated to himself, wiping the sweat from his palms onto his uniform trousers.

6:59 AM CDT
Onboard *Billesborg III*

The Royal Grenadian Coast Guard's team chief, Assistant Inspector Samuel Toppin, had arrived on the *Billesborg's* bridge and was going over the ship's paperwork. Everything appeared to be in order. Another team was looking over the ship's diagrams in preparation for their space accountability check. Soon, that team would be departing below decks.

Nearly all the ship's crew had mustered in the mess for a check of their identity papers. They had agreed that the ship's engineer would be allowed to stay in the engine room and that the two *Billesborg* crewmembers escorting the Task Force team searching the exterior of the containers would have their IDs checked once they were finished.

Two members of the boarding party began crosschecking identity papers, while two others started their search of the crew's cabins. Once in possession of the detailed ship's diagram, Corporal Ogilvie and his team headed downstairs to begin their accountability check.

Each team checked in with the *Antioquia's* Ops Center every couple of minutes. Onboard the *O'Bannon*, another fully armed boarding party of US Coastguardsmen stood by—prepared to race over to the *Billesborg* at the first sign of trouble.

Since all was proceeding smoothly and everyone was settling down into a familiar pattern, pulse rates were slowly returning to normal. Many started to suspect that the tip off would end up being a hoax—that yet again a search would come up empty.

Below decks, the team conducting the accountability check was suffering in the stifling heat. The still air in the bowels of the *Billesborg* was nearly 125 degrees Fahrenheit. Despite the unpleasant conditions, they stayed busy stretching out tape measures, adding the distances, and comparing the resultant figures with the known dimensions indicated on the engineering blueprints.

As the sweat dripped continuously off his nose, Corporal Patrick Ogilvie thought to himself, *it's too damn hot down here, let's hurry up and get this over with.*

"Hey Rupert, Andrew, come look at this!" he shouted to his teammates.

As his two fellow team members approached, Ogilvie shined his flashlight at a distant wall near the corner of the huge interior cargo compartment. As they got closer, their flashlight beams concentrated on a section that had a slightly different color than the surrounding bulkhead. At first glance, it appeared to be freshly painted. As they came within reach of the wall, they noticed charring and splotches of black soot. Someone had obviously used a blowtorch there quite recently.

"Hey Cap, we got us a fake wall down here!" Ogilvie excitedly reported over his radio. "Looks like it's time for a PDS. Please send over a couple of drills, borescope, and some welding equipment."

7:02 AM CDT
Operations Center Onboard the *Antioquia*

Back on the *Antioquia*, Fitzroy George almost fainted at what he had just heard. *Don't get carried away, Patrick,* he willed across the distance between the two ships. *Stay calm! Everything's just fine!*

In the excitement, Ogilvie had jumped the gun by requesting the welding equipment for a Potentially Destructive Search. It was not his job to order that kind of inspection. Furthermore, this was certainly *not* how they had practiced. A *PDS* would require approval from both the Master and the home company.

"Damn, I'd probably call for the welding equipment too. I sure as hell wish I was over there right now," admitted the very excited Coast Guard Lieutenant in the Operations Center. You could almost hear him add "lucky bastards" to the end of his last sentence. This young American had gone through too many false alarms in his Coast Guard career. Clearly, he was very jealous, and wished that he could have been on the boarding mission. They were about to hit pay dirt and he could just smell it.

George started breathing again, upon hearing the American's comment. Just as George's heart rate was recovering from the last radio transmission, a new one came over the speakers.

"*Antioquia*, team leader Toppin here. I have detained the First Mate, Philip Handfield. During an inspection of his quarters, we found an envelope hidden under his mattress. Mr. Handfield told us the envelope was not his and gave us permission to open it. The envelope contained approximately $12,000 US in cash along with a piece of paper with a name and two phone numbers. We have found no evidence that Handfield—or any other member of the crew—have paperwork declaring intent to carry over $10,000 into the US."

"Hot Damn!" yelled the US LEDET officer.

8:05 AM EDT
Strategic & Information Operations Center, FBI Headquarters Building—Washington, DC

"Get us that name and those numbers, ASAP!" yelled special agent Phil Drennan from inside the FBI's cavernous Strategic & Information Operations Center or SIOC. Located on the fifth floor of their Washington, DC headquarters, the enlarged and updated facility could hold more than 400 people when at maximum capability. The SIOC was equipped with enough command, control, and communications capability to monitor five major operations simultaneously.

Drennan was sitting amongst the group of desks and computer consoles devoted to the FBI's Organized Crime and Drug Division. On the wall across from his desk, one of the 5 by 15 foot video consoles was displaying a live video feed of the *Billesborg* boarding.

"Where's our Coastie?" he added, referring to the Coast Guard Liaison Officer permanently assigned to work with the FBI at the SIOC facility.

Special Agent Phil Drennan had been a member of this organized crime unit for almost five years. If any of the phone numbers found on the *Billesborg* matched the numbers on the phone tapping warrant he held in his hand; they would have a powerful new bit of evidence—providing yet another link between his list of bad guys and Colombian drug trafficking.

One of Drennan's colleagues frantically searched his online database for the phone number to the Coast Guard's Eighth District in New Orleans. He suspected that they would also be watching the ship boarding and might have already received the phone numbers. However, before he could locate the District's main number, the fax machine at his desk sprang to life. Glancing at the cover sheet, he saw the words "United States Coast Guard, District Eight, New Orleans, Louisiana."

"Hey Phil, here it comes!" he called over to his colleague.

Drennan and the small group of agents huddled around the fax machine impatiently watching the paper emerge. Even before the fax machine finished spitting out the paper, he had seen the name.

"Well I'll be damn. Douglas Veith is one of our guys—a fairly big player out in LA!" Drennan said recognizing the name.

Pulling the paper out of the machine, he then checked the new data from the *Billesborg* against the long list of phone numbers included in Veith's file. Recognizing both numbers, he continued, "…and the two phone numbers match cell phone numbers he's used recently."

Drennan sat down and picked up his phone. He needed to make a flurry of phone calls. That small scrap of paper from the *Billesborg* was a very important addition to their investigation.

After completing the first couple of calls, Drennan looked up and asked the group still monitoring the boarding, "Have they found the stuff yet?"

"Not yet, Phil. The Coasties are still down in the belly of the beast doing their thing," replied one of the agents.

"And now folks," said another, playfully impersonating a game show host. "Let's see what's behind wall number three. Bob, please tell us what Mr. Veith's special prize will be if we find drugs behind that wall."

"Well, Jim," continued another. "He'll receive an all-expenses paid visit to an exquisite federal prison, located in beautiful, downtown Leavenworth, Kansas!" Light-hearted laughter erupted throughout the SIOC in response to this impromptu touch of humor.

Come on. Drennan silently urged on the boarding party. *Let's find some drugs on that ship.*

7:27 AM CDT
Onboard *Billesborg III*

Once they knew the location of the wall to be opened by blowtorch, the *Dana-Dafra* Shipping Company had quickly assented to the Potentially

Destructive Search.   A Zodiac from the USS *O'Bannon* brought over the welding equipment and two engineers with the required expertise to use it.

Superintendent George had graciously accepted the American Navy's offer of support as well as their congratulations.   They were pleased that George's men had done such a great job finding that false wall so quickly.

All over the Task Force, sailors peered through binoculars trying to follow the action on the *Billesborg*. They could see nothing of course, as most of the action was occurring below decks in a large cargo compartment.

Toppin and his team watched the engineers set up a gas-powered electrical generator along with the rest of their equipment. After re-checking their position in the compartment with the ship's blueprints, they began drilling a hole in the steel wall. In a few seconds, the large, industrial-sized drill had bored a quarter-inch hole. The engineers then inserted a borescope into the opening.

All five men huddled around the small TV screen of the borescope as the picture was adjusted and finally came into focus. After a bright flash of light blanked out the screen, the picture stabilized and they all saw it—small packets wrapped in plastic, each filled with white powder.

"Damn!" said the young sailor. "I'll bet the whole wall is stacked with this stuff." Each of the men stepped back from the small screen and mentally calculated the expanse of the false cargo compartment wall in front of them. "That's one shitload of drugs we just found, guys!"

The sailors exchanged congratulatory high-fives and handshakes. They had struck pay dirt. This was no longer an exercise; they had actually accomplished a real-world mission and had found some no-kidding narcotics.

Inspector Toppin reached into the bag next to him and pulled out a small plastic box. The box had the letters "N.I.K." stenciled on its side. The NIK was the Narcotics Identification Kit, supplied by the US Coast Guard for making initial chemical identification of any contraband found during searches at sea.

"Let's get a quick atmosphere check before we cut a bigger opening," said one of the engineers.

After confirming that the atmosphere in the compartment was safe for using the blowtorch, the engineers began cutting an opening large enough to allow access to the carefully wrapped plastic bags. As the blowtorch began cutting through the wall, a large shower of sparks flew in all directions and acrid smoke began to fill the compartment. Fortunately, the fans the sailors had brought with them cleared away nearly all of the smoke and fumes. They finished the small opening in less than a minute. One of the engineers carefully reached inside the still red-hot hole and removed one of the packages.

It sure looked like cocaine, but they wouldn't know for sure until they did the NIK test. Toppin cut into the bag with a small knife, withdrew a small amount of the white powder and placed it in a test tube. After adding a few drops of liquid, he shook it for several seconds and compared the color to a small chart—not unlike the ones used to test swimming pool water. The telltale color change indicated that this was a particularly potent batch of high-quality cocaine.

"Looks like some pretty good coke here, gents," he said to the men huddled around him. "Go ahead and make us a larger hole so we can get to the rest of this stuff. I'll call the *Antioquia*."

Toppin then picked up his walkie-talkie and made another radio call. His message was clear and concise—and its impact on the Task Force electric.

"*Antioquia*, this is team leader, we are positive... I say again, NIK inspection checks positive for cocaine. Looking at the size of the wall they've put in, I'd say we're talking about at least 1000 kilos. Standby for update. We're removing the rest of the wall at this time. Over."

8:35 AM EDT
JOIC, SOUTHCOM—Miami, Florida

Listening to Toppin's radio report, SOUTHCOM's Joint Operations and Intelligence Center had erupted in a tumultuous volley of cheers and applause. The good guys had just scored a significant victory.

Sitting next to each other at a table near the back wall of the JOIC, General Wilcox congratulated General Stuart.

"Great job Mike! Looks like your folks have done a bang-up piece of work. Game, set and match!" Everyone within earshot of the two Generals shared in their laughter and good cheer.

The two men moved around the room shaking hands and congratulating everyone for a job well done. It certainly was a great day for the counter-drug mission.

John Carter, on the other hand, was not so sure how "great" the day had been. He turned to Gloria and told her in a lowered voice, "This was too easy. This can't be all there is to it."

Gloria nodded once and placed her finger over her lips. Moving closer to his side, she cupped her hands over her mouth and whispered in his ear.

"Now is not the time—stay quiet. You can let them know what you're thinking later; once we're in a smaller group."

The two Generals completed their walk around the JOIC and returned to the table near the back of the room. As General Stuart gathered up his cup of coffee and notebook, he put his arm around General Wilcox.

"Tell you what, Chuck; let's head back upstairs. Colonel Carter, Miss Saenz, looks like things have come together quite nicely."

Saturday

As the entourage headed back to the General's office, Colonel Michael Kennedy also left the JOIC. Had anyone been looking closely, he might have noticed a sense of relief reflected in Kennedy's face. He now needed to make sure two men—one in Cali, Colombia and the other in Washington, DC—were briefed on what he had just witnessed.

7:47 AM CDT
Onboard *Antioquia*

Back in the operations center of the *Antioquia*, spirits were high. George and his men had just completed one of the largest drug seizures in recent history. The sometimes-boring progression of the annual exercise had been interrupted in spectacular fashion by this "real world" operation. They were all justifiably proud.

After debriefing the events of the day with representatives from each member country, Superintendent George turned to a discussion of what lay ahead for the Task Force.

"So, we're all in agreement," continued George. "We have permission from the US to continue escorting the *Billesborg* and the drugs to Mobile. We will carry on interrogating the *Billesborg's* crew while we're enroute. Once the crew had been placed in the custody of the American authorities in Mobile and the cocaine offloaded, the Task Force will continue with our planned ship visit at the port."

"Should we transfer the cocaine to *Antioquia?*" asked the ship's Captain.

"Thank you for the offer, but for now, I think we should just leave it onboard the *Billesborg*. My men will have it under 24-hour guard; but I would be very happy if the other ships could augment my team in that mission."

"My government has instructed me to cooperate fully," replied the *Antioquia's* Captain. "How many of our crew would you like?"

"Oh, I think that a crew of two men, serving six-hour shifts would do the trick," replied George. "I believe our steaming time to Mobile will be about 12 hours. I should think our NCOs would be able to come up with a work schedule that would be appropriate."

"That's fine with us," replied the Captain of the *O'Bannon*.

"Very well, gentlemen. I think we should get underway," said George, standing up and shaking hands with the officers around the table. "This has been a very successful day and I'd say our men have earned a very lively port call in Mobile."

Meanwhile, in the *Antioquia's* brig, First Mate Philip Handfield was doing a credible job of expressing his innocence in the cocaine smuggling—a performance enhanced by the fact that he was indeed innocent. Less convincing, however, was his explanation for the events of Tuesday night and Wednesday morning.

He was trapped between the proverbial rock and hard place with respect to his absence from the ship. Once it had become clear that the false wall had been constructed and the cocaine put onboard on Tuesday night, the interrogators had asked him about his whereabouts. Reluctant to expose himself to a charge of dereliction of duty for skipping out on his watch, he had at first denied being absent from the ship. When that story had proven untenable, he recognized that he desperately needed an alibi to explain his whereabouts and prove his innocence. Eventually, he had changed his story and reluctantly admitted his dalliances with the high-class prostitutes—at least the parts that he could remember. His interrogators found neither story persuasive.

Before completing the first hour of interrogation, Phillip Handfield slowly came to understand how competently, carefully and completely screwed he was.

9:12 AM EDT
Office of General William C. Stuart, US Army—SOUTHCOM Commander—Miami, Florida

General Stuart escorted Carter, Gloria, and General Wilcox back to his corner office. As the group took their seats around the General's conference table, Stuart announced, "Well, I'd say that the boarding seemed to go off without a hitch. That was one major catch."

He was understandably satisfied with the conduct of the boarding party and the success of their efforts in finding the hidden cocaine. Before anyone else could comment, the General's intercom buzzed, it was his secretary, "I'm very sorry to disturb you, General, but you have an urgent phone call from General Aguilar. He's on line two."

"Thank you, Barbara. I'll take it here on speaker phone," he said, hitting the flashing button on the phone console in the middle of the table. "What's up, Rick?" he asked.

"Sir, I've just received a priority message from NSA. They've intercepted a call originating from a pay phone downstairs at the entrance to the building. Would you like me to come up and show you the transcript, sir?" asked Aguilar.

"No, Rick. I'll save you the leg work, go ahead and read it to me, we're all cleared in this room," replied Stuart, looking at the faces around the table.

"As you wish, General. The transcript is from a conversation picked up at 7:21 this morning. The unidentified individual calling from the pay phone is referred to as 'Voice One.' The called party has been identified as Army

Colonel James Elmore, currently assigned to the Joint Staff, J3 Counter-Drug Division. He's referred to as 'Voice Two' in the transcript."

"OK, Rick, go ahead," said Stuart noticing Carter's wide-eyed expression of astonishment upon learning that the NSA was recording his former commander's phone conversations. As Aguilar started reading the transcript, Carter couldn't shake the feeling that they were all being played like fiddles.

"Voice One: *Delta One*, this is *Delta Two*. I've just escorted *Delta Seven* into this building. Had a chance to talk with him, shortly after he arrived. I'm certain he knows nothing of the plan."

"Voice Two: (that's Elmore)," added Aguilar parenthetically to the transcript. "Why are you calling on this line?"

"Voice One: My office is too heavily populated right now."

"Voice Two: Roger. I'll let November know. Out here."

"That's it for the transcript, sir," said Aguilar. "NSA analysts have confirmed that Elmore is the second voice in the conversation, as they've been running ongoing taps of all his phone lines. NSA believes that *November* is a former US Army Sergeant, named Martin Newmann, who owns several businesses in Colombia. NSA does not yet know the identity of *Delta Two* or *Delta Seven*. But since—"

"Son-of-a—" Carter interrupted, catching himself just in time. "*I* know who they are!" barely able to keep himself from shouting.

"Who's speaking?" asked Aguilar over the speakerphone.

"Rick," interjected General Stuart, surprised by Carter's interruption. "I've got a former member of the DAO in Bogotá up here in my office along with his friend, Miss Saenz, and our former commander, General Wilcox. The speaker was retired Air Force Lieutenant Colonel John Carter. Go ahead, Col. Carter... you were saying?" Despite the fact that he disliked being interrupted by Carter, General Stuart referred to Carter's retired rank—substituting the shorter "Colonel" instead of "Lieutenant Colonel."

"I'm sorry, sir," Carter said to General Stuart, trying to regain his composure. Turning his head toward the speakerphone, he continued, "Sorry to interrupt you, General Aguilar. As General Stuart said, I was assigned to DAO Bogotá with Colonel Elmore. I know that *Delta One* is Colonel Elmore. And unless they've changed an old system we used down there; I also know that *Delta Two* is Colonel Michael Kennedy, and that *I* am *Delta Seven*!"

General Stuart stared at Carter in astonishment. "What do you mean, *you're Delta Seven*?" he asked, incredulously.

"Yes sir. I wouldn't have thought they'd use such a simple way of camouflaging our names; but all the officers in the Bogotá DAO used *Delta Alpha* call signs on the Embassy's radio system. In addition to our 9mm

Delta 7

Berettas, we always carried hand-held radios. Elmore was *Delta Alpha One*, Kennedy was *Delta Alpha Two*, and I was *Delta Alpha Seven*. They've obviously dropped the *Alpha* for brevity."

"Well I'll be damned," said General Aguilar. "General, I need to get that information back to Washington right away. Do you have anything else for me?"

"No Rick, thanks," said Stuart, ending the conversation. Without saying another word, Stuart pushed his secretary's intercom button and picked up the handset.

"Barb, did you notice whether Colonel Kennedy headed for his office after he finished escorting General Wilcox up here this morning, or did he go back downstairs?" the General asked. After a short pause, he continued. "You think he went downstairs. OK fine, thank you Barbara." General Stuart put the handset back and scribbled a note in the notebook at the table.

"I guess that's another loose end we'll have to take care of," Stuart said leaning back in his seat. "Too bad about Mike Kennedy. It would appear that there's an excellent chance that he's been providing the drug traffickers with intelligence about our counter-drug operations. If they were tipped off to the timing and location of our patrols, they'd be able to sneak around our ships and avoid detection. It's a good thing our Task Force was at the right place at the right time—and Kennedy didn't have time to get that information to his co-conspirators before we got to them. We'll have to pull his clearance and get an investigation started. It's a damn shame to see someone throw away his life like this."

Deep in thought, Carter was no longer listening to General Stuart. Michael Kennedy and Kelly Elmore were involved in drug smuggling. As the multitude of events and disparate pieces of information from the last several days swirled around randomly in his mind, Carter struggled to discern a pattern. He couldn't shake the feeling that they were missing something. There were too many unanswered questions.

"I'm sorry sir, but I think something's not quite right. It doesn't add up to me," Carter blurted out as soon as General Stuart stopped talking.

"I don't understand. What isn't adding up for you, Colonel Carter? Let's see what we know so far... First of all," General Stuart explained, counting with his outstretched fingers for emphasis. "We know that for some time, the NSA has been listening into a certain *Mr. N*'s phone conversations. Based on their intercepts and subsequent data cross referencing, they believe *Mr. N* is Sergeant Marty Newmann—now one of our cocaine salesmen-of-the-year working out of Colombia."

"Two: Newmann has been talking to known organized crime figures in New York—probably his buyers."

"Three: Colonel James Elmore—former head of our DAO in Bogotá, and now working at the Joint Staff—has been having fairly regular phone conversations with Newmann. NSA intercepts indicate that they were planning a major drug shipment."

"Four: Two former members of that same DAO in Bogotá are either dead or missing under suspicious circumstances. My guess is that further investigation will show that they too were somehow caught up with Newmann and Elmore."

"Five: Yet another of these former DAO officers, Colonel Mike Kennedy—currently serving on *my* staff—calls Elmore right *before* we find the cocaine on they've hidden on the *Billesborg,* to let him know that *you* have arrived here at SOUTHCOM. I can think of no reason why he'd sneak around and make that phone call to Elmore unless he too was working with the traffickers. Since you're sitting at this table trying to help us and since Kennedy said he didn't think you knew about the plan, I'm guessing that you're *not* one of them."

"Six: The NSA's phone taps led them to believe that there as a connection between the bad guys and the Grenadian Coast Guard Commander... that Fitzroy George was involved with the traffickers."

"Seven: Less than an hour ago, George and his Grenadians presided over one of the biggest cocaine interdictions in the history of this Command—supervised and monitored by the United States Navy and our onboard Coast Guard LEDET. I'd say that shoots NSA's contention that George was involved with the druggies out of the water."

"So, other than that, what are we missing?" asked the General, staring at Carter, waiting for a response.

"I'm sorry, General, but I can't put my finger on it. It's a feeling that we're not seeing things clearly. That we're missing something important. I keep returning to Fitzroy George. I still think he's the key. Jack Zaworski felt it was important that I knew that people were interested in my asking about George. And I'm afraid that Jack was murdered for sharing that information with me. Again, my mention of George's name in Grenada is what got me involved in this whole mess. Why would that upset anyone?"

"But George came through for us didn't he?" General Stuart insisted. "I mean if he were dirty, they wouldn't have found the cocaine... would they?"

"I agree that my argument sounds weak, General Stuart. I'm just convinced there's more to this story," Carter said lamely.

"Maybe the inter-agency crowd in Washington will have an update for us," interjected Wilcox, trying to give Carter some breathing room. "We better let DC look into this... tell them what we're—"

He was interrupted by a persistent buzz from the General's intercom.

"Go ahead, Barbara," said General Stuart.

"General, I have the Director of the NSA, Lieutenant General Marvin Hoyer for you on line three. He says it's urgent."

General Stuart excused himself and picked up the phone. After short conversation, he hung up, shook his head and then paged his secretary.

"Barbara, could you please have the J1 and J3 come up to my office immediately."

Stuart put down the phone, paused for a moment, then got up without uttering a word and looked out his office window. In the distance, he watched as a commercial airplane made its final approach into Miami's international airport. Stuart turned around and walked back to the small group at the conference table shaking his head.

"It looks like Colonel Carter was right to feel like we were missing something. Talk about a startling development. To tell you the truth, I'm having trouble believing what Marv Hoyer just told me!"

8:31 AM EST
Newmann's Hacienda—Cali, Colombia

"¡Misión cumplida!" or "Mission Complete," was the simple message Marty Newmann heard on his satellite phone.

"Everything secure?"

"Sí Señor. Everything on schedule. I will call again for the next step in agreement with the plan—still estimate tomorrow morning," the voice was speaking in very heavily accented and halting English.

"Are you making the news?"

"Yes, the US Navy has sent military reporters from one of his ships."

"I'm very glad to hear that. Good job!" said Newmann, ecstatic—his heart pounding as this unbelievably high-stakes poker game played itself out. So far, it was working.

Newmann was within sight of the finish line. Despite some small setbacks, everything appeared to be on track. The Joint & International Naval Task Force had found the massive shipment—a little over a ton of cocaine. Just as a fisherman happily hands over money for bait in order to catch fish, Newmann had spent well over a million dollars for his bait. Roughly half was for the cocaine and the rest for payoffs and other miscellaneous expenses. Setting up the construction of the false wall on the *Billesborg* and transporting the cocaine inside had been the one of most difficult tasks; but all had gone off without a hitch.

Hopefully, in the next couple of days, that now-swallowed bait would help them hook the largest single drug shipment "fish" that the world would ever not know about.

The arrival of the press at the scene of the seizure was the next trigger point in the plan. It would be a compelling story of a successful ship boarding and the resultant seizure of cocaine—which, after being broken down into one-gram packets, would have generated more than $200 million in street sales.

However, that paled in comparison with the main cargo they had recently placed onboard the *Billesborg*. Nine *thousand* kilos of high-quality heroin was currently underway—escorted by a phalanx of naval warships and under the watchful eye of the international press corps—to Mobile, Alabama. While the world celebrated one of the largest-ever cocaine seizures in the Caribbean, a much more valuable cargo would soon be unloaded and transferred to a warehouse, just north of the docks.

Carlos' brother, Mani, was Newmann's "eyes and ears" on board the *Antioquia*. In the excitement of the big bust, Mani had stealthily set up the satphone behind some equipment secured to the aft portion of the *Antioquia*. While the Task Force focused on the container vessel, Mani had called Newmann with the *misión cumplida* update. Part of that update was to confirm that the press had been informed of the cocaine seizure. That broadcast would serve as an unequivocal message to New York that the operation was proceeding according to plan and that the main shipment was safely on its way.

After receiving Mani's phone call, Newmann sat at his computer and opened his e-mail program. He then selected the e-mail he had prepared earlier, which contained the details of the numbered Swiss bank accounts. To ensure that the money transfer occurred expeditiously, Newmann had drafted the e-mail, encrypted it, and saved it in a well-hidden section of his computer's hard drive several days ago.

The subject of the e-mail was "The Simmons Family Meets Mickey!" Each copy had five photos attached, documenting the fun-filled vacation of a family from Concord, New Hampshire who had visited Disney World. The digital code in one of the photos had been altered to include a series of numbers, which were the primary and backup numbered accounts he'd set up at the bank in Geneva.

Newmann and the New York group had successfully used this system a few weeks earlier for the first wire transfer of five million dollars. For that transaction, he had sent one e-mail to one recipient, indicating the proper account numbers. Each of the Swiss bank accounts would be activated and used only once. That first e-mail had facilitated the initial down payment for the operation—earnest money that confirmed New York's interest in proceeding with this spectacular business transaction.

After checking the e-mail one last time, he had smiled and triumphantly pressed the SEND button—dispatching the encrypted message on its electronic journey to New York. Being thorough and meticulous, Newmann had then checked his e-mail program's SENT folder to verify that the message was on its way. As expected, it was right where he expected, confirming that it had indeed been sent. If all went according to plan, these two accounts would soon hold over $200 million dollars.

Since Marty Newmann was not completely in tune with the technology behind e-mail communication, he did not have an accurate picture of what his computer had just done. He was completely unaware that a copy of the e-mail had also gone to someone in Washington, DC—someone completely unassociated with Newmann or his business associates in New York.

This second recipient never expected to receive personal e-mail in his unclassified account, which was posted on his Agency's website. He had a large staff, which normally filtered all but the most important or interesting of the electronic missives sent to this account. This person was certainly not expecting to be hearing from Marty Newmann.

The second recipient was Lieutenant General Marvin W. Hoyer, United States Air Force, Director of the National Security Agency.

9:36 AM EDT
NSA—Fort Meade, Maryland

For the first time in their careers, Young and Hargrove had been called up to the Director's office for an urgent meeting. The Director had showed them a very interesting e-mail he had just received. They had both been in the room when the Director had called General Stuart in SOUTHCOM.

"They can't be *that* stupid... or that provocative. They had to do this on purpose," the Director said after hanging up with the Commander of the Southern Command.

The three of them went over what they knew about the baffling e-mail. It had been sent directly to the Director's e-mail account—the one posted on his résumé page on the NSA website. Outwardly, the e-mail had been sent from a generic account—like the ones favored by spammers. A quick examination of the hidden portion of the e-mail's header section revealed that it had been bounced off a commercial "dot.com" account registered to a Mr. Martin Newmann in Bogotá, Colombia.

The two had never seen an adversary be so careless. It was an almost impossibly stupid thing for Newmann to have done. Surely, he did it on purpose... or perhaps it was a red herring sent by someone else.

"Red herring or not," Hoyer insisted. "I want you to follow up on this

ASAP. I'll authorize all the computer time you need to check those photos. Let's see what you can find out. I want you to report directly to me as soon as you get something. Any questions?"

"No questions, sir. We're on it," said Hargrove, breathlessly, as the two hurried out of the office.

They almost sprinted down three flights of stairs and back to their office. All the way, they went over what they knew so far. The puzzle was beginning to fall into place. They knew that Marty Newmann had sent the e-mail. They were certain that Newmann was their *Mr. N.*

Although it was almost inconceivable, they strongly suspected that the e-mail photos might contain encrypted information related to the imminent drug transaction. Now that the Director was directly involved with their case, the vast computing power of the agency was at their disposal. If there were any hidden data in those photos, they would find it.

As the two arrived back at their office, they noticed the flashing light on the intercept computer. The light alerted them to the fact that high-priority intercepts had been recorded while they were upstairs in the Director's office.

"When it rains it pours!" said Young, preparing to replay the new intercepts.

11:38 PM AEDT
Sydney International Airport—Australia

On the third floor of Sydney International Airport's main terminal—far removed from the first two passenger-clogged floors—Australian Customs had a small office used for interrogation of suspect passengers. For the past hour, two Customs agents had been questioning a Panamanian citizen. From the moment they had found the cash, Fernando García Luna had felt a tremendous need to come clean and unburden himself of his secrets. He would tell them everything—on one simple condition.

"Please don't tell Panamanian Customs until my family has left the country!" he had begged. "They are waiting for my call before they come here. Even if I must go to jail for what I have done, please let my family come here to be with me. I will tell you everything I know if you allow my family to leave the country. I have much more information about drugs and money. I know names and faces. Please don't let them hurt my family," García had pleaded.

García had been petrified that the Australians would inform the Panamanian authorities of his activities before his family had left the country. He knew that as soon as the Colombian discovered that he had been betrayed, his family would be killed.

García's story was compelling. The three men shared a common profession, and the Australians had understood and, at least partially, empathized with García. His concern for his family was palpable and obviously sincere. Convinced that he was telling the truth, the agents had contacted their Regional Office in Sydney for guidance. Australian Immigration officials had agreed to allow García's family to enter the country on temporary visas. If García's information subsequently proved to be accurate, they would consider his application for permanent residence and request for immunity from prosecution.

Once informed of the Australians' offer, García had told them everything. His confession had covered every single detail and had continued non-stop for almost an hour.

Given the time-sensitive nature of the information, the highlights of García's confession made their way rapidly up the Australian Customs Service bureaucracy. In less than an hour, the Central Office in Canberra had passed along the information to their counterparts in US Bureau of Customs & Border Protection.

9:44 AM EDT
NSA—Fort Meade, Maryland

Young and Hargrove had been running in several directions at once for the past hour. First, they had forwarded Newmann's e-mail to the Cipher Division with instructions that they look for encoded messages inside the attached photos. Next, they had replayed the phone call *Delta Two* had placed to Elmore.

Finally, they heard the latest intercept. It was a phone call Newmann received from a satellite phone somewhere in the Gulf of Mexico. They had not heard the heavily accented voice of this caller before, and assumed that it must have been a collaborator onboard the *Billesborg*. After listening to the entire conversation, however, they were even more baffled.

"This keeps getting stranger by the minute, Bill. The caller says that the mission is complete... but then he talks about making another call for the next step. What 'next step' could there be after the Coast Guard confiscates all their cocaine? Then, Newmann asks if the press is there—the *press* for God's sake. The guy's just been busted... just had about a million bucks worth of coke taken from him, and he seems positively happy to hear the news. And to top it off, he wants the friggin' *press* there?"

"Between this surreal phone conversation and that e-mail to the Director... well, this is just totally messed up," agreed Young.

"Speaking of 'messed up,' I think it's time you and I headed back up to the Director's office to give him an update."

Just as they were getting ready to set up another meeting with the Director, the phone rang. It was the Cipher Division. They had decoded the information hidden inside the e-mail. Newmann had used a rather unsophisticated encryption program, which had been no match for the Division's computer power. In a matter of minutes, they had extracted the information from one of the photos. It was a series of characters, which they suspected were Swiss bank account numbers. The Cipher Division had already passed the information along to the Treasury Department, which was now in the process of working with Swiss banking authorities to identify who had set up the accounts.

As Hargrove hung up the phone, he turned to Young, shaking his head and said, "These guys are either the most stupid drug smugglers on the face of the Earth, or we're missing something... big time!"

10:01 AM EDT
US Bureau of Customs & Border Protection—Washington, DC

International Liaison Officer Robert W. Wyclith saw the message pop up on his computer console in the Operations Center of the US Bureau of Customs & Border Protection. In 2003, the Customs Agency was reorganized and placed under the Department of Homeland Security. Even though the Bureau's organizational focus had shifted more toward anti-terrorism and homeland protection, the counter drug mission was still alive and kicking. Given this morning's activity in the Gulf of Mexico, that seemed especially true today.

Wyclith had been monitoring the aftermath of the *Billesborg's* boarding when he received the message from Australian customs. Shifting his attention away from the reports coming out of the intercept, Wyclith almost immediately realized that this message might prove to be vitally important to their investigation.

```
    CUSTOMS AGENTS ASSIGNED TO SYDNEY INTERNATIONAL
AIRPORT HAVE APPREHENDED A PANAMANIAN NATIONAL
AFTER A ROUTINE SEARCH REVEALED THAT HE WAS IN
POSSESSION OF APPROXIMATELY $15,000 (USD) IN
UNDECLARED CASH HIDDEN IN HIS LUGGAGE.  SUSPECT'S
NAME IS BEING WITHHELD IN ORDER TO PROTECT HIS
FAMILY, WHO MAY BE ENDANGERED BY RELEASE OF THE
FOLLOWING INFORMATION.
    DURING ROUTINE POST-ARREST INTERVIEW, SUSPECT
PROVIDED DETAILED INFORMATION CONCERNING THE SOURCE
OF THE CASH IN HIS POSSESSION.  BASED ON THIS
INTERVIEW THERE IS REASON TO BELIEVE THAT
APPROXIMATELY 25 SHIPPING CONTAINERS ONBOARD THE
PANAMANIAN-REGISTERED CONTAINER SHIP, BILLESBORG
III, MAY BE CARRYING ILLEGAL NARCOTICS OR OTHER
```

CONTRABAND ITEMS. FURTHER, SUSPECT INDICATES THAT
THE CONTAINERS IN QUESTION WERE SHIPPED FROM PANAMA
BY A LOCAL OFFICE SUPPLY STORE NAMED PANAMAX.

CUSTOMS SERVICE WILL RELEASE MORE DETAILS ONCE
SUSPECT'S FAMILY IS UNDER THE PROTECTION OF LOCAL
AUTHORITIES HERE IN AUSTRALIA.

10:02 AM EDT
Office of General William C. Stuart, US Army—SOUTHCOM Commander—Miami, Florida

After receiving General Hoyer's "curve ball," General Stuart had added new players to the game. In addition to Carter, Gloria and General Wilcox, there were three additional individuals at the General's conference room table. Seated next to General Stuart and General Wilcox was the command's Chief of Operations (J3), Major General Steven W. Hayes, US Army. To his right was the Command's Chief of Intelligence (J1), Brigadier General Ricardo Aguilar, USAF. At the other end of the table, opposite General Stuart, was the Command's DEA Liaison Officer, Benjamin Tucker.

Several unorganized piles of reports and paperwork from the *Billesborg's* boarding were strewn over the table. Also, carefully guarded in General Aguilar's hands, was a folder with diagonal stripes and large TOP SECRET markings. The folder contained highly classified copies of the NSA's intercepts of Newmann's phone calls. Since access to these reports was restricted to those with special "code-word" security clearances, Aguilar was keeping a close watch over them.

The group had tried in vain to make sense of the perplexing e-mail received by General Hoyer at NSA. Did Newmann actually send it... and if so, why? Was he toying with them? In the end, the e-mail evoked more questions than it provided answers. They had finally decided that it was highly unlikely Newmann had sent it, because the Treasury Department had confirmed that the bank account numbers hidden inside were linked to genuine Swiss accounts—very likely his own. The consensus opinion was that one of Newmann's associates must have betrayed him and forwarded the e-mail to the NSA.

The discussion then moved to the next topic: Colonel Kennedy's communications with Elmore in the Pentagon, along with Elmore's connection to Newmann.

"I think he should be placed under arrest," said General Aguilar.

"There's not a lot of meat in those intercepts, Rick," replied General Stuart. "I don't think they give us enough ammunition to send him away yet. Of course, I *do* think we need to keep an eye on him."

"He's been in regular contact with a known drug trafficker. I think there's got to be something we can make stick," insisted General Aguilar.

"I don't think Kennedy is one of the ringleaders in this group. I'm more concerned about Superintendent George. We have the transcripts from NSA. Why was he communicating with Newmann in Colombia? It doesn't pass the smell test," added General Wilcox, who had stayed out of the conversation until this point.

"Well, I think any doubts we had about George's reliability were put to rest out in the Gulf of Mexico just now," answered General Hayes. "The Navy says his boarding party did a great job finding those drugs on that container ship. He's been running the whole show since the Grenadians assumed TACON during the boarding—".

"Wait a minute. Did you say the *Grenadians* had TACON for the boarding?" interrupted Carter, referring to the military's abbreviation of Tactical Control."

"Well, Yes. Legally—and officially—since the ship boarding took place outside US territorial waters, they had TACON from the moment the ship boarding started. Although we had several of our Coast Guard guys there, the boarding crew was primarily composed of members of the Grenadian Coast Guard," replied General Hayes.

"And they'll continue to exercise TACON until the container ship arrives in Mobile, and the drugs are offloaded?" continued Carter.

"No. The US Navy will resume TACON of the Task Force as soon as the actual ship boarding is completed. The plan right now is that the entire Task Force will be escorting the cocaine to Mobile. George will be in charge of the Coast Guard contingent that will stay aboard the *Billesborg* while they're underway. The Task Force will be rotating additional teams onboard the *Billesborg* to protect the evidence."

"Well, I'll be damned! So, George and his men will be on the *Billesborg*— and in charge of that ship—the entire time it's being escorted to Mobile. Right?" asked Carter.

"Well, yes. As is normally the case, the Coast Guard contingent handles all law enforcement issues until arriving at the port—where local officials and DEA take over. That's standard operating procedure, and that's what we're doing now. The Task Force and the *Billesborg* will be arriving in Mobile about twelve hours from now," replied General Hayes, a look of confusion on his face.

"Then that *was* their plan all along!" exclaimed Carter, hitting the table for emphasis. "While we're all slapping each other on the back, congratulating ourselves on the cocaine bust, George is going to be escorting the real cargo— whatever's in those containers—all the way to Mobile. That's got to be it."

"What the hell are you talking about?" said a frustrated General Stuart. "I thought we already went through this."

"I'm sorry, sir. Let me explain," said Carter frantically looking through the piles of paperwork in front of him. "Sorry for not making myself clear; but I think I've just figured out what's really going on. Have you seen what that guy the Aussies arrested in Sydney said about the *Billesborg*?"

"Yeah," replied General Stuart, once again irritated by Carter's interruption. "He said something about drugs being on the *Billesborg*. We already know that now. We've got the drugs."

"Right. But there's no mention of a fake wall. He says something about *containers*," said Carter, rifling through the papers on the conference table. "Here it is. Look!" Carter said standing up with the paper and walking over to the table next to Stuart. Carter pointed to the message as he read, "It says, '...reason to believe that approximately 25 *shipping containers*... may contain illegal narcotics or contraband.' And in the next sentence it says that 'the *containers* in question' were shipped by an office supply store."

"So what? Intelligence is never completely accurate. Maybe they just got it wrong in Sydney," insisted the General.

"No sir. We were *supposed* to find the fake wall and the cocaine. There's got to be something else—something *much* more valuable—in those containers!"

"What the hell are you talking about? We just found and confiscated several million dollars worth of cocaine. You're saying we were *supposed* to find it?"

"That's the only thing that makes sense, General. My involvement with this whole mess began when I asked about Superintendent George while I was in Grenada this past Monday. I didn't ask about him because I *suspected* him of anything—I was simply trying to make conversation with a Grenadian bartender. Newmann somehow found out that I had asked about George and considered that threatening. When I returned to Miami the next day, I had a surprise meeting with Jack Zaworski, a friend whom I haven't seen in years and with whom I served at the Defense Attaché Office in Bogotá. He came to Miami to warn me that I might be in danger and to talk me into going to Colombia. I'm afraid that Jack was killed because he came to Miami to warn me."

"Before I left for Cartagena, I made a few phone calls to try to get in touch with people who knew Zaworski from the DAO in Bogotá. When I called Bruce Meyers' wife, she told me that Bruce had been killed recently in Colombia under mysterious circumstances."

"When I got down to Cartagena to meet with Jack, he was probably already dead. So, because I asked about George, and then showed up in Colombia, Newmann must have considered *me* a threat to his drug smuggling plans. I'll bet the only reason Newmann didn't kill *me*, is that there would be too many dead members of that former DAO team in Bogotá. By killing me, there'd be *three* of us dead, he'd be leaving a trail right back to himself. So instead, he arranged to have me roughed up—and the guys busting my butt made it perfectly clear that I should get the hell out of Colombia."

"I left Colombia... but I didn't give up. I flew up to DC to try to get more information from my contacts in the area. While I was in Washington, I learned more about Newmann and his exploits in Colombia. I also got in touch with my former boss, Colonel Kelly Elmore up in the Pentagon. Elmore seemed to already know about Zaworski and Meyer, and even let slip details about my mugging in Cartagena. Finally, I find out that Elmore's been in touch with Marty Newmann, which might explain why he already knew about Bruce and Z's death as well as my getting beat up in Cartagena."

"Today, I've learned that yet another member of DAO Bogotá, Colonel Michael Kennedy—who is currently serving on your staff—has been in regular contact with Colonel Elmore, and that Elmore appears to be Newmann's main military point of contact. Kennedy would be able to provide both of them with valuable intel on SOUTHCOM's counter-drug operations. So, I'd say that the Sergeant is now in charge of the Colonels."

"Now... let's return to our hero of the moment, Superintendent Fitzroy George. Based on NSA intercepts, we know that the Grenadian Coast Guard Superintendent has kept in touch with Newmann over the past couple of months. And this morning, by some amazing coincidence, the very same Superintendent George just *happens* to be in position to assume command of a ship boarding that takes place way outside of his normal area of responsibility. More importantly, we find out today that Superintendent George is going to secure the evidence and provide a military escort for the *Billesborg* all the way back to the Mobile."

Carter paused and looked around the room. Everyone was intently listening to his every word. Gone were the looks of derision and impatience. They were with him now. It was all starting to make sense—to him *and* to them.

"General Aguilar mentioned earlier that in one of NSA's intercepts Newmann appeared to be happy when he learned that we had intercepted the *Billesborg* and found the cocaine. Newmann would have spent a lot of money to set up this operation," Carter continued. "I don't think he'd be happy to see it all go down the toilet. Well, it *hasn't*. The ship's manifest will tell us which containers were shipped by that office supply company in Panama. We've got to follow those containers!"

"What do you think is in these containers, Colonel Carter? You don't think it's a nuke, do you?" asked General Hayes, no longer questioning Carter's explanation of events.

"No, sir. They wouldn't need 25 containers for that. Plus, we've seen no indication that these guys are into terrorism. No, I think we're talking about a major… I mean *major* drug shipment. That number of containers could carry hundreds of millions of dollars worth of drugs. To ensure that the shipment arrived safely in the US without being detected, it would certainly make sense to spend a couple million dollars to arrange this whole cocaine seizure to divert us away from the real shipment."

"So if drugs are in the containers, why don't we start opening them now, and find out exactly what's inside them," said Stuart.

"No sir," answered General Hayes. "I don't think we can open up containers while the ship is at sea. It's too dangerous. They're all strapped down and someone could get hurt. I'll check with our Coast Guard liaison; but I'm pretty sure they'll want to wait until the ship arrives at port where they have all the equipment required to safely inspect them."

"Gentlemen… and lady," DEA Liaison Benjamin Tucker calmly interjected—acknowledging Gloria with a smile. "We suddenly find ourselves inside our adversaries' decision cycle. Because of that inexplicable e-mail Newmann—or whoever—sent to the NSA, we have a couple of Swiss bank account numbers, which just might be associated with this drug deal. If we act quickly, I believe we'll be able to set up a nice little sting operation for these bastards. The way I see it, if we let Newmann and his gang continue to believe we're oblivious to their plan, we would be in a position to spring a trap on them once the deal goes down. If those accounts are the 'Real McCoy,' we'll be able to monitor the transfer of funds. And *that* will implicate all the big fish."

"What you're suggesting, Benny, is that we should let George escort that stuff—whatever is in those containers—right into Mobile?" asked General Stuart.

"That's precisely what I'm saying, General. However, after we share this information with Washington, they'll set up quite a reception committee. I'm sure DEA, FBI, Alabama State and local law enforcement will have agents all over Mobile. Once we track down the shipping documents, we'll even know where the containers will be sent after they arrive in Mobile. They won't be able to hide that many containers; we'll stay right on top of them. As soon as the bad guys complete their transaction, I'll bet those Swiss bank accounts will reflect the transfer of money. After that, we move in, recover the drugs and bust everyone involved. I didn't go to law school, but I'd wager we'd have enough for several convictions."

"I like that plan, Benny. I'll let you get in touch with your bosses in DC, and I'll get the Pentagon into the loop. Washington has an awful lot of coordination and planning to do—and precious little time to carry it all out. They'll need the details of what appears to be Mr. Newmann's plan. I think Col. Carter has just figured out how to put together the pieces of this puzzle," said

General Stuart, patting Carter on the back. "All we need to do now, is to convince our two military plotters—Colonels Kennedy and Elmore—that we're blissfully unaware of their real objective. I'm going to have Colonel Kennedy come up here to escort General Wilcox and his guests out of the building. While he's with us, we'll act as if this is all over. Next, I'm going to order the JOIC to return to normal staffing, and I'm going to send everyone home. Rick, I want you to arrange for surveillance of our Colonels—at their homes and offices. We need to make sure that they don't catch wind of our little sting operation. If they *do* figure out that we're on to them, we need to be in a position to pull the plug on their communications with Mr. Newmann. Can you handle that with the appropriate agencies here and in DC?"

"Yes, sir," replied Aguilar. "DIA will have the required assets in DC, and we have enough personnel here to keep Colonel Kennedy under wraps."

"Good. Let me know if you need my horsepower to get things done up in DC," said Stuart, pointing to the shiny row of stars on his shoulders. "Is everyone ready for a little play acting?"

After General Stuart called his secretary to have her get Kennedy, General Wilcox leaned over towards Carter and said, "Well, John, I'm glad that I let you talk me into coming to my house last night. It also appears fitting—if this all pans out—that I got you a seat at this table. To be perfectly honest, your presence here this morning was not easy to arrange. I've used up most of the green stamps my retired rank afforded me. However, I feel certain that in the next day or so, it will prove to have been well worth the effort."

10:32 AM EDT
JOIC, SOUTHCOM—Miami, Florida

Michael Kennedy continued to go over the data coming in from the Task Force. There were several updates concerning their planned steaming schedule, reports of the disposition of the crew of the *Billesborg*, and a timetable for guarding the cocaine shipment. There was nothing in any of the reports that indicated the plan had been compromised. No one had shown any undue interest in the containers. Still, he needed to find out why Carter had shown up at the headquarters this morning. If only they had let him into the General's office with Carter, perhaps he would have been able to learn more about that particularly disturbing mystery.

Kennedy almost jumped out of his chair when his office phone rang. It was Barbara Malacari, the Commander's secretary. The General wanted to see him in his office immediately. For the second time that morning, Kennedy's heart pounded in his chest. Would this be the end? Had they found out about his involvement with Newmann?

Kennedy tried to calm himself for what might lie ahead. He took a deep breath and headed up the stairs towards General Stuart's office.

10:35 AM EDT
Office of General William C. Stuart, US Army—SOUTHCOM
Commander—Miami, Florida

"Come in, Colonel Kennedy," said General Stuart, smiling broadly. "We're just about finished up here. Before General Wilcox and his guests leave us, I wanted to congratulate you and your staff for the great job you've all done. We have just participated in one of the largest interdictions of cocaine in the SOUTHCOM's history. I'm very proud of the men and women of this Command. Job well done!" he said extending his hand towards Colonel Kennedy.

"Thank you, sir. We were just doing our jobs," said Kennedy with tremendous relief.

"It would appear that the cargo of cocaine we've just found onboard the *Billesborg* was the reason Col. Carter here, was roughed up in Colombia. Apparently, someone down there thought that he was still involved in the counter-drug business, and didn't want him sniffing around. Anyway, since our Task Force is now escorting the cocaine back to Mobile, it is the considered opinion of this august group that the fat lady is singing," Stuart said, as the group laughed.

"Since this *is* a Saturday," continued General Stuart. "I'd say we've all earned a well-deserved day off. I'm therefore *ordering* you, along with all the extra staff we've called in to monitor the boarding, home for the rest of the weekend to be with your families. Any objections?"

"No objections on my part," said General Hayes. "I've got a few golf balls left to send flying all over the Doral Country Club Golf Course."

"Sounds like an excellent plan to me," agreed General Aguilar.

"Colonel Kennedy," said General Wilcox, as he, Carter and Gloria, stood up and got ready to leave. "I extend my hardy congratulations to you and your staff. Too bad this couldn't have happened on *my* watch; but my time at the helm is long gone. If you'd be so kind, I'd appreciate you showing us out of the building."

"I'd be happy to, General," said Kennedy.

The group of officers shook hands, said goodbye, and left. Kennedy gleefully escorted Wilcox, Carter and the Colombian girl out of the building and into the waiting staff car. As the car pulled away from the front of the building, Kennedy was confident that everything was still proceeding pretty much according to the plan. It was time to go home, relax, and figure out how he was going to spend the money that would soon be coming his way.

12:20 PM EDT
Colonel Kennedy's Home—Weston, Florida

After returning home from SOUTHCOM, Kennedy immediately changed out of his uniform and into shorts and a T-shirt. As soon as he reported this morning's activities to Elmore, he would be heading east to take his boat out into the Atlantic waters off Fort Lauderdale. Kennedy was looking forward to relaxing and spending the afternoon fishing. Before landing a boat-full of fish, there was one last piece of business. He dialed Elmore's home phone number.

"Why are you calling me on this line?" Elmore asked, recognizing the caller ID.

"Stuart sent just about the entire staff home for the weekend. I was there in his office. They have completely swallowed the bait. They're convinced it's over, and so am I," confided Kennedy triumphantly.

"That's the same feeling I got when I left the Pentagon. The Joint Staff is racking this up as a tremendous victory for the CD community. I hate to admit it—knock on wood—but things are looking pretty positive."

"Yes, I'm beginning to think that this is actually going to work. If this goes off... well, maybe retirement is going to be a wonderful thing. To tell you the truth, I'm ready to call it quits. I've had it: sneaking around, working with Newmann, taking all his crap. As soon as that money shows up in my account, I'm putting in my papers and you can color me gone."

"Same here," agreed Elmore. "I'm going to maintain a low profile until this thing is over."

"Sounds good to me. Take care, Kelly. Keep in touch," said Kennedy without conviction, hoping that he would never again have a reason to contact Elmore.

1:14 PM EST
Newmann's Hacienda—Cali, Colombia

Marty Newmann was pacing back and forth in his office—going over the handwritten notes in the notebook he had just removed from his safe. He had just put a check mark next to the note indicating that he should verify that the bank in Switzerland was ready for the transfer.

Next, he had to confirm that everything was still on track out in the Gulf. He called Elmore at his Virginia home.

"I just spoke with *Delta Two*. They don't suspect a thing down there. It's the same thing up here, they have no clue what's really happening," Elmore had said confidently. He then continued, "As soon as that ship gets back, I expect to see something in *my* account ... got it?"

"Don't get too cocky. We still have a long way to go," replied Newmann. "Speaking of which... What has *Delta Two* learned about what *Seven* was doing at SOUTHCOM this morning?

"Oh yeah, I forgot about that... he was in their Operations Center during the boarding."

"You're shitting me!" yelled Newmann.

"No. Apparently, *Seven* arrived early in the morning with the former Commander. They had some Colombian girl with them. It was like they were on some tour or something."

"That's fucking bullshit! That's too big a coincidence. Did you find out what they were talking about? Did they know anything?" asked Newmann, furious.

"Calm down! Nobody knows or suspects anything. You're getting paranoid, Marty. Right before *Seven* and the General left the building, *Delta Two* was invited into the big boss's office. They were all congratulating each other on a job well done. Listen, if *Delta Six* didn't know anything—and I assume he didn't—then how could *Seven* know anything? They've sent everyone home for the rest of the weekend down there. This thing is a done deal!" said a very confident Elmore.

"I've got too much riding on this. I don't want to take *any* chances."

"Fine. I'll keep you in the loop. But like I said, everyone here is acting like it's over and they're all heroes. Stop worrying. *Seven* doesn't know anything, nor does anyone else in the Pentagon or down in Miami."

"All right, you do everything you can to keep on top of *Seven*. I don't want him to keep showing up in the middle of our shit!" insisted Newmann.

"OK, I'll let you know immediately if anything changes on my end," Elmore lied. He had done his job and all he planned on doing was to wait for his money.

2:26 PM EDT
Colonel Elmore's House—Mount Vernon, Virginia

Joyce Elmore was used to her husband locking himself into his office upstairs for hours at a time. He had installed a special safe there several years ago, and had periodically barricaded himself in his office working on one secret counter-drug operation after another. She was a bit surprised that the Pentagon would allow him to work on classified operations at home; but figured it was just part of his increased responsibility. What he did—at both the Pentagon and upstairs in his office—was off limits to her. She was comfortable with that arrangement, as were most military wives who spent years together with husbands constantly involved with classified programs.

Therefore, she had hardly noticed when Kelly had gone upstairs to answer Newmann's Satphone call. Nor had she noticed the unmarked van parked unobtrusively down the street from their modest two-story colonial home in Riverside Estates—just north of Mount Vernon, Virginia.

Unlike Joyce, the men inside the van knew the reason for Elmore's trip upstairs into his office. They were also privy to the entire conversation, as the technicians inside the van had just monitored Elmore's call to Newmann.

A few days ago, they had been lucky. Elmore had taken his family out to a local restaurant. While one team had followed the family to dinner, the other had stayed at Elmore's house. Once Elmore and his family were a safe distance away, they had broken into the house, hidden microphones in nearly every room, and tapped all the phone lines. About the time the Elmore family began their main course at the restaurant, they had already finished installing and testing all the listening devices and phone taps.

Sunday

You may have to fight a battle more than once to win it.

- Margaret Thatcher

Sunday

12:15PM CEST
Rothschild-Ferrier Bank, S.A.—Geneva, Switzerland

Philippe Rivière preferred to work weekends and nights. At those times, the bank was much less hectic than it was during regular weekday business hours, which usually allowed him to avoid interaction with clients. Rivière felt much more comfortable with numbers, account balances, and currency transactions. This Sunday morning was already proving to be the exception to the rule; he had been far too busy.

In his decades-long career with *Rothschild-Ferrier*—a near permanent fixture in the 200-year old Swiss banking industry—Rivière had witnessed the gradual change. In many ways, the change suited him. His bank, along with the entire Swiss banking establishment, had once prided themselves for providing their clients personal attention and service. Now that most transactions took place online, most of his clients never set foot inside the bank. Anyone with the $200,000 minimum deposit and the mandatory US $950 account setup fee could open a numbered account. There were few restrictions as to currency or nationality. Clients could count on the bank's complete discretion. In fact, based on the Swiss banking law passed in 1934, it was illegal for a Swiss banker to release information about his clients.

Over the past several years, however, in an attempt to combat money laundering associated with the huge sums of money generated by international trade in drugs and arms, the world's financial community had pressured the Swiss to amend their rules. Their system was deemed too lax and accommodating. As a result, Rivière was forced to comply with questions and requests from auditors and investigators who routinely swarmed around the bank. These people acted as if they had an inherent right to poke their noses into the bank's business and impose their wretched transparency. Philippe Rivière was keenly aware that transparency was precisely what many of his clients sought to avoid.

Just hours ago, Rivière had met with several of the regulatory busybodies. Appalled at their brazen disregard for centuries of tradition, Rivière had initially resisted their attempts to monitor several of his clients' inviolate numbered accounts. Unfortunately, these transparency-seeking investigators were armed with the required paperwork. They had warrants, a judge's signature, and authorization from the Swiss Federal Department of Finance.

Rivière's hands were tied. Resigned to the fact that he must now cooperate with the investigators, Rivière began to rationalize. Perhaps it was all for the best, as these particular customers had been monopolizing his time lately— sometimes calling more than once during the same day.

Just yesterday, for example, the American gentleman had called again from

174

Colombia, insisting on going over the details for an upcoming transfer of money. Rivière had ensured him that the new accounts were ready for activation and that the electronic routing information along with the account numbers and passwords had already been verified.

Even more bothersome, less than an hour later, someone else had called and insisted on going over the very same questions. *Don't these drug traffickers ever coordinate with each other?* Rivière had thought after the second phone call.

Rivière knew that Colombia (along with Albania and Nigeria) were "restricted countries." That designation meant that the bank was not allowed to set up numbered or pseudonym accounts for clients from those countries. The American, however, had provided documentation showing that his company was incorporated in the Bahamas. Up to now, Rivière saw no reason to divulge the apparent connection between these accounts and the people calling from Colombia. As long as law protected him, he could protect his clients.

The intrusive bastards from Interpol, however, were making him increasingly nervous. If events turned against him, Philippe Rivière had more than enough experience to come out ahead. If forced to choose between preserving the privacy of these particular clients and saving his skin, there was no doubt which option would prevail.

10:04 AM CDT
Wharf # 3—Mobile, Alabama

Dressed in the summer white uniform of the Colombian Navy, Manuel Hernández was standing with a small group of sailors from the *Antioquia*. Shortly after docking that morning, they had watched as DEA and local police officials had taken custody of the cocaine shipment. Mani had been relieved to escape the claustrophobic confines of the *Billesborg's* cargo hold, where he'd spent the last six hours guarding the seized cocaine. He and the other sailors were patiently awaiting word from the *Antioquia's* Captain that their long-awaited shore leave had officially begun. In the meantime, they continued to monitor the offloading of containers from the *Billesborg* while enjoying a couple of cigarettes and engaging in small talk.

As Mani and his shipmates chatted on the dock, his brother drove up to the wharf's front entrance and presented a forged press pass to the guard. With all the press at the dock area for the offloading of the cocaine, he was sure they would grant him access to the port facility. Finding a parking spot on the dock near the *Billesborg*, Carlos got out of his car and headed toward the crowd gathered next to the giant ship.

Mani spotted his brother walking toward the *Billesborg*. "Carlos!" he called with outstretched arms, walking briskly towards his brother.

"*Hermanito!*" said Carlos as the two gave each other the traditional *abrazo*-style bear hug. "It's so good to see you after all this time. Later tonight, after everything has been completed, I'll be inviting you to many drinks, my brother."

"It's been a very long time since we've been together. A few hours at a bar sounds like a great idea. I also hear that the American women are very nice!" Mani said with a smile. "Perhaps we will find some at the bar you've picked out for us."

"You've been at sea too long, Mani. Our Colombian women are more beautiful... but certainly not as quick to spread their legs for you like the American whores. We'll have time for that later. Let's go for a quick walk," Carlos said, putting his arm around his brother's shoulder.

As they continued walking away from Mani's shipmates, Carlos asked, "Do you have the list of the containers that are going to our warehouse?"

"Yes. They have already been taken off the ship. No one paid any attention to them. In fact, no one is looking very closely at *anything* coming off the boat. Instead, they concentrate on the wall and the cocaine. Soon the containers will be on their way. Are you sure you don't want me to go with one of the trucks?" asked Mani, desperate to be of service to his brother.

"No, *hermanito*. If I need anything else, I will let you know. There's no need for you to go with me. Stay here until they let you leave, and then go to that bar we talked about before... the one on the north side of the city, near the warehouse. You have money for the cab fare?"

"Yes Carlos, I have plenty of money and I'm going to spend plenty of it on drinks with my brother. I have been at sea for a while, you know," he said, still smiling broadly.

"The warehouse is only a few kilometers from here," Carlos added, ignoring the drinking invitation. "So it'll be a short drive for the trucks—15 or 20 minutes at the most. I will meet you at the bar after the containers have arrived safely. I only have—"

Carlos was interrupted by his ringing cell phone, which he immediately answered.

"Yes. Yes, we are ready. I'll meet you at the previously-agreed location. In ten minutes. Yes. Goodbye," Carlos said evenly and without emotion, folding up the cell phone and putting it back in his pocket.

"I have to go, little brother. I must return to Colombia tonight, once this is over. I want you to know that you've done every task assigned to you very well. I'm proud of you and your service to the Revolution!"

"You can congratulate me tonight at Jaime's Bar. Are you sure you have to return so soon? I want to hear all about your life," replied Mani, looking forward to a longer reunion with his big brother.

"Mani," said Carlos, placing his hands on his brother's shoulders and looking directly into his eyes. "If something should go wrong this afternoon... if the police should get involved, I want you to promise me something."

"What could go wrong? Everything seems to be going perfectly."

"Any operation can end badly, my brother. We must make preparations for any contingency."

"All right, Carlos. Of course, I'll do whatever you say."

"I want you to promise me that if anything goes wrong—if I can't meet with you tonight—I want you to stay here in the United States. Do not go back to your ship. Do not go back to Colombia. You have learned English. You must start a new life in this country. America is a huge country—large enough for you to disappear... to have a good life... to raise a family... to escape from the violence and death of Colombia."

"But Carlos, what about you? Won't you need my help?"

"Don't worry about me, little brother. I can take care of myself," replied Carlos.

"But I don't know anyone here, I—"

"No! You must promise me that you will stay in this country," insisted Carlos, surprised by the words he was saying.

For the first time in many years, and for this one fleeting moment, Carlos actually cared about another human being. Although it was true that they had been apart long enough to have become strangers; he felt that today, his brother might have become more important than the Revolution.

During his years of service to the FARC, Carlos had learned that any individual human life was less important than the overarching progression of history. Carlos never dwelt on his own mortality, nor did he think about those who had to die for the cause. The Revolution had to take precedence, and people had to kill and be killed based on its needs.

There was a time—in the distant past—when taking a life would have been unthinkable. After becoming part of the FARC, however, killing had become easier to justify. For a second, as he looked at his brother's innocent face, Carlos wondered what was actually motivating his actions now. Was it the Bolivarian Cause... or was it simply money and power?

As they embraced again, patting each other's backs, Carlos tried to clear his mind of these troubling thoughts. He must concentrate on his duty and what lay ahead.

"OK, Carlos," he heard Mani say. "I promise that I'll stay in this country if anything goes wrong. But nothing will go wrong. Everything will be perfect; and I will see you at the bar in a couple of hours."

"Adios. *Cuídate*, Mani, I'll see you soon."

"*Nos vemos, hermano*" called Mani cheerfully as he watched his brother walk back towards his car.

10:05 AM EST
Newmann's Hacienda—Cali, Colombia

"I can't take any calls now!" Newmann snapped at the guard outside his office, who was holding the cell phone. "No wait… who is it?"

"It's one of your company managers in Barranca, *Jefe*. He says he's being harassed by the local police and needs your help," said the guard, sheepishly.

"Fuck him. Tell him to fix it himself. I'm too busy right now!"

"Yes, *Jefe*," the guard said sheepishly.

Newmann was finding it very difficult to concentrate. This was the biggest investment venture he had ever undertaken and he had hardly slept for two days. He had put everything on the line, and his wealth—even his life—were now at risk. He couldn't take time to baby-sit clueless and spineless minions. He paid them well to run his businesses… for once; he'd have to let them do so without adult supervision.

Newmann's blood pressure would have been much higher if he had known what was happening around his house at that very moment—just out of sight of his guards. As Newmann waited for the final stage of the operation to play out in Mobile, another operation was beginning to take shape much closer to home.

As he nervously awaited the call from Mobile confirming the arrival and acceptance of the containers, several hundred Colombian soldiers had quietly and methodically encircled his large estate. The Task Force was primarily composed of elements of the 14th Brigade of the Colombian Army. In addition, there were over one hundred Colombian Special Forces troops from the elite *Fuerza de Despliegue Rápido* or FUDRA, Colombia's Rapid Reaction Force.

The head of the operation was the Commanding General of the 14th Brigade. He and the Colonel in charge of the FUDRA had just completed their final troop deployments. These two men—neither a stranger to combat—were preoccupied with preserving the element of surprise given the unusual constraints they faced this morning. Unlike any other military operation in which they had heretofore participated, they would not be controlling the timing of the attack. Instead, their assault would be triggered by events occurring outside Colombia—in Switzerland and the USA.

10:17AM CDT
Parking Lot near Wharf # 3—Mobile, Alabama

Tony D'Ambrogio was a young, tough and ambitious sub-capo in charge of the group who had come from New York. A trusted lieutenant of Joseph Tessuti, D'Ambrogio had put together a team of five security men and a chemist—whose job would be to test the potency of the heroin hidden in the containers.

He had done business with Newmann and Hernández before; but none of the three had ever met. Until this morning, they had always conducted their business over the phone or via e-mail.

Always cautious, D'Ambrogio's men had set up a perimeter of security—with an unobstructed view and clear lines of fire—covering the entire area surrounding the parking lot. They watched carefully as Carlos drove up, double-checking that he was alone, as agreed.

Just as planned, Carlos pulled into the open parking space next to the large limo in the middle of the nearly deserted lot. Two men were standing outside the limo. They motioned Carlos out of his car, frisked him and quickly checked him for a wire. Once they were assured that Carlos was unarmed and "unplugged," they opened the back door to the limo and ushered him inside.

"How are you doing, my friend?" asked Tony D'Ambrogio, as Carlos got into the back seat next to him. Carlos noted that D'Ambrogio was dressed for the part—wearing an expensive designer suit and stylish Italian leather shoes.

"I am fine. As I'm sure you already know, everything continues to go exactly according to our plan. The first of the containers will be driven out of the port facility in about a half hour," replied Carlos. "Will you be coming with us to the warehouse?"

"Yes, I'll be there with our *Doctor*," replied D'Ambrogio without emotion, referring to his chemist.

"That's fine. Your people in New York are ready to transfer the money, as soon as the *Doctor* has tested the shipment?"

"Yep. If this shipment is as good as you've promised, I think we'll both benefit from a continuing business relationship, my friend."

"That is our wish too," said Carlos, glancing down at his wristwatch. "It's time I went back to the dock. I'd like to watch the trucks leave for the warehouse."

"As you wish," D'Ambrogio said simply, gesturing to the door indicating that Carlos should leave.

Carlos opened the car door and walked the short distance back to his vehicle. As he got into the car, started the engine, and pulled out of the parking lot, his heart pounded in his chest. The moment of doubt and weakness he'd felt with his brother was over. He flashed back to his combat experiences in the jungles of Colombia. It was the same adrenaline rush, but a different battle. Service to the Revolution required dedication, sacrifice and—when necessary—alliances of convenience. D'Ambrogio and his masters in New York cared nothing for the oppressed people of Colombia. It didn't matter who or what they cared for; their motivations were irrelevant. The money they would soon transfer to pay for the heroin would be help enough for his country's poor. The money would allow the FARC to continue its armed struggle for years to come.

11:25 AM EDT
DEA Headquarters—Washington DC

The operations center in DEA's Washington, DC headquarters was at an exceedingly high level of activity. On the walls of the large conference room where DEA Special Agent Andrew Stabnick now stood, hung a series of diagrams, maps, and organizational charts. Three dozen agents moved busily about or sat in front of consoles—making phone calls, coordinating with the other agencies involved and updating maps to reflect the disposition of various law enforcement resources and personnel.

For the past 12 hours, the DEA—the government's lead counter-drug organization—had been burning the midnight oil. With great skill and patience, Stabnick had methodically transformed Benjamin Tucker's vague sting concept into a comprehensive operational plan. There were legal documents to write, coordinate, and have approved at international, national, state, and local levels. Communications nets had to be established and tested. Dozens of law enforcement agencies had to be quickly brought into the loop and provided points of contact within various branch offices of the DEA, FBI and other law enforcement organizations. Andrew Stabnick had indeed been a busy man.

Throughout the night, as he fleshed out his plan, Stabnick had repeatedly watched the track of the *Billesborg*, as it continued to move slowly northward towards the port of Mobile. The *Billesborg's* inexorable northward progress on the map was like a stopwatch without a stop button—relentlessly counting down the minutes remaining.

Stabnick glanced up at the large map of the Gulf of Mexico on the wall with tired, blood-shot eyes, and then arranged his notes on the lectern from which he'd soon be briefing the Administrator. He wished he had a little more time to prepare—time for a shower and a short nap too. The interminable cups of coffee he had consumed during the night were keeping him jittery but awake. Still, his body screamed for sleep.

Stabnick controlled his trembling hands by grabbing the sides of the lectern.

The DEA Administrator had just walked into the room and was taking her place at the head of the conference table. The time for planning was quickly running out. All the players were briefed, in position, and ready. Last night, before the marathon planning session had begun, the Administrator had asked for a briefing not later than one hour before the expected kickoff of the operation. It was "show time."

"Good morning Ms. Lemkin, ladies and gentlemen," Stabnick began as the Administrator took her seat and nodded in his direction. "This is the final pre-Op briefing for the takedown associated with the *Billesborg* and her cargo. I have just gotten off the phone with our Agent Phil Swann and FBI Special Agent Chris Ramsdell in Mobile. They report that all their assets are briefed and in position. We have also heard from Treasury that they are ready to go at the *Rothschild-Ferrier* Bank in Geneva."

"I'd like to give you an overview of the expected timeline for our operation today." Looking at his watch, Stabnick continued, "In about an hour, the last of the containers should have been taken off the *Billesborg* and hooked up to the shuttle trucks at the dock. We have several agents monitoring that process, and they continue to report that all appears to be on schedule. Once they're offloaded, our 25 containers will be hooked up to commercial 18-wheelers, and transported from the port storage facility to the Gulf Central warehouse outside Mobile. Since the Gulf Central Company only owns five of their own rigs, they contracted out for the additional twenty. Of those twenty contracted trucks, four will have drivers who are part of our team—one DEA, two FBI, and one Mobile police officer who had been working undercover in the area on another case. In addition to the drivers in the convoy, we have allocated 15 unmarked vehicles to track the convoy as it proceeds to the warehouse."

"Overall, we have six of our own agents and eleven FBI agents on site. The Alabama State Police and local Mobile Police Department are also involved. The head of security of the Mobile Port Authority has several of his most trusted employees keeping an eye on the *Billesborg* and the port in general. I'm confident that we have the manpower in place to monitor the containers the entire time they are in the port area. Furthermore, we have enough assets set up to follow the containers as they're transported from the port to the warehouse."

"In the area of the warehouse, we have over 50 law enforcement officers in position—ready for the takedown once we give the go-ahead. That go-ahead will be contingent upon the money transfer that we expect to monitor at the bank in Switzerland. As you know, the NSA has decrypted an e-mail communication between the traffickers, which contained bank account numbers linked to the trafficker in Colombia, named Marty Newmann. At some point—probably shortly after the drugs get to the warehouse—we expect them to test and accept the shipment. Once that happens, we're anticipating a money transfer using those Swiss bank accounts. Our Embassy in Berne has arranged to send their Legal Attaché and our DEA Attaché over to Geneva to witness the transfer. I spoke with our Country Attaché just before we got started here, and he reports that everything's ready on his end."

"We have set up wiretaps on the suspected buyers in New York and Los Angeles, as well as on Newmann's phones in Colombia. I'm therefore confident that we'll be able to monitor the transfer of the money and link that transfer to events in Mobile. Our lawyers have consulted with Justice, and have agreed that we'll have a compelling chain of evidence, which they feel will legally connect the buyers and sellers to the drugs in Mobile. As soon as we've documented the money transfer, we'll freeze the bank accounts and give the go-ahead for the simultaneous takedowns in Mobile, New York, LA and Colombia."

"Who's running the show in New York?" asked the Administrator.

"We're the lead agency for the apprehension in New York. They're all set and standing by for the 'go' order."

"And the Colombians? Are we sure we've kept the operation there confined to individuals in whom we have trust—Colombians who won't tip off this Newmann guy?" asked Lemkin, jumping ahead of Stabnick's briefing.

"The Colombians have elements of an Army brigade and an elite Colombian Special Forces unit—all under the command of an Army General. We've had several successful operations with both of these units and they have an excellent record of operations security. They've had Newmann's residence in Cali under surveillance for several hours now and have seen no indication that he's aware of what's about to happen. They've got his place completely surrounded, so even if word *does* get out, Newmann will not escape," replied Stabnick with confidence.

"Good," Lemkin said, nodding her head approvingly. "I'm sorry, I should let you go ahead and finish your briefing without interrupting you. But this is just too exciting!" she joked, rubbing her hands together—causing a round of subdued laughter around the room.

"No problem, ma'am... and I have to agree with you. I've never been involved in such a complex inter-agency and international operation— conceived, coordinated, and set up in so little time. Our staff, and the rest of the CD community have done a tremendous job over the last... what is it?" said Stabnick, again looking at his watch. "...12 hours or so. We've managed to piece together a near simultaneous operation in three different countries, and three different States. Yes ma'am, I must agree that this is pretty doggone exciting!"

10:37 AM CDT
Wharf # 3—Mobile, Alabama

The Port of Mobile stays busy twenty-four hours a day, seven days a week. Multi-story tall quay cranes deftly lifted containers from waiting ships and transferred them onto specially designed shuttle trucks. The shuttles then transported the containers to temporary storage areas near the docks. From these storage areas, the containers are then picked up by commercial trucks, loaded onto trains or transferred to other ships.

The Port of Mobile's Wharf Number Three was more hectic than usual this Sunday morning. In addition to the normal complement of dockworkers, shuttle trucks and containers, the dock was teeming with police cars and news crews. They were all there to monitor the offloading of one of the largest shipments of cocaine ever intercepted in the history of this Gulf port facility. Against this busy backdrop, news commentators were reporting on the Counter-Drug Task Force and their role in successfully intercepting the shipment. Local news channel reporters had already interviewed several members of the Task Force, including Superintendent George and his fellow Grenadians.

From a car parked across the street from the facility's entrance, Carlos Hernández watched for any unusual interest in their containers. He had just heard from his younger brother, who had called to report that all twenty-five had cleared Customs and would soon be leaving the port area. Seconds later, Carlos watched as the first 18-wheel truck—its cab festooned with the corporate logo of the Gulf Central Transportation Company—pulled up to the main security gate.

11:38 AM EDT
Dakota Apartment Building—Central Park West, New York

"Can you believe this shit?" said Joseph Tessuti, pointing at the television screen as he watched an attractive newswomen interviewing one of the US sailors.

"I don't know… this kinda scares the crap outta me. I mean, right there on national news, we're watching our shipment. Look at all those cops… and the military too. I can't believe this is all goin' down just like he said it would. It's like we got *everybody* on our side," agreed Giancarlo Carletti.

"Well, one thing's for sure. If this starts to unravel, we'll see the whole fucking thing on TV!"

Tessuti had been pushing the family to increase its business dealings with the American in Colombia. Over the years, he and Newmann had been conducting increasingly profitable operations. The shipment to Mobile, however, represented a massive expansion in their joint efforts. The bosses up the chain had been reluctant to support the deal initially; but they couldn't deny that Newmann had always delivered—his shipments were on time and on budget. If this deal were successful, Tessuti would be in a strong position within his family. His immediate boss, Giancarlo Carletti, was nearly at the point of accepting Tessuti's optimism.

"My guy, Tony, is down there at the warehouse. He says the first truck should be leaving the port right about now, and it'll all be at the warehouse in less than an hour. Knock on wood, but I think this damn thing is gonna work!"

"So, what if your guy Newmann gets greedy?" asked Carletti.

"I got that covered. I've worked out a deal with a group of paramilitaries down there. They're set up on a hillside, just out of sight of Newmann's house. If we give them the word, they'll be in there in a few minutes to pick up Newmann," replied Tessuti confidently.

"And they can handle any protection Newmann's got?"

"Oh yeah; don't worry. These guys have been fightin' the Colombian military for years. And they go both ways—sometimes they work with the drug dealers and the guerillas, sometimes they're against 'em."

"Well I'm glad *you* got all this shit figured out. Paramilitaries, guerillas… sounds pretty damn convoluted to me," admitted Carletti. "What about the money?"

"We got the money in our bank here—ready to be wired over to Newmann's Swiss account. So as soon as we hear from Tony that the stuff's as good as Newmann says; we'll be ready."

"Yeah, good thing CNN ain't broadcasting *that*. What a way to run a fucking drug deal!" They both laughed, and continued to watch the news broadcast.

10:39 AM CDT
Wharf # 3—Mobile, Alabama

As the first truck pulled up to the security gate, the well-fed Evergreen Security Company guard got out of the air-conditioned comfort of his small hut at the main entrance to the wharf complex.

"What in the world is going on in there this morning?" the guard asked the truck's driver, in a slow, southern Alabama drawl. After checking the container's bar code against the list on his clipboard, he continued. "I never seen this many police and news folks here before."

"They're sayin' it's a big drug bust or something," replied the driver calmly. "Hell, all them cops and news trucks are just gettin' in our way. I'm already running late. We gotta get this stuff to a warehouse north of town," said the driver, pointing his thumb back towards his cargo. "At least it looks like we'll make the evening news."

"Well, don't *that* make it all worthwhile! You have a nice day, and drive careful," said the guard over his shoulder as he walked over to open the gate.

Across the street, Carlos Hernández watched the first truck emerge from the security gate and start out towards the warehouse. Slipping his own car in behind the lumbering 18-wheeler, Carlos breathed a sigh of relief—it looked like this was really going to work.

While he concentrated on the busy traffic, Carlos did not notice that in a nearby parking lot, another man with a pair of binoculars was following the progress of the truck as it slowly shifted gears, heading away from the port.

Overhead several news helicopters jockeyed for position to film the offloading of the *Billesborg*. One of them, however, was more interested in following the rapidly-growing caravan of trucks heading toward the north part of town. From inside this unmarked helicopter a simple radio report was transmitted:

"Convoy is now leaving port facility, headed northbound on Telegraph Road."

10:43 AM CDT
Special Joint CD Task Force—Mobile, Alabama

"Roger," was DEA Agent Phil Swann's simple response to the report from the Agency's helicopter. His partner, FBI Special Agent Chris Ramsdell, had just left the office in his rental car heading toward the Gulf Central Warehouse. Swann was staying at the command center in Mobile with a couple of communications specialists to monitor and coordinate the entire operation.

Swann surveyed the mess around him in the room that had served as their planning center. Styrofoam coffee cups, overflowing ashtrays, and various piles of paperwork were the only remaining testament to the frenetic activity of the last several hours. Nearly everyone was now out in various parts of the city, ready to carry out their part of the operation.

Phil Swan had planned many a takedown in his career, but none as convoluted as this one. It was multi-faceted—involving individuals in several different countries. Here in Mobile, he was monitoring two simultaneous operations. First, was the extremely visible one related to the cocaine seized from the *Billesborg*—involving several uniformed officers and agents who would be openly displaying their status as FBI or DEA agents.

The other operation—the one that had kept everyone up most of the night planning—was much more complex and covert. The second one was more important because it involved the containers and their contraband.

Swann had structured his Task Force with the dual goals of keeping his assets visible in the area around the *Billesborg*—but hidden with respect to the containers and along the route they'd follow to the warehouse. At the warehouse itself, Swann had gone to great lengths to maintain the element of surprise while also ensuring that they had ample firepower for the takedown.

Perhaps the most troubling aspect of the entire operation was that it depended on events outside of their control. Everything hinged upon a financial transaction that they *hoped* would take place in Switzerland. In order for the sting to work, law enforcement assets had to delay moving out until after the group in Geneva had verified the exchange of funds. If anyone jumped the gun and tipped off the traffickers before they completed the wiring of the money, the plan might quickly unravel. Without that transaction, they would not have the ammunition needed to collar the ringleaders in New York and Colombia—the big fish would just swim away. If nothing happened in Geneva, they'd still have to pull the trigger on selected aspects of the operation. Swann mentally decided to cross that bridge if and when he got to it. One thing was certain: no one would leave that warehouse unless he was wearing handcuffs or zipped inside a body bag.

As he waited at the console—listening for radio updates and awaiting news from Switzerland—Swann continued to have nagging questions about the operation.

What if the expected financial transaction didn't occur? What if the account information hidden in the e-mail was a ruse or unrelated to this shipment?

Phil Swann hoped that they would soon have answers to these questions. In any case, there was no longer time for second-guessing. Everyone was briefed, in position, and ready.

11:06 AM CDT
Gulf Central Warehouse—Mobile, Alabama

The first of the trucks were pulling into the Gulf Central Warehouse's main entrance. In the area of the main gate, several men—wearing jackets that barely concealed the automatic weapons hidden inside—carefully monitored the trucks' arrival.

One by one, the trucks slowly pulled away from the main gate and continued towards the back of the facility, where other employees signaled each one into position at the warehouse loading doors. Once all the available loading bays were occupied, the rest of the trucks were guided into a tightly spaced line next to each other in the parking lot.

Inside the warehouse, Carlos Hernández watched as employees opened the huge sliding doors of each bay, removed the seals and locks, and then opened the first container.

As the door to the container swung open, Carlos saw miscellaneous pieces of office equipment and furniture neatly stacked from floor to ceiling. Several workmen set about removing desks, filing cabinets, computers and boxes from the container and carrying everything to the center of the near-empty warehouse. When the container was empty, Tony D'Ambrogio pointed to one of the desks and a couple of the workmen started taking it apart—removing its drawers, legs and top. As Carlos watched, the men removed plastic bags containing white power, which were taped to the back of each drawer and underneath the desktop.

At the same time, one of D'Ambrogio's men unraveled a long extension cord, plugging one end into a receptacle on the wall and the other into an apparatus, which he had placed on a table in the center of the warehouse. The device had several dials and a foot-long thermometer. Meanwhile, the chemist had set up a line of small vials containing chemicals on the table.

By the time D'Ambrogio's men had set up the testing equipment, warehouse workers had removed about 20 bags of heroin and stacked them next to the disassembled desk. D'Ambrogio picked one of the bags out of the stack and brought it over to his chemist, who then cut it open, removed a spoonful and divided it up into several small samples. Everyone watched intently as the "Doctor" sprinkled some of the heroin onto a circular piece of glass, which he then placed onto the apparatus.

"Relax, gentlemen," he said to the group around him, watching his every move. "This is going to take a while. I've got to check the precise melting point of this stuff. I've also got to check for the presence of compounds *other* than heroin ... and I can't do that if I hurry the process."

"Take all the time you need," D'Ambrogio said without emotion, glancing at his watch. "We've got all day."

The chemist continued dividing the rest of the samples, placing them into several test tubes, into which he added drops of chemicals from the various vials. After five minutes of dropping, shaking, tinkering and measuring, he finally rendered his verdict.

"243.5 Celsius—right on the button. It's very good. In fact, that's some of the purest *H* I've field-tested in a very long time," he said, pokerfaced.

"It would appear that you have delivered what you promised," D'Ambrogio said, nodding his head to Carlos. "I will give New York the go-ahead," he continued, opening up his cell phone.

Sunday

7:21 PM CEST
Rothschild-Ferrier Bank, S.A.—Geneva, Switzerland

Near a row of computer consoles in the bank's international trading floor, a group of men stood in a semi-circle staring over the shoulders of several *Rothschild-Ferrier* account specialists. Along with Philippe Rivière were the bank's head manager, an official from the Econ section of the US Embassy in Berne, the Embassy's DEA Country Attaché and the Legal Attaché. The Swiss had sent a deputy director of their Financial Security Office and an Interpol official. Based on the information provided by the Americans, the group was hovering around two computer consoles waiting intently for the expected activity in one or both of the numbered bank accounts they had recovered from Newmann's e-mail.

At 7:22 PM, a call came in from New York. The group listened intently as the bank employee began the transaction.

"Yes, I'm ready to carry out your instructions... We are to transfer $200 million dollars U.S. from account number 329945466 to account 586758449. Is this correct? Your password, please? Very good, sir. One moment, please."

The password was correct, and the account number matched the one of the series of numbers scrawled in notebooks of the officials. Everyone watched silently as a few keystrokes sent $200 million worth of electrons through cyberspace.

"Your transaction has been completed, sir. May we provide you with any other service? Thank you very much indeed, sir. Goodbye."

At the completion of the call, there was a moment of silence as they took in what had just transpired. For the purposes of this quasi-judicial proceeding, they had the all evidence they needed. Arrest warrants had been issued and were ready to be served in New York and Los Angeles. In Cali, Colombia, several hundred Colombian soldiers were waiting to attack. Last, and certainly not least, there was a large number of cops "locked and loaded for bear" in Mobile, Alabama.

The takedown was a *Go*.

11:22 AM CDT
Gulf Central Warehouse—Mobile, Alabama

On the roof of a building just across the street from the Gulf Central Warehouse, FBI Special Agent Chris Ramsdell was watching the activity with a pair of binoculars. Through the earpiece he was wearing, he heard the execute order from Phil Swann.

188

"Give the signal, we're a go!" said Ramsdell softly over his radio. He then crawled back from the edge of the roof, jumped up from the prone position, and sprinted towards the stairs at the other side of the roof.

Just as he was reaching the stairs, he heard the signal from across the street: five long retorts of the horn of one of the trucks outside the warehouse. As Ramsdell bounded down the stairs—three and four at a time—he knew that upon hearing that signal, four of his associates would be jumping out of the trucks with their weapons drawn and ready. During the short delay between the radio call and the horn blasts, the four had put on blue windbreakers to help their compatriots identify them as friendly and grabbed their weapons from under seats or out of lunch boxes.

Outside the warehouse, several police cars came careening through the wire-meshed fences. There was an instantaneous transition from calm to chaos. Some of the men in the warehouse begin shooting at the police and agents rushing into the warehouse and its surrounding property; many others gave up immediately or ran away without firing a shot.

Hearing the commotion outside, Carlos sprinted toward the front window of the warehouse and saw the police cars racing through the parking lot. Outside, there was chaos and gunfire in all directions—not unlike some of the larger battles he had experienced in Colombia.

"*¡Hijo de puta!*" he cussed loudly.

Turning his attention back inside the large open area of the warehouse, Carlos saw that everyone's gun was drawn and eyes darted about the room nervously—no one knew who the traitors were amongst them.

"Fuck this," yelled D'Ambrogio, bolting towards one of the open loading bay doors. No one stopped him. In the midst of the shouting and confusion, Carlos heard a deafening blast as one of the side doors of the warehouse exploded open. Less than a second later, there was another explosion—this time from behind. Looking at the door where he'd heard the latest explosion, Carlos saw two men wearing blue windbreakers rush in—their weapons at the ready.

One of them yelled, "FBI! Put down your weapons!"

Carlos brought his pistol up into the firing position... but before he could shoot, his body shuddered—as if someone had bumped into him with a full head of steam. Inexplicably, Carlos' world began to decelerate—like the slow-motion rerun of a televised soccer game. Within seconds of the impact, he began to have trouble breathing, as if he had the breath knocked out of him. He felt a stinging sensation in his left shoulder blade. His mind barely registered the continuing series of loud explosions, which echoed eerily in the cavernous warehouse. Slowly, Carlos lowered his head and looked at his hands—in the left hand was the cell phone... in the right, his unfired pistol. He was puzzled by the fact that neither hand appeared under his control—refusing to respond to his mental commands. Powerless, he watched the phone and pistol begin a slow-motion descent to the floor.

As his left knee hit the concrete, Carlos noticed an expanding splotch of red on his shirt—which had somehow become ripped. As he fell sideways towards the floor, it appeared that someone was slowly turning the warehouse's light rheostat towards a darker setting.

The high-velocity slug had entered just below Carlos' left shoulder blade and continued through his chest—its speed only partially diminished by the tissue in its path. By the time it reached the front of Carlos' chest wall, the slug was still traveling at nearly 500 feet per second. Carlos' sternum had been no match for all that kinetic energy and it had exploded outwards at impact—leaving a large, but survivable exit wound. However, on its way through his chest, the slug had sliced through his aorta. His heart was now frantically pumping blood into his chest cavity in a futile effort to keep him alive.

His body rapidly losing its battle with death, Carlos peered out into the darkness with unseeing eyes. His last thought was of Mani.

"*¡Cuídate, Mani!*"

"Take care of yourself, Mani," he tried to whisper. Amidst the continuing noise and confusion in the warehouse, no one heard his last words.

7:25 PM CEST
Rothschild-Ferrier Bank, S.A.—Geneva, Switzerland

The atmosphere on the *Rothschild-Ferrier* trading floor had just begun to return to its normal dull drone of ringing phones and voices carrying out various financial transactions. The transfer of money, which had set so much into motion, had taken only seconds to complete. All that remained was to freeze the account owned by the American in Colombia.

As they prepared to carry out the procedures necessary to freeze Newmann's account, the Embassy's econ officer had joked that those funds might be frozen for quite some time. He went on to suggest that there would certainly be scores of lawyers in several countries fighting over that $200 million for years to come.

Without warning—and before they had frozen the accounts—the balance began counting down rapidly towards zero. Everyone stared wide-eyed at the screen.

"Freeze it! Goddamn it, Freeze it!" they shouted desperately in four different languages.

Even before they stopped yelling, it was already too late. The balance in Newmann's account was $342.

11:26 AM EST
Newmann's Hacienda—Cali, Colombia

"What the—what's happening to my fucking money?" Newmann bellowed.

A stream of cusswords echoed throughout his large hacienda accompanied by the sound of his fist repeatedly slamming the computer keyboard. Newmann watched helplessly as his Swiss account balance decreased towards zero. He was dumbfounded that his moment of triumph had been cruelly stolen from him. But by whom?

Up to now, nearly everything had proceeded as they had planned. Retracing the events of the last few days, Newmann began to consider the possibility that John Carter was to blame—that he had somehow uncovered their plan.

Newmann's cell phone rang—startling him. He looked at the caller ID and recognized Carlos' number. Yanking the phone open, he shouted, "What the hell is going on? Carlos? Carlos?"

There was no answer... only static. "Carlos? What's wrong, I can only hear static." Pulling the phone away from his ear, Newmann verified that the signal strength was strong.

"Carlos! Carlos!" he yelled fruitlessly. Listening carefully, he suddenly realized that it was not static he was hearing—it was gunfire. Staggered, Newmann gazed at the computer screen and his cell phone, unable to process the implications.

At that moment, the quiet outside his home was interrupted by an eruption of heavy gunfire. Newmann reeled around, violently pushing away from his desk—sending his chair flying over on its side behind him. His face contorted with rage, he ran out of his office and into the main hallway.

"Carlos?" he repeated one last time into the phone. "What the fuck is going on?" he yelled to the guards.

"The outer perimeter guards say they're under attack by Colombian Special Forces, *Jefe*," answered one of the wide-eyed guards, listening to the frantic shouts on his radio. "They have great numbers and air support."

"I'm calling the Front's headquarters. We need help now!" Newmann whirled around and ran back into his office.

"I need you NOW!" Newmann screamed into the radio, attempting to communicate over the sound of helicopters, explosions, and gunfire outside.

11:27 AM CDT
Jaime's Bar—Mobile, Alabama

Manuel Hernández sat alone at a table at the far end of the dark barroom. Above the bar, an ancient TV with a faded, snowy picture tried its best to provide the proper sporting ambiance for the patrons. Mani watched as two unknown boxers pummeled each other while the announcer breathlessly described the action in rapid-fire Spanish. No one in the bar was paying any attention to the battling pugilists. There were about a dozen other customers—in small groups of two or three—engaged in various animated conversations. They had all raised the volume of their voices in an attempt to compete with the noisy television.

Mani had gone over his brother's instructions many times since he had left the port. He was anxiously awaiting their reunion... it had been so long since they'd had any time together.

A few minutes ago, however, he had heard the sirens.

He hoped that they were unrelated... an accident... a fire... some other emergency. However, the sound had only intensified. Unable to shake a horrible feeling of dread, Mani had gone outside to see what was happening. Away from the noise of the bar, he had been able to hear the intermittent and unmistakable sound of gunshots coming from the direction of the warehouse—only a few blocks away. That could only mean one thing.

Mani continued to walk past the bar's parking lot, onto a deserted side street. He took out his cell phone and dialed his brother's number. There was no answer.

My brother is strong and brave and will return just like he said he would, he prayed, walking back into the bar. Returning to his table, Mani struggled to overcome a growing sense of panic, sorrow, and... loneliness.

9:28 AM PDT
Santa Monica Freeway—West Hollywood, California

The handcuffs holding Douglas Veith's hands tightly behind his back were making him extremely uncomfortable. Minutes earlier, he had been sound asleep in his West Hollywood home. Never one to awaken before noon, Veith had been out partying the night before. He had not even heard the cops until they had flung open his bedroom door and dragged him from bed. Before he knew what was happening, they had slapped him in handcuffs, placed him under arrest, read him his rights, and brought him out to the street. Outside, there had been a half a dozen cop cars and DEA agents. He was quickly led over to an unmarked black sedan and thrown into the back seat.

Agent So-and-So continued to ask him bullshit questions as they sped westward on the Santa Monica freeway, "So, Mr. Veith, why did your name and phone number show up in a container ship with 1000 kilos of cocaine hidden inside? Can you explain that?"

"No, I can't explain, because I don't know what the fuck you're talking about," Veith protested—in this case honestly. He had been through the drill many times before, and his lawyer had counseled him to say nothing to an arresting officer.

"When do I get to make my phone call, asshole?" he snapped at the DEA agent dismissively.

"Later," the agent replied simply.

11:31 AM EST
On a hilltop, west of Newmann's Hacienda—Cali, Colombia

From his hilltop position, two kilometers to the west of Newmann's hacienda, Captain Fernando Azcárate peered incredulously at the scene below. Not only could he see the various armored vehicles move rapidly towards the hacienda during the initial minutes of the attack, Azcárate was close enough to hear the cacophony of gunfire and explosions as the attack progressed. In the skies above, he watched the circling Colombian Army Blackhawks—at times flying almost directly over his position. His unit was well hidden, however, and had not been spotted by the choppers.

Azcárate was in charge of two dozen members of the *Autodefensas Unidas de Colombia* (the United Auto-Defense of Colombia or AUC), a Colombian paramilitary organization. The night before, he and his men had reached their current position—a heavily wooded section of the hills west of Cali. They had arrived under cover of darkness in three rented vans. The tall trees in the area had provided adequate cover for both his men and their vehicles.

The operation being carried out by the Colombian Special Forces in the valley below was quite impressive to Azcárate's military-trained mind. Although he had seen the movement of many military vehicles in the area, he couldn't bring himself to believe that they would be setting up a strike on the same target until it was too late. Up until the start of the attack, Azcárate had been waiting for his cell phone to ring—ordering him and his men down the hill to assault the same compound. For some reason, the Colombian military had beat him to the punch, and his own operation was now completely out of the question.

A week earlier, Captain Azcárate had received a phone call from an Italian man in New York City—a man with whom he had done business before. The

Italian wanted him to be ready to enter Marty Newmann's compound, grab him, and transport him to a safe house outside of Cali, where they would await further instructions. The Italian had handsomely compensated Azcárate and his men just to be there this morning—promising an even more significant sum if they successfully snatched Newmann.

From the moment the bullets began to fly around Newmann's compound, Azcárate knew his job was over. Therefore, to ensure that the satellite cell phone maintained its charge, he had turned it off and placed it back into the canvas bag hanging from his shoulder. Surely, the Italian could wait a few more hours to learn that someone else had taken care of Mr. Newmann.

12:33 PM EDT
Dakota Apartment Building—Central Park West, New York

It was a dull, overcast and blustery day in Manhattan. Pedestrians braving the biting cold that afternoon on the city's sidewalks did not notice the convoy of vehicles heading north up Eighth Avenue—they were just part of the normal, never-ending bustle of New York traffic.

Across from the Dakota Apartment Building in Central Park, nine undercover agents—each dressed in different attire to allow them to blend into the crowd—waited for the order to move out. A street vendor selling hotdogs and two of his customers were stationed across the street from the Dakota, where they could monitor everyone going in or out of the building. The vendor glanced at his watch as he rubbed his hands together in an attempt to stay warm.

A group of three joggers ran along the sidewalk in front of the stand. No one noticed that they had been running in circles for the past hour. Furthermore, the earphones they wore were not playing music. Instead, they were tuned to a radio frequency reserved for the FBI.

Suddenly, two-dozen men leapt from the fleet of vehicles that had just come screeching to a halt in front of the Dakota. They wore jackets with letters on their backs: FBI, DEA, and NYPD. One of these men carried their most powerful weapon: a sealed indictment and arrest warrants for several prominent New York businessmen who currently lived in the building.

Giancarlo Carletti, Joseph Tessuti and their bodyguards emerged from the Dakota building and were escorted into the back of the waiting government vehicles—their faces hidden under jackets, hands, and newspapers.

The only thing Joseph Tessuti could think of was…

The money! That bastard took our goddamned money. Then, to top it off, the fucking Feds get here before I can get Azcárate moving down in Cali. So help me, as soon as our lawyers get us out of jail, Marty Newmann is one dead son-of-a-bitch.

11:42 AM EST
Newmann's Hacienda—Cali, Colombia

The shooting had steadily intensified outside Newmann's home. He could now hear the impact of individual bullets on his home's exterior walls. Although the reinforced concrete walls and bulletproof windows were keeping the steady-growing battle safely outside of his residence, they could not block the sound of the fighting raging on the perimeter.

The Colombian Army was serious this time. There seemed to be an entire battalion of soldiers fighting his security force. The FARC had provided over forty fighters to protect this important member of the Revolution. Newmann knew that they would fight the Colombian Army to the end and would do their best to protect him and the information in his office.

The escalating noise outside, along with the fact that he could no longer contact his security detail indicated that the battle was not going to end well. It was time to carry out the emergency destruction of the data in his office. He called to several of the guards that were looking nervously out of the windows in the living room.

"Come in here! I need help in my office," yelled Newmann over the gunshots and explosions.

Newmann had two choices. Since the thick armored walls of his office had been constructed to withstand a heavy mortar attack, he could use it as a safe room. Once locked inside, he could wait out the attack until re-enforcements arrived.

Alternatively, if all appeared to be lost—and that appeared to be the case this afternoon—the walls would contain the blast from the plastic explosives placed throughout the file cabinets and computers. FARC engineers had installed this failsafe mechanism to safeguard the valuable information stored inside.

Newmann never gave much thought to the explosives rigged in his office. The FARC had sent one of their explosive experts to set up the safe room many years earlier. It had taken several days to install all the explosives and the wiring system to activate them.

At the time, Newmann had told Aliria that he was installing an anti-intrusion system. She had apparently bought the story, and had befriended the explosives expert—making sure that the servants brought him food and drink as he worked in the room.

It was becoming more and more obvious that Newmann had only one course of action. He *must* protect the vital information inside his office at all costs. Slowly and deliberately, he went over the simple steps that he had committed to memory so long ago.

One—Arm the system with the switch inside his office.

Two— Open the safe and place the contents on the floor. This was necessary, the explosive expert had explained, because the safe was strong enough to protect its contents from the blast.

Three—Close and secure the office door.

Four—Enter the six-digit code into the control box outside the office and press *Enter*. The control box was connected to his computer, and was designed to scramble all the data on his hard drive.

Finally, after a 30-second delay—BOOM!

Newmann recalled that the expert had assured him that the office was designed to contain the explosion without damaging the house's interior. Newmann never believed it, and assumed that if the time ever came, he would be as far away from that damn office as his legs would take him in 30 seconds.

As Newmann and his guards busily set about preparing to set off the explosives, a strange calm settled over the house. The gunfire had subsided.

"*¡Apúrense!*"

"Hurry up!" he yelled, tossing the last of the papers from the safe on the floor. They scurried out of the office and turned to shut and lock the door. It took two of them to push the massive door into the closed position and secure its two large dead bolts. Newmann entered the required code, and pressed the *Enter* key. As he turned around and sprinted past the front door, he was thrown to the floor by a tremendous explosion.

For a split second, Newmann thought the explosives in his office had detonated prematurely. Through the dust and debris, however, Newmann watched as several soldiers rushed through the gaping hole that used to be his front door. He recognized the distinctive camouflaged uniform of the Colombian Special Forces. Suddenly, shots rang out and two of his bodyguards slumped towards the floor. As Newmann lay transfixed and motionless, one of the soldiers calmly walked up to each of his remaining guards and delivered a *coup de grace* pistol shot to their foreheads.

Newmann suddenly remembered the office… and the explosion. How long had it been since he had entered the code? The explosion was going to occur any second now; he had to get away from that door.

"*¡Suéltenme, hijos de puta, tengo que alargarme de aquí!*" he yelled, struggling to free himself from the soldiers as they held him tightly and forced handcuffs onto his wrists. Newmann could not clear his mind of the vision of that heavy steel door flying into his body—catapulted by the force of the imminent explosion. He had to get out of there.

The soldiers ignored Newmann's ranting and quickly yanked him off the floor and out the mangled remains of the front entrance. Once outside, Newmann closed his eyes, as a swirling maelstrom of grass clippings and dirt from his front yard were whipped painfully into his face. A very noisy Blackhawk helicopter was landing, amidst what appeared to be hundreds of Colombian Army soldiers. Newmann also noticed the bodies of most of his security unit. They had obviously been hopelessly outnumbered and outgunned.

The door to the Blackhawk was already open, and Newmann was quickly shoved inside. Seconds later, as the chopper lurched into the air, he stared at the remains of his once elegant home. As the smoldering ruins disappeared behind them, Newmann felt an overwhelming sense of dread rush over him.

The office... there was no explosion. Oh my God, I never heard the explosion. The bastards have it all and I'm a dead man.

Newmann was having a difficult time comprehending the enormity of what had just happened. The money was gone. His house was gone. Somehow, he had even failed to destroy the information in his office—information that would destroy him. His mind swirled with the possibilities—frantically trying to figure a way out of his current predicament. Finally, as the buildings of downtown Cali became visible through the Blackhawk's windows, another thought popped into his mind.

Aliria. Where is my wife?

Sunday... one week later

Hell hath no fury like a woman scorned.

From the play,
"The Mourning Bride"
by William Congrev

Unknown location

Although its initiation had been accelerated by events beyond her control, Aliria Newmann's plan had worked flawlessly. The money had stayed in the Swiss bank account long enough to seal the fate of her husband. Either he would stay in jail (if Colombian or American authorities continued to hold him), or either the Mafia or Cartel would eventually kill him. Although she preferred the former outcome, Aliria had to admit that she would not be too troubled by Marty's demise.

Aliria had long known that her husband was responsible for the deaths of many people. He was not the type to pull the trigger himself. He would simply order others to do the dirty work. After years of Marty's abuse, and with the help of Jack Zaworski's reassuring influence, Aliria had begun to climb out of the emotional shelter she had built around herself since childhood. Slowly and methodically, she had put together a strategy that would remove Marty from her life and start her off on the road to her own independence.

Aliria's plan took advantage of her comprehensive knowledge of international banking procedures. An ability Marty never even suspected of her. When it came to her association with her father's bank, Marty had falsely assumed that she had served in some menial secretarial position. He seemed incapable of attributing any intelligence or business acumen to his wife—or any other woman for that matter. Ever since he had left Karen and amassed great sums money and power, he became accustomed to dominating the women around him. That was the way he had always treated Aliria—more his property than his wife.

Once she had figured out how to take the money, she needed an escape plan *and* a way to cover her tracks. Colombia's continuing violence provided the perfect backdrop. Kidnappings were an almost daily occurrence in Colombia—a common method of fundraising for the FARC and other groups fighting the Colombia government. Aliria had decided to stage her own kidnapping.

On the same day she had set up Marty's computer to send the incriminating e-mail to the NSA Director, she had also placed a credible trail of evidence among the files in his office documenting her abduction. She left detailed electronic notes on Marty's computer outlining his negotiations with the kidnappers. She used real names and phone numbers taken from Newmann's FARC and business files. With any luck, the fake kidnapping would keep Colombian investigators busy tracking down false leads for several weeks, giving her enough time to cover her tracks and mask her true whereabouts. Finally, before she left the office, she had disconnected the explosive devices from the control box outside Marty's safe room as the FARC's explosive expert had shown her several years earlier.

If he survived, Marty would certainly figure out that she was behind both the disappearance of the money and the phony kidnapping. If he were still alive, he might try to convince whoever was holding him that she had made up the whole kidnapping thing. But who would believe him?

Although Marty would no longer be a threat, Aliria realized that she was unlikely to resume a normal existence. In fact, she fully recognized that she might have to spend the rest of her life in hiding. She had stirred up a nest of extremely lethal hornets, and they would never stop looking for her.

In the meantime, Aliria was a very busy woman—manipulating scores of ever-changing bank accounts, spread throughout the world's banking network. The vast majority of this money—nearly a quarter of a billion dollars—was tainted by blood and drugs. Because of this, she would not keep it for long. She had already transferred tens of millions of dollars to a well-known Catholic charity association in her country, *Cáritas Colombiana.* Other charities throughout the world would also be receiving generous contributions over the next few weeks.

Keeping all that money moving in the right directions would require most of her attention for the next several months. Subconsciously, she recognized that by focusing on the electronic flow of funds, she was also avoiding coming to grips with the implications of her recent actions.

Her life had changed in so many ways, and it wasn't solely because of the money. Eventually, she'd have to deal with the unexpected discovery from a week earlier—the astonishing secret she had found tucked away amongst the records of her father's financial empire.

Onboard *Juguete del Calamar*—off the north coast of Cartagena, Colombia

Gloria was at the helm of the *Juguete del Calamar*. Carter sat close by, adjusting the genoa sheet. Over the past week, Carter and Gloria had been teaching each other how to sail. Carter was quickly mastering the art of skippering a sailboat and was enjoying every second. In many ways, it was similar to flying—keeping control of a moving vessel while constantly accounting for the effects of winds and lift.

"What do you think happened to Newmann's money?" Carter asked Gloria, as he watched her guide the sailboat skipping energetically through the ocean in the stiff morning breeze. "And what about his wife, Aliria? Do you think there's any chance that the kidnappers will let her go, now that Marty's in jail?"

"Somehow, I think she's just fine," said Gloria mysteriously, with a Mona Lisa smile. "As for the money, I think we'll find out about that soon enough."

200

If Carter had known the reason for Gloria's smile, perhaps the sky would have appeared a bit brighter. It had been a week since Carter had come back to Cartagena to settle Z's estate. As he had promised during their meeting in Miami, Jack's handwritten will had left everything to Carter. As expected, the estate consisted almost entirely of the *Juguete*, along with a few of his belongings onboard.

Within a few days, Carter would have to make a decision about returning to the US. Gloria had suggested that he stay with her in Colombia. They could live well in Cartagena with the money he had already saved, along with his military retirement pay. It was also true that they had enjoyed every minute of the last week spent on the *Juguete*. For the moment, he was in no hurry to make a decision and was quite happy to stay right where he was.

While Carter remained tentative and still uncommitted, Gloria was certain what she wanted for her future. *Her* future was sitting next to her in the *Juguete*. Whether they were in the US or here in Colombia, she would be happy as long as they were together.

Gloria had recently learned several things that would significantly influence her future. If the future evolved the way she hoped, what she had learned this morning would be an important part of *their* future. For the hundredth time that day, she reached down and felt for it inside the front pocket of her shorts. It was still there.

It all began earlier that morning, when she had gone to her bank's Cartagena branch to get some cash. After presenting her identification, the teller informed her that a safe deposit box had been opened in her name a few days earlier and that she needed to complete a signature verification card before she could use it. Gloria told the teller that this must be a mistake, as she had made no such request and did not even *live* in Cartagena. The teller had insisted that there was no mistake and recommended that she speak to the bank's vice president.

Intrigued, Gloria had filled out the required paperwork and gone downstairs with the bank official to look inside the box. After he removed it from its slot in the wall, the bank officer brought the box into a small private room, placed it on a table and left her alone. Filled with curiosity, she had opened the box and discovered that it contained a lone envelope with her name handwritten on the outside.

With trembling hands, she had carefully opened it and removed the handwritten letter. As she unfolded the paper, a photo dropped out. It was a small picture of Aliria Newmann and her father—Gloria's former boss— Ramón Escobedo Valeria.

Puzzled, she stared at the photo for a few seconds, wondering why it had been given to her. Finally, she put the photo on the table and began to read the letter.

Sunday... one week later

My dear Gloria,

There is so much I need to tell you. How I wish I could talk to you face to face. I hardly know where to begin... so I'll just start.

Do you remember the first time we met? It was at the American Ambassador's residence in Bogotá. You came to the reception that night with my father and me. I remember being a bit surprised that of all the bank personnel, father picked you to go with us that evening. I also recall that my father was acting a bit strange and nervous the entire evening. Now I know why.

Father passed away two weeks ago. We had never been particularly close. I guess neither of us has been very good at showing emotion. Anyway, in the process of piecing together his will, the estate and his finances over the past couple of weeks, I found a surprise. Amongst the complex collection of investments, trusts and other financial instruments, I discovered that a few years after I was born, father's lawyers created and funded a particularly well-hidden trust. It was set up to provide significant and regular payments to Alma Saenz. As soon as I saw the name, I knew who she was and what that trust fund represented. As I expected, birth records confirmed that Alma is your mother. Given the circumstances, dates, etc., I'm quite certain that a DNA test would confirm that my father, Ramón Escobedo Valeria, is also your father... that you are my half sister.

So much of the past now makes sense to me, and perhaps this news will help unravel some of the mysteries of your life as well. Based on the way you carried yourself while working at the bank, I'm quite certain you had no idea who he really was. I'm sure that your mother had her reasons for keeping this information from you. I guess we all have our reasons for keeping secrets.

Oh how I wish I could have told you these things in person. Unfortunately, that just can't happen yet. Perhaps soon, we can get to know each other and become real sisters. I cannot guess when that will happen; but I know in my heart that it will happen someday. Not knowing how long that day will be postponed, I decided that you had a right to know the truth about our father sooner, rather than later. That's why I'm telling you this now.

I'm sure you know that father was quite comfortable financially. His estate is almost entirely debt-free, and he left nearly everything to me in his will. The trust fund I mentioned before will continue to provide your mother with income for the rest of her life. However, I believe that as his child, you should have been included in his will too. For whatever reason, he did not see fit to do so. I have decided to rectify his error and have begun to set up accounts in your name representing half of what he left me.

There are more financial details to share with you, and I will return to that subject at the conclusion of this letter. For now, permit me to move on to recent events regarding Marty Newmann, Jack Zaworski, and me. We both know that John Carter and Z were very close. However, I don't see how you could have known about my relationship with Z, so that's where I'll take you now.

Z and I enjoyed many wonderful hours together on the Juguete. He was such a straight-forward, honest and easygoing person—unlike anyone I've ever met before. Even today, I can't really explain my feelings for him. He was always there for me—listening to my complaints, comforting me, and understanding my concerns. In many ways, I guess I considered him the father I never really had. At other times, he was more like a lover to me. Without even realizing it, he gave me back my life.

Eventually, it began to sink into my thick skull, how horrible my existence had become as Mrs. Marty Newmann. Z was the first man to truly open up my heart. I began to realize that Marty never really loved me... and never would. I think I can safely say that through Z, I was feeling love—or at least a capacity for love—for the first time in my life. It was exhilarating to feel that power.

Perhaps Z helped me discover myself and to think for myself. That's why, about a year ago, I began to put together a plan that would rid me of Marty, and allow me to start over. I began taking money from Marty's Cartel accounts. They never completely trusted him, and would routinely have his accounts checked by their own accountants. My father taught me well, and I was able to use Marty's money without him (or them) being able to discover what I was doing. Each time they checked out his books, Marty came off looking like a genius. It ended up that I was much more suited to the job than he was, and my profits greatly exceeded what his would have been. No one in the Cartel—including Marty—ever figured out what I was doing. Marty's money was never important to me. It was, however, the only weapon I had to use against him.

Originally, my plan was to invent a scheme that would make it look like Marty had stolen money from the Cartel and the Mafia gangsters with whom he had been doing business. Having removed Marty from the picture, I thought I might be able to start a new life... maybe even to run away with Z. I always assumed that I would have more time to figure it all out.

Tragically, Marty took Z away from me—away from you and John too—before I could be sure what my feelings were for him. Oh, how I miss him now!

As I write this, it seems like ages ago that Z left on that last trip to Miami. He desperately wanted to warn John about Marty. Z understood that Marty would never set him (or me) free. He always suspected that one day, he might become a liability and therefore expendable. We both lived with the knowledge that eventually Marty would probably kill one... or perhaps both of us. We recognized the danger... but what could we do? Marty had become very powerful and dangerous.

I never shared my plan with Z. I knew he would never agree to run off with me while Marty was still alive and in the business. I'm pretty sure he preferred to maintain our arrangement as it was.

In case you're wondering, our "arrangement" never included sex. We certainly enjoyed the occasional stolen moment... holding hands during sailing lessons... talking about our lives. But that was it.

I also feel that you and John should know that Z talked incessantly about John. I'll bet John never knew it; but since those days when we were all together in Bogotá, he has been Z's best and most cherished friend. Other than me, John was the only person that he ever trusted completely. That's why he made out his will the way he did.

So there you have it, my sister. No matter what happens, I will remain quite busy for the next several months continuing to dispose of the money I've recently taken under my control. Eventually, I'll settle father's estate and divide it with you. More importantly, I look forward to our first family reunion and getting to know you.

Finally, in order to you have sufficient funds while I continue to arrange my finances, I've set up a bank account for your immediate financial needs. The bank manager will be able to help you access the funds. I know him and trust him explicitly.

All my best,

Your sister, Aliria

She had spent almost an hour down in the bank's small vault, reading and re-reading Aliria's—her sister's letter. Finally, she carefully folded it up and placed it back in the safety deposit box. She then gently slid the photograph into her pocket and called for the bank officer. After he had returned the box into its slot in the wall, she had left the bank and walked home—lost in a bewildering fog of confused emotions.

The letter, along with the events of the last several days, had profoundly changed her life. For the first time, she knew the truth about her father's identity. She had also learned that she had a half-sister. Several times on the way back to the marina, she thought of her mother, realizing that they would soon have to have a *very* long talk.

Gloria also tried to come to grips with the fact that she was about to inherit a significant, but undefined quantity of money. She wondered how much it would turn out to be, and how it might affect her life. Finally, and most importantly, she thought of John Carter.

Over the last week together, she could see unmistakable signs that he was finally opening up his heart to her. With each passing day, she became more hopeful that he would decide to stay in Cartagena. She was sure that in time, she might finally be able to show him the depth of her love.

As she continued to guide the *Juguete* along its course, Gloria once again moved her hand down to her pocket. She could just feel the small snapshot under the fabric of her shorts. She wondered what it must have been like for Aliria the day she had placed it in the envelope along with her letter.

"Why don't you take over for a while, *Señor* Carter, I've got a few things to share with you," she said, relinquishing the helm to Carter, who moved silently over to the helm.

As Carter took control of the *Juguete*, she moved closer to him, feeling comfortable and protected as he pulled her close with his free arm. The two sat quietly together as the boat bounded along in the wind and waves—they belonged in each other's arms.

Carter looked down at Gloria's tear-filled eyes. He gently wiped one of the tears from her cheek.

"What's the matter, darling? Don't like my sailing?"

"No, it's just that I'm so happy, I feel like crying," she explained.

"Believe me Gloria; I know exactly how you feel."

Glossary

AEDT	Australian Eastern Daylight Time (GMT +11: Sydney)
AIRA	Air Attaché
ALUSNA	US Naval Attaché
ARMA	Army Attaché
AST	Atlantic Standard Time (GMT -5: Grenada)
AUC	*Autodefensas Unidas de Colombia* (United Auto-Defense of Colombia); a Colombian paramilitary organization
CDT	Central Daylight Time (GMT -6: Mobile, Gulf of Mexico)
CEST	Central European Summer Time (GMT +2: Geneva)
COGATT	Coast Guard Attaché
CT	Counter Terrorism
DAO	Defense Attaché Office: pronounced with the letters "DAO"
DAS	Defense Attaché System
DATT	Defense Attaché: the ranking member (normally a full Colonel) of the DAO
Devil Dog	Nickname for US Marine. According to Marine Corps legend, during the World War I, German infantry referred to the tenacious fighting of the US Marines by calling them *Tuefelshunde* or Devil Dogs
DIA	Defense Intelligence Agency
DIAC	Defense Intelligence Analysis Center
EDT	Eastern Daylight Time in the USA (GMT -5)
Eldorado Canyon	Code name for 1986 Raid on Libya
ELN	*Ejercito de Liberación Nacional* (National Liberation Army): Colombian guerrilla group
EST	Eastern Standard Time (GMT -6: the local time in Panama and Colombia—not corrected for Daylight Savings Time)
FAO	Foreign Area Officer. Military career specialty involved with overseas service.
FARC	*Fuerzas Armadas Revolucionarias Colombianas* (Revolutionary Armed Forces of Colombia): pronounced as a word, FARK; Colombian guerrilla group
GMT	Greenwich Mean Time (also known as Coordinated Universal Time, or UTC)

HARM	High-Speed Anti-Radiation Missile; pronounced as in the English word "harm"; an airborne missile used to defeat anti-aircraft missile sites.
HMCS	Her (or His) Majesty's Canadian Ship
ICE	Immigration and Customs Enforcement: now part of the Department of Homeland Security
JIATF-South	Joint Interagency Task Force – South. The first four words are turned into an acronym pronounced "Jyat-if"
JOIC	Joint Operations Intelligence Center. An operational staff organization at the combatant command level synthesizing intelligence and operations data from various government sources.
PDT	Pacific Daylight Time (GMT -7)
NCO	Non-Commissioned Officer: An enlisted member of the armed forces.
NIK	Narcotics Identification Kit
NSA	National Security Agency: primary US electronic intelligence-gathering agency
OPORD	Operations Order: orders carrying out a military operation
RPG	Rocket-Propelled Grenade: shoulder-fired anti-tank weapon, similar to a bazooka.
TACON	Tactical Control: command authority granted to subordinate unit. Pronouced "Tay-con"
TFR	Terrain Following Radar: used to guide aircraft over all kinds of terrain in all types of weather, can be coupled directly to the airplane's autopilot for "hands-off" flying
UNITAS	From Latin for "Unity," a long-running, multi-national exercise primarily involving naval units from the US, Europe and Latin America.
UNREP	Underway Replenishment. Seaborne transfer of gas and other supplies.
WSO	Weapon Systems Officer, always pronounced "Wizzo." In the F-111, sits in the right seat—in most other tandem-seat fighters, sits behind the pilot
Zodiac	Rubber-hulled skiff with outboard motor used by US Coast Guard. Also called a RIB, for Rigid Inflatable Boat

Acknowledgments

Although I had long thought about writing this book, it would never have taken shape without the dedication, love, prodding, encouragement, consoling and editing of my wonderful wife of 30 years. I owe her a debt of gratitude, which I shall endeavor to repay over the rest of our lives together.

Next, I must give thanks to my daughter Nicole for her expert editing and brainstorming. My daughter and wife teamed up to make me consider some important options about the development and depth of my characters. She's also the artist behind the design of the cover of this book.

Captain Aaron Davenport, US Coast Guard also deserves credit for his assistance. Aaron's real-world experience has helped make the ship boarding action more believable. He also pointed out some glaring geographical errors in an early draft of this book. He is currently at sea with the United States Coast Guard helping secure our borders.

As this book is truly a family affair, I'd also like to thank my uncle, John V. Cathcart (who passed away recently), and my father-in-law, Larry Cowper—both of whom provided much inspiration, encouragement and advice in the early stages of this process—when I wasn't at all sure that writing a novel would be worth the effort.

If you have any questions, comments or would like more details on the Delta 7 experience, please visit my website: www.Delta7Book.com.

Made in the USA